DANGEROUS

and UNSEEMLY

A Concordia Wells Mystery

K.B. Owen

Dangerous and Unseemly
A Concordia Wells Mystery

Formatting by Debora Lewis
arenapublishing.org

ISBN-13: 978-0-9889974-0-0

For
Joan Considine Owen
You inspired this book. We miss you still.

Acknowledgments

It's a great time to be a historical author, with the wealth of digitized historical material available on the world wide web. For anyone interested in the background research that went into the writing of this book, I've shared some wonderful primary and secondary sources on my website, **kbowenmysteries.com**. I'd love to see you there.

Even in our internet age, however, a writer needs to turn to real people– for facts, advice, or moral support.

This page is to thank those people.

To Professors Susan Pennybacker and Andrew Walsh of Trinity College, Hartford, CT, and author Jan Whitaker, who helped keep my characters out of questionable establishments by providing information about respectable Hartford tea shops for women.

To Bert Johansen, co-author of *Hartford County Trolleys* and one of the directors of the Connecticut Trolley Museum, for the fascinating and enormously useful details about Hartford's streetrail system in the 1890s. It was gratifying to make the trolley car Tuscan red.

To my agents, Miriam Goderich and Jane Dystel, who first believed in this project, even in the face of setbacks, and helped shape it. No author could ask for better professionals in her corner.

To Yassine Belkacemi at DGLM's digital publishing program, who fielded many, many questions with professionalism and expertise, and cover artist Niki Smith, who patiently endured multiple tweaks and revisions along the way and produced such a wonderful end product.

To Kristen Lamb and the generous community of fellow writers known as WANAs, who provided advice and support. We are truly not alone.

To author Michael J. Sullivan, for his invaluable expertise during the early stage of querying this book.

To author Mary Morrissy, for her wonderful mentoring, and the ladies of S.P.E.—you know who you are!

To my sons, Patrick, Liam, and Corey, who pitched in when deadlines were tight, and kept me grounded; to my parents-in-law, Steve and Lyn, who provided loving support; and to my parents, Ag and Steve, who listened, sympathized and encouraged during all the bumps along the way, just as they have done with all of my endeavors.

But most of all, I want to thank Paul, my partner and my love. This would not have been possible without you.

K.B. Owen
January 2013

Chapter 1

Hartford Women's College
February 1896

Perhaps one could grow accustomed to the sound of female shrieks at dawn, but Professor Concordia Wells thought otherwise.

Today, an out-an-out caterwauling yanked her from sleep. *Mercy! What now?*

Groping for her eye glasses and wrapping herself in a shawl against the morning chill, she listened. Please not another mouse. It was remarkable how one small creature could produce such an uproar. Last week's intruder had led them a merry chase before Ruby trapped it in the dustbin.

She tucked her feet under her, just in case.

Overhead came laughter and the babble of voices mixed in with the wails.

Concordia rolled her eyes in exasperation and sprang out of bed. No matter what had them in a pucker *this time*, she had to get them quiet in a hurry. With Willow Cottage being closest to DeLacey House, the residence of no-nonsense Lady Principal Hamilton, the disturbance was bound to reach her ears. Concordia was the cottage's teacher-in-charge, and responsible for these students. The last thing they needed was Miss Hamilton descending upon them.

She didn't even bother to find her slippers, but stomped out of the room, her hair trailing in a fraying braid down her back. She groped her way up the steps in the dim early-dawn light.

Drat! She smothered a yelp as she stubbed her toe on a step.

Reaching the first freshman room, the pain gave her additional fury as she flung open the door to a group of squalling girls.

"Stop that noise *at once!*" she hissed. "Do you want to bring the lady principal down upon our heads? Do you remember the last time this cottage was put on restriction for unseemly behavior?"

Startled, the girls stared, mouths open at the sight of the wild-haired, angry Miss Wells, hopping and rubbing her toe as she glared at them. Concordia didn't realize that her appearance was more frightening at the moment than the abstract threat of restriction.

"That's better." At least, there weren't as *many* freshmen wailing now. Maybe they still had a chance to avoid the lady principal's wrath. Concordia whipped out of the room and knocked on the door of the Head Senior, Miss Crandall. A bleary-eyed Charlotte Crandall stuck out her head.

It was amazing what seniors could sleep through, Concordia thought.

"Miss Crandall, can you help me get these freshmen settled down? Heaven only knows what has them in a twist this time." Concordia knew she could count upon Miss Crandall, whose unruffled demeanor and quiet decisiveness carried weight with her peers. She would make a good teacher someday, if she chose that path.

Miss Crandall suppressed a sigh as she pulled on her mantle and followed Concordia to the freshmen bedrooms.

It took only a glance in the rooms of the sniffling girls—the pulled-out drawers, the cluttered vanity tables in more disarray than usual—for the Head Senior to appreciate the situation.

"Ah," the girl said, face clearing in understanding, "it's Glove Night. That's the problem."

"And what, pray tell, is *Glove Night?*" Concordia demanded. This last question sent up a fresh wail from one of the students, who was quickly hushed by the others.

Concordia was new this year to Hartford Women's College. But every school has its own set of customs and quirks, and she had seen her fair share of student high jinks in her previous teaching post. She knew she wasn't going to like the answer.

"It's a prank the sophs play on the freshies. It usually happens in January, when we've returned from the winter recess," Miss Crandall explained, smothering a yawn. "The sophomores slip into the freshmen bedrooms during the night and abscond with all of the dress gloves they can find. Then the freshies have to hunt them down."

Concordia groaned and closed her eyes. Splendid. A scavenger hunt for stolen gloves. This would not end well.

"Where would they be hidden?" she asked. The freshman girls, some tear-streaked but all of them quiet now, huddled around Concordia, barefoot and still in their night dresses.

Miss Crandall smiled. "Oh, all over campus." She ticked off the list on her fingers. "Broom closets, the dining hall pantry, the ornamental fountain in the quadrangle–at least that's *drained* in the winter–between stacks of books on the library's shelves..."

The senior girl broke off as Ruby Hitchcock, Willow Cottage's house matron, huffed down the hall toward them. She was a short, stocky woman of middle age, at the moment clad in a dressing sacque and threadbare slippers.

One quick look told her the whole story. "Ah, Glove Night," Ruby said, nodding.

"Why am I the last person to know about this?" Concordia demanded.

Ruby gave a chuckle and waved the girls back into their rooms. "You'd best get dressed for chapel. It's getting late. Go on, now!"

The girls pouted but shuffled down the hall.

Miss Crandall looked out the hall window at the brightening sky. "Ruby's right, there's not time to retrieve the gloves before morning chapel–the sophs usually plan it that way, frankly–so the girls will have to go bare-handed for now, and look for them later."

That was going to be distressing for the gloveless girls, Concordia knew: appearing in chapel bare-handed was akin to walking among the congregation bare*foot*. It simply could not be done without drawing attention to oneself. She could only hope that the usually-strict Lady Principal would be understanding in this case. But this was the same woman who required the girls to be suitably-gloved when they stood in front of the class to read their themes aloud.

With a nod of thanks to Miss Crandall, Concordia followed Ruby back down the stairs.

Does this happen every year?" Concordia asked the matron.

Ruby nodded. "And those hiding places–the crazier the better, it seems," she said. "They're always trying to out-do each other. A couple of years ago, when Miss Crandall was a sophomore herself–she was a wild one back then–we found the gloves dangling from the *beams of the chapel* when we walked into the service." She shook her head at the memory. "Land sakes, I could'n believe my eyes. Three dozen pairs of gloves, hanging from the ceiling. No one ever figured out how they managed *that*, but the custodian had quite a time of it, even with the tallest ladder, taking them all down."

"Don't the freshman try to guard their gloves? Hide them away?" Concordia asked.

"Oh, yes, the shrewd ones do," Ruby answered, grimacing. "Sometimes the sophomores are right wicked, though, and wait a while, until the girls relax their guard."

Concordia sighed. Right wicked, indeed.

Time to get dressed and face the day ahead. They still had chapel to get through.

Chapter 2

"It will be fine. Everyone will understand," Concordia soothed, as a distraught freshman balked at going through the chapel doors.

The girl sniffed. "Why do those sophomores have to be so *cruel*, Miss Wells?"

Another freshman—also gloveless—tossed her head and glared in the direction of the smirking sophomores. "Well, I for one do not give a jot about it."

Once inside the vestibule, however, the young lady's bravado failed her. She thrust her hands into her coat pockets and leaned closer to Concordia. "We should be able to find the gloves soon, don't you think?" she whispered.

Already straining with the effort of propping open the plank-style doors for the lagging girls, Concordia grunted and prodded them through.

Just get through chapel. Then the worst of the drama will be over.

Memorial Chapel, now almost half a century old, was one of the original buildings from the 1850s, when the college was first founded as a ladies' seminary. Its Gothic-revival features gave the structure a sense of boundless height, from the pointed-arch windows and doors, to the vaulted ceilings and steep gables. The chapel proper was made of wood, with ornate scrollwork moldings throughout the interior. The asymmetrically-adjoining bell tower was constructed of local limestone, and topped with a crenellated parapet that made it look like a miniature castle. It had taken a few weeks of passing the building before Concordia could approach it without stopping to stare.

She followed the students as they filed in. As was the custom, the formal procession started with the senior faculty, then the students by their class: seniors, juniors, and so on. The younger faculty, Concordia among them, came in behind the freshmen, in order to shepherd any stragglers. That meant Lady Principal Hamilton would be near the front, and not likely to notice the gloveless freshmen, at least for a little while. She noticed a lot of the freshman girls from other cottages had their hands thrust in pockets. The residents of Willow Cottage hadn't been the only victims, apparently.

Strangely, the usual orderly line into the chapel seemed to disintegrate. From her position in the back, Concordia heard gasps and the chatter of excited voices, as the girls in front crowded along the steps leading up to the altar.

Concordia pushed past the students, to where the other teachers stood, staring.

Perched atop the table sat a group of crudely-sewn dolls, their likenesses rough but recognizable: of the school's President, Dean, and Lady Principal, along with Miss Bellini, Miss Jenkins–and Concordia observed an unflattering but unmistakable rendition of herself, complete with red yarn hair and drawn-on eyeglasses. The figures were lined up neatly, save for one.

The back of Concordia's neck prickled at the sight of the doll-figure of Lady Principal Hamilton, flung on its back, a knife through its heart. Gloves littered the floor at the altar's base.

The sophomores had, at last, outdone their predecessors.

Chapter 3

"At least the freshmen won't have to hunt for their gloves," Miss Pomeroy remarked cheerfully. Gertrude Pomeroy, a classical languages instructor, inevitably found a sunny side. She didn't look very professorial, though, with her fluffy hair, round baby face, and chubby cheeks. Her wire-rimmed eyeglasses were all that saved her from looking like a china doll instead of a professor.

The faculty had assembled in the front parlor of DeLacey House, the women's residence for senior faculty and administrators, to discuss how to respond to the chapel incident.

DeLacey House had been named after a generous patron of the college's early expansion project. The building was not only a residence; it accommodated students and guests for those college events customarily held by the lady principal. The Saturday afternoon string quartet, for example, was a favorite on campus.

The parlor fire had been hastily stoked, but the heat had not really penetrated the chill. Concordia rubbed her hands together in an attempt to warm them, and looked around the room.

The interior décor was decidedly formal, with tall paneled ceilings, several upholstered settees and chairs in dark velvet, and a grand piano in the corner. The faded draperies were the only discordant note in the room. Most ladies would never have allowed their draperies to get in such a state. But the college's finances were tight enough, she knew.

As Concordia continued idly looking around her, she noticed that both President Richter and Ruth Lyman, the college's bursar, were missing from the group. She knew that Miss Lyman was a chronic over-sleeper and would be happy to have missed the drama, but she wondered at President Richter not being here, or at chapel, this morning. That was unusual.

Concordia glanced at Miss Hamilton. She, too, was new to the college this year. Tall and angular, with hazel eyes and graying blond hair pulled back at the nape, she exuded a calm, effortless authority, born of her years as headmistress of a prestigious girls' academy. Immediately after the chapel discovery, Miss Hamilton had quickly squelched what she termed "an indecorous display of hysterics," and sent the girls back to their cottages in the charge of the resident matrons.

No doubt Miss Hamilton was accustomed to curbing similar *indecorous displays* in her former post, Concordia thought. Yet she thought it unlikely Miss Hamilton had ever encountered a likeness of herself impaled on the end of a knife.

Sitting next to Miss Hamilton was Edward Langdon, the dean. He matched the lady principal's calm demeanor, although not her dignified air. He was a large man, with a decided paunch that bulged his jacket and strained the buttons. Miss Hamilton looked over at the dean, who stood and waited for silence.

"We have directed the custodian to clean up the chapel," he said. "The head teacher from each cottage will return the gloves."

"What about those… figures?" Miss Bellini asked. She was a petite woman, with dark hair and eyes, a beautifully fashioned nose completing the classic Roman features of her face. Today, she sat huddled into her shawl. Her usual olive complexion had taken on a sallow tinge.

"I will be keeping those," Miss Hamilton answered. "Perhaps there is some information to be gleaned from them."

Dean Langdon continued. "Resuming our schedule quickly will serve to diminish the pranksters' satisfaction. I know that you ladies tend to dwell on such drama," he smiled, oblivious to the scornful looks sent his way, "but we cannot allow this to–"

"I grant you, Mr. Langdon, that some of our students may derive some thrill from this event," Concordia interrupted, ignoring Miss Hamilton's warning frown, "however, that should be ascribed to their immaturity, rather than their gender. The prank is disturbing, to say the least. Did you not notice the violence of feeling expressed toward Miss Hamilton?"

Concordia dropped her eyes and self-consciously smoothed back a loose strand of hair. *Drat, she was in for it now.*

Dean Langdon looked only mildly surprised. "Miss…?"

"Wells," she answered. *The man still didn't know her name?* She'd been here for months.

"Yes, Miss Wells, I intended no insult, my dear, I was merely inserting a bit of humor into the meeting."

A very *little* bit of humor, Concordia thought. She adjusted the spectacles sliding down her nose.

"Miss Hamilton, President Richter, and I will see to disciplining the offenders." The dean looked over at Miss Hamilton. "No word yet from Arthur?" She shook her head.

"Well, ladies," Dean Langdon said, gathering up his coat, "I must attend to a few things. I'll leave you to figure out the schedule." With a little bow, he left.

Miss Bellini sniffed in disdain. "'Dwelling on drama' indeed. Pah! Men!"

Concordia smothered a laugh.

"We have no time for personal animosities, Miss Bellini," the lady principal chided. "There are plans to be made."

Lucia Bellini flushed in annoyance.

Miss Pomeroy spoke up in her high-pitched voice. "Of course, Miss Hamilton, the presence of the knife is disturbing, but otherwise it seems to be a harmless…"

"Harmless? Have you taken leave of your senses, Gertrude?" Miss Cowles, the librarian, interrupted. Her long, thin nose quivered. "Unbalanced minds are at work here."

Several teachers exchanged anxious glances.

"Where is the bursar? Is she ill?" one teacher asked.

Miss Hamilton pursed her lips in disapproval. "Perhaps, although I wasn't notified. I'll check on Miss Lyman shortly. At the moment, we must decide upon our course of action."

"Perhaps each teacher should question the residents of her house," Concordia offered. "After all, the girls in question would not only have needed to sneak into freshmen bedrooms, they would have had to slip out of their cottages, travel across the grounds, get into the chapel, and then return without being detected. Someone must have noticed something unusual."

Miss Hamilton nodded in approval.

Miss Bellini added, "Those dolls—they would take time to make, would they not? Perhaps other girls may have noticed a bit of the sewing, even if they did not understand the significance of it back then?"

Miss Hamilton nodded again. "Very well. But I would suggest that we make it a casual, less intimidating sort of enquiry. Approach students with whom you have an established relationship of trust. We shall proceed from there."

The gathering broke up soon thereafter, with the decision to resume classes in the afternoon. The lady principal urged the faculty to stay vigilant. "Any violation of the ten o'clock rule should be swiftly dealt with."

Concordia put on her jacket and tried to slip out with the other teachers when Miss Hamilton called to her. "Miss Wells, a moment please."

Concordia, pausing, saw sympathetic glances cast her way as the others left.

"Let us go to my office," Miss Hamilton said, shrugging on a finely-tailored jacket of antique gold, with bronze velvet facing on the lapels to match her skirt. It made Concordia's own nobby blue wool, which she considered quite smart-looking when she bought it last year, seem dowdy by comparison.

They stepped out the door to a temperate February day, especially welcome after the bone-chilling temperatures of last night. Concordia appreciatively breathed in the sharp scent of damp earth, a promise of spring to the winter-weary. The lady principal set a brisk and nimble pace. Concordia, more diminutive in build, struggled to keep up with her longer strides, and dodged the melting snow piles edging the path with considerably less grace. Her view more often than not was that of Miss Hamilton's tall, straight back as she fell behind.

They were approaching Founder's Hall, a two-winged brick structure which housed the library, study rooms, a faculty lounge, and offices. Known simply on campus as "the Hall," it was as old as the chapel and constructed in the same gabled, vaulted Gothic style. The college had quickly outgrown the Hall's early purpose as a classroom building and had to construct another, as well as a badly-needed larger dining hall. These buildings formed an open quadrangle that was the heart of the campus. There was a pond on the far side of the building cluster, a favorite for skating parties this time of year. Although perhaps not for long, she thought, glancing at the warning ropes strung across one section of the pond, where the ice had softened.

Concordia loved the blend of old and new on the campus, the two-fold sense of legacy and progress. It was a small college by most standards, with three hundred current students, approximately half of whom lived in the six residential cottages, with the rest traveling daily from town by street rail. Yet the school boasted many of the same modern comforts as the larger women's colleges in the region, such as upgraded electric lights and steam heat. The school also claimed a roster of esteemed professors among its faculty, particularly in the subjects of physics and moral philosophy. She was fortunate to be teaching here.

Concordia was so preoccupied that she nearly collided with Miss Hamilton, who had finally stopped beside the door to the Hall. Fortunately, that lady seemed equally distracted, as she checked her watch.

"Oh, dear, it's later than I thought." Miss Hamilton shook her head. "I'm afraid I don't have time today, Miss Wells, but there are matters that I wish to discuss at our earliest opportunity. I have a task in mind for you. You are finished with classes as of three o'clock tomorrow, I believe?"

Concordia nodded. How the lady principal managed to keep the schedules of three dozen faculty members in mind was a feat she could not contemplate. There were times when she had difficulty remembering what day of the week it was.

"Splendid. Three o'clock tomorrow, in my office, if you please," Miss Hamilton said. "Now, if you'll excuse me, I'm late for an appointment."

As Concordia watched her hurry inside, she wondered what the lady principal could possibly want her to do.

Chapter 4

"Composition books out, ladies." Concordia turned to the large chalkboard behind her on the instructor's platform, and wrote out the day's assignment for her "Masters in English Poetry" students.

With a rustle of skirts, satchel flaps, and a number of stifled groans, the sophomores began copying the essay question. A few squinted at the board; the weak daylight filtering through the leaded-glass windows of Moss Hall did little to brighten the room. Concordia switched on the electric lights along the walls. She caught a whiff of burnt filament as a bulb behind her flickered and went out. She suppressed a sigh. *Third one today. Gas lamps are more reliable than this faddish invention.*

Discontented murmurs in the back corner of the room caught her attention.

"Yes, Miss Landry; you have something to contribute on the subject of Mr. Wordsworth's *Preludes?*" Miss Landry and her cohort, Miss Spencer, were a popular duo. Give them any latitude, Concordia had learned, and discipline in the classroom would quickly degrade.

Miss Landry was a pretty, brown-haired girl, with a snub nose and a demeanor to match. The girl assumed an aggrieved air. "Oh, Miss Wells, Wordsworth is such a *grind.*"

Several students nodded their agreement. Miss Spencer managed a pretty pout.

"When are we going to study someone *exciting*–and *radical*," she continued, "such as Lord Byron?"

Concordia had been expecting some sort of mutiny from the girl; it had been weeks since she last staged a rebellious display.

"One's course of studies should not be determined by popularity, Miss Landry," Concordia answered evenly. "Mr. Wordsworth shaped an important poetic tradition, and was England's poet laureate, both of which you should know by this point."

More sighs.

Concordia plowed on. "We cannot proceed to Lord Byron and his company until you and your fellows show mastery of today's writing theme. Furthermore, I am expecting better work from the class than I have seen heretofore."

There was an uneasy shifting in seats.

She drove her point home. "I cannot countenance sloppiness—neither sloppy thinking nor sloppy handwriting. This is not a 'snap course,' ladies."

After a pause she pointed to the question on the board.

"You may begin writing."

As the students bent over their work, Concordia wondered if her rebuke had any effect upon Miss Landry and her set, each of them the product of long-established New England upper-society families. These particular girls were part of a new breed of privileged young ladies: those here for the "college experience." It was the social life of the college, rather than the pursuit of higher learning or a vocation, that mattered to them.

Such a phenomenon produced dismay among the older women professors. Concordia had listened to a number of lamentations on the subject in the professors' lounge. Miss Cowles, who had an opinion on nearly everything, was particularly vocal.

"These young things have no idea how the women before them have fought to get a college education," Miss Cowles said, spectacles quivering down her thin nose in her agitation. "My poor mother, the good Lord rest her soul, lived in terror that I would return home from college a raving lunatic. She believed everything she read in *Harper's*, especially the Clarke article–remember that one?–about the damage that academic study can produce in a young lady's brain. Oh, the rows we had!"

Concordia recalled her own struggles with her family when she wanted to attend college. Although she was younger than Miss Cowles, the early ideas about a woman's "limited" intellect still lingered.

Another teacher chimed in. "I agree with you, Jane. I find it exceedingly odd that now it is *fashionable* for these society girls to go to college, but, oh, not to study, mind you. If we are not careful, women's colleges will be in danger of becoming social clubs."

Concordia didn't believe the situation was quite so dire, but she had kept her opinion to herself. There was no denying that, for at least some of these young ladies, college life was a round of teas, frolics, dances, clubs, and boys.

And, lately of course, pranks. Concordia found her thoughts straying to yesterday's incident, and Miss Hamilton. How did she feel about a knife being plunged into her effigy? Why hers, and no one else's? Such overt hostility was perplexing. Concordia could think of nothing the woman had done to provoke such a response. The knife suggested spite, rather than harmless mischief.

It had been a relief, at least, to find one matter resolved, upon President Richter's return yesterday afternoon. According to the faculty gossip chain (Miss Bellini was an excellent source of information), Richter had little to say about the prank when it was reported to him, and had, in fact, been rather brusque in the face of Miss Hamilton's questions. He had a meeting with the trustees, and that was the end of the subject. He did, however, express concern over the disappearance of Miss Lyman.

No one knew where the bursar could possibly be. She wasn't in her office, or her faculty quarters; she had not been seen by anyone, nor had she left word about a family emergency requiring her to leave campus. By all accounts, she had seemed upset lately, so perhaps a family crisis was to blame. But why depart without notice of any kind?

Word spread throughout campus that the lady principal had sent telegrams to Miss Lyman's immediate family this morning, inquiring as to her whereabouts. President Richter, reluctant though he was to contact the police and invite negative publicity for the college, pledged to do so if the bursar had not been heard from today.

Concordia suppressed a sigh and, checking her watch, brought her attention back to the task at hand.

"Pass your papers forward, please."

She continued with the lesson as she collected them.

"Perhaps you would find Mr. Wordsworth more interesting if you had made yourselves better acquainted with his biography. You would have learned that he was quite the radical in his youth, and supported the cause of the French Revolution."

She suppressed a smile as the students leaned forward more attentively. Wordsworth, a revolutionary? Perhaps he was not such a grind, after all.

"He and his fellow activists," Concordia continued, "William Godwin, Mary Wollstonecraft, and Thomas Paine, among others, dreamed of a society of equals, with a government run by the consent of the people, for the common good. But Wordsworth found, to his horror, that the Revolution had turned their dream for France into a bloody nightmare." Concordia quoted from memory:

> *"Friends, enemies, of all parties, ages, ranks,*
> *Head after head, and never heads enough*
> *For those who bade them fall...."*

"Some of you may recognize Wordsworth's allusion to the guillotine. Turn to Book Ten of *The Prelude*, beginning with line 307," she directed.

As the students flipped through pages, Concordia turned her attention to the instigator.

"Miss Landry, you may begin reading aloud."

Miss Landry, momentarily bested, stood and smoothed her skirt, and began.

A shriek from outside stopped the recitation and sent Concordia and the girls rushing to the windows.

The disturbance came from the pond, just below. With a quick glance at the sight of hand-wringing girls crouched at the pond's edge, Concordia snatched her jacket.

"Fetch the custodian and tell him to bring a long pole. Quickly!"

Open-mouthed, Concordia's students watched her dash out of the room.

Chapter 5

Week 3, Instructor Calendar
February 1896

Concordia half ran, half slid down the snowy hill to the pond, gloveless and jacket flapping, hands and feet already chilled by the time she reached the scene.

It was a skating party of four girls, half of whom had fallen through the ice and were flailing in the water in the middle of the pond, the other half flailing just as ineffectually on dry land.

"Stop that caterwauling *at once*, or so help me, I shall push you in to join your companions," Concordia snapped.

Her threat–or the fact that she had flung a clump of snow at their heads for good measure–served to quickly settle the girls down.

"You–go get more help–and blankets." One young lady scurried off.

Concordia looked across the ice to where the other two, Miss Dellawan and Miss Patterson, had fallen through. Miss Dellawan had by now managed to pull herself out of the water and lay in an exhausted, shuddering heap. She was in no condition to help her companion, still struggling in the water. Concordia could see Miss Patterson trying for a hand-hold along the slick edge of the ice, breaking off fragile bits, which only widened the hole she was in. The girl would go under soon, from sheer exhaustion and the weight of her skirts.

"Pass me the end of that rope," Concordia directed Miss Gerald, pointing to the caution rope which had sectioned off the thinning ice. The heedless girls had obviously taken it down in order to skate. One end was still tied around a tree trunk.

Wrapping the free end of the rope around her arm, Concordia cautiously stretched out on her stomach along the ice, as she had seen a cousin once do when rescuing the family's sheepdog at Aunt Florence's farm. "It distributes your weight, so you're less likely to fall through," he'd explained.

Let's hope this works. She pushed herself forward across the ice, testing to see where the surface would hold her weight. Her progress seemed agonizingly slow, and the ice made alarming creaking noises. Once, a section caved beneath her torso a few inches, soaking her breathless in icy water.

Concordia looked over at Miss Patterson. Her head was still above water, thank goodness, but she was barely moving.

"I'm c-c-coming!" Concordia called. "Float on your back if you c-can!" It was surprisingly difficult to shout while lying on one's stomach. She could barely get a breath between her chattering teeth, and her midsection had gone numb. But she was nearly there.

"Miss Wells!" a voice shouted.

She turned on her side to glance back to shore, where her class had now gathered, along with Mr. Drew, the custodian. He gestured to a ladder that he had tied to another rope. "This shud do better for ye!" Carefully, he slid it out ahead of him on the ice as he crawled towards Concordia, who continued to edge cautiously toward Miss Patterson.

By this point she was in arm's-reach of the girl, who was fading in and out of consciousness. Sliding as close as she dared to the hole, Concordia lunged and grabbed the young lady's collar, gasping as her own face and chest were doused.

Despite the girl's sodden skirts, she was buoyant enough for Concordia to pass the rope under her shoulders and tie a clumsy knot. Her fingers were too numb for anything better. She hoped it held.

"Pull!" she called to the growing crowd on shore. Several sets of hands smoothly pulled the rope. Soon Miss Patterson, revived and sobbing in relief, was safe in a cocoon of blankets.

Mr. Drew and the ladder had reached Miss Dellawan, who was shaking uncontrollably. Concordia slid over to them, took off her damp jacket and wrapped it around her. "Lay f-f-flat on the l-l-ladder," she told the girl.

"Sorry I couldn't get to ye sooner, miss," the custodian said, helping her with Miss Dellawan. "I knew it was a ladder ye *really* needed–better'n a pole–but somebody'd moved it from the Hall's back shed. Took a bit o' time to find."

Concordia could only nod stiffly. She felt as if she would never get warm again. And she must be a sight. Her hair had come out of its pins, she had lost a boot somewhere, and her wet skirts clung to her legs.

At last, they all reached safety to a chorus of cheers, and more helpfully, blankets. Amid the profusion of thanks, tears and embraces, all Concordia wanted was to go back to the cottage to change into dry clothing.

"Miss **Wells**."

That stern tone could only belong to one person.

Sure enough, there stood the lady principal, wearing an expression colder than the pond water that saturated Concordia and the miscreants. The crowd dispersed, suddenly recalling engagements elsewhere. Only Concordia, Mr. Drew, and the soon-to-be-disciplined band of four remained.

Concordia suppressed a groan. She remembered that her appointment with Miss Hamilton was–*now*.

Miss Hamilton had turned her attention to the girls. "Can you walk? Good. Go directly to the infirmary and wait for me there. And count your blessings that we have quick-thinking staff to keep you from killing yourselves."

Dripping, sniffling, and trailing the ends of their blankets along the ground, the offenders shuffled off to the infirmary. Concordia was tempted to sniffle and shuffle off, too. Instead, she wrapped her blanket–and what remained of her dignity–more firmly around her.

"I know I've missed our appointment, Miss Hamilton, but if I c-c-ould just ch-ch-change–" *Drat.* She couldn't stop shaking.

"Let's get you back to your cottage, Miss Wells, before you catch your death. We'll discuss this"—she gestured vaguely at the pond, ropes, ladder, and Concordia's stockinged foot—"later." She picked up a muddy boot lying on the ground and held it out. "I believe this is yours."

As Concordia sat on the ground to put her boot back on and the custodian cleaned up the discarded rope, Miss Hamilton looked out over the pond.

"We should prohibit skating here the rest of the season. These girls have no sense. Mr. Drew, could you—" She broke off in mid-sentence, as she caught sight of something on the far side of the pond, partly obscured by low-hanging tree limbs. She paled.

Concordia followed her gaze, and caught her breath. Directly below the tree's shadow, amid another break in the ice, was a rounded, clothed hump.

"Mr. Drew." Miss Hamilton's voice held just a hint of a quaver. "Fetch the president. And the police. We have found Miss Lyman."

Chapter 6

Week 3, Instructor Calendar
February 1896

Apparently a great deal of effort is involved in extricating a body from a frozen pond, a fact that Concordia and others on campus wished they need never have learned. After the unusually warm day, the ice wasn't strong enough at that end to withstand a man's weight, but there was still plenty of it to hamper efforts to get a boat through. A team of policemen and firemen, with ropes, ladders, and hooks, worked into the evening before successfully pulling the unfortunate lady's body from the water.

The faculty, shaken by the discovery, kept the students inside their cottages, away from the scene, until the body was taken to the city morgue. President Richter had the sad task of informing Miss Lyman's family and meeting her brother there.

Later, at a hastily called faculty meeting, a bedraggled-looking Arthur Richter returned from the morgue with more sad news.

"It looks as if Miss Lyman's death was not an accident. It was a deliberate act to end her own life," he said, his voice hoarse from a bad case of laryngitis. He sat down, absent-mindedly rubbing a scratch along his temple.

"Is that what the police believe?" Miss Hamilton asked, amid background murmurs of shock and distress.

"That's not yet what they are saying *officially*," the president said, struggling to project his voice into the room, "but I spoke with the chief of police. Miss Lyman's boots were not clad in steel runners for skating, and a fabric sash from the skirt she was wearing was tied around one ankle. He hypothesizes that she was trying to weigh herself down in the water, but after her death, the sash snagged on something sharp and broke off the weight. The coroner found a wound to her head, where she struck one of the rocks, as she…went under," he finished, with a shaky breath and a fit of coughing.

The poor man, Concordia thought. To be ill, and dealing with such tragedy, too.

"But there was no note in her rooms," Miss Hamilton protested. "I looked for one myself in her quarters, before we found her. I was trying to determine if she had a family emergency."

Richter cleared his throat and squeaked, "I wondered that, too. The police chief said suicides don't always leave notes."

Concordia felt a twist of pity for Miss Lyman, but wasn't shocked by the news. It had seemed unlikely that Miss Lyman's death was an accident. The bursar had been missing since the early morning of the chapel incident, but had attended supper the night before. That meant she must have gone out on the pond in the middle of the night.

Although Concordia hadn't known Ruth Lyman very well, it seemed far-fetched that the bursar would have gone skating in the middle of a frigid night, and *alone*. Even if she had accidentally fallen in, wouldn't someone have heard her cries for help? And now, the sash found around her ankle made suicide a clear conclusion.

And in turn, suicide suggested that Miss Lyman's feelings of guilt over the college's financial problems had proved too much for her to bear.

Much like an embarrassing relative one does not like to acknowledge, the shaky financial status of Hartford Women's College was a condition that could only be ignored for so long. The problems had begun with the stock market crash–dubbed the "Panic of '93"–three years before. The resulting run on the banks had plunged the entire country into the worst economic depression it had ever suffered. Even now, there was still debate about whether President Cleveland's opposition to the free coinage of silver had prolonged the depression, or had, as he asserted, saved the financial viability of the Treasury.

It was common knowledge that Hartford Women's College had shared in the misery, sustaining heavy losses, and that President Richter felt responsible for advising the trustees to invest college funds in railroad stocks just before everything had spiraled out of control.

From there, it was said, the college had suffered additional financial setbacks: unpaid invoices, inexplicable money transfers that could not be tracked satisfactorily, a sold parcel of college-owned land that did not fetch the price originally thought. Although the bursar had done her best in such a crisis, accounting books were ill-kept during that chaotic time, when emergency funds had to be moved quickly. Concordia had heard the board of trustees was still trying to untangle the mess, even as the college struggled to pay its current bills.

No one had blamed the bursar, although there had been talk of hiring an outside accountant. Now, of course, someone would be taking over the dead woman's former responsibilities.

Poor Miss Lyman. Could this have driven her to act so desperately?

But that led to more questions. *Why go to the pond to end it all? And why now?*

The students and staff grappled with these questions over the next week, as discussions, conjectures, and regrets circulated. The police interviewed staff members close to Miss Lyman. Concordia was glad she was not among *that* group. She had never spoken at length with a policeman before, and the thought made her a little uncomfortable. Even the sight of the two uniformed men on the college campus this week seemed strange. It was an unsettling reminder that all was not as it should be.

At a school as closely-knit as Hartford Women's College, there are very few secrets, and soon Concordia learned the gist of the police interviews.

Several close associates of Miss Lyman had reported noticing a recent moodiness and preoccupation in the lady; even Arthur Richter, when pressed, had reluctantly acknowledged that he'd wondered if the bursar was suffering from melancholia, but had dismissed the idea.

What could we have done for her? seemed the current refrain on everyone's lips. A memorial service was held, in which only praise was spoken; nothing about her mistakes or struggles, or suspicions of the mishandling of funds.

In that manner, Miss Lyman's death was pronounced an unfortunate suicide and quietly pushed out of the way, questions unanswered. And yet, Concordia was uneasy. She never liked unanswered questions.

Chapter 7

A few days after the memorial service, Concordia had her long-delayed meeting with the lady principal.

Miss Hamilton made one brief mention of the pond rescue that preceded the discovery of Miss Lyman.

"We will not be taking any more chances," she said, with a meaningful look at Concordia, "will we?"

Miss Hamilton sat tirelessly straight, her crisp white shirtwaist showing not a sign of crease or wrinkle. Concordia surreptitiously smoothed her skirt and tugged at her cuffs. "Miss Patterson would not have lasted much longer. I had to act."

"Perhaps," Miss Hamilton said, "and I am grateful to you for rescuing her, at considerable risk to yourself. However, it strikes me as reckless and ill-considered on your part. I expect my staff to comport themselves with more decorum. Leave the heroics to others, Miss Wells. We certainly don't wish to lose more staff."

"Yes, ma'am," Concordia answered meekly.

"This is your first year, is it not?" the lady principal asked, in a change of subject.

"It is my first year *here*," Concordia said. "I held a teaching post before at my alma mater. Mr. Young recommended I apply for this position."

Nathaniel Young, a family friend, was on the board of trustees for Hartford Women's College.

"But Hartford is the city of my childhood, so I am not new to the area," she added.

In general, Concordia was glad to be back in Hartford. She had missed the familiar haunts, the bustle of the downtown district, and the handful of friends she had left behind. Her younger sister Mary, now married, lived in affluent Asylum Hill, barely two miles from the college. To the surprise of both, their renewed communication had begun to produce a friendship that had eluded them as children.

But Concordia's homecoming was not entirely congenial, which was to be expected. Her mother, widowed years ago, still lived in their childhood home, also nearby. Concordia had made one obligatory attempt to visit, only to be coldly rebuffed. She had not made a second attempt.

Miss Hamilton broke into her thoughts. "It is difficult for someone new, the adjustment. Especially for an administrator. This too is my first year at the college, as you know, and I have had to learn about the people I work with; determine who is reliable, who is not, and make best use of people's strengths."

There seemed to be no good response to this, so Concordia didn't offer any.

"You are no doubt aware that Miss Banning is too ill to return to teaching," Miss Hamilton continued.

"I hear her rheumatics are troubling her in this weather," Concordia said. Miss Banning had taught history at the college since its inception nearly twenty years ago. Her retirement was almost certain now, but the lady seemed to dither about whether she was really retired or not.

"We have been able to borrow professors from Trinity College to teach her classes," Miss Hamilton continued, "but we have found no one to take charge of the senior play. I was hoping you could--"

"But I am only a junior instructor," Concordia protested, knowing now where this was leading. "Really, I know very little about directing student plays."

Leading the senior play would not have been the job of a new professor, as it was considered a prestigious duty.

Hartford's elite attended the performance, and the seniors thought of it as the crowning glory of their college years.

In Concordia's mind, it was a prestigious pain in the neck.

"Nonsense," Miss Hamilton said, "I have reviewed your background. You had stage experience as a college student, besides having taught the Shakespeare play they will perform. I will give you Miss Banning's address in town, should you need to confer with her. She is well enough for visitors, I hear."

Concordia thought frantically of possible excuses as Miss Hamilton rummaged through a drawer and pulled out a key. "Ah–here, Miss Wells," she said, passing it over, "I am promoting you to temporary senior faculty status for the rest of the term. This unlocks the auditorium and most of the common buildings."

Concordia looked down at the key; it was heavy and ornate, with a medallion of the college's seal attached to it. She experienced conflicting sensations of pride and alarm.

But she wasn't ready to concede defeat, yet. "There must be someone else, surely? I already supervise the literature club and the bicycling club. How would I have time for the senior play?"

The lady principal's lips twitched at the reference to the bicycle club. Except for winter weather, the avid cyclists took to the paths regularly. President Richter was less than enthusiastic–dismayed might be a better word–to see the young ladies wobbling about the campus on their machines, clad in bicycling suits of shortened skirts and bloomers.

"An upperclassman can lead the literature club, Miss Wells. I'm sure you know of someone adequate for the position. As for the bicycling," Miss Hamilton added with a straight face, "no doubt you will still find the time."

Concordia walked back to Willow Cottage, lost in thought. Miss Hamilton was a difficult woman to refuse.

Directing the senior play would be a substantial drain on her time. In addition to her teaching duties, her responsibilities as live-in chaperone–surrogate mother, really–made the concept of *leisure* seem laughable. With the term beginning inauspiciously enough with Miss Lyman's death, Concordia could tell it was going to be a difficult semester.

Events would prove her prediction to be painfully correct.

Chapter 8

If you can look into the seeds of time
And say which grain will grow and which will not,
Speak then to me.
                                    Macbeth, I.iii

Week 4, Instructor Calendar
February 1896

In her sitting room, Concordia settled into a well-worn padded armchair to get re-acquainted with the Shakespeare play the seniors had selected for this year's performance.

Macbeth. Also known as "the Scottish play" and "the unlucky play." Unlucky for her, certainly. Concordia grimaced. She doubted that the elite of Hartford society were ready for a tale of gore, violence and witchcraft, not to mention a haranguing female as one of the leads.

There was a knock on her door.

"Come in!" she called.

Ruby Hitchcock leaned in. "A lady to see you, Miss Wells." This was followed by a crash overhead. "I'll see to that. They're likely cooking fudge again," she said, and hastily left, muttering, "I'm gettin' too old for this nonsense."

Concordia frowned as she headed for the front parlor. Indeed, the odor of burnt chocolate was strong out here. Thank heaven for Ruby. Concordia knew she would take a firm hand against illegal cooking in the rooms. Although the lady grumbled a good deal, Concordia had learned very little flustered her. Perhaps it came from being thrown back upon her own resources as a young widow after the Civil War, making her living however she could—as maid, cook, and seamstress, among other occupations—before becoming a fixture at Willow Cottage, when the seminary-turned-college abandoned its single-building dormitory system for the more domestic "cottage" arrangement. The years of hard work had roughened Ruby's hands, certainly, but beneath matron's crotchety exterior, she had a genuine fondness for the girls in her care.

Concordia straightened her collar and smoothed her hair before opening the door to the parlor.

"Sophia! What are you doing here?" she cried in delight, embracing the young woman in front of the fireplace.

Sophia Adams had been a childhood friend of both Concordia and her sister Mary. Mary, before her marriage, had occasionally helped with Sophia's charity work. Sophia was also active these days in the suffrage movement that was gaining ground in the area.

Upon second glance, Concordia noticed that the pale skin under Sophia's eyes was smudged with shadows, and her clothing, a simple walking suit of gray worsted, hung more loosely upon her slender form.

"You must be working too hard, Sophie. Have you been well?"

Sophia shook her head. "I've come to take you back to Mary. She's quite ill."

Concordia felt her stomach lurch. "But I thought she was better now." She leaned against the writing desk. "How bad is it this time?"

Mary had been in ill-health for several months, since her return from her three-month bridal tour in southern Europe. The bouts of abdominal pain and weakness usually abated after a course of medicine and rest. When Concordia had last seen Mary, just after the New Year, she seemed better.

"Doctor Westfield is calling it another 'episode,'" Sophia answered, grimacing. "But I'm concerned that it's something more. Mary cannot keep anything down now, and her fever is worse. I think even the judge is worried."

That was certainly saying a great deal, Concordia thought, since Mary's father-in-law viewed succumbing to physical illness as a lack of mental fortitude. A little indisposition would do him some good, in her opinion. Perhaps it would have a humbling effect.

Concordia dreaded her encounters with Judge Armstrong. The two of them disagreed fervently about women's education, vocation, and right to vote, and had taken up battle during past visits. There would be no avoiding him now.

But that wasn't the only person she sought to avoid.

"Has Mother been told?" Concordia asked.

Sophia shook her head. "She's visiting Aunt Florence out in the country. They got a lot of snow yesterday, and I haven't been able to get word to her."

"But don't worry," Sophia added, misreading Concordia's sigh as one of distress, rather than relief, "I'll keep trying."

After packing a valise and giving Ruby a note for Miss Hamilton, Concordia and Sophia set out for Mary's home.

Hartford's street rail had a stop within walking distance of the college. The trolley ride would take them along Main Street through the business district, and across Asylum Avenue, to stop a block from where Mary lived.

"Henry has the carriage. He's still downtown," Sophia explained. "I volunteered to bring you back on the trolley rather than wait."

In Concordia's view, the Hartford Street Railway was more efficient than navigating crowded evening streets in a private vehicle, especially now that the city had switched over all of its lines from horse-drawn cars to the new electric-propulsion. Within minutes of waiting, they caught a glimpse of the streetcar as it approached, the signature Tuscan red with cream-tinted trim gleaming in the dying light of winter dusk. She and Sophia gave the conductor their nickel fares, collected their transfer tickets to the Asylum Line, and settled themselves on the benches as the trolley lurched into motion.

From Main Street, Concordia saw the Connecticut River waterfront in the distance, dotted with smoke stacks from the Colt factory. The mingling smells of coal smoke and stagnant water had receded by the time they approached the City Hall Post Office stop. From there, they switched cars for the briefer trip along the Asylum Avenue line.

Concordia caught glimpses of the closely packed tenement buildings of the East Side, three- and four-story shoddy structures propped haphazardly alongside one another, with clotheslines stretched across narrow alleys and rear yards. Sophia worked with families in this section.

"How is your work going?" Concordia asked Sophia, to keep her own thoughts diverted.

Sophia made a face. "Frankly, not well. Oh, there have been small successes—the Harrity family was able to move out of those awful tenements and into a decent home. Our settlement house was able to find work for Mrs. Harrity—she's recently widowed. But there are so many others. Women especially, and their little ones—with no schooling, not even reading and writing. The children can't go to school because they have to earn money for the family. They get work in the thread and loom mills, but it's back-breaking work for a child, and they are paid a pittance. Everyone in the family works, but it's barely enough to keep body and soul together."

Concordia could see Sophia's distress, and was about to change the subject when Sophia continued in a fierce whisper, leaning closer:

"Do you know what some of these women have to resort to, just to put bread in their children's mouths? Do you realize what peril they expose themselves to, from disease or brutality? And men use them—for sport, for pleasure, for some proof of manliness." Sophia gave a hollow laugh. "We shun the women who act in desperation, but not the men who take advantage of them for amusement. And yet we consider ourselves genteel and civilized?"

Concordia shifted uneasily. She had no answer. She had always assumed that streetwalkers—there was no doubt whom Sophia was alluding to—were morally weak creatures, and perhaps too lazy to perform respectable work. She had never really considered the question before.

"These evils come home to roost. That is the way of things," Sophia said softly, standing up as their stop approached.

Judge Armstrong's house, like most others in Asylum Hill, was an impressive structure: asymetrically-proportioned, painted slate blue with creamy gingerbread trim, with peaked roofs and gables of the Gothic-revival cottage style once popular in the '40s. Before they reached the door, it was opened by a nervous parlor maid, ushering them in and taking their coats.

"Have Mr. Armstrong or the doctor arrived yet?" Concordia asked.

"No, miss. But Mrs. Armstrong is keen to see you."

Sophia put a reassuring hand on Concordia's arm. "I'll wait in the parlor. I think Mary wants to see you alone."

Concordia nodded. She was in for a long night.

Chapter 9

Sleep that knits up the raveled sleave of care.
II.iii

Week 4, Instructor Calendar
February 1896

Concordia sat beside Mary's bed, straightening the crumpled covers. Even in a laudanum sleep, Mary was curled up tightly, protectively, around her abdomen, as if bracing herself against spasms of pain.

When in good health, she was a pretty, blond-haired young woman, with a heart-shaped face and a mild temperament. Her illness, however, had furrowed her brow, made her complexion sickly and her hair lank and dull against the pillows.

Concordia wrinkled her nose. The stuffy room smelled strongly of carbolic acid, despite the lavender the maids had tucked under the mattress and carpets. She wished she could open a window.

She reached once again to wring out wet cloths for her sister's forehead and neck. Mary had been awake that first night, but talking exhausted her. She had not been alert for much of the past two days.

Mary murmured and turned in her restless sleep. Concordia fumed. That quack of a doctor, an old friend of the family that Judge Armstrong insisted on consulting, prescribed nothing but useless tonics and powders. We're on the brink of the twentieth century, should we not be able to do more?

Henry should have consulted a specialist long ago. But Mary's husband of six months deferred to his overbearing father in nearly everything, including when to seek further help for his ailing wife.

Concordia found the entire household exasperating. Henry's mother had died in his infancy, so there was no mother-in-law to supervise Mary's care. A household of men in charge? She shuddered. They failed to understand that Mary required better tending to her hour-to-hour needs than what the inexperienced maid, Nancy, could give.

Some of her frustration, Concordia knew, was directed inward. She felt guilty for not paying closer attention to her sister, or spending more time with her. It was obvious now that Mary had deliberately concealed the seriousness of her condition. But why?

Mary's behaviors and preferences had long baffled Concordia. As girls, they had been worlds apart. Concordia inhabited a realm of ink-stained hands and dusty books, where libraries were delightful and dinner parties torturous; Mary lived in a world of manicures and fashion magazines, where social calls were the breath of life and dead poets a yawning bore. There was little common ground.

Then Concordia left for college, a defiant and disgruntled nineteen-year-old. Her mother took to her bed for a week.

If only their father had been living; he would have championed her dream of college and smoothed the way for her. He had been the scholar of the family, the one who had given Concordia her name, for the Roman goddess of harmony.

"Harmony" had been an apt descriptor of her relationship with her father, but with no one else. Concordia never returned to live at home.

Mary was sixteen when Concordia left. By the time she had completed her college degree, her sister was all grown up. Hesitantly at first, they began exchanging polite letters, which were soon filled with happy news of Mary's upcoming marriage to Henry Armstrong.

It was an ideal match; Henry, like his father, was trained for the bar, and was on his way to making a name for himself among Hartford's privileged set. Mary fit well with his ambitions; she would make a pretty wife and a charming hostess.

Both families supported the union. Concordia attended the ceremony, seeing her mother for the first time since she had left home. Nothing had changed between them. Mother was as cold and uncommunicative as ever, which provoked Concordia into baiting her, with talk of the women's movement and her own scholarly pursuits. Even as she found herself behaving this way, Concordia wondered why on earth she was deliberately making a bad situation worse.

Concordia and Mary, on the other hand, found it easier to get along as adults than they had as children, and looked forward to the possibility of visits and outings now that she was teaching at Hartford Women's College. But it wasn't working out that way, between Mary's ill-health and Concordia's teaching duties.

Shaking her head, Concordia resolved to spend more time with her sister, once she had recovered. She would not take such opportunities for granted again.

"Miss Concordia," a soft voice interrupted her thoughts. Nancy was in the doorway, carrying a tray.

"Just set it down over there." Concordia gestured toward the nightstand.

"Yes, miss… but… I also came in to tell you that Doctor Westfield is here."

Nancy turned her head as she spoke, for the good doctor followed closely on the heels of the maid's announcement, saying, "Ho… Miss Wells! Good to see you, my dear!" in the sort of jovial voice that seemed much too loud for the sickroom. Concordia wondered if he startled his near-death patients back to life through sheer volume.

The man was as large as his voice, and walked in a waddling, side-to-side fashion that set his coattails swaying. He had a wide, generous mouth, reddened nose, and kindly eyes. Although Concordia didn't consider him the right choice for Mary's physician, he seemed likable enough.

Mary was starting to wake, blinking and looking up at him in confusion while the opiates cleared. She glanced across at Concordia, reaching out her hand. It was surprisingly cold. Concordia chafed it gently.

"Doctor Westfield has come to check on you, dear," she said. "I'll be out in the hall, and I'll come right back in when he's finished." Mary reluctantly let her go.

Concordia felt as if she had been in the sickroom for an eternity, but dusk was just beginning to stretch through the long hall windows. She looked at the bare bones of trees along the avenue, casting black and gray shadows upon the frozen ground. It was beginning to snow again. The New England landscape looked as bleak as she felt.

She jumped when the front door bell sounded in the stillness. Knowing the staff were otherwise occupied, Concordia went downstairs, opening the door to a familiar face.

"Nathaniel!" she exclaimed. "This is a surprise!"

Nathaniel Young was an older man, with a head of thick, wavy brown hair heavily streaked with silver. He was of her parents' generation, and had been a steadfast presence during Concordia's and Mary's childhood years. To Concordia, he seemed like a favorite uncle, one who would chastise the children for jumping on the sofa, with a wink and a smile.

He was shivering, and his voice was thick with worry. "Sophia sent me a note about Mary. How is she?"

Concordia led him to the parlor fire before answering. They sat, Concordia making sure that Nathaniel perched on a chair closest to the warmth.

"Dr. Westfield is with her now." Concordia tried to put more reassurance into her tone than she actually felt about this news.

"What does he say? This is the fifth such attack she has had, Concordia, did you know that? What in the world is wrong with her? Why do they not consult another physician?"

Concordia grimaced. "I have asked Henry the same questions, and I only get evasions. I know he's reluctant to defy his father's wishes."

She patted his hand. "But I will keep pushing him to seek another opinion. I promise."

"Will I be able to see her tonight?" His eyes were hopeful.

She shook her head. "The doctor typically gives Mary a sedative in the evening. He says sleep is the best remedy." She kept her opinion to herself regarding *that* truism. She stifled a yawn and rubbed her stiff neck.

"Then I should go," Nathaniel said, rising. "You need some rest, too, my dear. You *will* send word when she can have visitors?"

"Of course," she promised.

When he left, she watched him through the window, head bent against the swirling snow. Even after all these years, she thought, he is a staunch family friend.

As tired as she was, sleep did not come easily that night. Perhaps it was the watching and worrying over Mary; perhaps it was successive nights in a strange bed; perhaps it was the unfamiliar noises—the creaks of the house, the sighing of the wind in the trees.

When she at last drifted asleep, she had strange, fitful dreams. The creaks became footsteps; the sighing became toneless murmurings. The air grew cold as she seemed to glide along corridors, opening doors that led to more passageways, following the sounds. At last, she came upon a door that opened into a room.

Her room. She saw herself in bed, asleep. And across the room, a small, white-gowned form, stretching out a pale hand.

"*Uhh-nehh, uhh-nehh.*"

Her heart thudded madly in her chest. She wanted to run, wanted to scream, but she was immobile.

The apparition silently crossed the room and approached the bed, growing closer, closer...

Concordia awoke to the sound of her own shriek. Bolting out of bed, she turned up the lamp with trembling fingers, and inspected every dark corner of the room.

She was alone.

Chapter 10

A soft knock on the door and the clatter of crockery woke Concordia the next morning.

"How is Mary?" she asked, sitting up and rubbing her eyes. After that awful dream, she had dozed a little, but it wasn't nearly enough.

Annie set down a tray of toast and fragrant tea—*Light of Asia* blend, a favorite of hers. The dollar-per-pound cost, however, was too exorbitant for a teacher's salary. Concordia usually made do with Oolong or Ceylon.

Annie's usual smile was absent this morning. Her teeth tugged nervously at her lower lip. "The missus is no better, Miss Concordia." She hesitated.

"What is it?" Concordia slopped tea into the saucer.

"Oh, miss, no, she's no worse neither," Annie was quick to reassure her, blotting up the spill, "it's just that Nancy is mighty worried, and with not knowing how to take care of a sick 'un, she don't know whether she's coming or going a'times."

Nancy had joined the household as Mary's maid once the couple had returned from their honeymoon trip. Annie was protective of the younger girl, and had helped her learn her new duties. But beyond that, Annie couldn't help her much; she was kept busy enough as the cook's assistant. Occasionally, when a guest stayed in the house, as Concordia had, Annie took on additional maid duties, trading a flour-dusted cotton apron for a crisply-starched lace one.

"What we really need is a nurse. I'll speak to Mr. Armstrong about it—*again*," Concordia said.

Annie straightened up from her smoothing and folding of clothing articles that Concordia had strewn in her fatigue of last night, and gave her a grateful look, mixed with an expression of—something else? It was so fleeting that she wasn't sure she had seen it at all.

After Annie left, Concordia dressed quickly, hoping to catch Henry before he left for downtown. She crouched beside the bed to retrieve a shoe.

A small piece of painted wood under the bed skirt caught her eye. Concordia picked it up. It was a spinning top, its wide round base coming to a small point in the center, a thin stem above, gaily painted with red and yellow stripes.

But what was a child's toy doing in her room? She frowned. There were no children here in the house. She tucked it in her skirt pocket to ask about later.

Concordia was barely in time to waylay Henry. She didn't appreciate conducting the conversation by the front door, but he seemed ill-disposed to budge. Successive wakeful nights had etched lines around his mouth. His thinned face made his eyes look large and luminous. Although he was older than she, it gave him a vulnerable, boyish appearance.

"Yes, what is it? I'm late," he said impatiently.

Concordia tried the direct approach. Her temper was too frayed for tact.

"Henry, you must engage better care for Mary. It is obvious that Doctor Westfield is out of his element. Can't you see that she's only getting worse? And you cannot expect Nancy to shoulder the burden for her care. She's just a girl. You know that Mary needs a specialist and a nurse."

Conflicting emotions crossed his weary face: anger, frustration, worry.

"I have already decided to call in another professional," he said defensively. "He should be here sometime tomorrow. Later, we'll see if a nurse is advisable."

He left, adding under his breath, "What happens now? Heaven only knows."

By the afternoon, Concordia was relieved to see that Mary was resting more comfortably. Nancy was sent to bed, nearly asleep on her feet. Concordia restlessly paced the floor of Mary's room. After three days in the Armstrong house, with little more to divert her mind from the sickness and worry than watching the dust motes settle, she was eager to return to her classes. Heaven only knew how behind they would be, even with another teacher taking over in her absence. But someone needed to stay to take care of Mary.

"Concordia."

She turned to the bed. Mary was awake.

"Mary! How do you feel?" She sat down beside her.

Mary smiled weakly. "I have been better. Where is Mother?"

"She's still trapped at Aunt Florence's, dear," Concordia answered.

Mary gave a sigh. "She misses you, Concordia. She's too proud to admit it, but I can tell."

"I doubt *that*," Concordia retorted.

"You believe that you and Mother are so dissimilar?" Mary said. "I think not. Both of you are stubborn, and carry a long grudge. *You* must be the first to make amends. She is too…set in her ways… to do it."

Concordia shook her head. "You forget how she treats me, Mary. I cannot."

"*Can* not, or *will* not?" Mary persisted. "After I am gone, the two of you will only have each other."

"Tut-tut—you're not going anywhere," Concordia said soothingly.

Mary gave her a steady look. "Try—for me?"

Oh, alright, we'll see. I cannot promise," Concordia grumbled. Mary always knew how to get her way.

Deciding not to push any further, Mary changed the subject. "There's something else you can do for me."

"What is it, dear?"

"Take a look in the attic. No, really," Mary said, in answer to Concordia's puzzled expression. "There have been... noises, coming through the ceiling, in the middle of the night."

Perhaps the dream of last night was still fresh in Concordia's mind, for Mary's words produced a chill at the base of her spine.

She shook off the first ridiculous thoughts that sprang to mind. "What sort of noises?"

"Shuffling, mostly, and occasionally a slight scraping sound." Mary gave a shaky laugh. "I know it sounds crazy, but it's been happening too often this past week for it to be a dream, Concordia. I asked Annie earlier if she would go see, but she looked so alarmed—guess the attic *is* rather gloomy, and she seems the superstitious sort—that I dropped it. When I asked Henry, he acted as if I'd lost my wits."

Concordia patted Mary's hand. "Of course you haven't. Big houses have noises, that's all, and with your illness, and the laudanum the doctor has prescribed, it would be strange if you *didn't* hear things." Perhaps she was trying to reassure herself as much as her sister.

Mary shook her head stubbornly. "It's not the medicine, or my condition. There was someone, some... *thing*, up there."

Concordia felt that quiver of fear inching up her back again. "Did Henry search the attic after you told him?"

"He *said* he did, and saw nothing out of the ordinary. But I want *you* to look, Concordia. You're the only one I can trust."

There was a pause. Mary gave her another pleading look.

"Well, I can certainly look around," Concordia said, standing up and straightening her skirts, "but I doubt that I'll find anything." Except dust and spiders, she thought with a shudder. Heaven knows what condition the fifty-year-old attic would be in.

"Be careful," Mary said. Her lips trembled. "There's one other thing I didn't tell you—about the noises." Her voice dropped to a whisper. "Once, I thought I heard a voice. Garbled. It didn't sound—quite human."

Chapter 11

With Mary's parting words undermining her courage, Concordia hesitantly climbed the narrow back stairs to the Armstrong attic, her bedside lamp in hand. Although it was the middle of the day, the small attic windows would not provide enough light for her to make a thorough search.

And it should keep ghosts from sneaking up from behind, she thought sarcastically. *Let's be sensible, old girl.* She would scare herself witless by her own fancies.

The narrow door opened easily on well-oiled hinges. The attic, though certainly gloomy, seemed to have been vigorously dusted recently, to Concordia's surprise. Her limited experience with attics led her to expect a grimy and neglected jumble of household goods, the detritus of previous occupants and grown children. But the items here were neatly stacked, and allowed plenty of room for movement, if one crouched. Concordia cast her lamp around, making a face at the layers of hideous wallpaper panels, leftovers used to insulate the attic walls. They were peeling in places, and she could see decades of unfortunate décor choices: Neo-Gothic prints of trefoils and towers, garish Rococo designs festooned with gilt and curlicues, the frenzied florals of an Art Nouveau pattern.

The contents of the attic were the sort that one would expect: a wood-and-leather hobbyhorse that Henry had no doubt played with as a little boy; trunks filled with cast-off clothing, one old night-shift sticking out of a corner; an assortment of umbrella stands, hat-racks, and end tables; even a worn mattress propped on its side.

Hadn't she searched enough? She was obviously the only person here. She could report back to Mary and put her fears to rest.

Still, something about this room didn't feel right. Perhaps her disturbing dream of last night, combined with Mary's suppositions, preyed upon Concordia's imagination.

Reluctantly, Concordia continued toward the back of the attic, farther from the sunlight filtering through the narrow window, farther from the only door out of the room.

It was dusty at this end of the room, and a shifted trunk had left its outline. Concordia's heart lurched as she noticed something else: a thin string attached to a wood handle, painted in familiar-looking red and yellow stripes.

Setting down her lamp, Concordia crouched to pick it up. Pulling the top from her pocket, she compared the two. There was no doubt that they were a set. After a couple of clumsy attempts from remembered childhood days, she finally got the top to spin. She idly watched its point make thin swirl marks in the dust as she considered what the presence of these items could mean.

From her vantage point so close to the floor, she could now see similar swirl marks, undisturbed. She frowned. *Someone has been here.*

A movement caught her eye. With a startled squeak, she turned toward the door. It was softly closing by an unseen hand.

"H-h-hello?" she called out, scrambling to get up, but—*bother!*—her skirts hampered quick movement.

By the time she made it to the door, she was too late. The stairs and corridor outside were empty. Who had been spying on her?

She could at least talk to Mary about what she found. After one last glance down the empty hall, Concordia put the spinning top and string in her pocket and headed to her sister's room.

But their talk would have to wait. Mary was asleep. Stroking Mary's light hair as it lay tousled on the pillow, Concordia noted the relaxed delicacy of her sister's face, her easy breathing. She was sleeping more easily than she had in days.

Concordia felt hopeful. The specialist would know what to do. Thank heaven Henry had finally developed a backbone and was getting his wife the care she had long needed. She wondered what Judge Armstrong had to say about Henry's act of defiance. Fortunately, she had not encountered him since her arrival.

As if conjured by her thoughts, the sound of a throat clearing made her turn to see that very man standing in the doorway. Although getting on in years, the judge was still a commanding presence: tall, muscular, and barrel-chested. His florid complexion emphasized the startling contrast between the pure white of his hair and his black brows, which settled into a perpetual frown. Whenever Concordia was in the judge's company, which thankfully was not often, she could not help but stare at those eyebrows.

Concordia accompanied the judge into the hall and closed the door. She stifled a sigh. Whatever he wanted, she resolved not to be goaded into an argument this time.

"Your mother will be arriving soon," he said.

Concordia looked up at him, struggling to avoid the eyebrows. The attempt was futile. There they were, frowning down upon her, as if they had a life of their own.

"But I thought she was still stranded at Aunt Florence's," she said in surprise.

"Miss Adams managed it somehow," the judge said with a derisive snort. "Upstart young woman. Thinks she can intrude her ideas upon other people."

"She *is* resourceful," Concordia said, smiling.

The judge scowled, and the brows drew close to touching.

"'Resourceful' is of little use when you young 'career women' lack the feminine instinct to take proper care of my daughter-in-law," he said sharply. "Perhaps if you had paid attention to your true vocation, Concordia—which is *hearth and home*–and left behind these faddish notions of doing a *man's* job, you could better care for Mary. Your mother's arrival cannot come soon enough for *me*. She, at least, has the maternal instincts necessary to tend to your sister."

"Had you engaged a proper *professional*," Concordia retorted, "a 'career woman' such as a nurse, Mary would have had better care all along."

The judge's reddish complexion was now taking on a purplish tinge.

"I know, at least, that *your* presence is no longer needed," he sneered. "You are free to return to your school and cram more useless knowledge into those empty-headed girls."

Abruptly, he walked away, leaving her seething.

Chapter 12

Present fears are less than horrible imaginings.
I.iii

Week 5, Instructor Calendar
March 1896

The trolley ride from the Armstrong house back to Hartford Women's College briefly diverted Concordia from her thoughts. She boarded a crowded morning streetcar, standing during the early part of the trip, stretching to grasp a nearby hand strap, feet already aching from her pointy-toed boots. If only women's fashions would take pity on a lady's foot and forgo these ridiculous shapes.

At City Hall Square, many of the office workers disembarked. Concordia sat down in relief, adjusting her spectacles for a better look through a frost-etched window. This section was the hub of downtown Hartford, and the bustle of the city had an appeal all its own. Even on a cold winter morning there were people outdoors: street vendors setting up for business with their rickety hand carts, expressmen loading packages onto wagons for delivery. She could hear the boisterous shouts of newsies, mixed with the thin, high-pitched calls of children selling chewing gum and shoelaces. Main Street was crammed with these, along with bicyclists and pedestrians.

The trolley car continued north, leaving the noise of the inner city. Concordia's thoughts returned to her sister. What was making her ill? Why was a new doctor only *now* being called? The Armstrong family could afford the best specialists and nurses, and Henry certainly wasn't near with a dollar.

Concordia had to reluctantly concede that the judge was right about one thing: Mary would receive better nursing at the hands of their mother than she could give. Her mother's arrival yesterday was a relief, although the two of them exchanged the most perfunctory of greetings.

Mrs. Wells had brought with her the trusted housekeeper who had cared for Concordia and Mary through many a childhood illness. It seemed a good idea to have extra help, but Judge Armstrong sent the housekeeper away, refusing to allow anyone but family.

Why?

With all the commotion—and tension—of her mother's arrival, Concordia missed the chance to talk with Mary about what she had found in the attic. She honestly didn't know if it was important or not. The toy could have been dropped a while ago. Perhaps previous guests of the Armstrongs had brought a child with them, who had wandered off. Perhaps it was going to be a gift, and had fallen out of a pocket. She should have asked one of the staff before she left, but she just wanted to make a quick exit. She'd had enough of that household.

They were approaching the stop for the college. As she caught sight of the Memorial Chapel tower in the distance, her thoughts turned to the problems the college was having. The chapel prank. The loss of Ruth Lyman. The financial difficulties. Hartford Women's College had a lot of obstacles to overcome this year.

Concordia gathered up her belongings as the trolley slowed.

As she approached the center of campus, she saw students milling about in front of the Hall.

Her heart sank. Please heaven, not another crisis. Although the girls were exasperatingly mischievous this semester, Concordia found herself hoping it was simply a harmless practical joke.

Once she had sidled past students on the third floor stairs, her valise bumping awkwardly against her knees, Concordia could see that the disturbance was centered in front of President Richter's office. Miss Bellini and Miss Pomeroy were shooing a dozen or so girls in the adjacent hallway. Beyond them, President Richter and Dean Langdon were in close conversation as Miss Hamilton pulled something from the door and inspected it.

The president and dean were a study in contrasts: the latter, large and rumpled, with mismatched garments selected for comfort and convenience rather than style; the former, long-limbed, trim and nattily dressed.

"Out you go, now, Miss Babcock, Miss Dellawan, Miss Connors. All of you: out, out," Miss Pomeroy said, propelling the girls by their elbows, as they craned their necks to see.

"Ooh, Miss Pomeroy, we just want to know what's going on," a girl begged.

Miss Bellini, too, sternly waved them back toward the stairs, but the corners of her mouth curled in a hint of a smile and her black eyes glittered with barely-disguised interest.

"You heard Miss Pomeroy, *signorinas*. We have much to do here, and we do not need you all—what is it? Under the foot," Miss Bellini said. She dropped her voice a bit. "I promise—later I will tell you all, *sì?*"

Just as Concordia set down her case to help, the air was pierced by the sound of a metal whistle. All turned toward the stairwell. In the stunned silence, the white-haired Miss Jenkins, coach's whistle around her neck and hands on hips, called out:

"Basketball practice in ten minutes, ladies! What are you doing there, gawking? Get moving!"

Before one could say "foul shot," the hallway was cleared. Miss Jenkins, a satisfied smile on her lined face, followed the girls out.

"That woman is a gem," Miss Pomeroy murmured. She made a half-hearted attempt to tuck strands of frizzy brown hair back into their pins.

"What has happened here?" Concordia asked. She looked over at Miss Hamilton, holding—was that a knife? She felt a little sick.

The lady principal was the single point of utter calm among the agitated group. President Richter, standing beside her, was staring at a torn piece of paper that he held between trembling, tobacco-stained fingers. Dean Langdon shifted uneasily from one foot to the other as he read over the president's shoulder.

"There was a note on his door," Miss Pomeroy said, "held in place by that letter opener." She pointed to the object in the lady principal's hand. Concordia breathed a small sigh of relief. They didn't need any more knives.

Miss Bellini nodded. "One of my students, she was coming to see me in my office, yes? She let out a scream when she saw it." Miss Bellini rolled her eyes. "The young ladies, they are so dramatic."

"Of course, that brought everyone running," Miss Pomeroy picked up the thread of the story. "And word spread like wildfire after that. President Richter came, and found that his office had been rummaged through."

"Did anyone see who it was?" Concordia asked.

Miss Bellini shook her head. "My door was only partly open. I saw nothing."

"I was also in my office," Miss Pomeroy said, "but I was so engrossed in my translation of Charlemagne that I noticed nothing before I heard the scream."

"What does the note say?"

"I saw it," Miss Bellini said. Her dark brows furrowed in concentration. "'Beware. Next time a real stabbing could happen,'" she quoted.

Even the placid Miss Pomeroy looked troubled. "Why would someone do this? What can it mean?"

Concordia shook her head. "One thing is clear: we have moved beyond irksome practical jokes."

Chapter 13

Week 5, Instructor Calendar
March 1896

"Two pranks in ten days is an outrage, especially after Miss Lyman's death," President Richter thundered. He had recovered from his bout of laryngitis, and was as loud as ever. He turned to the lady principal. "Miss Hamilton, what has been done to catch these girls? Have you made *any* progress?"

It was just after the evening meal, and the staff, most still in their dinner attire, had gathered in the spacious parlor of Sycamore House, which housed the president, dean, and visiting male professors. Fires in the hearths at each end of the room cast dancing shadows upon worried faces.

Concordia could sympathize with his frustration, although she bristled with the barely-restrained urge to defend the lady principal. It certainly wasn't Miss Hamilton's fault.

But the strain was taking its toll on Arthur Richter. Looking closely at the president, sitting in a large wing-back chair across from her, Concordia saw the web of creases spreading beside his eyes, and the sagging flesh under his chin. His mouth, nearly bloodless, twitched, and his restless fingers drummed upon his knee.

Concordia remembered Arthur Richter from her childhood, when he and her father, poring over a rare book find together, would puff away at their pipes until their library at home was thick with a bluish-white haze. The smoke never bothered her. Sometimes, Mr. Wells indulgently allowed Concordia to stay and listen to them talk. The memory was still strong.

Arthur Richter had been appointed President of Hartford Women's College eight years ago, stepping in after the death of the college's very first president. Some were surprised when Richter accepted the position. It was common knowledge that, as a former trustee, he had objected to the 1878 collegiate conversion of what had been the Hartford Ladies' Seminary, citing the views of experts–prominent physicians, religious and civic leaders–that women's minds were constitutionally different from men's, and that a young woman risked damaging her "delicate apparatus" with arduous study.

But change was inevitable. Women's colleges had been springing up in the area like crocuses in a winter thaw–New York's Vassar College in 1861, Massachusetts' Wellesley and Smith Colleges in 1875–and enrollment at Hartford Ladies' Seminary had dropped off drastically. The evangelical fervor of preparing women for motherhood or the teaching profession, which had been the original driving force of the seminary more than two decades earlier, had been replaced with more modern sensibilities. The early generation of women scholars had proved that they possessed the aptitude for serious study. Demand for such institutions was increasing. The Hartford Ladies' Seminary was lagging behind the times, and its trustees knew it. Thus, Hartford Women's College was born.

Now, with Richter as president, Concordia could see that he was in a unique position to control the direction of the college in its second decade. Under his leadership, the college had maintained some of the seminary customs designed to train young Christian women in decorous behavior and family life: daily Chapel, formal dinner dress, once-per-week (chaperoned) social visits, and strict enforcement of bedtime curfew, widely known as the "ten o-clock rule." Male costume for student plays was not allowed, and the student basketball teams only recently were permitted to play in modified skirts and bloomers. Only irrepressible youth could have managed athletic endeavors in full skirts, she thought.

Concordia looked around the room and noticed Miss Bellini, her shoulders hunched under a paisley shawl, distractedly plucking the ends of its fringe in her lap. It must be unsettling to realize that the prankster had struck again nearly at her door.

The wall sconces—electric, now—had been switched on in the growing dusk, so Concordia could see even into the far corner, where she observed a familiar-looking man. She could not quite place him. She thought she knew all the teachers by now. He certainly was handsome, and knew how to dress well. His suit, made of finely-woven French wool, fit his lean frame too well to be anything but custom-tailored. He was seated in a chair against the wall, his long legs leisurely crossed, looking quite relaxed, despite the tension in the room. Concordia felt as if she could look at him for hours.

She took her mind off fanciful thoughts when she sheepishly realized that she had missed a large portion of the discussion.

"Could we not bring in a private inquiry agent?" Dean Langdon suggested.

Several people shifted uneasily in their chairs.

President Richter shook his head vehemently. "The public exposure would be detrimental to the college. Between Miss Lyman's untimely death and rumors about the college already in circulation before that, such a public action in this matter could irrevocably damage the school's reputation."

Concordia saw the lady principal and dean exchange glances. They knew the president was referring to the college's financial problems.

The meeting concluded, with very little decided (as happened with most large meetings, Concordia thought). She smothered a yawn. Back to Willow Cottage, and to bed.

Miss Hamilton, however, had other plans, and caught up to her before she could slip away.

"Miss Wells, I know you must be tired, but we have much to discuss. Could you meet me at DeLacey House? I will be there shortly."

How could Concordia object?

Chapter 14

In the dark, DeLacey House looked massive and looming, but as Concordia approached to ring the bell, the fieldstone facade and deep front porch of the structure gave it a sort of hominess. She could imagine comfortable rockers set out in the milder weather, and pots of cheery geraniums along the railing.

Concordia took a good look around as she followed the maid through the ground floor of the residence, past the open doors of the parlor and library. The décor seemed a mix of domestic practicality and stately style: ornate panellings and tall, medallioned ceilings cohabited with well-worn afghans draped across divans and sewing baskets tucked into out-of-the-way corners. Concordia cast a longing eye toward the library's floor-to-ceiling bookshelves before following the maid upstairs to the lady principal's quarters.

Miss Hamilton's sitting room had overstuffed chairs flanking a hearth and a cheery fire. Concordia saw more books—books stacked haphazardly on stools, books on tables, books in the corners of the room. Most importantly, Concordia spied a tray laden with tea and muffins. They smelled wonderful. In all of the excitement, Concordia hadn't realized how hungry she was.

She also hadn't known that another visitor waited for Miss Hamilton. As she approached the fire, she found herself face to face with that remarkably handsome man she had noticed at the meeting. She paused awkwardly.

The man straightened his cuffs, an amused smile tugging at the corner of his mouth.

She was about to say something when Miss Hamilton walked in, still in her silk dinner dress of china blue. Obviously, she was having a busy evening. "Ah, I see the tea tray has already come." She gestured to Concordia. "Mr. Reynolds, may I present to you Miss Wells, whose classes you have been teaching these last few days. Miss Wells, Julian Reynolds."

The man made a quick bow. "Miss Wells, a pleasure."

Concordia recovered her voice. "I'm pleased to make your acquaintance, Mr. Reynolds. I'm most grateful for your help."

Julian Reynolds extended a well-manicured hand, and clasped hers warmly—and just a shade longer than necessary—for an initial acquaintance. She felt a flush bloom across her cheeks.

Up close, he looked older than she had initially thought, with fine lines around his eyes and mouth. He had one of those classical Grecian profiles, accented by straight sandy hair and deep blue eyes. The effect was breath-taking.

Oh, stop it, she thought crossly. You're not the type to go swooning over an attractive man like some silly schoolgirl. She was tired of craning her neck to look at him, anyway. She took a chair farthest from the fire. It was getting warm in here.

"No doubt you and Mr. Reynolds will find a convenient time to discuss what went on in your absence, Miss Wells," the lady principal said.

"Any time would be fine with me," he responded with a smile. His voice was as pleasant as the rest of him, but Concordia wasn't sure she liked his smile—it had a self-satisfied, mocking quality that made her uncomfortable.

Miss Hamilton continued briskly, "I have asked you both here in order to help uncover the identity of the mischief-makers. It's even more urgent, now." She looked around, and sighed. "But I left them in the other room. Excuse me."

Mr. Reynolds settled back and waited. Concordia, uneasy with the silence, asked conversationally, "Have you taught before, Mr. Reynolds?"

Reynolds reached for a teacup, offering it to her. "I have, Miss Wells. I currently run the business of my late wife's family, but before then, I had taught—here and there. Your classes were no trouble. In fact, your students were most cooperative." He smiled again.

Concordia didn't doubt it. She remembered now where she had seen Mr. Reynolds. It was last fall, and he had been teaching Miss Banning's classes during one of her rheumatic attacks. Concordia remembered the buzz among the girls, who dubbed him "Professor Dashing." Her own students would fall right into line.

Miss Hamilton returned, carrying the effigies from the Glove Night prank. The knife had been removed from the lady principal's figurine.

"I have examined these closely," she said, handing each of them a doll. "Tell me what you observe."

"What are we looking for?" Reynolds asked impatiently, holding the effigy of Arthur Richter with some distaste, "I'm hardly a dollar-a-day private detective."

Although Concordia could understand Mr. Reynolds' aversion to being associated with detectives—they were an unsavory lot, after all, and ready subjects in lurid novels and yellow journalism—she thought he was being unduly fussy about the matter.

A look of annoyance crossed the lady principal's face. "Anything unusual about the fabric or decorative parts. Whatever will narrow our search for the perpetrators."

"Can we truly assume that the two incidents are connected?" Concordia asked. "Perhaps someone took advantage of the first incident and sought something in President Richter's office."

Miss Hamilton nodded her approval. "An excellent point, Miss Wells. It would indeed be a mistake to make such an assumption until we have more facts. However, if it is *not* a mere student prank, then it is even more imperative that we find the culprits."

Miss Hamilton had a point. Someone bold enough to target the president's office must be desperate indeed. But desperate for what?

Concordia turned her attention to the figure in her lap, of Miss Bellini. The basic body of the doll was constructed of white muslin—someone had sacrificed an old nightshift, she guessed—and was dressed in navy-colored sateen with a lavender floral print. It would have made a pretty shirtwaist, she thought, fingering the cloth. Certainly, it wasn't cheap material. The doll was also dressed in cut-up lace antimacassars, no doubt to represent the shawls Miss Bellini liked to wear. The maker had used ordinary black yarn for hair. The facial features were crudely drawn in ink, and the stuffing looked to be old quilt batting.

"Most of these materials could have come from anywhere, Miss Hamilton," Concordia said, looking up. She pointed to the sateen. "Except, perhaps, this. But I haven't seen anyone wearing a dress or shirtwaist of this fabric. How could we find it?"

"Your seniors will be making their costumes soon for the play, will they not?" Miss Hamilton countered.

"You mean that when material for the costumes is collected, we may find this fabric, and connect it to the guilty party?" Concordia asked. It was an intriguing idea.

Reynolds glanced up in interest. "Are there other distinctive fabrics here? I have to plead ignorance about the subject, ladies."

Miss Hamilton turned to the other effigies on the table. Concordia's doll was dressed in gingham of a light pink tint. As if she would ever wear such a color, Concordia thought scornfully. She wondered if the fabric was chosen deliberately, so as to make the doll's red hair even more atrocious. Any lady cursed with hair of that particular shade knows that she cannot wear pink. Unfortunately, gingham was an all-too-common fabric.

The others— wool, percale, serge—were also widely used. Miss Hamilton held up her own effigy. It was dressed in black taffeta, the fabric embroidered with a pattern of tiny black leaves. "Here is another possibility," she said, passing it to Concordia.

She tried to ignore the large gash in the upper body of the figure as she examined it.

"Where is the knife?" she asked. She looked at Miss Hamilton, hoping she hadn't distressed her by the question.

Mr. Reynolds shifted uneasily in his chair, probably concerned, too, with Miss Hamilton's reaction.

But if Miss Hamilton was bothered by the query, she gave no sign. "I returned it; it was one of the college's kitchen knives," she answered, taking back the figure and giving it an absent-minded pat as she set it aside.

Checking his pocket watch, Reynolds stood. "If you will excuse me, I will say good night. Ladies, this has been a most instructive evening."

Miss Hamilton chuckled after he left. "Poor man. He wouldn't know a bolt of French lawn if it flattened him on the street."

"Then why involve him?" Concordia asked.

Miss Hamilton offered Concordia the muffin plate. "I want another set of keen eyes looking for these fabrics. We will be seeing more of Mr. Reynolds on campus this semester," she explained. "I have prevailed upon him to take over your literature club, to free you for play rehearsals."

Concordia thought it likely that literature club meetings would be well-attended in the future, if "Professor Dashing" was going to preside over them.

"Doesn't he have other matters to attend to? He mentioned running a family business," she said, helping herself to a muffin.

"Mr. Reynolds' wife passed away last year," Miss Hamilton explained. "He wants to stay occupied, and I understand that his business concerns are not very time-consuming. He's one of the college's trustees, and good friends with President Richter. It seemed a beneficial arrangement."

Miss Hamilton poured tea for both of them and took a muffin herself. They sat in companionable silence for a while, watching the play of the firelight on the polished hearth, until Miss Hamilton asked, "You have certainly had a difficult week, Miss Wells. How is your sister?"

Concordia felt a lump rising in her throat, and first took a sip of her tea. "No better, I'm afraid. Her husband is consulting a specialist."

Miss Hamilton raised an eyebrow. "Another specialist? It must be a difficult malady." Concordia's sister had been ill for some time; naturally, the lady principal assumed a specialist had already been consulted.

Carefully keeping the anger out of her voice, Concordia tried to explain the delay without voicing her own doubts.

But Miss Hamilton was quick. "So you believe that something more deliberate is going on in connection with your sister's illness. Do you suspect... poison?"

Having taken that inopportune moment to drink her tea, Concordia nearly choked over Miss Hamilton's blunt question. How could Miss Hamilton calmly talk of such things? Yet it was clear by Miss Hamilton's face that she was quite serious.

"That can't be!" Concordia protested, when she managed to find her voice again. "This is not some three-decker sensation novel; it is my sister's life. She certainly did not marry into a family of murderers."

Miss Hamilton was silent for a moment.

"I realize I spoke rather frankly, my dear," she said finally, "nevertheless, you have a mystery on your hands. Perhaps we should arrange for more time away so you can better oversee your sister's care. Mr. Reynolds can take over your classes again."

"But I have just returned!" Concordia said in dismay. She could not bear facing the Armstrongs again so soon, especially after her last row with the judge.

"Our mother is with her now," Concordia continued. "She can care for her better than I could. I would prefer to wait, Miss Hamilton."

The lady principal gave Concordia a long look.

"Very well," Miss Hamilton said, "but keep in mind things aren't always what they appear."

"What about Miss Lyman's death?" Concordia asked. "Is that what it seems? Do you believe she died by her own hand?" The question had been bothering her, especially with this latest incident. Could the bursar's death be connected to the pranks and threats?

Miss Hamilton pressed her lips together thoughtfully before answering. "The coroner has ruled the death a suicide, but still, I find it troubling. I simply don't know what to think."

Concordia left shortly thereafter, pleading fatigue.

She walked along the lighted path back to Willow Cottage, all too aware of how quiet and lonely the grounds were at night. The ten o'clock curfew had long passed, and the campus was dark, save for the paths and an occasional glow coming from a window in the faculty residences. Frost rimming the stones along the walkway sparkled like tiny shards of glass. She shivered from more than the cold. What if someone was out here now, planning more than mischief?

Feeling foolish, she quickened her pace nonetheless, and was relieved to reach the front porch of Willow Cottage. She was fumbling for her latchkey when a voice breathed close to her ear, "Miss Wells."

With a yelp, Concordia leapt back from the door and into the arms of Julian Reynolds, as he stepped from the porch shadows. His arms tightened to steady her.

"I beg your pardon, Miss Wells!" he cried, his face a picture of concern. "I didn't mean to startle you."

"Well, you did, Mr. Reynolds," Concordia replied crossly, righting her spectacles and trying to calm the wild thumping in her chest. "You may let go of me now, if you please."

"What is it you want?" she asked shakily, after he had released her.

Before Reynolds could answer, a light came on inside the hallway, a bolt was shot back, and Ruby opened the door.

"Miss Wells, and Mr. Reynolds!" she exclaimed. "Good heavens, what is going on?" She gave them each a stern glance. Even clad in dressing gown and homely felt slippers, her hair in a long graying braid, the squat-figured Ruby was a formidable presence.

"Mr. Reynolds was simply seeing me safely to the door," Concordia said, attempting to make her grimace pass for a stiff-lipped smile. "Good night, sir."

Reynolds took her hand in a gallant farewell gesture. "Shall we meet then, during your free period tomorrow?"

Ruby frowned. Concordia freed her hand. "Eleven o'clock. Classroom three," she said curtly.

With Reynolds gone and the door firmly latched behind him, Concordia apologized to the matron for waking her. "The lady principal wanted to see me."

Ruby's face softened. "It's all right, miss. I don't think any of them hoydens upstairs were woke up. You'd best go to bed," she said, as Concordia covered a yawn. "You've had a long day, for sure."

Judging from the soft footfalls and whispers above Concordia's head as she settled down to sleep, Ruby was wrong about the girls not being awakened. She wondered drowsily what the students would make of her being seen in the company of the handsome "Professor Dashing" so late at night. For now, she was too tired to care.

Chapter 15

What's done cannot be undone.
V.i

Weeks 5 and 6, Instructor Calendar
March 1896

Concordia awoke to the thunder of twenty pairs of feet clattering down the wood steps. As she hurriedly dressed to join them for breakfast and morning chapel–drat these boots!–Ruby called to her, tapping on her door.

"Coming!" Concordia called.

Concordia couldn't hear the muffled response, so she yanked the door open, still clutching boot and button hook.

"Ah, miss," the matron said, eyes straying to Concordia's stockinged foot, "the lady principal sent word that you be allowed to sleep."

Several of the students filing past Concordia's door gave her coy smiles. Undoubtedly, last night's porch scene with Mr. Reynolds would provide fodder for several days' worth of student gossip.

"I'll get 'em to their breakfasts. That won't take no doing, to be sure," Ruby said with a grin, and closed the door behind her.

The week that followed brought a hectic routine that Concordia found oddly soothing. There were a few crestfallen faces her first day back to class when "Professor Dashing" failed to make a reappearance, but there was plenty of excitement when she announced that he would be conducting future literature club meetings.

As promised, Mr. Reynolds did meet with her to discuss her classes.

"My, Mr. Reynolds, you have covered an impressive amount of material in such a short time," she said in surprise, looking over the lesson plans he had copied out for her. "They are nearly finished with the Romantic poets in the Masters class, and the Milton class will soon be ready to start on *Paradise Lost*. However did you manage it?"

He smiled, the corners of his blue eyes crinkling. "You have such charming girls, Miss Wells. Do you know how hard they work? And without complaint, too. I was absolutely besieged during my office hours: students coming for tutoring, or questions, or simply seeking more intellectual depth to the topic. Quite impressive."

"Ah," was all that Concordia could trust herself to say. She doubted that such diligence, nay, *enthusiasm*, was the result of Milton's or Wordsworth's appeal. She hadn't the heart to disillusion him, though.

"But I have kept you talking for much too long!" Reynolds exclaimed. "You must allow me to take you to the faculty lounge for some tea. Shall we?" He held out his arm.

She was about to protest that, no, she did not require any tea. Yet she found herself blushing as she took his arm and accompanied him to the lounge.

During the next week, Concordia encountered Mr. Reynolds on several other occasions: in the classics reading room, in the student dining hall, and once, to Concordia's annoyance, in the midst of play rehearsal. Since a scant nine weeks now remained until the performance, it was her custom to meet in the evenings with the cast members, to determine what the major players had done with their lines thus far, and work out assignments for the remaining minor roles.

The night Mr. Reynolds visited—to "see what our brilliant senior class would be performing this year," he said—the girls made squealing fools of themselves and competed for attention.

There was no doubt about it, the man was a distraction. Little progress was made *that* evening. While she couldn't deny feeling flattered by his interest, she found it perplexing. Concordia had looked in the mirror often enough to know that she did not fit any classical standard of beauty. She had neither the height nor the flawless complexion—her mother had *promised* her freckles would fade—and red hair was certainly not in fashion this year, nor likely to be in the near future. So why was Mr. Reynolds being so attentive? Was he lonely after the death of his wife, or did he merely suffer from excessive gallantry?

In the meantime, her sister's condition was unchanged. Sophia wrote to Concordia nearly every day. The specialist had indeed come from Boston. However, he had left after just a few days, and Sophia had not been able to find out why. Had the doctor abandoned the case as hopeless?

But Concordia did not have much opportunity to meditate further upon either the mystery of Mary's illness or Julian Reynolds's attentions. In addition to her courses and play rehearsals, the doings at Willow Cottage were sufficient to keep her and Ruby occupied in their scant spare time. It was Willow Cottage's turn to host the president's Tea, and during the course of the week the girls were in a flurry of excitement, vigorously cleaning and polishing, snipping endless recipes for scones, muffins, and other dainty edibles for the dining hall's cooks to make, contributing pillow cushions and other bric-a-brac from their rooms to pretty up the parlor. Silk dresses were brushed, gloves mended, and shoes polished.

It was a source of pride for the students to play hostess to President Richter, who spoke glowingly of the teas as an example of "refined Christian womanhood." (Apparently heathens did not drink tea). What Arthur Richter did not realize was that the teas had become a competition of sorts among the cottages to see who could outdo the others. Not a ladylike, or Christian, goal.

Soon it was the Saturday afternoon of the tea. Concordia planned to leave afterward to visit Mary— and discovered what the specialist had learned. In the meantime, she needed to supervise her girls, so that the event proceeded smoothly. She was proud of them—they all looked well-groomed, and were, so far, conducting themselves in an uncharacteristically lady-like manner. She knew that the influence of their Head Senior was partly responsible for their success.

She looked over at the composed Miss Crandall, every strand of her smooth brown hair in place, arranged snugly at the nape of her neck. Such a style served to emphasize her strong, square jaw line, a feature that Concordia found incongruous in the girl, as it hinted at rebellion where there was none. Although Ruby *had* described the senior as once "a wild one," Concordia remembered. If so, she'd certainly matured in the past two years.

Miss Crandall was seated (one might say wedged, as there was hardly room for all twenty girls and their guests in Willow Cottage's parlor) between President Richter and Miss Hamilton on the settee. As she chatted, the girl passed teacups and plates to others with smooth, practiced movements, clearly comfortable in such a setting. And no wonder, having been raised in the wealthy Crandall household, where such niceties were as essential to one's education as Moral Philosophy. Concordia thought of her own abilities at that age, and suspected that she would have been more likely to dump the tray of scones in Richter's lap.

He seemed to be enjoying himself, smiling amiably at the girls, encouraging what he saw as their strides toward domesticity. Yet Concordia noticed shadows under his eyes, and his long, stained fingers fidgeting restlessly with a teaspoon.

"I must say, my dear young ladies, I am most impressed by your preparations," Richter commented, casting an approving eye around the room, taking in the newly-swept hearth, the shining wood surfaces, the carefully-laid tea tray.

"It is gratifying to see that you keep your faith and your home duties close to your hearts, even here at the college," he continued, looking again at the "God Bless Our Home" sampler prominently displayed over the mantel. No one volunteered the fact that Miss Drake had pulled it from the depths of her trunk in honor of the occasion. No doubt it would find its way back to obscurity after the tea.

Richter kept the conversation on light-hearted topics, and the girls followed his lead. The time seemed to drag on. Has it only been half an hour, Concordia wondered, surreptitiously checking her watch again. She reflected upon the smaller teas that she and the other professors hosted for their students, where stimulating discussions were the norm, and the time flew by. And what a wide range of topics—not just the school subjects one might expect. The students were, surprisingly, interested in current events, politics, even international affairs. She remembered one discussion about the overthrow of Queen Liliuokalani, and whether the United States should have better considered the proposal to annex the new Republic of Hawai'i. Concordia had known nothing about that part of the world. Then there was the debate about the Pullman railway strike—should President Cleveland have intervened the way he had, sending in federal troops to end it? What about the workers, who were protesting reduced wages for twelve-hour workdays? That had been a particularly spirited discussion.

The students have lively minds, Concordia thought, looking around the room at each of her girls. She had developed protective feelings toward them. She hated to think that any of them would be considered unladylike for wanting to discuss matters of greater import than which spring bulbs were emerging, or plans for the next dance.

Her eyes rested upon Miss Hamilton, looking most elegant today in a gray taffeta with black braid trimming at the waist and hem. The lady principal, in turn, was closely observing both the president and Miss Crandall. Her face conveyed a watchful stillness that reminded Concordia of a cat, poised to strike when the mole emerges from hiding. Concordia suppressed a shudder.

President Richter looked up and caught Concordia's eye, giving her a silent nod of approval. She smiled, relieved that the tea was nearly over—without incident. Soon she would be able to turn her attention to other matters.

She had sent word to Henry in advance, so the Armstrong carriage was waiting for her at the campus gate when she was ready. Once the driver settled her comfortably, they were on their way. Concordia was anxious to see Mary again, although she was wary of sharing the house with both Judge Armstrong *and* her mother, even for so short a time. It would be a chilly reception.

She knew something was wrong as soon as they approached the house. An empty buggy was standing in the street; Concordia recognized it as Doctor Westfield's. The front door had been flung wide open, and no one had yet thought to close it. Concordia stumbled out of the vehicle before the driver could help her, and ran into the house.

Chapter 16

Out, out, brief candle!
V.v

Zion Hill Cemetery
March 1896

Concordia stood next to Mary's grave as the minister read the prayer. The March wind tugged at her hat, and dried her damp cheeks. It was difficult to stand for so long. Her head throbbed and her legs ached. Her mother stood next to her, rigid, dry-eyed, and pale.

Perhaps they should not have come. She had seen a few eyebrows lifted in surprise upon their arrival. Concordia knew that many still held to the custom that women—even female relatives—did not attend the graveside service of a departed loved one. But she *had* to come today, even if no one else understood. She could at least keep watch over her sister this final time, when she was put to rest. Her mother, surprisingly, had insisted upon accompanying her.

She looked at her mother. Mary had been so like her: the same heart-shaped face, light blue eyes, and golden hair, her mother's now streaked with silver. Both women had been beauties in their time. For Mrs. Wells, time and grief had faded the red of her lips, pulled the skin of her neck into loose folds, veined her long slender hands with blue. She looked fragile, standing out here in the wind, as if a strong gust might knock her down. Protectively, Concordia reached for her hand, which was snatched away. Concordia felt a lump rise in her throat, remembering their argument the day before.

"Mother, you know I detest that woman. She isn't here to offer condolences—oh, certainly, for the sake of appearance, she will. She is here to gather fodder for gossip and to satisfy her busybody curiosity. Visit with her all you like—it is your house, after all—but do not require *me* to come down. I will not."

Mrs. Wells' lips compressed into a thin line. "No, of course not," she scoffed. "Heaven forbid you support me when I need you. All these years, you have done as you pleased. You have not visited or even written."

Concordia clenched her fists within the folds of her skirt as she took a deep breath.

"I tried to visit, when I came back. And you *know* why I stayed away to begin with," she said evenly. It took an effort of will not to scream in frustration.

"You made my life miserable," Concordia continued. "I could not be who you wanted me to be. I could not be like Mary. I never can."

Her mother choked back a sob. "That girl was the delight of my life. And now… she is… gone." Mrs. Wells groped again for her handkerchief.

Wordlessly, Concordia went back in her room and shut the door.

Concordia looked over the funeral gathering. The Armstrongs were gathered closest to Reverend Elliot. Henry, his face even paler in severe black, kept his gaze fixed on the ground. Judge Armstrong, his brow furrowed, scowled at the poor minister, who had lost his page in the wind.

Beyond the immediate family, she recognized President Richter, Nathaniel Young, and Julian Reynolds. A subdued

Sophia Adams, who cared not a jot for social convention, was standing behind them.

When the service was concluded, the mourners began to disperse. Arthur Richter approached, frowning–in concern, or disapproval? Concordia could not tell. Mrs. Wells stretched out a gloved hand, which he held and gently patted.

"Letitia, you and Concordia should have spared yourselves this distress. It was not necessary to make an appearance here. Death, while unfortunate in one so young, is a fact of life, after all. I understand she had been ill for some time."

"We appreciate your concern for our well-being, Arthur," Mrs. Wells responded stiffly. "Thank you for coming. I remember how you doted on Mary, during your visits with my husband."

This was merely politeness on her mother's part, Concordia knew. Arthur Richter's visits when her father was still alive were confined to the library, a place of little interest to Mary. Concordia's own intrusions upon those sessions, while welcomed by her father, had been scarcely tolerated by Richter.

Arthur Richter nodded. "Indeed. Mary was a charming child. I will always remember her as a little girl, in a pinafore two sizes too large for her."

He gestured toward Mr. Reynolds, who had joined them.

"Concordia, Miss Hamilton wanted me to inform you that Mr. Reynolds here will continue with your classes until you are ready to return. Take all of the time you need to set your family affairs in order, my dear." With a bow, he left.

A breeze blew a lock of Julian Reynolds' blond hair rakishly across his brow as he clasped Concordia's hand. Even through the gloves they each wore, the warmth of his hands enfolding hers was comforting. In that moment, she felt a disconcerting urge to be gathered up in his arms and cry without stopping.

She pulled her hand away and took a breath to collect herself. "I do appreciate your help, Mr. Reynolds. It...should not be much longer. We have a few more tasks to attend to. I intend to return to classes by the end of the week."

Mrs. Wells, still standing next to Concordia, swayed slightly. Time to get Mother home; it had been a grueling day. Making their apologies to Mr. Reynolds, they headed for the carriage. Sophia caught up to them, helping Concordia prop her mother, who was sagging quickly.

"Allow me to assist you, Miss Wells!" Reynolds called out, hurrying after them. By this point, Concordia and Sophia were standing beside the vehicle, the driver wrestling open the door against the wind. Concordia clutched her hat, eyes watering, and with the other arm helped ease her mother in.

Mr. Reynolds, breathless and arriving too late to be of help, gave a rueful smile.

"Well, at least I caught up with you before you left. I forgot to mention that we should meet to discuss your classes. Could you perhaps come to my residence one afternoon this week when you are free? I would not want to presume upon a household in mourning."

Concordia frowned. Who makes social arrangements in a cemetery? But she knew Mr. Reynolds had a point. It might also be pleasant to see him again, under less somber circumstances.

"Sophia," she said, turning to her friend, "could you accompany me to Mr. Reynolds's house in a few days?"

Sophia, though puzzled, agreed.

"Excellent," Reynolds exclaimed, taking Concordia's hand again, "I will wait to hear from you."

Concordia stepped into the carriage, working to settle the folds of the dull black crape-lined dress she had borrowed from her mother. It was too long for her and had been hastily pinned. She suspected that at least some of the pins had worked themselves loose. She winced when her suspicion was confirmed.

As they put the cemetery behind them, Sophia was the first to speak. "What an odd gentleman!"

Concordia smiled weakly. "Perhaps. I don't know what to think, honestly."

Sophia thrust out her pointy chin and gave an unladylike snort. "Well, *I* do. Look out for that one."

Seeing that her mother had fallen into an exhausted sleep, Concordia did not reply. She was puzzled by Sophia's words. Mr. Reynolds had been nothing but a gentleman, showing a sincere, albeit inexplicable, interest in her. It was her own feelings she had to be wary of.

The carriage ride from Zion Hill Cemetery to her mother's house in the South Green neighborhood was short. Sophia had volunteered to stay with Mrs. Wells while Concordia remained at the Armstrong house to go through Mary's possessions, something she knew her mother could not bear to do. Henry had abdicated all responsibility for the dispersal of his wife's belongings. Concordia could not decide whether he was too callous to care, or too deeply grieved.

She also had another, more formidable task, one that she kept to herself; to discover what the Armstrongs had to hide about Mary. If Concordia was to have any peace about her sister's death, she had to know the truth.

Once assured that Mother and Sophia were in the care of the attentive housekeeper, Concordia drove on to Asylum Hill. She looked out idly as the carriage drove through Bushnell Park, where budding willows and the emerging crocuses dotting the ground reminded her that spring was coming. A spring that her sister would not see.

Concordia's eyes blurred as she struggled to shake off these thoughts. She would need all of the composure she could muster in order to face the Armstrongs.

Chapter 17
Our fears do make us traitors.
IV.ii

March 1896

The afternoon after the funeral was a lonely one. The household was quiet, with Henry and Judge Armstrong ignoring Concordia and one another, and retreating to their rooms. After sharing a cottage with twenty lively girls, Concordia was unaccustomed to empty silences. She needed bustle and noise; if she couldn't have that, at least she could find something to occupy her.

Concordia went into Mary's dressing-room. It still possessed the character of its owner, with Chantilly-lace curtains and the lingering scent of rose-water. The vanity table held neatly arranged brushes, combs, and a monogrammed hand mirror—Concordia's wedding gift. She picked it up. Water drops began to spatter its surface.

How did she think she could do this? She crumpled to the floor, buried her head in her arms, and wept.

It was dark outside when she was roused by wind-lashed branches scraping along the roof tiles. The soft *pfft, pfft* against the window meant the rain that had been threatening all day had started at last.

Floors were not meant to be slept on, Concordia thought, wincing at the stiffness in her back. She blew her nose noisily in her handkerchief. Feeling better now, she resolved to at least *start* sorting through Mary's belongings, late though it was.

She opened the armoire, admiring the array of silk wrappers, soft wool skirts, shirt-waists sporting the popular leg-of-mutton sleeves, and traveling suits, some tailored in the latest fashion of masculine shoulders and military-like braid. There were also tea gowns and ball gowns in shimmering colors of aquamarine, cerise, silver, and rose. Most of these would be given away. Mary had been slimmer than she, and Concordia certainly had no social occasion that called for a gown.

Amid the *swish* of silk and taffeta and sounds of the storm buffeting the house, she almost missed it: a series of pattering sounds above her head. She froze, heart thumping.

She listened. A further *scrape* and *creak* sent goose bumps shivering along her arms. Had that been overhead as well? It was difficult to tell. Was this what Mary had heard, when she pleaded with Concordia to search the attic? Or was *she* now the one imagining things?

Firmly thrusting away thoughts of ghosts, or madness—this house was getting on her nerves—Concordia stepped into the hall. Annie was just coming down the passageway, obviously in search of her.

"Ah, miss—I thought you might be here," she said. "The judge and Mr. Henry don't need any of us tonight, and I wanted to see if you wanted anything before I go to bed." Brow furrowed, she looked closely at Concordia. "You did'n eat much today, miss, if you don't mind my sayin' so. Can I fix you some toast, maybe?"

Concordia was touched by her concern. "I'll be fine, really. I was wondering, though—have you heard any unusual noises tonight? I've been hearing something that sounds like it's coming from the attic."

"Ya don't say?" Annie paled. Mary was right, Concordia thought, Annie *is* a bit superstitious. "Can't say I have, miss, but that storm sure is loud, with them trees knockin' around. Are you sure it weren't that?"

"Well, I'm not sure," Concordia said, "but it seemed to come from right overhead."

Annie thought for a moment. "Could be squirrels," she said finally. "Last spring, there was a whole nest of them. Made a big mess."

"I suppose," Concordia said doubtfully.

"The grocer's boy is comin' in the morning," Annie said. "I'll get him to look. You won't catch *me* going up there if there's any critters, that's for sure. Well, g'night, miss."

"Good night, Annie."

Somewhat reassured, and hearing nothing after that beyond the wind and the rain, Concordia resumed her sorting. Soon she had Mary's clothes divided into piles on the bed, the brightly-colored silks gleaming in the light. She pushed a few hairpins back in place, and stretched.

What next? She glanced around the room. Mary's jewel case was perched atop the armoire. She could go through that. Mary wasn't one to wear excessive ornaments, so it shouldn't take long. That would do for tonight.

Concordia hesitated when she opened the case. There were more pieces than she had anticipated. She recognized a few girlhood keepsakes of Mary's, including a sterling silver bib pin, a christening gift from their grandmother. Concordia cherished her own pin, from so long ago. She would have to make sure that Mother got Mary's.

The rest of the jewelry pieces, however, were unfamiliar. Which items were gifts from Henry -- things that might have sentiment attached?

Concordia sighed. Should she disturb Henry? Had he retired for the night? She could at least go downstairs to see. And a cup of buttermilk might be nice.

As she reached the landing, Concordia noticed Dr. Westfield's coat and medical bag in the front hall, carelessly tossed on the high-back chair. He obviously arrived after the staff had retired for the night. The doctor's coat would have been hung up neatly, not left like that.

Concordia stood uncertainly on the bottom stair. What was the doctor doing here? Was Henry ill from his grief?

As she was debating what to do next, she heard a voice raised sharply. Concordia followed the sound to the library door. She looked along the corridor first before leaning closer to listen. She was placing herself in a ridiculous position if someone caught her with an ear to the keyhole. Fortunately, she had changed out of mourning—the dress rustled terribly—into a quiet wool skirt.

Only snatches of the conversation were audible.

"Frankly... disappointed... where were...." The voice belonged to an angry Judge Armstrong.

The voice which murmured a reply was Dr. Westfield's, Concordia could tell, although she could not make out the words. *Tarnation!* She straightened up from her crouch. What little she had heard suggested that Judge Armstrong was unhappy with Dr. Westfield for missing—what?

Perhaps the funeral service. Concordia had noted his absence, but one assumes with doctors that a pressing medical call is to blame.

She had to hear what was going on.

What other doors or windows would there be? She remembered the library as quite large. And unmistakably a *man's* room, with its deep burgundy velvet draperies, dark leather chairs and the lingering scent of pipe tobacco. Not a flower vase in sight.

In this weather, prowling out-of-doors was out of the question. But she remembered there were other interior doors, including....

She frowned in concentration. *Yes.* The judge kept his rarest books in a curtained alcove at one end of the library, to protect them from dust and sunlight. Annie told her it used to be part of the housekeeper's pantry, originally intended as a combination storeroom and sitting room for the head of the staff. If so, there *should* be a connecting door between the alcove and the pantry, accessible through the kitchen.

She hurried toward the kitchen. Peering in, she sighed in relief. Empty. She crossed to the pantry door and pulled slowly on the latch, testing the hinges for creaks. She slipped inside. As there was no light within, she groped for the alcove door. Finally, she found it, and softly eased it open.

Concordia hardly dared to breathe as she stepped into the library. She was now separated from the room's occupants by the floor-to-ceiling velvet curtains in front of her. The alcove was not deep; she had to brace herself against a wall of books to avoid fluttering the curtains.

"…precious few patients left to keep you so occupied, Adam." The caustic voice was Judge Armstrong's.

"You already have what you wanted from me." Doctor Westfield sounded weary, and bitter. It was not at all the jovial, booming voice she was accustomed to hear.

The judge laughed. "We've helped each other over the years, or don't you remember?"

"How could I forget?" Dr. Westfield answered. "I live with it every day."

There was silence.

Dr. Westfield continued, "Who else have you *helped*, Matthew; what knowledge do you use against other poor devils to get what you want?"

"I seem to remember that it turned to your advantage," the judge replied tartly. "Is what I've asked in return so outrageous? Simply sign the certificate, and keep your speculations to yourself."

There was a pause, and the judge continued, more gently, as Concordia heard Dr. Westfield weeping, "It was too late to do anything more for the girl, Adam. It is better to let the matter rest."

Concordia's chest tightened so that she could hardly breathe. Her first angry impulse was to run out of her hiding place and demand an explanation.

But something made Concordia stay where she was. Not cowardice, she hoped, although her heart was pounding and her mouth had gone dry, but her sense that neither man would have told her the truth if she confronted them. The judge would be only too happy to show her the door and forbid her return.

Then she would learn nothing more. She had to find another way.

A knock on the library door nearly made Concordia fall headlong into the curtains. There was a moment's pause—the judge giving the doctor a chance to regain his composure, Concordia guessed—before she heard the door open.

"Oh." It was Henry's voice. "I didn't know you were engaged. I came in for a book."

"I was just leaving," Dr. Westfield answered in a flat voice, "Goodnight."

Concordia heard the door shut behind him.

"The doctor seems upset," Henry said.

"What do you expect?" Judge Armstrong snapped.

"I'm here to get the Tennyson book, not trade barbs with you, Father."

Concordia realized that Henry's voice was getting closer. Please heaven the book wasn't back *here*.

"You keep it in the alcove, do you not?" Henry asked.

Of course it would be, Concordia thought, rolling her eyes. The curtain fluttered and she could see his fingers curl around the fabric. She braced herself, throat constricted.

"You'll have to find something else," the judge answered. "The Tennyson is at the bookbinder's for repair."

Concordia's knees quavered as she watched Henry's fingers loosen their grip and disappear from sight.

After what seemed an eternity, both men left, and Concordia found herself in darkness. She waited a few more minutes before cautiously slipping out of the library and up to her room, milk forgotten.

Back in the safety of her bed, she lay awake for a long time, staring at the ceiling.

The next morning was the start to yet another damp and blustery day. When Concordia came down to breakfast, still yawning from her wakeful night, Judge Armstrong and Henry were already at the table, sharing pages from *The Hartford*

Courant. Concordia had to restrain herself from glaring at the judge. After all, she wasn't supposed to know they were concealing something from her. Fortunately, the judge paid her little attention, instead lowering his black brows over an article in the paper. She was relieved to be spared the difficulty of making polite conversation. They ate in silence, save for the occasional clink of a spoon against a china cup.

Concordia finally spoke, keeping her tone level. "Henry," she said, "I need your help in identifying some of Mary's personal items."

Henry looked up. His dark, red-rimmed eyes looked dull against his pale face. "I'm afraid, Concordia... I can't..."

The judge cleared his throat, and Henry glanced over at his father. "Perhaps," Judge Armstrong said, "we are being selfish in keeping Concordia here unduly long. She has her teaching to resume, and work is the best cure for grief. Help her this morning, Henry, so that she can finish more quickly." He returned to his paper.

Concordia stared at the judge, her mouth open in surprise. Judge Armstrong never spoke of her work, save with a sneer. Now he *respected* her time and responsibilities? Was he trying to be rid of her before she found out too much? But how could he even know that she had discovered something? She didn't think the judge would be so calm if he knew where she had been last night.

Henry looked equally surprised by the judge's directive, but merely nodded.

After breakfast, Henry accompanied Concordia to Mary's dressing room. He briefly hung back in the doorway, as if reluctant to enter the room, but recovered and joined her at Mary's dressing table. Concordia opened the jewel case. "I can't identify these," she said, pointing to a lower tray of earrings, neck chains, and brooch pins.

They went over each one. The last piece, pushed to the back of the tray, was a gold-filigree brooch pin. Concordia plucked it out. "This is beautiful," she murmured, running her fingers lightly over the pearls inset at each corner. "Is this your gift?" She handed it to Henry.

Henry frowned as he examined the brooch closely. "No. I've never seen her wear this. This is not an heirloom from your family, perhaps? But then, why did she not wear it?" he mused. "It's a stunning piece."

Concordia leaned over to look at the pin again. It must have cost at least twenty dollars, about a month of her teaching salary. "I don't know. I could ask my mother," she said finally.

Henry passed the brooch to her. "Show it to her. Keep it if you like," he said. "It means nothing to me." He looked away, his thoughts already elsewhere. Concordia put the brooch in her pocket for the time being.

"If we are finished here, Concordia, I have other matters to attend to." He rose stiffly. His grief was aging him, she noticed. He moved like an old man, as if every joint were painful. She felt profoundly sorry for him.

Finally, late into the night, Concordia finished in Mary's room. She tidied the piles, packed a few items she thought Mother would want, and wrote instructions for the dispersal of the rest. It was a relief to be done, and to leave the Armstrongs in the morning. As if the company of Judge Armstrong and Henry wasn't bad enough, there was something about the house itself that chilled her.

Looking around the room once more, she had the feeling she had overlooked something, but she couldn't think what.

In the silence, the soft creak was unmistakable this time. It was *not* the rain outside.

Nor is it a squirrel or a mouse, she thought grimly. *Someone is up there.*

She was going to settle this, once and for all.

Chapter 18

March 1896

The Armstrong attic was not a congenial place even on a sunny day, as Concordia well knew, so it was with a thumping heart that she approached the attic stairs, lamp in hand, so late on this miserable rainy night.

As before, the knob turned easily and silently, although the wooden steps creaked loudly enough to be heard over the steady drumming of the downpour outside. The sharp smell of rain, filtering through the eaves, mingled with the usual smells of mothballs and dust.

Her breath caught in her throat. Was that a glow, at the end of the attic?

As she paused, uncertain what to do next, a figure detached itself from the gloom, coming toward her. Concordia yelped in terror and backed away.

"Miss! Miss Concordia! It's just me!" Annie said in a strained whisper.

"Annie! You scared me to death!" Concordia cried. "Whatever are you doing here?"

"Shhh. I don't want to disturb no one," Annie said in a low voice, moving toward the door. "I was checking to see how much room there was fer the missus' trunks, seein' as how yer nearly done packing them. I'm sorry to scare you."

"*Uhh-nehh, uhh-nehh.*"

The sound was chilling, and familiar. Concordia pushed past a protesting Annie, and stooping low, made her way to the back of the attic.

A white-gowned figure–the one from her dream, Concordia realized with a shock–crouched in a corner, terrified.

"Annie, what in heaven's name is going on?" she demanded.

It was a child–a boy of perhaps eight years, although Concordia, not knowing much about children, was only guessing as to his age. He was a handsome child, with a full head of glossy black curls, wide eyes, and delicate pointed chin. He rushed over to Annie, flinging his arms around her skirts. "*Uhh-nehh.*"

Annie clasped him protectively, giving Concordia an apologetic look. "Can we get him out of the damp first, miss, before I tell you about it? I was just comin' to get him."

Indeed the child, barefoot and clad in a thin night shift, was shivering.

"Let's go to my room. It's nowhere near the judge's or Henry's bedrooms. And I assume they know nothing about this," Concordia added dryly.

Annie shook her head.

"There's a nice fire in there," Concordia said to the boy, in a softer tone. He looked at her blankly. Annie turned to the boy and made gestures which he seemed to understand, as he readily followed them out of the attic.

"What's wrong with him?" Concordia whispered.

"He's deaf, miss. Been this way since he were a baby and got scarlet fever. He's my brother."

"Oh." Why in heaven was a deaf child hiding in the Armstrongs' attic?

Once safely in the room, Concordia stoked the fire and turned up the lamps. The boy flinched at first when Concordia tried to put a blanket around his thin frame, but must have realized that here was a friend. Once he was snuggled close to Annie, he gave Concordia a tentative smile, gesturing rapidly.

"What is he doing?" Concordia asked, puzzled.

"It's a sort o' language for deaf people, miss. They're teaching it to him at the 'sylum. I'm learning some, too. He's saying 'thank you'."

Concordia knew what asylum Annie meant—the Hartford Asylum for the Education and Instruction of the Deaf and Dumb. It was only a few blocks from here, and had been founded more than eighty years before, for the training of deaf children. The neighborhood of Asylum Hill had been named for it.

"He's been saying things, too," Concordia said, "I thought all deaf people were mute."

"There's nothin' wrong with Davey's voice, that's fer sure," Annie said, with a fond tousle of the boy's hair, "and when he's mad he can yell somethin' fierce. He jus' can't hear what he's saying, so it comes out all garbled."

"But he can say *Annie*," Concordia said, realizing what the repeated *"Uhh-nehh"* meant. It had been part of her dream—but not *all* of it a dream, she now knew. Mary had undoubtedly heard it too, during those wakeful nights of illness.

Annie nodded. "He could say that when he were a baby, before he got sick. I guess he still remembers that."

By this time, Davey had fallen asleep in Annie's lap.

Concordia went to the door, looked down the hall to make sure it was empty, and closed it again. She turned back to Annie with a stern look.

"Do you realize how badly you frightened me—and Mary, in the last week of her life—by keeping your brother here?" She looked over at the sleeping child. "Put him in my bed for now, and then we have to talk. I want the whole story."

"I'm ever so sorry, miss," Annie began, when Davey had been settled comfortably. "I did'n mean to give you and the missus such a fright."

"What is he doing here? How long has this been going on?" Concordia asked.

Annie sighed. "Fer a couple o' weeks now. The 'sylum got a terrible outbreak of influenza. They sent the healthy ones home, and shut down the school and took care of the sick ones 'til it was over. I'm glad Davey did'n get sick, but I been tearin' my hair out trying to figure what to do w' him."

"You haven't any family here?" Concordia asked.

Annie shook her head. "Can't afford the train fare to send him back home, and there weren't no one to go w' him, anyway. He sure can't go by hisself. I had him w' some other boys at a boarding house off and on—one of the teachers is takin' care of them—but he's been fighting w' some of the others lately, and she can't abide that."

Concordia looked over at the angelic face of the sleeping boy. It was difficult to imagine Davey as an aggressor.

"Strange, ain't it?" Annie agreed, catching her glance. "I think he's been picked on, but he won't let on."

Concordia walked over to her wardrobe and rummaged in a pocket. "I gather this is Davey's?" She held up the wooden top and pull string.

Annie's eyes lit up. "Ooh, he'll be so happy. He's been missin' that. Where'd you find it?"

"He must have dropped it by the bed when he visited me one night. I thought I was dreaming. And the string I found in the attic."

Annie's mouth formed a small "o" and she shifted uncomfortably. "Sometimes I'd let him play in the attic, when I worried he'd be seen in my room. But mostly, I try to keep him with me at night. It's been real hard," she said apologetically.

Visions of the boy wandering into Judge Armstrong's bedroom in the middle of the night made Concordia shudder. Annie was playing with fire.

"He can't stay here anymore, Annie. You know that. You could lose your place if the Armstrongs see him."

"I know, miss. Thank the stars the 'sylum is lettin' the students back tomorrow."

Concordia looked once again at the source of all the trouble. The boy slept deeply, his face a picture of utter calm. Thank the stars, indeed.

The next morning, Concordia prepared to leave for her mother's house. She would stay there a few days before returning to the college. Only a few days, she reminded herself. Surely she could manage that. She paced the floor of the front parlor, waiting for the coachman to arrive.

While it was a relief to have answers to the mystery of what had been going on in the attic, she had found out frustratingly little about her sister's death, which was her true purpose. In the time since Concordia had eavesdropped on Dr. Westfield and the judge—more than a day ago now—the doctor had officially declared Mary's death the result of endocarditis, an infection of the heart valve. There seemed nothing sinister in such a malady.

Upon waking this morning—Annie having smuggled Davey back up to her own room—Concordia realized what had been missing from Mary's possessions when she sorted through them: her sister's personal correspondence. And perhaps a diary of some sort, too. Ever since they had been little girls, Concordia and Mary had been encouraged to keep a journal. Concordia had soon tired of the exercise, claiming (petulantly, she was sure) that there wasn't anything exciting enough in her life worth writing down. Mary, however, faithfully wrote in her diary nearly every day, and would most likely have kept up the practice in adulthood.

Concordia had not been able to find Annie or Henry this morning to inquire about it. Annie was no doubt taking Davey back to the asylum school—and not a moment too soon, in her mind—and Henry must have left for work early. She certainly wasn't going to ask Judge Armstrong. Should she ask one of the staff?

"Miss Wells?" A hesitant voice broke into her thoughts. Concordia turned to see Nancy in the doorway. She held out a small scrap of paper. "For you, miss."

It was a note from Annie.

"Thank you, miss, fer helping me," she wrote. "Today's my haff-day. Could we meet at Brown Thomsons at 11 clok? There're some things I'm not easy in my mind about. I think you should know."

Concordia checked the mantel clock. She had just enough time. Thankfully, the coachman was now pulling up to the door.

She grabbed her valise and hurried out, giving the driver her new destination.

Chapter 19

Every Hartford native was familiar with the Brown Thomson Company on Temple and Main Streets, in the heart of the downtown shopping district. It was the largest department store in the city. Like its competitors, G. Fox and Sage Allen, Brown Thomson had its humble origins, decades before, as a dry goods dealer. These days, the store reminded one more aptly of an elegant lady primped and ready for callers. On previous visits Concordia had marveled at the polished floors, gleaming counters, and neatly arranged displays, laden with goods from the world's four corners. Today, she walked by it all without a glance, her meeting with Annie uppermost in her mind. Her heart pounded in anticipation. What did Annie have to tell her? Could she answer her questions about Mary? If so, why had she not spoken before?

The Ladies Restaurant at Brown Thomson's was a welcome alternative to more questionable eating establishments, where a respectable woman would never go unaccompanied. Concordia had dined here before, although she was careful to avoid the expensive entrée selections.

The room hummed with subdued conversation. Concordia chose an out-of-the-way corner table, laid like all the others with crisp white linen and dainty lace napkins, and ordered tea and cake for the two of them.

As she waited, her thoughts skirted around the same questions: what had been wrong with Mary? And whatever it was, why was Judge Armstrong working so hard to conceal it? Could he have been poisoning Mary, as Miss Hamilton had so boldly suggested? Had Mary known, but been helpless to save herself?

But each of these questions pointed to the hardest question of all: why? It was the brick wall that kept her from seeing everything else.

She was about to call for a fresh teapot when Annie finally came, wearing a modest brown dress with matching felt hat and low heels. Having seen Annie only in her domestic's garb of gray dress, cap, and apron, Concordia almost didn't recognize her.

An alert waitress came over with a fresh pot and their food.

"How is Davey?" Concordia asked.

Annie flashed a wide smile. "Oh, he's just fine, now. He's so happy to be back at school. I think I'll finally get a good night's rest for the first time in a dog's age."

"I can imagine that," Concordia murmured.

"Thank you again, miss, for all you done," Annie added. She hesitated, smoothing her skirt and picking an invisible fleck of lint from it.

Concordia waited, holding her impatience in check.

Finally, Annie plunged into the heart of the matter. "I keep thinking there was something wrong with the missus that them men don't want no one to know about." Annie shook her head in frustration. "I been wanting to tell you, and then after what you did for me an' Davey, I knew I ought to say something. But I can't figure out what's wrong. But there's *something*. I sure hope you don't think I'm crazy, miss."

Concordia certainly understood how the girl felt. "You're not crazy, Annie. Let's figure this out together. Between the two of us, maybe we can find an answer."

Annie nodded, fortifying herself with a sip from her tea cup. Leaning closer, Concordia walked her through Mary's illness, symptom by symptom, as it developed over the months. Pain. Fever. Nausea. Bleeding.

"Wait a moment." Concordia hadn't seen a wound of any sort. "What kind of bleeding?"

Annie shifted uncomfortably. She dropped her voice to a bare whisper. "Like a lady's cycle, miss. But it were for a long time. We had all them linens to clean, so we couldn't help but know."

Concordia started, realizing that her own sense of modesty, and squeamishness, were to blame for missing this important detail. She customarily left the sickroom whenever the bed was being changed or her sister was to be examined. She could kick herself now.

This symptom was obviously important, but Concordia was at a loss to explain it. What did a female indisposition have to do with the heart valve infection that caused Mary's death?

A wild idea occurred to her. Could there be a poison that produced this effect? But the notion was absurd. This was not a bookstall penny dreadful one reads on a train. And what did she know of poisons?

Could Mary have been mistreated by her husband, perhaps brutalized by him? It was a repugnant thought. Everything she knew about Henry rebelled against the idea. And the fever would make no sense, if that were the case.

There was another possibility. Concordia looked over at Annie.

"Could Mrs. Armstrong have given birth to…a stillborn child?"

Although Concordia was certainly no expert in the matter, it would account for most of Mary's symptoms. The pain, the bleeding, the fever. But why go to such lengths to hide it? To lose a child would be a misfortune, certainly, but hardly a source of scandal.

Annie gave a shocked gasp. "No, Miss Concordia, that's impossible!" Several heads turned toward their table, and Annie dropped her voice.

"I would a' known, miss. No one could hide something like that."

Concordia let that go for the moment. "Tell me about the visit from the specialist—what's his name?"

Annie dutifully took Concordia through what she could remember: the relief they all felt that the missus would now be taken care of; the arrival of Dr. Samuels, the well-to-do gentleman with his fancy Boston mannerisms; the brief first visit, followed by a second, much longer visit, where everyone else, except Dr. Westfield, was told to leave the room; and a final, heated argument behind the study doors between Dr. Westfield, Judge Armstrong, Mr. Henry, and the Boston doctor. Annie couldn't hear what was said, but she remembered that it ended with Dr. Samuels storming out of the study. He left so quickly that she barely had time to hurry ahead to hand him his coat, medical case, walking stick, and hat before he was out the front door.

"The judge was in a fine pucker for days after that," Annie said, "stomping around, yelling at everybody for the least little thing."

Concordia was silent for a while. The Armstrongs and Dr. Westfield had strongly objected to Dr. Samuels's medical opinion. Why? She looked up at the maid, who was watching her hopefully.

"Our next step is to contact the specialist. I will do so right away," she said. Annie looked disappointed.

Concordia, too, was less than confident about her course of action, although she saw few options. Most doctors, understandably, were reluctant to breach patient confidences, even that of a deceased patient. Nonetheless, she had to convince Dr. Samuels to do just that.

Annie had re-pinned her hat in place and was gathering up her gloves and pocket book when Concordia remembered something else.

"Annie, do you know if Mary kept a journal? I couldn't find one when I was going through her possessions. In fact, I couldn't find a scrap of personal correspondence anywhere."

Annie looked puzzled. "Now, that's kinda odd," she said, "'cause I know she got letters. When they was away on their tour in Europe, we had a whole stack of 'em saved for when she got back."

"But I don't know about a jernal," she continued. "She used to be writing at her desk a lot when she weren't sick. I couldn't say if it was a jernal, miss. I'm sorry."

Concordia bit her lip in vexation. They didn't seem to be making much progress. She tried one last idea.

"Do you think you could look around the house for a journal, and any of her correspondence? Without...the Armstrongs' knowledge?" She felt hesitant about asking Annie to snoop in her employer's house. She didn't want to get the girl in trouble.

But Annie's eyes lit up. "O' course! Ladies feel secretive about their private writing. Maybe the missus hid hers somewheres."

Concordia felt her spirits lift a little. Annie's enthusiasm was infectious. "Yes, it's quite possible," she agreed.

Annie stood to go. "Then that's what I'll do," she said decisively. "If she had one, I'll find it."

Concordia, too, stood. She grasped Annie's hand. "Thank you. But do be careful."

Chapter 20

Nothing is but what is not.
I.iii

March 1896

Concordia and her mother were preparing for yet another round of condolence calls. They had received more calls in this past week than Concordia had in the last two years. She had forgotten how insulated the college environment was in comparison with the rest of society; at Hartford Women's College, it was inclination, rather than necessity, that would prompt one to stir outside the campus gates.

Most of the callers were her mother's friends, an irksome assemblage, who seemed to delight in commenting upon the unseemliness of Concordia's vocation. Many of them embraced the misconception that women's colleges were a veritable breeding ground for anarchists and liberals.

"I wonder at you, Letitia, allowing your daughter to consort with such people," one triple-chinned matron said, after helping herself to another teacake.

"I find Concordia's fellow teachers to be entirely respectable," Mrs. Wells said primly. Her long, slender hands delicately worked the tiny sugar tongs to pluck a cube for her tea. As a child, Concordia had been fascinated by those fluid movements, and had thought her mother the most graceful woman in the world.

"A number of them have sent notes of condolence, and have been quite kind," her mother went on. "Concordia's students come from the most upstanding families in the area, Agatha."

Concordia, startled by support from this unexpected quarter, looked over at her, but received no answering glance.

But their well-fed guest was not finished with the topic. "Our dear Reverend Burrows only last week informed us of a most *alarming* trend–apparently, most of these college girls do not go on to *marry* and have children! 'Race suicide,' he called it."

Whatever do you mean, Mrs. Griffith?" Concordia asked, with a touch of impatience.

The lady gave a smug smile, enjoying her role as bearer of ill tidings. In her enthusiasm, she made an abortive attempt to lean forward, only to be thwarted by a tight corset, which gave a mutinous rasp of coraline and elastic stretched to the breaking point. She resettled herself, and the danger passed.

"Well, I've known it all along," Mrs. Griffith answered, huffing to catch her breath. "Just look around, at our own city! The foreigners are copiously producing their own kind, while the numbers of white children are in decline. It is only a matter of time, young lady, before we are absolutely overrun!"

Concordia blinked in surprise. Mrs. Griffith must be dipping into the sherry a bit too often.

"Now, Agatha, really," Mrs. Wells interjected feebly.

"Mark my words," the lady continued, wagging her finger, "those indolent Catholics and Hebrews will be taking over, if we don't protect our own interests."

Concordia refrained from pointing out that "indolent" people wouldn't be stirring themselves to take over much of anything. Instead, she gritted her teeth and offered more scones. It was a relief to them both when Mrs. Griffith finally left.

There were a few agreeable callers. Sophia Adams came by daily. Surprisingly, Concordia's mother seemed to have a soft spot for Sophia, despite their philosophical differences. Concordia would have expected that the modern Sophia, with her reformist views on women and social issues, would provoke her mother beyond tolerance, but Sophie had a winning way about her, and Mother would just smile indulgently when she talked about her work at the settlement house. Concordia wondered if perhaps she could learn something from Sophia.

Nathaniel Young also paid a visit. The poor man was looking haggard. While he was as well-groomed as usual, his silver-streaked wavy brown hair neatly smoothed to the side, his eyes lacked their usual sparkle and his face had a pinched look. He was taking Mary's death as hard as the rest of them.

He declined refreshments, but sat down to ask about their well-being, and Concordia's future plans.

"I will be returning to the college in a couple of days, after I pay a few obligatory calls," Concordia answered. She suppressed a sigh. It could not be soon enough. She and her mother had maintained an exhausting civility toward each other since the funeral.

"Oh? Whom are you visiting, my dear?" Nathaniel asked.

"Miss Banning, tomorrow. I dearly need her advice on preparations for the senior play."

Concordia didn't mention that she would also be paying a call on Mr. Reynolds. She wasn't ready to discuss him, yet. For some reason, she thought Nathaniel and her mother would disapprove, although she wasn't sure why. She certainly didn't want them to get the wrong idea about her and Mr. Reynolds.

"Ah, Margaret Banning!" he exclaimed, smiling. "Have you met her? No? Well, you will find her an unusual woman."

Concordia had heard similar comments. She had a vague recollection of Miss Banning from an early fall faculty meeting, shortly before the lady's ill-health had forced her to give up her teaching duties. Concordia hoped the visit would not be tedious, with the old lady complaining of her various aches and pains.

Miss Banning's house was a modest brownstone along the quieter eastern end of Capitol Avenue. As she rang the bell,

Concordia braced herself for the meeting, squaring her shoulders and settling her spectacles more firmly upon her nose. She had dressed carefully, choosing her best traveling suit of dark gray, the bolero jacket trimmed in decorative buffalo-red braiding with velvet-faced lapels of the same accent color. She hoped that she looked the part of a junior colleague. She wasn't sure she felt that way.

A woman much too old for parlor maid duties helped Concordia remove her hat and scarf. Concordia glanced around the narrow hall. It was furnished simply, with a single high-back chair, umbrella stand, hat rack, and small table. The floor was bare. Obviously, not a front entrance that catered to many visitors. There was not even a mirror for a lady to check the state of her hair, or a plate for receiving calling cards. Miss Banning was a woman who suited her own needs, apparently.

But Concordia was not prepared for the state of the parlor. While the hallway was bare of furniture and ornamentation, the parlor was a jumble of décor and collectibles in the old Victorian style of excess. The oriental carpet was room-sized and ornately worked; the window dressings were elaborate swathes of fringed dark green velvet fabric, which barely admitted light into the room; the surfaces were littered with china figures, alabaster vases, and embroidered pillows. There was even an unfortunate stuffed bird under a glass dome, Concordia noted with a grimace. She didn't know what to look upon first. The room was uncomfortably warm, and smelled of dried flowers and multiple cats. As proof of the latter, several felines dozed in front of the hearth.

She saw movement. Miss Banning, seated near the fire, waved a cane imperiously at her.

"I'm too old to get up," she said, her voice strong but reedy, "just sit down over here, young lady, so I don't have to keep looking up at you." Concordia complied, shifting aside a pillow on a chair farthest from the fire. A well-fed orange tabby jumped into her lap. Concordia unceremoniously dumped it back on the floor and brushed off her skirt, drawing a throaty laugh from her hostess.

"You'll have to excuse Caesar, Miss Wells. That's his usual spot," Miss Banning explained. She gave the beast an indulgent look, as he settled himself at the old lady's feet.

Miss Banning was as extraordinary-looking as the room. She was a small woman, as Concordia had remembered, with large bottle-glass spectacles perched on her nose, and gray hair that peeked out from under a lacy breakfast cap of Swiss muslin, perhaps fashionable two decades ago. It was impossible to determine her figure, thin or stout; she looked as if she wore an entire dry-goods store on her back. Concordia couldn't tell where the layers ended and the woman began. She didn't look like any history professor she had ever met.

Margaret Banning was giving Concordia a more frank appraisal, as she rang for tea.

"So, you're the one who has charge of the senior play now, eh?" Miss Banning commented. She looked at Concordia intently, her eyes wide and distorted through her glasses. "I hope that Hamilton woman knows what she's doing. You don't look much older than a senior student yourself. How are you going to control that passel of young brats?"

Concordia, still reeling from the lady principal being dubbed "that Hamilton woman," and not at all certain she *could* handle the seniors, sat, silent. She flushed with irritation.

Miss Banning moved on to another topic. "What do you think of our new Lady Principal, Miss Wells? I've been hearing interesting reports of her."

"I admire her, of course," Concordia responded tentatively.

Miss Banning was unimpressed. "Humph. 'Admiration is the daughter of ignorance.' Benjamin Franklin. I don't want platitudes, girl. What do you *really* think?"

Concordia considered her answer. She was not sure what she thought of Miss Hamilton. She felt rather intimidated by the lady principal.

"She is undoubtedly strict, but seems to be fair," she said finally.

The old lady shot her a keen glance. "Know anything about her background? Where she comes from?" Her sly smile hinted at something more.

The chair creaked as Concordia leaned forward. "Whatever do you mean, Miss Banning? Miss Hamilton has impeccable credentials. It is common knowledge that she was headmistress at Forsythe Academy, a most prestigious girls' school."

Miss Banning snorted. "And how long has it been since she left that position? *Seven years.* Did you know *that*, my smart young miss? I think not. But she has led everyone to believe it was more recent than that."

"It is of no consequence," Concordia said dismissively, although she would not admit to the old busybody that she was curious about it, too. "She has the necessary credentials, nonetheless."

"But no one *knows* anything about her life during these past seven years, before she came to the school," Miss Banning persisted. "Do you not find that strange? What has she been doing? For all we know, she could have been in prison all that time."

Concordia knew it would be rude to laugh in her face, and restrained herself. "I don't believe we have to worry about that," she said mildly. "But we should respect Miss Hamilton's privacy, don't you think? She has dealt with some trying circumstances lately." Concordia wasn't sure how much Miss Banning knew of the incidents at the college, although word of Miss Lyman's death had undoubtedly reached her.

Miss Banning grunted. "Ah, yes, the bursar's death. Most trying for her, I'm sure. And those pranks, too. Hardly surprising, however."

"What in heaven's name do you mean by that?" Concordia said sharply.

Margaret Banning, surprised, gave a long, yellow-toothed smile. "Nothing takes place in a vacuum, my dear young lady. How well do you know the history of the college, and of the people who run it? *When the past no longer illuminates the future, the spirit walks in darkness.'* de Tocqueville."

"But these were student pranks, Miss Banning," Concordia protested. "The students have little 'history' at the college. And Miss Lyman, unfortunately, succumbed to melancholia and died by her own hand."

"Perhaps," Miss Banning countered, "but I doubt our sharp-eyed lady principal is convinced of the suicide, or thinks that mere student high-spirits are involved in the campus pranks. And you would be more naïve than I take you for to assume it, either."

The old lady waved her cane wildly in the air to emphasize her point. The cats scattered, then placidly resettled themselves.

Miss Banning continued, warming to her theme. "'A man's affairs become diseased when he wishes to cure evils by evils.' Sophocles. Ever read Sophocles, Miss Wells, hmmm? Or do you just read those moony English poets? No substance to them at all."

Concordia refused to rise to the bait, although the woman was certainly trying her patience. "Which man's affairs, Miss Banning?" she pressed. "Do you know who is responsible for the problems at the college? Did Miss Lyman die at the hand of someone else?"

Margaret Banning shook her head stubbornly. "I have no proof. One can damage a person's character through ill-advised accusations. 'It takes many good deeds to build a good reputation, and only one bad one to lose it.' Franklin again. You would do well to read him."

"However," the woman continued, noting Concordia's vexation, "there is nothing to prevent *you* from making your own discoveries. You seem to be a lively sort. Use that head of yours, girl. 'The measure of a man is what he does with power.' Plato. Who has power at Hartford Women's College? The students? Hardly." Miss Banning gave a wheezy laugh.

Concordia shifted restlessly in her chair. She had come here to discuss the play, not parry with the old lady and her sly hints. And yet, Miss Banning was voicing questions that had been troubling Concordia. But how would she go about finding answers?

Her musings were interrupted by the same maid bringing in the tea tray. It was elaborately laid and exceedingly feminine: embroidered tea cloths, a matching set of translucent bone china, thinly-sliced sandwiches, delicate pastries. Wordlessly, the maid set down the tray with a decided *thump*, turned and left them to their own devices.

What an odd maid, Concordia thought. She poured the tea, spicy and fragrant, while Margaret Banning, in a pointed change of subject, began discussing the senior play.

They discussed role assignments, costumes and sets. They also talked about Concordia's greatest challenge: raising the quality of the students' portrayals. Concordia had realized, in the few rehearsals she had conducted so far, that most of the students were giving rather wooden performances, especially the senior in the lead role of Macbeth. This was where she needed the most help.

Miss Banning grunted in disapproval. "A sad want of imagination, Miss Wells," she said. "They are still thinking of their parts as words on a page! You must get them to conceive of these people as *real.*"

"Take Macbeth, for instance," she continued, leaning forward, eyes gleaming, "people forget that he begins as a brave and noble man, and a trustworthy one, while others around him show their traitorous and cowardly natures. That is how he first finds favor with the king and becomes Thane of Cawdor. Yet, what happens to him?" she asked Concordia, much as a teacher would ask a student.

Concordia responded promptly: "He is tempted, and succumbs to his desire for power. He chooses evil, which gradually consumes him, until he cannot turn back."

Miss Banning made a noise of approval, adding: "Yes! Our 'hero' becomes the play's villain, quite quickly. Why? His weakness—ambition. *I have no spur/To prick the sides of my intent, but only/ Vaulting ambition, which o'erleaps itself,'* he says. Evil begets more evil."

Concordia understood all of this, and had already tried reviewing the themes and characters with the seniors. She didn't see how this would help her.

Margaret Banning thumped her cane for emphasis. "He is *human*, like the rest of us," she said. "No matter how kind, well-intentioned, or amiable we may be, we are each equally capable of malice, under the right circumstances. Get your students to imagine *that*, and even better, to imagine a specific person, which reminds them of their characters."

She gave a mischievous grin. "I can think of a number of people, right under your nose, missy," she said, belligerently pointing her cane at Concordia, "who would fit that description."

Chapter 21

This castle hath a pleasant seat; the air
Nimbly and sweetly recommends itself
Unto our gentle senses.

I.vi

March 1896

The next day, Sophia accompanied Concordia on her last obligation before she was to return to the college: a call upon Mr. Reynolds. He lived along Washington Street, amid the expanse of mansions dubbed "Governor's Row." As this section bordered the South Green neighborhood, it was close enough to Mrs. Wells' house for the two of them to walk.

Each was wearing her most flattering walking costume for the visit. Sophia looked quite stylish in a dark forest-green plaid suit, its skirt lined in rustling taffeta, and the jacket smoothly fitted at the waist to soften her angular frame. Concordia wore her favorite, a slate-gray Eaton suit. It was older and slightly out of fashion, but the tailored jacket created a slimming silhouette, while the wide and deeply-cut lapels, lined in black broadcloth to match the trim along the skirt's edge, drew the eyes upward to one's face.

After considerable reflection, Concordia had decided not to wear mourning for Mary after the funeral. While the practice was customary for widows, there was no prescribed etiquette for other family members who were mourning a loss. She did not require an outward show of her grief to know how she felt, and such a display would only prompt unwanted questions and pitying looks, which she could not abide.

The walk was a pleasant one. Typically, March in Hartford does not let go of winter easily; yet today was a rare day of early warmth, when the ground is coaxed into shrugging off its shroud of brown and gray. Bright patches of green were more abundant in the front yards they passed, and the trees were dotted with buds. Concordia, however, walked by it all in preoccupied silence. Between Miss Banning's remarks, the doubts she felt about Miss Lyman's death, and the secrets the Armstrongs were keeping from her, there seemed to be a great number of things she did not understand. What was her next step?

Sophia ducked to avoid a low-hanging tree branch, which threatened to snag the ribboned edging from her hat. "I know that Mary's death is troubling you," she began hesitantly, stealing a sideways glance at her friend.

Concordia felt a now-familiar twist in her stomach as she tried to explain her feelings. "I know I'm not the only one to lose a loved one in the blush of her youth," she answered, "but Mary's death doesn't make sense to me. I just wish I understood it. Perhaps then I could be reconciled to losing her? I don't know."

"It's regrettable that you and Mary didn't have more time together, to grow closer," Sophia said. She hesitated, as if to add something more, but by then they had reached Julian Reynolds' house.

The Reynolds mansion was one of the largest of the row. And one of the most dramatic, in Concordia's eyes. It was in the Italianate style, with ornamental cornices under wide, overhanging eaves, windows and doors topped with Roman arches, and balconies symmetrically flanking the sides of the house. Crowning the whole was an elaborate cupola.

Sophia and Concordia exchanged looks. "A bit intimidating, isn't it?" Concordia observed.

Sophia gave her a scornful glance. "Nonsense," she said, stepping forward to ring the bell. Concordia, however, noticed that Sophia straightened her jacket as they waited.

Concordia was just beginning to wonder if they should ring again when the door was opened by a petite young parlor maid. She was blonde, and pretty, though clad simply in a gray dress and white apron.

"Please to come in?" the girl said in heavily accented English. She collected their calling cards and gestured toward the front parlor.

"I tell Mister Reynolds," she declared, hurrying down the hallway and leaving them to find their own way.

Concordia saw the same puzzled look on Sophia's face that must have been on her own. She had expected Reynolds' parlor maid to match the grandeur of the house: experienced, polished in manners, dressed in a lacy cap and apron rather than a plain uniform. This girl was obviously a recent immigrant, German or Swedish to guess by her accent.

Through the doorway of the parlor, Concordia looked around the room, noting how different it was from Miss Banning's establishment. It was unquestionably modern and elegant in taste, much like its owner. A delicate vine pattern, with muted tints of olive and cream, papered the walls; India fabrics and inlaid lacquer tables added an exotic note to the room. There was very little bric-a-brac. A grouping of framed photographs held pride of place on top of the piano.

Julian Reynolds came down the hallway to greet them. Attired as he was in black morning coat, patterned tweed trousers, and a beautiful waistcoat of Prussian blue, he exuded a stylish air of at-home informality. Concordia felt a little catch in her throat.

"Ladies, welcome," he said. "Please, be comfortable!" He tutted over the sight of Concordia and Sophia hovering uncertainly in the parlor doorway, and ushered them into the room.

"I am so sorry," he said, "Olga is still learning her duties. My former maid abruptly decided to quit and get married, flighty girl! This new girl was the best I could do on short notice. My wife used to hire the servants," he explained.

It must be quite difficult to adjust to a widower's life, Concordia thought. She wondered why he had not yet remarried.

"Were you and your wife married for very long, Mr. Reynolds?" Sophia politely inquired.

"Five years, Miss Adams," he replied. "Alas, she died before we had any children. I do have one nephew, whom I get to see on occasion. I manage his trust fund for him. Delightful boy."

He took a frame from the piano and handed it to them. It was a side profile of a youth, with longish wavy hair and sparkling eyes, his mouth crooked into a hint of a smile.

"He is my wife's nephew, actually. I was an only child," Reynolds said, passing another photograph over to them. The woman had a candy-box sort of prettiness: a soft, oval-shaped face, framed by wisps of the same wavy pale hair. Her self-assured smile suggested a life that was very much what she had expected it to be.

"They are very like," Concordia said. She gave them back to Mr. Reynolds, who carefully placed them on the piano, picking up another to show them.

"And these are my parents, taken shortly before their deaths. I am sorry to say that I'm the only one of my family left."

"That must be very difficult for you," Concordia murmured sympathetically. She looked closely at the photograph, noticing how the slant of light played across eyes and cheekbones. She could see the son's features in the father.

"Who was the photographer?" she asked, passing it to Sophia. "The lighting is skillfully done."

Reynolds beamed with pleasure. "I took those photographs, Miss Wells," he answered. "Photography has long been a hobby of mine."

Sophia shifted in her chair, and Concordia was reminded of the purpose of her visit.

"I regret that we cannot stay long, Mr. Reynolds," she began, "perhaps we should discuss the classes..."

"But I must show you more of my photograph collection!" Mr. Reynolds exclaimed. "It would not take long. We can do both in a short time: I will get my albums, as well as the list of assignments and grades that I have compiled for your classes."

He jumped up and left the room before Concordia could protest.

Sophia groaned. "'Album*s*?' Is this necessary?" she asked impatiently.

Concordia made a conciliatory gesture. "I don't want to be rude to the man. He has done so much for me, Sophie."

Sophia, resigning herself to the inevitable, settled herself more comfortably in her chair.

A quarter of an hour went by, without Mr. Reynolds reappearing. Concordia, feeling restless herself, decided to go looking for him.

"Unorthodox behavior, Concordia, to be sure," Sophia said with a grin.

"How much longer do you want to wait here?" Concordia said peevishly. She opened the door and glanced down the hallway. It was empty.

She walked along corridors, calling tentatively, "Mr. Reynolds?" It was such a large house, Concordia soon realized, that it was useless to call to him.

There were more doors than she could keep track of. She began opening them at random, losing her caution as she proceeded through the first floor. The air became chill toward the back of the house; why were there no fires in any of these rooms?

The state of the back rooms was quite different from the front parlor; here the furnishings were older, the carpets more threadbare, a thin layer of dust accumulating on the surfaces. Concordia ran her finger absent-mindedly along a bookshelf in what was probably the study, frowning at the smear on her glove. How to account for the neglect taking place here?

She heard footfalls overhead. She should not be here; Mr. Reynolds would be embarrassed to know that she had seen the condition of these rooms.

"Looking for something, my dear?" came an amused voice. Heart in her mouth, Concordia turned to see Mr. Reynolds, his arms full of bound volumes. Obviously, the footsteps she had heard overhead had not been his. Carefully, Reynolds set down the books and crossed the room in swift strides. Concordia backed up a few steps, where she was stopped by a wing chair.

"I... I'm s... sorry, Mr. Reynolds," she stammered. He stopped in front of her, *close* in front of her. She could feel his breath on the top of her head. Was he angry with her? She couldn't tell.

Julian Reynolds reached out and gently brushed back a loose strand of her hair. Like a trapped rabbit, Concordia froze, her heart beating wildly.

"Miss Wells..." he hesitated as footsteps approached. Sighing, he dropped his hand and took a few steps back.

"Mister Reynolds, sir, I make tea for your company?" The parlormaid had appeared at the door, and gave the two of them a quizzical look.

"Yes, Olga, that would be fine," he answered, turning around.

"Where is the sugar, please?" Olga asked.

"I'll wait in the parlor," Concordia said quickly, as Reynolds went with Olga in search of the sugar.

"Ugh! Look at the dust on the back of your skirt," Sophia commented, when Concordia returned.

"I'll explain later," Concordia said. She swatted at her skirts, and settled herself back in her chair as Julian opened the door.

"Here we are!" he said brightly. He placed the albums in front of her, along with her grading book and a pile of student themes. "It took me a little while to find everything. Thank you for indulging me, ladies. I would truly appreciate your opinion of the photographs," he said, addressing both women, but his gaze lingered warmly on Concordia. She flushed.

She realized that her best chance of recovering her composure was to stop looking at Mr. Reynolds and instead turn her attention to the albums. They were beautifully bound, in supple burgundy leather. Concordia turned over one of the volumes to look at the back cover. *The Signal Printing Company.* A local business? They did excellent work.

The rest of the visit passed uneventfully. Finally, she and Sophia took their leave. The late-afternoon sun streaked the clouds in deep shades of pink as they walked. Concordia described what she had seen of the house, carefully omitting her encounter with Mr. Reynolds.

Sophia was quiet for a while, thinking. "There is a simple explanation," she said at last. "Reynolds cannot manage a household. It shouldn't be surprising. Men aren't very good at it, you know; although," she continued, her determined chin thrust forward, "they will need to learn, since modern women will be taking on new responsibilities of their own."

Concordia recognized a favorite subject of Sophia's, echoed by her fellow settlement house activists. Personally, Concordia doubted that, if *she* ever married, her husband would assume any domestic tasks so that she could follow a career. She would not be offered a teaching position, anyway; she didn't know of any college that hired a married woman. And then–*mercy!*–there would be children to manage.

"Perhaps," she said wearily. She would be happy to return to her uncomplicated life back at the college tomorrow.

Chapter 22

Weeks 9 and 10, Instructor Calendar
March/April 1896

Concordia's vision of a quieter and simpler life back at school was at least a brief reality, as she had returned during the students' spring recess. Many of the faculty and administrators scattered during this time as well. Only a few students, those who could not travel home because of distance, remained in the care of the house matrons.

Concordia was content to work uninterrupted during the week. Besides grading midterm examinations and student themes, she also spent time composing a carefully-worded letter to Dr. Samuels, asking for information about her sister's illness. She felt better after sending it off. Annie had not yet contacted her about the search for Mary's journal or letters, and Concordia chafed at the wait. She tried not to think about the earlier plans she and Mary had made for Concordia's spring recess—the exhibit at the Wadsworth Atheneum they had wanted to see, the shopping they would have done together.

The tranquility on campus was broken soon enough, as April brought its cacophony of bird calls and returning students. Concordia was immersed once again in the day-to-day routines of campus life: meals, chapel, classes, meetings, teas, rehearsals. She had not seen Mr. Reynolds since her visit to his house in town.

Concordia still flushed at the memory of their encounter in that dusty back room. What would have happened if Olga had not come in? What would she have wanted to happen? That question made her blush even more, so she firmly set it aside.

There was one activity in particular that Concordia had been looking forward to, now that the warm weather was making its return. On one temperate afternoon, she opened her wardrobe to pull out her bicycle outfit, complete with jacket, skirt, bloomers, leggings and cap. She felt a familiar rush of excitement as she put them on. This would be the first time in months that she had been able to ride. It was an odd feeling to wear the outfit, after so long a time; it showed a shocking amount of leg, which took a little getting used to.

After pinning her hair beneath the cap and casting a dubious glance at the mirror, she pushed her machine through the door, and headed for the paths. In the distance was the bell tower and clock. Although the bell had fallen into disrepair and been removed long ago, the tower's clock still worked. Concordia squinted, shading her eyes for a better look. Almost three. More than an hour before she would have to return and change for dinner.

Concordia was a skilled rider, having bicycled for several years. Soon the awkwardness of being on the machine after so long ebbed, and her greatest challenge was dodging the clumps of students who were also out enjoying the sunshine. She made her way to the less frequented back pastures, which were seamed with smooth dirt tracks.

The air moving across her face was a delight, and soon Concordia found her mind freed from its worries, content to follow the tender green hills on the horizon, to fill her nostrils with the scent of new growth. This was as close as one could come, perhaps, to flying....

"Ho! Watch out!" A voice sharply brought her attention back to the trail, which she had drifted from. She saw a young man dive for safety. Concordia swerved, braking hard, which caused her to tumble head over handlebars. She felt a painful wrench to her shoulder. Worse yet, she heard the sickening *crunch* of a bent bicycle frame as it tumbled, riderless, down the hill.

The young man stooped over her, his face creased with concern. "Are you all right, miss?" he asked, helping her to her feet. "That was a nasty spill you had."

"Yes, yes, I'm fine," she answered, grimacing as she rubbed her shoulder. "It was my fault. I wasn't minding the path."

Concordia righted her spectacles. Miraculously, they had stayed on her face. She took her first good look at the gentleman, who had bits of brambles and dried grass stuck to his hounds-tooth tweed jacket and trousers. "I'm so sorry!" she exclaimed. "Are you injured?"

"Not at all," he reassured her, with a smile at her equally bedraggled appearance, "we seem to have escaped serious harm. Which is more than I can say for your bicycle, unfortunately." He gestured down the hill.

"Oh, no!" Concordia exclaimed, looking down at her ruined bicycle, which lay on the embankment below, the stream washing over part of it. She started to scramble down to get it, ignoring the pain in her shoulder.

The gentleman stopped her. "Please, allow me. You can rest here," he pointed to a blanket, upon which several books and a picnic hamper rested.

Concordia didn't protest, and sank gratefully unto the blanket. As he climbed down to fetch her machine, she re-pinned her straggling hair under the cap. She found her eyes straying to the stack of books. The one on top caught her eye.

Burton's College Chemistry. Hmm. Hardly light reading. Who brings a chemistry book on a picnic? He was a Trinity student, no doubt. But why picnic alone, on a women's campus? Had she broken up a planned tete-a-tete?

He reappeared a few minutes later, now damp and muddy, dragging her bicycle. It looked far worse than he. The fender was smashed flat against the rear wheel, whose wooden rim had split; the chain and pedal seemed inextricably entwined. The horn and parcel basket were missing—no doubt washed downstream by now. He laid it down and sat beside her.

"Whew!" he panted, out of breath from the exertion. He wiped his hands on his handkerchief. "I don't think it's irreparable," he commented, as she looked over the bicycle in dismay, "in fact, I have a friend in the machine shop at Trinity College who can try to fix it for you, if you like."

Concordia could not help but laugh out loud. This man, a stranger to her, whom she had nearly run down, had seated her comfortably, fetched her bicycle, and now offered to have it repaired.

He appeared momentarily disconcerted, but soon was chuckling himself. Perhaps he was relieved she wasn't complaining of her injuries, or fainting.

Finally Concordia was able to gasp out a response. "I...am...most grateful...Mister—?"

"Bradley. David Bradley, at your service, miss," he finished, with a mock gallant bow. Concordia, giving him a longer look, noticed that he was close to her own age. He could not be called a handsome man; he was perhaps a bit shorter than average, but well-built and muscular. His face was his most appealing feature, with heavy black lashes over brown eyes, and a dimple in one cheek when he smiled, which was often.

Concordia realized that the silence had been lengthening. "Are you here visiting a student, Mr. Bradley?" She must sound quite matronly, asking such a question. But the staff was charged with screening male guests and their business on campus.

Mr. Bradley gave her an amused grin. "Hardly, Miss—?" Now it was his turn.

"Oh—sorry! Concordia Wells. I teach English Literature and Rhetoric." Her tumble must have rattled her brains.

"Wonderful! We are colleagues, then. I teach the senior Chemistry Seminar here this semester; I also teach Chemistry and Physics at Trinity."

Concordia must have looked doubtful, for he added, "And don't tell me that my youthful good looks make it impossible for me to be old enough to teach, because," he teasingly pointed a finger at Concordia, "the same could be said for you, my good miss." She laughed.

With the sun on her back easing her sore shoulder, she was content to linger, sharing the apples and cheese from his hamper. For close to an hour, Concordia and Mr. Bradley talked about work and students. Soon the subject of the pranks came up.

The young man grew serious. "I hope the culprit is caught soon. It's quite worrisome."

"But nothing has happened since last month," Concordia said. Before Mary died, she added to herself.

Bradley hesitated. "There has been another incident since then. Miss Hamilton has kept it quiet."

"How do *you* know? What incident?" Concordia asked.

He hesitated. "It was just before the spring recess. Miss Hamilton offered to loan me a book from her library. When I followed her in, we found her rooms in chaos. Books and papers disturbed. Someone was quite desperately looking for something."

Concordia was quiet for a while, digesting this new information. Why was the lady principal a target?

The springtime sun started sinking lower toward the horizon. She regretfully stood and brushed off her skirt. "I have to get back."

Mr. Bradley jumped up and righted her bicycle, looking it over critically. "You can't possibly ride this now. Let me carry it back with you."

She thanked him, and they proceeded across the fields to Willow Cottage.

Her shoulder felt better by the evening, when she met with a much-depleted senior cast for play rehearsal. She was losing some of her students to basketball practice tonight. Basketball practice and rehearsal times didn't usually conflict—she had tried to avoid that—but the hotly contested Junior-Senior game was coming soon. Miss Jenkins, true to her single-minded nature, had decided that additional practices were needed for the players. Ever protective of her girls, she had even used her own money for new gymnasium attire, as the old uniforms had been mended until they were threadbare. President Richter had refused to provide school funds for the purpose. "As tight-fisted as they come," Miss Jenkins had complained, to anyone who would listen. It was pointless to remind her that the school was already in financial difficulties.

Everyone at school would attend, along with many trustees and town residents, creating a standing-room-only crowd in the gymnasium. The students were quite keen for the game. Concordia had heard the story of a student last year who, ill with whooping cough, had tried to slip out of the infirmary to attend. She didn't get far, of course, before her coughing gave her away.

Concordia hoped that she could keep her students on task, both in rehearsals and the classroom. This time of year was rife with distractions: besides the basketball game and the play, there was the upcoming Senior Spring Dance, a formal affair which drew many of Hartford's most elite families. And then there was the suffrage rally next week. For some unknown reason— Concordia expected a facility usage fee might have been involved, President Richter had decided to allow a rally on campus, marking the first time that the Women's League had obtained permission to hold such an event at the college. The settlement house ladies were hosting the rally, with Sophia Adams as the keynote speaker.

Her thoughts were interrupted by a student stumbling over her lines.

"Miss Osgood," Concordia called to the offender, "It is *not*
'Away, and hide the time with fairest show
False heart must hide what the false face must know.'

"It is
'Away, and *mock* the time with fairest show
False *face* must hide what the false *heart doth* know.'"

Concordia stifled a sigh. If Macbeth can't keep her lines straight, they were done for.

Louise Osgood looked sheepish, and began again.

Chapter 23

Over the next few days, anticipation of the upcoming rally began to build. It was the primary topic in the faculty lounge, drawing heated opinions on both sides.

"And why should we not have the same voting rights as men?" Jane Cowles asked one afternoon, when several of the teachers, along with the lady principal, were taking a tea break. "We make important decisions every day of our lives. Are we not to be entrusted with choosing our leaders?" The tip of her long nose twitched even more than usual, and her thin frame was rigid with anger.

"Wyoming has had full voting rights for women for more than twenty years now, before it even became a state," another teacher said. "And just recently, Colorado extended the franchise to women."

"Wasn't Utah's admission to the union an interesting development," Miss Pomeroy added, jumping into the discussion, "with their leaders banning polygamy *and* granting women the vote, nearly simultaneously? They have certainly become progressive in the past year."

Given Miss Pomeroy's single-minded absorption with French literature, Concordia was surprised that the lady was even aware of Utah's existence. The woman's placid demeanor was difficult to penetrate. Not a crease or frown puckered her round, cheerful face, whether the subject was politics or the latest translation of *La Chanson de Roland*.

Miss Jenkins gave a derisive snort. "*Utah?* 'Progressive' is not a term I would use, Gertrude. It took six attempts before the territory was granted state status. The Mormon elders were forced to outlaw polygamy, *finally*. And giving Utah women the franchise merely solidifies the Mormon voting base. It was a politically expedient move."

Miss Pomeroy nodded and stared off into space, Utah forgotten.

There was an awkward pause before Miss Bellini picked up the original thread of the discussion.

"Women are not *naturally* political beings," she argued, with a pointed look in Miss Jenkins' direction. Her olive skin flushed with the heat of debate. "Why should we become involved in areas that men can manage quite capably?"

Miss Jenkins rolled her eyes. "Their competence remains in doubt in *my* mind. Our leaders devise ways to make the rich even richer, and the poor more desperate than they were before. We have corruption at nearly all levels of our government. Thank goodness Mr. Cleveland is putting a stop to *some* of it. But we should not have to depend upon the *men* to elect such people. It isn't right that we do not have a hand in the decision."

Miss Bellini would not cede the field so easily. "But as Signorina Cowles has said, we women make important decisions every day, do we not?" she argued. "Our sphere of influence—it is wide—as teachers, mothers, advocates. We help the poor. We make the lives of others better. That is all of the power we need to have. Too much power—it brings trouble," she ended with a frown.

Miss Jenkins, fiddling abstractedly with the cord of her whistle, didn't dignify Miss Bellini's claim with an answer.

Concordia had been reluctant to join the discussion, but felt the need to interject a middle position. "Some of the suffragists have argued," she began carefully, recalling her talks with Sophia, "that women as voters would bring more balance to the process. If one takes the position that women are naturally maternal" (here Miss Cowles grunted in disdain), "and more invested in the future of a society that their children will inherit, then they are *better* able than men to select leaders who would contribute to the greater good."

Miss Cowles jumped back into the discussion. "It is the principle that matters to me," she said. "Do you know that at this moment, legally, women are classified with children, idiots, and criminals? How can one argue that women have power when we are placed in this position?"

"Ladies, please," said Miss Hamilton, silent up to this point. Although sitting at her ease in a rocking chair and balancing a sandwich plate on her lap, her sharp glance brooked no argument. "We will have plenty of opportunity for discussion at the rally."

Several of the women settled back to their tea, although Miss Cowles, tight-lipped, stalked out of the room.

Miss Jenkins attempted a change of subject. "So, Miss Wells, who was that handsome young man I saw walking back with you from the fields the other day? I feel as if I've seen him on campus before."

Concordia involuntarily flushed. "Mr. Bradley. He teaches the Chemistry seminar here."

Miss Hamilton gave Concordia a quick glance, but said nothing.

Miss Bellini, though, was happy for a distraction. She leaned forward in interest. "Ah! Have you known him long? How did you meet?"

Concordia shifted in her chair. She decided to opt for honesty. "I ran him down. Almost," she quickly added.

They were all familiar with Concordia's zeal for bicycle-riding. The resulting laughter dispelled the tension in the room, and soon after, Concordia managed what she hoped was a dignified exit.

As Concordia made her way back to Willow Cottage—she really did have essays to grade—she thought about Mr. Bradley. The day after her unfortunate spill, he had come, true to his word, to collect her bicycle. He had also taken the opportunity to ask her to join him the following week for a picnic lunch.

"Without the bicycle this time," he said teasingly. She found herself agreeing to go.

Mr. Bradley possessed a warmth and sense of humor that Concordia found endearing. She felt at ease in his company. He certainly did not make her heart beat faster or her breath catch in her throat the way Julian Reynolds' presence did, but she did not need *that* additional complication. In fact, Concordia had not seen Mr. Reynolds since her return to campus. She wondered if the gentleman was avoiding her.

She was quickly disabused of that notion, however, when she approached the door to her quarters. Propped carefully beside the lintel, for all the world to see, was a single red rose. A note lay beside it. The seal was broken.

With trembling fingers, Concordia picked up the note. As she read, she felt her face grow hot with embarrassment.

> *Your beauty makes this rose blush in shame. I am just returned from business, and I long to see you again.*
>
> *Fondly,*
> *Julian*

Splendid. Someone—likely more than one person—had read the note. The rumors about her and Mr. Reynolds would be fanned back to life now. Please heaven the lady principal didn't hear of it.

Why did men have to complicate things so?

Chapter 24

But swords I smile at
Weapons laugh to scorn,
Brandished by a man that's of a woman born.

I.vii

Week 10, Instructor Calendar
April 1896

The day of the rally was unusually warm for a Hartford April. Concordia had just finished dressing when there was a knock on her door.

"Yes?" she called out. Sophia Adams let herself in, giving Concordia a hug. She was dressed in her rally finery: a tailored dress of dotted white lawn, with a high lace collar, sleeves buttoned to the elbow, and narrow folds of bias satin at the skirt.

"So, Sophie, are you ready to face the lions?" Concordia joked.

Sophia looked subdued. "How are you, Concordia?"

Concordia knew what she meant. "I still think of Mary," she said quietly. "I won't stop looking for answers. She deserves that."

Sophia nodded. "I've done a great deal of thinking, too. There is something I want to discuss with you, regarding Mary—" she sighed, looking at the watch pinned to her lapel, "but I have final preparations to oversee. Can we talk in the morning? I'm staying at DeLacey House tonight. The faculty reception after the rally will end late, so it seemed prudent to stay the night."

"Can't you tell me what it is now?" Concordia asked. "Why the delay?"

Sophia simply tipped her chin at a stubborn angle and shook her head. Concordia could get nothing more from her, as she edged out the door and waved good-bye.

The Hartford Women's League, a local branch of the National Equal Rights Party, had decorated the college auditorium in suffrage colors: white, purple, and green. Even with all of the fans turned on, it was getting stuffy as more people came, ushered to their seats by women wearing bright sashes emblazoned with the motto "Knowledge is Power."

There was a group of women from the *Hearth and Home Ladies Society* in the back of the auditorium, quietly holding placards protesting the rally: "Women Should Not Want to Be Men," and "Male and Female *He* Created Them."

The students were all comporting themselves with dignity, giving the protesters curious glances and seating themselves with only a low buzz of excited conversation.

The administrators, trustees, and faculty processed onto the stage next, with the Hartford Women's League members close behind. Concordia found herself seated along one wing of the stage, with Julian Reynolds right in front of her. She would recognize his sand-blond hair and elegant back anywhere. He turned around and winked impertinently. She dearly wanted to discuss the imprudence of leaving notes of a personal nature in plain view, but here was not the place. That would have to wait.

"What are your views on women's suffrage, Mr. Reynolds?" Concordia asked instead.

"Excuse me, sir?" a soft, feminine voice interrupted. It was Miss Howe, one of the settlement house ladies. A very pretty young woman, Concordia could not help but notice, taking in her curvaceous figure, glossy brown hair and creamy skin. Reynolds rose from his seat politely and gave Miss Howe a long, warm look that set Concordia's teeth on edge.

"We need a tall gentleman to re-attach the banner in the hall. A corner has come down. Would you mind?" Miss Howe blushed charmingly.

"Delighted." He bowed to Concordia. "If you will excuse me," he said, and followed Miss Howe off the stage.

The auditorium was filling quickly. Looking around, Concordia saw others who appeared as restless as she. Nathaniel Young inspected his fingernails. Miss Hamilton repeatedly checked her watch. Dean Langdon was staring into the distance, a dreamy look on his face. On such a beautiful spring day, he was undoubtedly eager to return to his garden plot.

None of the staff who felt a personal objection to the event was required to attend. Yet, surprisingly, Concordia saw that Miss Bellini was here. Perhaps the conversation in the lounge had sparked her curiosity. There were others she had not expected, either, especially Judge Armstrong and Dr. Westfield. She realized that they were, of course, here in their capacity as college trustees. Perhaps the judge hoped his presence would have a restraining influence upon Sophia, so that her speech did not go beyond what had been agreed upon. Concordia smiled. If so, he obviously did not know that "upstart young woman" very well.

Dr. Westfield's attention was turned toward the judge, and Concordia could understand why. Judge Armstrong's face, despite the usual fierce scowl and active eyebrows, had a sickly pallor. He held himself rigidly in his chair, but his hands shook a little as he gripped a sturdy walking stick decorated with an ornate lion's head knob. She frowned. She had never seen him look ill.

Concordia's attention was diverted by the sight of Margaret Banning lumbering over to a seat on the stage, trailing wraps and shawls in her wake. A few gallant males collected the scattered layers and restored them to her. With barely a nod, Miss Banning settled herself into a chair and began to study the room with a sharp eye.

Everyone knew ahead of time that President Richter would not attend—he would only capitulate so far—so the duty of introducing the speaker fell to the lady principal. After members of the league led the students in a rally song, Miss Hamilton stood.

Without much ado, she introduced Sophia. If the students had expected Miss Hamilton to give any indication of her own views of women's suffrage, they were sadly disappointed.

Sophia Adams stepped up to the podium. How very like they are, Concordia realized, as Sophia and Miss Hamilton greeted one another: the same height, the same slender build and erect posture, the same angular shape to their faces. Sophia's hair was a bit lighter than Miss Hamilton's perhaps, and she was, of course, younger than the lady principal. Yet the overall likeness was striking. Concordia had not noticed it before.

"L'il lady! I say!" came a loud, boisterous voice. A young man, standing in the back, was approaching the stage, although *lurching* toward the stage would have been a more accurate description.

"Y'ud have my vote, Sophia dearie!" he leered. Quite a seedy-looking individual, Concordia thought, repulsed. His dark hair was greasy and uncombed, his face had several days-worth of beard stubble, and his suit, though undoubtedly expensive, was creased and rumpled, as if he had repeatedly slept in it.

Both Nathaniel Young and Dean Langdon stood up at the same time. Sophia, cheeks flushed and eyes wide in recognition, took an involuntary step back from the podium. The lady principal, who had not yet taken her seat, grimly advanced toward the man.

What was Miss Hamilton doing, Concordia thought, alarmed. Did she not realize how dangerous he could be?

Barely six feet from the lady principal, the man stopped at the bottom step to fortify himself from a flask.

"Pow'er to the ladies! Put 'em in charge of e'rything!" he bellowed, after a long swallow.

Before Miss Hamilton could confront the drunkard, Young and Langdon jumped from the stage, grabbed the man by both arms, and frog-marched him to the exit.

The audience erupted into cheers.

"They are all yours, Miss Adams," the lady principal said, with a stifled sigh of relief.

Sophia, composure returning, stepped forward as the noise subsided.

"Thank you, Miss Hamilton. I and my fellow league members appreciate the opportunity to speak with you all today," she said, looking out over the crowd. "When we stand together, we can succeed. But many wish us to fail." She glanced toward the back of the room, at the *Hearth and Home* group of protesters.

Concordia was struck by those words: *Many wish us to fail.* Could that be the motive behind the incidents at the college? Could they be looking at this from the wrong point of view? Everyone had assumed that the pranks were petty attempts by students to lash out at authority; could someone in *power* be behind it instead? But what about the bursar's death? Could she have gotten in the way of someone's plans to sabotage the school? Instead of falling through the ice by accident, or throwing herself in as a deliberate suicide, could someone have killed her and put her body in the pond?

She looked over at Margaret Banning. What was it she had said during their visit several weeks ago? *"The measure of a man is what he does with power.' Who has power at Hartford Women's College? The students? Hardly."*

Who would wish the college to fail? Who had power? Concordia felt a little sick. She did not like the direction her reasoning was taking her.

But the incidents had abated recently; nothing new had happened since the students had returned from spring recess. And no one else had died. Perhaps she was worried over nothing.

She focused her attention on Sophia once again. Enthusiasm radiated from the woman like ripples on a shore.

One could not help being swept up by it. *When we stand together, we can succeed.*

Chapter 25

Week 10, Instructor Calendar
April 1896

"A most impressive address, Miss Adams," Miss Hamilton commented. A more intimate group of faculty, along with a few administrators and trustees, were gathered in the DeLacey House dining room. "You handled yourself beautifully. I apologize for the unfortunate disruption."

Sophia, blushing, waved aside the apology. "Do not concern yourself, Miss Hamilton. One disturbed young man is not enough to stop our work. It means so much to us to be able to bring our message to your students. Perhaps we could discuss the formation of a junior suffrage league at your college?"

Concordia saw Miss Hamilton's lips contort into what could have been either a wry smile or a grimace. "Let us take smaller steps to that end, Miss Adams."

Sophia leaned eagerly toward the lady principal, heedless of her cheese plate and glass of punch. "We are trying to make a difference in *all* aspects of women's lives, you understand, Miss Hamilton. Consider your own faculty, for instance. Why only appoint unmarried women? That is not an issue for the male professors that you hire. Why should it be different for the female professors?"

Miss Hamilton responded easily. "Our women professors are charged with the safety and well-being of the female students committed to our keeping. These are responsibilities that the male professors do not have."

"Pah!" Sophia did not try to hide her contempt. "You are *trained* to provide these young women with a college education;

that is a job only you can do. *Any* responsible adult woman could act as their chaperone."

Miss Hamilton grew thoughtful. "Your point is well taken, Miss Adams," she said finally.

"There is much to be done for our sisters, in all walks of life," Sophia pressed, her voice getting louder and more vehement. "Women are being exploited every day; their health and even their reason are suffering as a result."

Concordia noticed that Nathaniel Young and Judge Armstrong, who were helping themselves to the buffet, stopped, and looked over at Sophia in surprise. Sophia's intensity could be a bit startling sometimes.

It was late when the gathering broke up. Concordia came over to Sophia to say her good-byes.

"Remember, I want to talk with you tomorrow," Sophia said.

Concordia nodded. She could not imagine what Sophia had to tell her. She was tempted to press her again, and not wait. But she knew how stubborn her friend could be. "We can have breakfast at Willow Cottage. Eight o'clock?" Tomorrow was a Saturday, so she had more free time.

"Good," Sophia answered. Concordia gave her hand a quick squeeze, and left.

The next morning brought a steady, gray, and chilly downpour. New England springs were notoriously inconsistent, Concordia thought with a sigh. She looked out at the dismal scene, wanting to retreat back to bed, but she had to prepare for Sophia's arrival. As she got ready, she remembered something that Mark Twain, Hartford's most famous resident, had written years ago:

I reverently believe that the Maker who made us all makes everything in New England but the weather. I don't know who makes that, but I think it must be raw apprentices in the weather clerk's factory. The people of New England are by nature patient and forbearing, but every year they kill a lot of poets for writing about "Beautiful Spring."

When eight o'clock came and went without a sign of Sophia, Concordia put on her boots and mackintosh. No doubt Sophia had become entangled in some earnest debate with one of the faculty at DeLacey House and had lost track of the time.

Slipping her hood over her head, she ducked out into the rain. She nearly collided with Mr. Bradley (she seemed to be doing a lot of that sort of thing), who was pushing her newly-repaired bicycle ahead of him down the path.

"Why on earth are *you* here?" Concordia asked him, astonished.

He gave her a sheepish look, made all the more ludicrous by the rain plastering his dark hair against his head and dripping down his nose. "Seems silly, doesn't it?" he said. "Delivering your bicycle in the pouring rain? I have business that takes me to Boston for a few days, so I wanted to make sure you got it back before I left."

As they hastened back to Willow Cottage to stow away her bicycle, Concordia explained her errand.

"I'm looking for Sophia. She was supposed to meet me nearly an hour ago. I think she might have been delayed at the faculty house."

"Let's go, then," Bradley said. "I'll walk with you."

They set out again for DeLacey House. Concordia and Mr. Bradley had not gotten very far along the path, however, before they heard a moan coming from the hedge.

"What was that?" Concordia asked. "A cat?"

Mr. Bradley looked grim. "No." He ran to the hedge, where two paths intersected, stooping over to look. Concordia hurried to follow.

"Oh, dear Lord, no!" she exclaimed. It was Sophia. She had a large gash on the side of her head. A pool of blood, blurred by the rain, was collecting under her ear. She was white, and motionless.

Chapter 26

Week 10, Instructor Calendar
April 1896

"She's still breathing," Mr. Bradley said, leaning over Sophia.

"Thank heaven," Concordia whispered, her chest constricted in fear. Sophie looked so very pale, lying there. "We have to get her inside," she urged. Concordia's rain hood had slipped back, but she ignored it. She pushed aside the wet locks straggling across her eyes, and looked around for possible help. No one, of course, was outside in this weather. She and Mr. Bradley would have to manage by themselves.

Mr. Bradley recognized the same thing. "I would rather not be moving her, but we cannot leave her out here in the wet. I don't feel any broken bones," he said, carefully probing her neck and limbs. He gently gathered Sophia in his arms. Concordia hurried ahead of him to open the door to Willow Cottage.

"In here," she said, gesturing to the settee in the parlor. Ruby came bustling down the hallway at the sound of voices, her apron still on and her calloused hands dusted with flour.

"What on earth...?" At the sight of the dripping couple and the unconscious Sophia, Ruby sucked in her breath sharply.

"Ruby," Concordia said, "send some of the girls for the lady principal and the infirmarian. We'll need towels and blankets, and a hotter fire in here." Ruby scurried off.

She turned to Mr. Bradley. "I have to send you out of the room now, David. Ruby and I need to get her wet clothes off. It may already be too late to keep her from developing a chill."

She looked over at the young woman. "I should have gone looking for her sooner," she said, shivering.

David frowned. "It's not your fault, Concordia. And you need to get dry, too. I don't want you to become ill."

But Concordia was already pushing him out of the door, as Ruby came in with blankets.

He stopped at the doorway. "Her injury looks more serious than Miss Jenkins can remedy," he said quietly. "I should fetch a doctor for her."

Concordia knew he was right. "Do you know someone nearby?" she asked.

"What about Dr. Westfield? I believe he's attending the trustees' breakfast at Sycamore house at the moment. One can't get any closer than that."

"No! *Not* Dr. Westfield," Concordia replied firmly. She'd already lost her sister under the doctor's care; she wasn't going to lose her friend as well. "Oh, I can't explain, David," she said, in response to his puzzled expression, "just find someone else, *please.*"

"Very well," he said reluctantly. "I know a doctor not far from here, off of Wooster Street. I'll be back as soon as I can."

He hesitated in the doorway. "I would feel better if you locked the door behind me."

She did.

Chapter 27

Week 10, Instructor Calendar
April 1896

Concordia, Mr. Bradley, and Miss Hamilton waited in Concordia's sitting room. They had been ordered to stay out of the way as Miss Jenkins and Dr. Musgrave, the physician that Mr. Bradley had found, attended to Sophia. Ruby was occupied with keeping the all-too-curious student residents of Willow Cottage in their rooms.

Concordia, now in dry clothing, cradled a cup of strong tea that Ruby had brought for each of them before disappearing upstairs. She looked over at Mr. Bradley, who was toweling his hair. His shoes and jacket had been placed in front of the hearth, wisps of steam coming from them as they dried.

"Mr. Bradley, why don't you sit closer to the fire?" Concordia invited.

He complied, but answered with a grin, "I liked it better when you called me 'David.'"

Concordia flushed, replying tartly, "No doubt you did, *Mr. Bradley.*"

Miss Hamilton stifled a laugh. The gentleman did his best to look chastened.

Miss Hamilton broke the silence that followed, bluntly putting forward the question they were all considering. "Who do you suppose attacked Miss Adams, and why?"

Concordia shifted uncomfortably in her chair. She would never become accustomed to Miss Hamilton's candor. The lady principal was a study in contradictions: unreadable at some moments, and blazingly forthright in others, all while comporting herself with an unflustered, dignified air.

"It might have been an accident," Concordia said tentatively.

Miss Hamilton shook her head. "Unfortunately no, Miss Wells. I checked the path where she was found; there was no rock, or other object, which could have caused her wound. The weapon was carried away by the person who wielded it. We must be realistic, as unpleasant as it is."

Miss Hamilton was right. Concordia sighed. As soon as she had locked the door behind Mr. Bradley, she knew there was something to fear. It was foolish to pretend the danger wasn't real.

Mr. Bradley leaned forward. "One possibility is that someone resents her suffrage work. I understand that there was a protest group at the rally, and even a drunken lout who tried to disrupt the event? I wasn't able to attend, but I certainly heard of it. It would not be surprising if Miss Adams has made enemies."

Miss Hamilton frowned. "That could give the president, and others who share his opinions, more reason to ban such events in the future. If Miss Adams was indeed a target because of her activities, it may be deemed too dangerous to involve the campus any further."

Concordia was quiet. Dr. Musgrave seemed to be taking a very long time with Sophia.

"What do you think, Miss Wells?" Miss Hamilton asked.

Before she could answer, there was a polite knock, and Mr. Reynolds stepped into the room. The rain must have stopped, Concordia realized, because he was perfectly dry, and as immaculate as always. What a contrast to poor Mr. Bradley, she thought, looking over at that gentleman. He was drying out nicely, but his hair had a wild curl to it. The odor of wet wool hung in the room.

Mr. Reynolds had noticed David Bradley and paused, puzzled, until Miss Hamilton said, "This is Mr. Bradley, one of our part-time instructors. He and Miss Wells discovered Miss Adams lying under the hedge. Mr. Bradley," she continued, gesturing to Reynolds, "this is Mr. Reynolds, one of our trustees."

The two men exchanged wary glances and curt pleasantries. Mr. Bradley continued drying his hair. Reynolds promptly ignored him, turning to Concordia.

"I came over from the trustees' breakfast as soon as I heard," he said, sitting beside Concordia and taking her hand, which prompted a lift of the eyebrow from both Miss Hamilton and Mr. Bradley. "It is so unfortunate! Your dearest friend!"

While Concordia felt comforted by the warmth of his hand, she pulled away, afraid that such sympathy would cause her to lose her composure.

"Who could have done this?" she asked, her voice trembling.

Reynolds cleared his throat. "Actually, I've been thinking about that on my way over here." He hesitated.

"Yes, Mr. Reynolds, what is it?" Miss Hamilton asked.

"Well, I've been wondering if the attack upon poor Miss Adams is part of the whole of what has been happening at this college," he answered finally.

"How is it possibly connected, except by geography?" Bradley quipped.

Reynolds gave him a frosty glance, then turned to Miss Hamilton. "Suppose Miss Adams was not the intended target," he continued, "perhaps the attacker mistook Miss Adams for someone else." He looked steadily at the lady principal.

Miss Hamilton looked surprised. "Mistaken for *me*! Surely not."

Concordia sat up straighter. "Yes, I've noticed it, too. You and Sophia do look remarkably alike. I recall observing the similarity at the rally yesterday."

"But I must be at least– hmm," here Miss Hamilton hesitated, "twenty years older than Miss Adams!"

"But in low light, with the rain coming down in sheets? Her form and carriage could have been easily mistaken for yours," Reynolds pointed out.

Miss Hamilton sat silent, and thoughtful.

"What about Miss Lyman?" Concordia asked, disturbing the silence. "Could her death have been—"

There was a knock at the door. Dr. Musgrave came in, accompanied by Miss Jenkins. Concordia's stomach lurched when she saw the blood upon Hannah Jenkins' infirmary apron.

Dr. Musgrave was a small man, elderly and gruff in manner. He was dressed in the standard attire of a local town doctor: black morning coat, stethoscope bulging from the right pocket; gray worsted trousers, water stains fading around the cuffs; sturdy leather oxfords with worn heels.

The doctor began without preamble. "The young lady's condition is very serious. She has not regained consciousness, and I do not know if she will. There is no fracture to the skull as far as I can determine, but there is a great deal of swelling. She hit her head as she fell, thus compounding the injury."

"Can you surmise what kind of weapon she was struck with?" Miss Hamilton asked quietly.

Dr. Musgrave answered, "Most likely, it was something compact but heavy, with some sort of irregular edge that lacerated the scalp. The attacker hit her just above her right ear, from behind."

Concordia felt the backs of her eyes prickle. "Is there *any* hope?" she asked.

The doctor's eyes softened in pity. He cleared his throat. "In a few of these cases, yes, the patient *has* recovered, at least partially. A complete recovery is rare," he added gently. "But she is young, and strong, and those factors are in her favor."

"Miss Hamilton," he continued, "since the young lady is in such grave condition, she should not be moved very far. I recommend that she be moved—carefully, mind you—only as far as your campus infirmary." He gestured to the infirmarian. "I have given instructions for her care to Miss Jenkins. I can also provide you with the names and addresses of competent private nurses."

"I will return to check on her tomorrow," he said to Miss Jenkins, who nodded.

"I will take my leave of you, then. I am behind on my rounds." Dr. Musgrave bowed, and left.

"What will happen now?" Concordia asked Miss Hamilton, as the doctor closed the door behind him.

"President Richter has spoken with the chief of police," the lady principal said, her brows creased in a troubled frown. "I expect they will be sending someone here shortly."

Miss Hamilton's prediction proved correct. Sophia had scarcely been settled into her infirmary bed before Concordia and a nearly-dry Mr. Bradley were summoned (rather like naughty children, Concordia thought) to Miss Hamilton's office, where a Lieutenant Capshaw was waiting to question them.

Capshaw rose from his seat when they entered. He was a tall, gaunt man, with wavy red hair and a neatly-trimmed mustache to match. Concordia noticed that he stooped over slightly when upright, as if continually searching for something he might have missed. The downward slant of his brows, heavy-lidded eyes, and bent head conveyed an air of perpetual melancholy. He wore the standard wool tunic of his profession, with brass buttons running down the front in a double row. His cap had been set aside.

With only a perfunctory introduction, the lieutenant pulled out an oft-folded wad of paper, crumpled and worn along the edges, and a tiny nub of a lead pencil. Once they were seated, he addressed Concordia.

"Now, miss," he began carefully, as if fearful that she would erupt into hysterics at any minute, "we only need a wee bit of information from you, nothing at all to worry about."

Concordia looked over at Miss Hamilton, who lifted an eyebrow in amusement.

"You needn't treat me with kid gloves, Lieutenant," Concordia answered. "I promise I will not have a fit of the vapors."

Mr. Bradley's lips twitched. Capshaw turned as red as his hair.

"Very well," he continued, clearing his throat. "I believe, Miss Wells, that you were expecting Miss Adams the morning of her attack? What time would that be?"

Concordia explained the arrangements she and Sophia had made, and how she had become concerned when the prearranged time had come and gone.

"So you went out into the downpour to look for her? Was that wise? You could have caught a chill, or ruined your dress."

Concordia wondered which consideration the lieutenant thought was more pressing to a lady: risking a cold or spoiling one's attire?

Capshaw did not seem to expect an answer to the question. He turned to Mr. Bradley. "And why, sir, were *you* walking about in the pouring rain? Is this a practice on college campuses with which I am unfamiliar? Not being a college man myself, of course."

Mr. Bradley gave a rueful smile. "I was returning Miss Wells' bicycle to her. It needed some repair."

Capshaw pursed his lips thoughtfully. "Indeed." He looked at Concordia as if she had grown a second head. "You *ride* one of those machines?" He shook his head. "Extraordinary. Do you often ride your bicycle in the rain, miss?"

Concordia was startled. "Of course not," she snapped.

"Then why was Mr. Bradley venturing out in the rain to bring it to you, when a sunny day would have suited better?"

Mr. Bradley stood up. "I can explain, lieutenant."

Capshaw waved him back into his chair. "Yes, I would very much like to hear that explanation, Mr. Bradley, although I think we needn't keep Miss Wells any longer." He stepped over to the door and held it open for her. "Thank you, miss. You may go."

Concordia got one last look at the exasperation on David Bradley's face as she left the room. Poor Mr. Bradley.

Chapter 28

You have displaced the mirth, broke the good meeting
With most admired disorder.

III.iv

Week 11, Instructor Calendar
April 1896

"'Be this the whetstone of your sword.'" Malcolm began.
"'Let grief
Convert to anger; blunt not the heart, enrage it.'"

Malcolm (otherwise known as Mabel Davis) paused, looking at Concordia.

"Good, Miss Davis," Concordia responded. "Since our Macduff is currently at basketball practice, I will read her part:
'O, I could play the woman with mine eyes
And braggart with my tongue!
Bring thou this fiend of Scotland and myself;
Within my sword's length set him.'

Concordia looked up expectantly. This was where the girl had stumbled before.

Miss Davis answered easily:
"'This tune goes manly.
Come, go we to the King. Our power is ready;
Macbeth is ripe for shaking, and the powers above
Put on their instruments. Receive what cheer you may.
The night is long that never finds the day.'"

"Excellent!" Concordia was relieved that they had proceeded through the fourth act so smoothly tonight. The seniors were certainly applying themselves.

"That will be all for this evening," she said to the girls, "but remember—we still need fabric for costumes. Ask the other students in your cottages, too. I want everyone's contribution by the end of the week. *Before* next weekend's basketball game," she emphasized.

Concordia followed the students out of the auditorium, switching off the electric lights as she went, and locking the side door they had come through.

The evening, though clear, was cool. Even in April, the ground quickly returned to its late-winter chill after sunset. Concordia could see her breath. She shivered, and picked up her pace.

She wanted to stop at the infirmary to check on Sophia, who, a week now after the attack, had not yet regained consciousness. At least she had not developed a fever from her exposure; the doctor was of the opinion that she hadn't been outside for long.

Concordia hoped the policeman was making progress. She hadn't spoken to either the detective or Mr. Bradley since the day of the incident, although she'd heard that Mr. Bradley had at last gone to Boston. He must have been able to finally allay the policeman's suspicions. The notion of Mr. Bradley attacking Sophia, while holding a bicycle in the pouring rain, was absurd. But the lieutenant struck Concordia as a very thorough man.

But was Lieutenant Capshaw any closer to answering the questions that had been keeping Concordia awake all week? Who had attacked Sophia? Was she the intended target, or was it Miss Hamilton? And why? Concordia doubted that suffrage activities could spark such a violent response.

Miss Hamilton as a target made more sense: her quarters had been searched; a knife had been left in her effigy and no one else's. And yet, this was only the lady principal's second semester at the school; how could she have made an enemy so quickly?

And was the assault connected to Miss Lyman's death? Had Sophia's attacker actually killed Ruth Lyman, and made it look to be a suicide? But again, why? Sophia and Miss Lyman had never even met.

Miss Hamilton and Miss Lyman, on the other hand, had worked very closely together on college business. Were administrators being targeted? If the attacker had picked the wrong victim this time, would he try again?

"Concordia!"

She jumped as a tall, lean figure emerged from the shadowy path to her right. It was Julian Reynolds. He had an uncanny ability to catch her unawares. She breathed a sigh of relief.

"Mr. Reynolds, hello," she said weakly.

"'*Mr. Reynolds*?' I thought we were better friends than that," he said, capturing her hand and drawing closer. "You must call me Julian. We are more than mere acquaintances, are we not?" He smiled down at her, and stray lock of his sand-blond hair fell across his brow. Concordia resisted the sudden impulse to smooth it back.

"Ye-es, of course—Julian. But whatever are you doing here?" It was nearly the students' bedtime hour.

"Our beloved Literature Club," he answered. "Those girls are certainly avid readers! We talk about all sorts of things, besides books. They are quite the gossips."

Concordia laughed. "You are only just discovering this?"

He grinned. "Actually, no. When I taught Miss Banning's classes, I found that to be the case as well. You ladies are not good at keeping secrets."

Concordia bristled at such a remark, but decided to let it pass. "I really must go. I want to visit Sophia before retiring."

"You shouldn't walk alone on campus at night." Reynolds frowned. "I'll accompany you."

Concordia was about to protest that she could take care of herself, but recent events made her hesitate, and take his proffered arm.

"Did you like the rose?" Reynolds asked as they walked.

"It was lovely–Julian. But you cannot leave such tokens and ardent notes out for all to see–and read. It could compromise my reputation. You don't want that, do you?"

"Of course not!" Reynolds paused and made a mock gallant bow. "You have but to say the word, m'lady. I shall restrain myself in the future."

Concordia smiled to herself. He *was* quite charming.

The private duty nurse was with Sophia when they arrived. She stood up from the bedside and handed them the visitors' log sheet to sign. Sophia was looking much better, her breathing more regular.

"Her eyelids have been fluttering," the nurse said cheerfully. "Dr. Musgrave is hopeful that she may eventually become conscious."

"Wonderful," Concordia breathed, sitting beside her bed.

"You cannot stay very long," the nurse reminded her.

All too soon, they had to leave. Julian walked her back to Willow Cottage. The night air was chillier still. Her light wrap offered little warmth, and Concordia's teeth chattered despite herself. Julian shrugged off his coat and put it around her shoulders.

"Thank you," she blushed. The garment smelled of an exotic cologne she could not identify, but it was pleasant. She smiled up at him, but he was looking away, his thoughts elsewhere.

They walked along in silence for a while, with only the sounds of their boot heels along the pavement audible in the stillness.

"That man–Bradley–have you known him long?" Julian asked abruptly.

"No." Concordia was puzzled by the question. There was more silence, until they had reached the porch of Willow Cottage.

"How do you know him, if I may ask?" Julian persisted.

Concordia wasn't sure that she liked his tone. He sounded jealous, and proprietary.

"You may ask," she replied tartly, "but I'm not sure I care to answer." She handed back his jacket. "Thank you. Good night." She put her hand to the latch.

What happened next took Concordia by surprise. In a moment, she found herself gathered in his arms. She gave an alarmed squeak as he lowered his face toward hers. Then he kissed her.

She involuntarily relaxed. *What was she doing?* Part of her mind frantically protested the kiss; the other part, what the minister called the "Eve" of a woman's nature, had almost expected it, and found it quite agreeable. Had she not been waiting for this, since the time he surprised her in the back room of his house?

The moment was brief, although it seemed to stretch, suspended. He was smiling when he gently let her go. Without a word, Concordia fumbled for the latch, stepped into the hallway, and did what any well-bred lady would do in such a circumstance: she closed the door in his face.

Chapter 29

To beguile the time,
Look like the time.

I.v

Week 12, Instructor Calendar
April 1896

"So much fabric!" Miss Pomeroy exclaimed, as she helped Concordia sort through the piles of donated cloth. Miss Pomeroy came from a family of accomplished seamstresses, and she would make many of the costumes for the play.

"And it's only Wednesday," Concordia said. "We could get more in the next two days." While Concordia appreciated Miss Pomeroy's help in sorting, she had hoped to go through the piles herself first, so that she could note which fabrics came from which students. She remembered Miss Hamilton's plan to track down the effigy-makers. Unfortunately, she had found nothing of interest yet.

Miss Pomeroy laughed out loud.

"What is it?" Concordia asked, glancing over.

"They do mean well, they really do, but sometimes these girls simply aren't thinking!" Miss Pomeroy said, grinning, chubby cheeks pushing up her wire-rimmed eyeglasses. She held up a segment of light pink gingham. "Can you imagine Lady Macbeth in *this*?"

Concordia's heart beat faster. "Who turned that in?" she asked, forcing herself to remain calm. Gingham was a common fabric, after all.

Miss Pomeroy pursed her lips thoughtfully. "One of the sophomores—I'm not sure which."

Concordia tried to hide her impatience. Miss Pomeroy's slow, plodding approach to everything, combined with her mild demeanor, could be irksome. She delved further down into the pile of fabric that Miss Pomeroy had been sorting through.

Soon she had found the two distinct fabrics they were looking for—the navy sateen with its lavender print (another unlikely candidate for Lady Macbeth's costume), and the embroidered black taffeta. "Were these all contributed by the same person?" Concordia asked.

Miss Pomeroy nodded. "Let me think—I've had her in my Introductory French class—lively girl, rather tall.... Yes. Phoebe Landry. Why? Is it important?"

"I'll explain later," Concordia said, bundling up the fabrics and rushing out of the room.

Within the hour, Concordia sat in her office, waiting for a knock on her door. When it came, it was a hesitant tapping.

"Enter!" she called.

Miss Landry and Miss Spencer walked into the room. Meredith Spencer seemed the more nervous of the two, plucking at the folds of her skirt, looking around as if she expected something to jump out and bite her. Miss Landry, though wary, comported herself with something close to her usual aplomb.

"We were told you wish to see us, Miss Wells?" she asked smoothly.

"Sit down, ladies." Concordia stretched her hand out toward the pair of chairs in front of her desk, positioned to catch the light from the window. She wanted to see their faces clearly. Miss Landry calmly smoothed her skirt as she sat, while her cohort Miss Spencer perched uneasily upon the other chair.

"Do you know why I sent for you, Miss Landry?" Concordia asked.

Miss Landry looked amused. "Fashion hints, Miss Wells?" she said, looking pointedly at Concordia's pleated white shirtwaist and durable navy serge skirt. Miss Spencer let out a groan and slunk into her chair.

"Hardly." Concordia pulled out her own effigy and held it up. "I would pay little heed to fashion advice from someone who would dress a red-head in pink gingham. The others here are somewhat more becoming, however." She pulled out the other dolls, except for Miss Hamilton's. Concordia also produced the remnants collected for the costume-making.

Miss Spencer muttered, "We're done for now." Miss Landry looked pale, but spoke with bravado.

"All right, not fashion hints, then. What are you going to do with us?"

Concordia ignored her question. "Here's a particularly fetching outfit," she continued, pulling out Miss Hamilton's effigy, dressed in the embroidered black taffeta. She clucked her tongue in mock dismay over the gash in the doll's midsection. "But what a shame; it has been ruined! Here, take a look," she said, passing the doll to the girls. Miss Landry held it reluctantly.

Concordia's voice became hard and brittle. "Are you responsible for the knife found in this doll, Miss Landry?" She fixed the now squirming girl with a stern look.

Miss Spencer, meanwhile, abandoned all caution, flinging herself out of her chair in agitation. "Never, Miss Wells! We were playing a joke, yes, but we are not *depraved*."

Concordia kept her gaze steadily upon Miss Landry, paying scant attention to Miss Spencer's histrionics. "Let me tell you what I think, Miss Landry."

Miss Landry gave an exaggerated sigh, and shifted in her chair. "If you must, Miss Wells."

Concordia continued. "I believe that, for the first time in your young life, you have found yourself in an environment where you are not permitted to do as you wish. Before coming to Hartford Women's College, you had no doubt been petted and spoiled"—another groan from Miss Spencer—"and given your own way in everything. But here, we expect you to exhibit self-control, and apply yourself earnestly to your studies. You have resented this, and have lashed out by making disrespectful likenesses of those in authority over you."

By this point, Miss Landry was no longer looking Concordia in the eye, but was instead staring out the window just beyond her shoulder, blinking rapidly. Miss Spencer was holding her head in her hands.

"However, this was not base enough for you," Concordia continued. "You had to further lower yourself, and distress others, by stabbing the likeness of the lady principal..."

"Stop!" Phoebe Landry cried, her composure crumbling at last. Tears trickled down her face. "Miss Wells, I swear to you, none of us put a knife in Miss Hamilton's doll! We were shocked, too. We don't know *how* it got there. The dolls were just supposed to be a jolly joke," she pleaded. "We wanted to impress the seniors, and beat the Glove Night prank they pulled when they were in our year."

"Surely you have heard about the sophomore class hanging the freshmen gloves from the chapel beams two years ago?" Miss Spencer chimed in.

Concordia did not answer them immediately as her mind raced through the possibilities. A separate person responsible for the knife in the doll?

It made a kind of sense, she realized. What had bothered her the most—the knife—didn't fit in with her experience of high-spirited students. It suggested a different sort of mind at work.

She would have to trust her intuition. "Tell me how everything happened, who participated, and who knew about it."

When they were done, Concordia had the names of six co-conspirators. The girls asserted that no one else but this group knew about it ahead of time. "We are very good at keeping secrets," Miss Spencer declared proudly.

Now it was time for Concordia to dole out punishment. "Miss Hamilton and I have decided to put your skills to good use, ladies. You and your fellows will meet me in the

Sophomore Study this Saturday, at one o'clock. Bring your sewing kits," she added as she gestured for them to leave.

When they had gone, Miss Hamilton came into Miss Wells' office to find Concordia slumped in a very unladylike position in her chair. She looked up at the lady principal. "You heard everything, I hope?"

Miss Hamilton looked amused. "Oh, yes, indeed, Miss Wells. Nicely done."

"But we still don't know about the knife," Concordia pointed out. "I believe the girls are innocent of that."

"As do I," Miss Hamilton said. "I have my own ideas about the knife that I will look into."

Concordia made a face, thinking back over the interview. "Was I too severe with them? Some might consider what I said to be unforgivably harsh."

"Perhaps," Miss Hamilton said, "but I'm sure they will forget about it.

"By the time they are grandmothers," she added as she left the room.

Concordia laughed.

Chapter 30

If it were done when 'tis done, then 'twere well
It were done quickly.

I.vii

Week 12, Instructor Calendar
April 1896

There was great excitement on campus at the approach of Saturday's junior-senior basketball game. The game of basketball had been only recently devised, played mostly by local Young Men's Christian Associations. Concordia was amazed by how quickly it was becoming popular among the women's colleges, too.

There was certainly no lack of enthusiasm on *this* campus. Several upper-story cottage windows displayed hand-lettered signs of support for the teams. Banners were springing up throughout the grounds, in the college's colors of green and gold. Students were wearing either green or gold bands around their arms to show their allegiances to the juniors or seniors. The faculty remained carefully neutral.

Although Hartford Women's College was not as strict as Smith College and other institutions about banning male spectators at the event, it was made clear that any male visitor caught whistling or shouting lewd comments to the players would be immediately escorted from the gymnasium. Further, in accordance with uniform rules, no girl was permitted to step outside the gymnasium building in her game attire.

Concordia regretted that she would be unable to attend the event. Miss Hamilton had decided that Miss Landry and her band of offenders would serve their detention for the glove night prank during the game; perhaps the penalty would be more keenly felt. Concordia had volunteered to oversee their work.

Word of the sophomores' punishment had circulated widely, to the chagrin of the culprits. Concordia's senior students were unhappy to learn that Miss Wells would be missing their game. Charlotte Crandall was one of them.

"But you *must* come, Miss Wells!" Miss Crandall said, her square jaw set in disapproval. "Can't someone else mind those sophomore brats? We need you to cheer for us!"

"You know it would be improper for me to take sides," Concordia admonished. She looked around the nearly empty library and continued in a low voice, "but I'm counting upon you to defeat the juniors this year. Otherwise, they will be insufferably full of themselves. It is for their greater good, you know."

Charlotte Crandall nodded gravely. "You are right, of course, Miss Wells. It is our duty." She grinned. "But you *will* come to a small gathering that I'm planning afterward?"

"I'll be there," Concordia promised.

On Saturday, about an hour before the start of the game, eight glum-looking girls filed into the Sophomore Study in Founder's Hall, where Concordia was waiting for them. On a table behind her were piles of fabric not needed for costumes.

"Since you have demonstrated an inclination to hand-sew dolls for your own amusement," Concordia explained, "we have decided to put your skills to use for a greater good. Today, you will be making dolls for the poor and indigent children of Hartford Settlement House." She proceeded to give them basic instructions as to what was wanted, and set them to work.

The lady principal stopped by a short while later. Concordia stepped into the hallway to speak with her.

"The girls seem industrious," Miss Hamilton commented. "I am on my way to the gymnasium, but I wanted to see how you are faring. Any trouble?"

Concordia shook her head. "They are remarkably cooperative. I don't anticipate any problems."

"Good," Miss Hamilton answered, then, gesturing toward the study door, added, "Before I forget— avoid closing this door completely. The knob has been sticking, and the custodian tells me that he has not been able to purchase the replacement part yet." And with that, she was gone.

As the students worked, the silence in the Sophomore Study was punctuated by faint sounds from the gymnasium across campus: a coach's whistle, a cheer from the crowd. More than once, one of the girls would sigh and turn her head to the open window.

Miss Landry came over to Concordia with her first finished doll. Concordia looked it over. "Nicely made," she commented, noting the even stitching. She looked up at Miss Landry and smiled. "I would like to see the same care given to your academic work. You are a bright student."

Concordia was astonished to see tears start in the girl's eyes. "Miss Landry, what is wrong?" she asked quietly. Miss Landry shook her head mutely. Several students looked up from their sewing.

"Let's go out to the hallway," she said, leading the tearful girl.

"Continue with your work," she called over her shoulder to the other students. At the end of the hall, they sat down on a bench outside the lady principal's office.

"What is wrong?" Concordia asked again, passing over her handkerchief.

Miss Landry wiped her eyes, then looked Concordia full in the face. "D... d... do you really think I'm smart?" she asked gravely.

"Of course," Concordia said, puzzled, "surely people have told you so before? That is why you are here."

Phoebe Landry gave a bitter laugh, fighting back more tears. "That's not what Mother and Papa say. I am not here to be a *bookworm*, as they put it. Mother expects me to make *beneficial* connections while I am here. Several acquaintances of Mother's have their daughters at the school, you know, so she thought this would be suitable for me, too."

"Has anyone else in your family attended college?" Concordia asked. Perhaps talking to a different family member would be of help.

"Besides Father? Oh, yes. My two older brothers. But it was different for them; *they* are quite clever, you see, being boys. Papa was always very strict about their studies. They went to Harvard. When they came home for holidays, they told me what a jolly fun time it was there. I was *so* excited to be going to college, too!"

Miss Landry paused and looked at Concordia, frowning. "But it's not at all what I expected—the girls are so *serious* here. It's more work than I ever thought." She wiped her eyes once more, calmer now.

"Does your father not inquire about *your* studies?" Concordia asked. Miss Landry shook her head.

Concordia thought about this. She remembered arguments from family and acquaintances when she announced her own intention to attend college.

Higher learning won't help you become a better wife and mother.

No one wants to marry a bookish woman.

You could ruin your health with all that studying.

She could recall the unwanted advice, too, from those who were cautiously in favor of the idea.

Take only domestic subjects, Concordia dear.

You must be sure to form advantageous friendships to help you later in life. Isn't Doctor Willoughby's daughter attending Wellesley? Perhaps you should go there.

The latter piece of advice was obviously Mrs. Landry's own rationale for sending her daughter to Hartford Women's College.

So what happens to a young lady enrolled at an academically rigorous college, expecting "jolly fun," Concordia wondered. In the face of such demands, she might assume that she would not be equal to the work. That would explain Miss Landry's rebellion, disdain, and lack of effort. Why make the attempt when one was sure of failure?

Phoebe Landry was looking at her expectantly.

"Miss Landry, I can assure you that you are capable of outstanding work," Concordia began, "but *you* are the only person who can believe it, and act upon it. That is entirely your own decision to make, not that of your family."

Miss Landry was about to answer when they heard a sound, like a dull *thud,* from inside the lady principal's office.

There isn't supposed to be anyone in there, Concordia thought.

"What was that?" Miss Landry's eyes widened.

Concordia stood up and cautiously tried the door to Miss Hamilton's office. Locked. She stood on her tip-toes and looked in through the narrow glass door panel. The office was empty. She could see that the window behind the desk was partly open, but they were on the third floor, so no one could have come in that way. She looked to the floor by the desk. A small book was lying face down. She sighed in relief.

"A draft must have knocked a book from Miss Hamilton's desk," she said, turning away. "We should return to the Study." There was something different about the office, but she couldn't place it.

Back in the Sophomore Study, the students were making progress. During the next half an hour, Concordia walked around the room, more to avoid falling asleep than for the sake of vigilance. As she passed the door at one point, however, she noticed an odd smell. She tried opening the door. It wouldn't budge.

"Bother!" she muttered under her breath. She had forgotten about the lady principal's warning, and had shut the door behind her when she and Miss Landry came back. The knob was stuck. They were locked in.

As embarrassing images ran through her mind that involved yelling out of the window to a passerby to come and release them, she realized that they had a more serious problem. The smell was becoming stronger, drifting in around the edges of the door.

Smoke.

Chapter 31

Concordia turned back toward the room. "Ladies, pack up your belongings," she said, forcing herself to remain calm. "Miss Spencer, open the window as wide as you can. See if anyone is out on the grounds." She kept trying the knob, hoping it would turn. She banged on the door, too, and gave it several good sound kicks. Nothing helped.

"There's no one outside, Miss Wells," Meredith Spencer called out nervously. "The game must still be going on."

They all went over to the window. Concordia could see that the grounds were, indeed, deserted. Foregoing the dignity expected of a professor, she leaned as far out of the window as she could and bellowed for help at the top of her lungs. The girls looked impressed, and followed suit.

"Help! Help!" They all yelled, in vain, until their voices were hoarse. There was no one to hear them.

The smoke was getting thicker in the room, the smell sharp in the backs of their throats. Concordia checked the study door again. She dragged over a chair and stood upon it to look through the narrow transom. There was now a distressing glow coming from the end of the hallway. The door felt noticeably warmer. And it was still stuck fast.

"Miss Landry, bring those remnants over here, please," she said.

Phoebe Landry scooped up an armful of fabric and moved quickly to the door, where she and Concordia, who had finally given up on getting it open, stuffed cloths as firmly as they could around the edges. Perhaps this would give them some time.

Concordia went back to the window, looking for a way down. The prospects were not promising. To her right, the brick was smooth, and bare. To her left, there was a dubious-looking growth of old ivy that reached past their third story window. The vines were fairly thick. She reached out and gave one of the sturdier vines an experimental shake. Mercifully, it didn't budge. Would it hold her weight? Was the rest of the vegetation equally secure?

They were all coughing by this point, and Concordia's eyes were stinging. She would have to risk it.

But first she grabbed the water pitcher and soaked scraps of muslin for each girl. "Breathe through these if you need to, and stay by the window. We must remain calm," she said. Her own heart was hammering hard within her chest.

As if on cue, one of the girls began crying hysterically. Concordia heard a sharp slap. "Compose yourself!" Miss Landry yelled at the girl, who sniffled and quieted down. Not the approach she would use, Concordia thought, but apparently an effective one.

To free her legs as she straddled the window sill, Concordia bundled up her skirts in front of her. One of the girls tittered as she caught a glimpse of cambric drawers. It's not every day that one gets a peek at a teacher's undergarments, presumably. Concordia swung her other leg over the sill, pivoting her body to face the building wall. Instinctively, she looked down. That was a mistake, she realized, as a lurching wave of vertigo gripped her for a moment. She took a deep breath as she planted both feet firmly on the ledge beneath the window.

Here I go.

Grabbing with one hand the thickest vine she could reach, she leaned away from the support of the window frame, seeking a second handhold in the ivy. Committed now, she stepped off the ledge.

For a sickening moment, it felt as if she were hanging in oblivion. Her arms and shoulders strained from the unaccustomed exertion. She heard gasps behind her. Then her momentum swung her toward the denser part of the ivy, where she wedged her feet wherever they could find a hold.

Concordia heard the vine creaking under her weight, and the flutter of wings as indignant birds were startled out of their nests. She gave a shriek as one flew past her head. Although she moved as quickly as she could, steadily scaling down the wall, her progress seemed excruciatingly slow. She could feel the plant giving way in places, the smaller suckers pulling out of the bricks completely.

Her skirts were an irksome encumbrance. She had to keep pausing and twitching them out of the way when they hampered her legs. She felt a rip as her underskirt caught something sharp. *That's my second best one,* she thought ruefully.

She was about five feet from the ground when she heard a shout from above her. The girls were pointing frantically to the doubled-over ivy above her head. Concordia jumped, and the entire plant came down beside her with a splintering crash and a cloud of debris.

Coughing, she looked back up. Smoke was pouring out of the window at this point, and all eight girls were crowded at the opening, trying to lean out as far as possible for air. She gave a quick glance toward the gymnasium on the far side of campus. Still no one outside yet, and it was too far for her to run to get help in time. At that moment, a closed window farther along the wing shattered from the heat. One of the girls screamed.

The storage shed—yes! There should be a ladder there!

She remembered the ladder the custodian had used on the frozen pond. It seemed ages ago. It *should* extend just far enough.

Concordia stumbled around to the back of the building, tugging and pulling at the cumbersome ladder in the depths of the shed, stifled sobs coming from her throat.

Please heaven she had enough time.

After a couple of attempts, she got the ladder propped against the wall.

Concordia called up to them. "Two girls—hold the ladder steady! Come down one at—"

The rest of her instructions were drowned out by the frenzied ringing of the fire bell, coming from the firehouse of Engine Company 7, half a mile away at Main and Capen Streets. Someone must have seen the smoke. Turning, Concordia saw half a dozen men running up the hill to help, and more people streaming out of the gymnasium. Even the players—still in their short skirts and bloomers—swarmed towards the disturbance. Meanwhile, Miss Landry nimbly made her way down the ladder, Miss Spencer waiting at the top, as Concordia continued to steady it from below.

In moments, large, firm hands took hold of the ladder. A voice said reassuringly to Concordia, "All right, miss. We'll get 'em down. There now, just let us take the ladder from ye."

In the end, they had to pry the ladder from her grip, because she couldn't seem to let go.

Chapter 32

Bear welcome in your eye,
Your hand, your tongue: look like the innocent flower,
But be the serpent under 't.

I.v

Week 12, Instructor Calendar
April 1896

"Stop fidgeting!" Miss Jenkins said in exasperation. "I'm not finished with you."

Concordia, still smelling of smoke but now in blessedly clean clothes a couple of hours later, stood impatiently in her sitting room as Hannah Jenkins applied iodine to the assortment of scratches on her arms. The brick wall had done a fair job of scraping her right hand, too, which was wrapped in gauze. She winced as Miss Jenkins found tender spots.

"There," Miss Jenkins said, satisfied. With a quick murmur of thanks, Concordia hurried from her room to the parlor.

The first startling sight was that of her *mother*, of all people, sitting beside Miss Hamilton on the sofa, a tea tray in front of them. Lieutenant Capshaw was there, too, perched gingerly on the edge of a creaky antique rocker. He stood politely as Concordia entered.

"Mother! Why in heaven are *you* here?" she exclaimed, ignoring both the lady principal and the policeman.

She braced herself for the expected caustic reply, but her mother, who had visibly paled at the sight of Concordia's bandages, instead clenched her trembling hands more tightly in her lap.

Miss Hamilton, patting Mrs. Wells' hands, gave Concordia a sharp look, her hazel eyes clouded with disapproval. "Your mother attended the game today and, like the rest of us, saw the rescue. Naturally, she was concerned for your well-being."

Concordia didn't know which was more remarkable: that her mother had come to visit her at Willow Cottage, solicitous of her welfare, or that she had, apparently willingly, attended a *women's basketball game.*

"I appreciate your concern, Mother. I'm fine, really," Concordia answered, feeling a twinge of guilt. "But I don't understand why you were there to begin with."

Some of her mother's spark had returned. "There are many things about me that you do not understand, Concordia," she said coldly. She stood. "I do not care to explain myself in front of a *policeman.*"

"Thank you for the tea, Miss Hamilton," she continued, turning to the lady principal. "I shall see myself out."

Once the front door had closed with a sharp *click*, the ever-patient Lieutenant Capshaw finally spoke. "So, Miss Wells, another incident," he began, as if she were responsible for causing him trouble. "I will need to ask you some questions, miss."

"Of course," Concordia said, with a quick glance in his direction before addressing Miss Hamilton, "but first, tell me— are the students all safe?" Concordia, feeling dazed and lightheaded after help arrived, had only a dim recollection of what had happened immediately afterward. There had been a great deal of shouting, she remembered, and she had a general impression of people getting in one another's way, calling out contradictory instructions. Then, mercifully, the steam-powered pumper truck had arrived, and the volunteer firemen had taken over.

"Yes, Miss Wells," Miss Hamilton answered, "the students are all safe, thanks to your cool-headedness—and impressive acrobatic abilities," she added, with a small smile.

Miss Hamilton continued, shaking her head. "I regret that a defective door knob rendered such a feat necessary." She shuddered.

Concordia sank down into a chair, weak with relief. She looked up at the detective. "Where did the fire start, Lieutenant?" she asked.

"In Miss Hamilton's office," he answered.

So someone *had* been there, Concordia thought, feeling a chill creep up her back.

Capshaw pulled out his paper wad and pencil stub. "Now, miss, if you could tell me about this afternoon?"

Concordia recounted what she remembered. She told him about the sound that she and Miss Landry had heard, and that she could see no one from her vantage point. Besides, the door had been locked, so she thought nothing more of it. No, she could not gauge how much time had elapsed from that point until the time she noticed the smoke.

Finally, Capshaw took his leave, shaking his head in disappointment. Concordia turned to Miss Hamilton. "We need answers, Miss Hamilton. Who was in your office? And why? The fire was deliberately started, yes?"

Miss Hamilton sighed. "It was, indeed. With all that has happened, I fear we'll have to close the school. The president has called a staff meeting for this evening at Sycamore House." She stood up to leave. "Let us talk more at the meeting. I have matters to attend to in the meantime. Oh, and your presence is required upstairs."

"Upstairs?" Concordia repeated blankly.

Miss Hamilton's mouth twitched. "Miss Crandall's room. You are quite the celebrity now, Miss Wells. I do not think that they will be denied." And with that comment, Miss Hamilton left.

Concordia climbed the stairs to the Head Senior's room. It was humming with conversation, and the door was flung open before she had a chance to knock.

"It's Miss Wells!" she heard a girl say excitedly. She was escorted to the only upholstered chair in the room. There were at least a dozen seniors; Concordia did not know the tiny room could possibly hold so many people. From her sitting position, it looked like a sea of skirts—reds, browns, plaids; cottons, twills, taffetas—surrounding her.

"So, Miss Wells, how do you feel?" one of them asked her.

"I'm fine, really," Concordia responded, as Charlotte Crandall handed her a cup of cocoa.

"You never told us your mother was such a good egg," another girl chimed in.

Concordia blinked. "I beg your pardon?"

"Ooh, yes, Mrs. Wells—wasn't she nice?" one senior began a side conversation with another. Sometimes students have the attention span of a flea, Concordia thought in annoyance.

"...she was able to settle Meredith right down, and you know that's awfully hard to do, once that girl gets a wind up her sail..."

"...and she spoiled that pretty lace handkerchief of hers in helping Elsie get the soot off her hands..."

"...did you see that one soph—I forget the girl's name—just *sobbing* on her shoulder?"

Concordia listened in bewilderment. She must have been more dazed after the rescue than she had realized. She seemed to have missed quite a bit.

And perhaps, too, she didn't know her mother as well as she thought.

Miss Crandall, ever the attentive hostess, noticed that Concordia had become quiet. "Are you sure you're feeling all right, Miss Wells?"

Concordia roused herself. "Yes, I'm fine. But I *do* have one concern."

There was a murmur from the girls. "What is that?" Miss Crandall asked, with an uneasy look.

Concordia looked around the room. "Who won?"

Charlotte Crandall beamed. "Who else?" she answered exultantly.

Chapter 33

*There's no art
To find the mind's construction in the face.*
I.iv

Week 12, Instructor Calendar
April 1896

The mood of that evening's meeting was quite different from the exuberant senior gathering. Looking around Sycamore House's crowded dining hall—a larger space than its parlor, where the staff had met before—Concordia saw that this was much more than a faculty meeting. Tonight, the trustees were also in attendance. Rarely did the trustees and college staff meet. Concordia felt a grip of panic. Had they already decided to close the school?

President Richter was drumming his thin, restless fingers on the tabletop in front of him. He looked around the room gravely, lost in thought. Miss Hamilton and Dean Langdon were seated beside him, talking quietly together. As mismatched as they seemed in appearance and temperament—the lady principal, coolly elegant in her tailored suit of marine blue, and the dean, bulging out of a rumpled black worsted suit that had seen better seasons—they made a good working pair, Concordia realized. They seemed to have developed a rapport that enabled them to work together without the typical power struggle one often sees between administrators.

Looking around the room, Concordia realized it was more likely that one of these people, rather than an outsider, was responsible for what was happening at the college. But who? And why? She knew—and liked—all of these people.

Margaret Banning had said something about it, when they were discussing *Macbeth*. She thought back. What was it?

No matter how kind, well-intentioned, or amiable we may be, we are each equally capable of evil, under the right circumstances.

It was a chilling thought.

The president stood, and the room became quiet.

"I will give you the good news first," Richter began. "No one was seriously injured by the fire." At this, he looked over at Concordia. "I must commend Miss Wells for her quick thinking under such distressing circumstances. We are grateful to you." Concordia flushed.

"Further," President Richter continued, "the Hall has not been structurally damaged by the fire, although the east wing will be closed for repairs for an extended period. Fortunately, this will not affect the ground-floor library," Concordia saw Miss Cowles breathe a sigh of relief, "but it means that the staff will be sharing offices throughout the rest of the term. If there is one," he added, mouth compressing in a grim line. "The fire was no accident. Miss Hamilton has suffered considerable loss— of both property and peace of mind—because she is the target of some malicious person. We believe that poor Miss Adams was attacked last week because she was mistaken for Miss Hamilton in the dim light, and now this has happened. If we cannot find the person responsible, and put an end to this, we will have to close the school. Our students' safety must come first. I welcome your questions, and suggestions." Richter sat, looking expectantly around the room. There was a moment's silence, and then the room buzzed with discussion.

Concordia knew she should be listening, but she found herself strangely disconnected from the hubbub around her; the result of her fatigue, she guessed. She watched gestures and facial expressions most acutely, but paid little heed to what was said, as if those around her were speaking another language. She noticed that Miss Bellini, cheeks flushed and dark eyes sparkling with animation, was watching President Richter intently. Miss Hamilton displayed her usual utter composure, hands resting quietly in her lap as she listened. Dean Langdon, strangely, appeared animated one moment, then silent the next, looking back and forth between the lady principal and the president, bobbing up and down in his seat in order to do so. Miss Pomeroy's usual cheerful countenance was more of a vacant smile.

The trustees known to Concordia seemed much the same: Nathaniel Young and Dr. Westfield, each exuding compassion and concern; Judge Armstrong, haughty, ill-tempered, his skeptical black brows drawn up until they seemed to touch the edge of his hairline. He was looking in better health today than he had at the rally, Concordia noted. His hands were steady, and his face had better color.

Julian, arriving late, had slipped into the dining hall and stood near the door. It was the first time she had seen him since last week, when he had kissed her. He glanced over at her, then looked away with barely a nod. Concordia felt her face grow hot. Was he angry with her for shutting the door, literally and figuratively, in response to his amorous display? A pity, but she had to make clear the difference between offering attentions that were appropriate and those that were not. She was not prepared to lose her position at the college because of him.

The meeting was drawing to a close by the time Concordia came out of her reverie.

"So we are agreed," President Richter was saying, "that the college will remain open—for the time being—but we will employ additional watchmen to patrol the grounds. Further, no student will walk to activities alone after dark, and all doors must be locked."

"Police scrutiny into the fire may suffice to deter more incidents," Nathaniel Young pointed out. Concordia wasn't so certain. No one else bothered to respond to this hopeful comment, either.

"But would not families take their daughters out of school, even if we continue the semester? We have had so much tragedy here, have we not?" Miss Bellini.

President Richter frowned in irritation. "For the moment, the attack upon Miss Adams is largely unknown, and I have prevailed upon the fire chief to keep the circumstances behind the fire confidential. We are allowing the public to believe that it was an unfortunate accident. It is our best course of action for the time being. And we certainly can't be held responsible for the unfortunate actions of an unbalanced woman who took her own life."

Mention of Miss Lyman's death sent prickles along Concordia's spine. She remembered her own doubts about the suicide, at the rally and just after Sophia's attack. Was there a deranged person on the loose at the college?

But if so, it was not a madman one could easily identify. Such a person would have to deliberately make Ruth Lyman's death look like a suicide as he dumped her in the frigid water; stalk a young woman in the rain to inflict what was meant to be a mortal blow to the head; select Miss Hamilton's office out of all others to hide in and then set fire to. While Concordia could not make head nor tail of the connections, she knew there was an intelligence here, wickedness rather than insanity.

Time was working against them. They needed answers, and quickly.

The meeting ended soon after, as the day had been an exhausting one. One of the last to leave, Concordia lingered. She hoped to ask Miss Jenkins how Sophia was recovering. She could see the white hair and trim figure of Hannah Jenkins, in close conversation with Miss Pomeroy, on the far side of the room. Should she interrupt? Judging by the older woman's gestures and the quick, excited lilt to her voice, the high points of the basketball game must be their topic of conversation. They could be quite a while.

Giving up, Concordia left by a side door. The garden of Sycamore House would put her on the path directly to the cottages.

As she passed the gazebo, she overheard the angry voices of Edward Langdon and Arthur Richter. They had obviously not noticed her through the lattice enclosure. Concordia shamelessly stepped behind a shrub to listen.

"I know what you have been doing, and I will make sure you regret it. You are threatening the security of this college." It was Richter's voice, shaking with rage and betrayal.

Langdon was equally furious. "You don't know what you're talking about, Arthur—I have only the well-being of this college at heart. Can *you* say the same?"

The hoot of an owl stopped their conversation, and Concordia slipped away before they could discover her.

Chapter 34

Week 13, Instructor Calendar
April 1896

After chapel services the next morning, Concordia had time to visit Sophia before she and Mr. Bradley were to meet for their picnic.

It was the perfect day for an outing. She passed clusters of students, sprawled casually upon the grassy areas, basking in the sunshine. Several were accompanied by gentleman friends, who were permitted to visit on Sunday afternoons. Concordia caught snatches of light-hearted conversation about the basketball game, the upcoming dance, the senior play. The fire of the day before was no match for spring fever.

Many girls waved to her as she passed by. Concordia forced a small smile as she waved back. She was not accustomed to being so popular. The price of swinging out of windows? Mercy! They wouldn't catch her giving a repeat performance any time soon.

The argument she had overheard last night in the garden came back to her as she walked to the infirmary. She had been too exhausted last night to spend any time thinking over the exchange—she didn't even remember laying her head on the pillow—but now she found it baffling. Why would the president and Dean accuse each other of wrongdoing, in the most bitter of terms? President Richter had used the phrase "what you *have been doing*"—not "what you have done." An ongoing sequence of acts?

The infirmary smelled of lemon wax polish. It was dim compared to the dazzling sunshine out-of-doors, and Concordia hesitated in the doorway to adjust her eyes. A welcome sight greeted her: Sophia, sitting up in bed, awake.

"Sophie," Concordia breathed.

"It happened just this morning. But—she *is* suffering from gaps in her memory," the nurse warned.

Sophia did seem bewildered. She looked at Concordia, frowning in concentration. Then her expression cleared. "Concordia."

"Yes, Sophie! Oh, we have been so worried about you." She clasped Sophia's hand.

"Do you remember what happened?" Concordia asked, sitting beside her bed.

Sophia frowned again, and shook her head, gingerly. "No. The nurse and Miss Jenkins have asked me, too, but I can't remember. They said that I was attacked. Do you know who? Or why?" Her eyes, wide in distress, looked searchingly at Concordia.

Concordia grimaced. "No, dear, I'm afraid I don't know. None of us knows. But there is a police lieutenant investigating. He will want to talk to you now that you are awake."

"Only after *I* say it is advisable," a firm masculine voice growled. Concordia looked up to see that Dr. Musgrave had arrived.

The doctor swiftly sent Concordia to the outer room so as to make his examination. She wondered if she should leave when Miss Jenkins walked in.

"Ah, Miss Wells, you are just the person I was looking for," she said. "Let me take a look at your hand." She pulled Concordia over to a chair in brighter light, and began unwrapping the dressing. "Isn't it wonderful that Miss Adams is awake?" she asked.

"It's a relief, yes. Do you think that she will completely regain her memory?"

Miss Jenkins was looking closely at Concordia's wound, giving a satisfied grunt. "I will apply a fresh bandage today, and then I want you to return every day, for the next several days, to have it changed. After that, we can remove it and allow the abrasions to continue healing in the open air."

"Miss Jenkins?" Concordia prompted. Was she avoiding the question?

The infirmarian gave her a somber look. "It's difficult to say. These things take time. And sometimes gaps remain, especially regarding the incident itself."

"So she may never be able to tell us who attacked her."

Miss Jenkins sighed, but said nothing. They both knew it was not really a question.

With a promise to return later, Concordia thanked the infirmarian and walked back out into the sunshine.

"How are you feeling?" Mr. Bradley asked Concordia as he helped her get comfortably settled. He was dressed in high picnicking style today, she thought, noting the jaunty straw boater hat he had just set aside. He had eschewed his usual tweeds for a pair of light linen trousers and coat of blue pin-check cotton. She couldn't help but notice that the effect was quite stylish.

She was also impressed by his picnic preparations. A great deal of thought was obviously put into it: the comfortable site under a pink-blossomed cherry tree, quiet but not isolated; the well-laid linens and plates, cups already poured to brimming with cool lemonade. Much like a side-show magician producing one wonder after another from a seemingly bottomless carpetbag, Mr. Bradley continued to pull more comestibles from a basket. Fruit, muffins, thinly-sliced cucumber sandwiches—*cucumbers in April? Has he raided someone's hot-house?*

He passed her a cup. "You had quite an experience, I understand."

"I thought everyone in Hartford had attended the game and saw my clumsy scale down the wall." She glanced down at her bandaged hand. "You weren't there?"

Mr. Bradley shook his head. "Unfortunately, no, although I'm quite impressed."

Impressed wasn't the word she would have used, Concordia thought. *Unladylike, hoydenish,* or *impulsive,* more likely. Or, to borrow a more polite term of Miss Hamilton's, *indecorous.*

"Do the police have any idea who set the fire?" he asked, breaking into her thoughts.

"Hmm–no. I think not. The police lieutenant asked us numerous questions yesterday–you remember Lieutenant Capshaw?"

"How could I forget? I seemed to be his principal suspect in the attack on Miss Adams. He kept me for another hour after you left. I had no idea that delivering a bicycle in the rain constituted nefarious activity."

"Well then, be grateful that you were *not* on campus yesterday, or he would have you in shackles already," Concordia teased. As she reached for a napkin, the cuff of her three-quarter sleeve fell away, exposing more of the scratches beneath.

"May I see?" The sight of her injuries had a sobering effect on him. He reached for her arm, holding it gently. She drew in a shallow breath. Her skin tingled where his fingers touched.

As he dropped his head to look closely at the marks, she noticed the dark hair curling at the back of his neck. She had a sudden, disconcerting urge to comb it with her fingers.

Land sakes, spring fever was affecting her, too.

When he let go, she expelled a breath and tugged on her sleeve.

"Well!" she said brightly, gazing out over the hills, "I'm famished. Shall we try those sandwiches you brought?"

Mr. Bradley had his head in the recesses of the basket already, pulling out squares of wax paper. With a small smile, he wordlessly passed one over.

They ate in companionable silence for a while, the sunshine filtering through the newly-leafed trees and casting a warm glow upon the breeze-rippled grasses below.

Mr. Bradley broke the silence. "How is your friend, Miss Adams?"

"Oh!" Her thoughts had been far away. "Much better, in fact. She was awake this morning, isn't that wonderful?"

"Really? Does she remember the attack at all?"

She shook her head. "No. That day is a blank."

"How frustrating. The culprit certainly seems to have luck on his side," Mr. Bradley said, frowning thoughtfully.

Concordia sucked in her breath. Sophia's attacker may not be content to rely upon luck much longer. She could still be in danger, especially once it was known that she was awake. *Why didn't any of us think of that before?* She would have to talk to Miss Hamilton right away.

"Mr. Bradley, this has been delightful. Unfortunately, I have to go." Concordia started packing up the napkins from their meal, shaking off crumbs.

"Of course," he said, standing up, "but there was something that I wanted to ask."

Concordia paused.

He took a deep breath. "Do you have plans to go to the Spring Dance next week?"

She nodded. "I am required to go, to make sure the students—and their gentlemen friends—behave themselves. Why?"

"What I mean is—would you accompany *me* to the dance? Unless someone else has asked you," he amended.

Concordia hesitated. Certainly no one else had asked her, she thought. She half-expected Julian to have done so by now. He'd had ample opportunity. Perhaps he was still sulking.

Mr. Bradley, on the other hand, was a man with whom she felt comfortable. Conversation came easily between them. There could be nothing wrong with attending the dance as colleagues and friends.

It might even be fun.

Concordia realized that the silence had been lengthening as Mr. Bradley waited for an answer. "I would be delighted." She smiled.

With an even wider grin, he swung the blanket and hamper over his arm and accompanied her down the hill. They parted ways at the quadrangle, Mr. Bradley heading for the front gate and Concordia for DeLacey House. She had to find Miss Hamilton.

She had not gotten very far, however, when she encountered Miss Bellini, sitting on a bench at the far side of the quadrangle, smiling at her. Concordia stifled a groan. Miss Bellini had most certainly seen her walking beside Mr. Bradley, with basket and blanket. She would draw the obvious conclusion. There was no avoiding her now.

"Signorina Wells!" Miss Bellini called out, hurrying over to catch up.

"Hello," Concordia responded faintly. She reluctantly slowed her pace.

Miss Bellini fell into step beside her, black eyes gleaming with interest. "That young man, Mr. Bradley, is it not? He is certainly most agreeable."

"Yes." Concordia was not about to encourage the conversation.

"Ah! You must not think me—what is it?—*nosy*," Miss Bellini continued, "but in my home country, the villages are small, and we are interested in—happy about—each other's *amores*. A college can be very much like a village, can it not?"

Concordia relaxed a little. Miss Bellini was not teasing her or acting with malice, but was expressing a genuine delight over a possible romance. Concordia found herself blushing.

"Really, Miss Bellini, there is no *amore* between Mr. Bradley and myself. We are simply friends," she said firmly. This idea needed to be squelched before it developed into a rumor.

But Miss Bellini was not to be thwarted. "A nice suitor should also be a friend, no? Who knows? Perhaps he will ask you to the dance."

When Concordia flushed an even deeper red, Miss Bellini laughed in delight. "So, he *has* asked you! And you have accepted, yes? But that is wonderful! Do you have a dress?"

Concordia realized with dismay that she did not own a ball gown; it had not mattered before, when she was planning to stand on the periphery to monitor her students. She had nothing to wear!

Miss Bellini must have recognized the look of panic on Concordia's face. She patted her arm soothingly.

"Do not worry! I have several gowns. You can look, and borrow one of mine. We are of a similar size, yes? Perhaps a little alteration, and you will be ready!"

Concordia smiled in gratitude. After making plans to visit her later, Concordia made her excuses and hurried away to locate Miss Hamilton.

The lady principal was not at DeLacey House. "I believe she went ta the infir'mry, Miss," the housemaid told Concordia.

Drat! She had just walked past the infirmary. She had no choice but to double back.

Breathless, she finally reached the infirmary, where Miss Hamilton was in discussion with Miss Jenkins, Sophia, and the private duty nurse. Miss Hamilton looked up as Concordia entered.

"Miss Hamilton, I came to warn you that...I mean...I don't think Sophia is out of danger," she blurted out.

"Do sit down and compose yourself, Miss Wells," Miss Hamilton said. "We have been discussing that very issue."

As Concordia pulled Miss Jenkins' desk chair over to the bed and sat down, Miss Hamilton continued.

"Miss Adams is safe as long as her attacker continues to believe that he is in no danger of being identified. He would not feel secure, however, in believing that Miss Adams, once conscious, would fail to remember the attack upon her, although that is what has happened. Therefore, we must engage in a little charade, and pretend that Miss Adams is still unconscious."

"Who knows about Miss Adams' present condition?" Hannah Jenkins asked.

"Besides those of us here, of course, only Dr. Musgrave. I have already spoken with him, and he has agreed that it is a wise precaution." Miss Hamilton turned to Sophia. "Unfortunately,

Miss Adams, this means that we will have to restrict your visitors to those of us already privy to the secret."

"I'm afraid that we will have to add Mr. Bradley to the list as well, Miss Hamilton," Concordia said apologetically.

Sophia started. "Do you mean Lawrence Bradley?" she asked.

"No, *David* Bradley," Concordia said, puzzled.

"Oh, I see," Sophia murmured.

"What about the police detective, Miss Hamilton?" Miss Jenkins asked, "Surely we must inform him?"

"I can tell him nothing," Sophia said wearily. "I do not remember that morning at all. Can we not delay notifying him?"

Miss Hamilton nodded her agreement. "Dr. Musgrave did not want Miss Adams, in her delicate condition, disturbed by persistent questioning. I cannot see that there is anything to be gained by immediately informing the lieutenant. In fact, if the policeman is seen coming to the infirmary, people will assume the very thing we are trying to avoid: that Miss Adams is indeed awake and being questioned."

Concordia thought of something. "We are supposing that the attacker knows Sophia survived. What would he have done next? How could he be certain that Sophia was unconscious? I'm wondering if he has not already made sure of her condition after she was brought here."

Miss Hamilton looked at Concordia with respect. "An excellent point, Miss Wells." She turned to the infirmarian. Do you have a log of all of Miss Adams' visitors, Miss Jenkins?"

"Of course." Miss Jenkins looked over at the nurse, who passed a clipboard to the lady principal.

"Hmm. Miss Adams seems quite popular," Miss Hamilton commented, handing the log to Concordia.

The log continued on a second sheet of paper. There were no strangers on the list: faculty, a few administrators and students, and members of Sophia's settlement house. Even Mr. Bradley had visited Sophia this past week. Concordia found that surprising, although she did not know why. She looked at the nurse. "Would someone be able to see Miss Adams *without* signing the log?"

"Certainly not," the woman replied, offended.

"Well, perhaps someone paying a professional call," Miss Jenkins corrected her. "Dr. Musgrave certainly doesn't sign in."

"Yes, but he doesn't count," the nurse argued. She hesitated a moment. "If you mean *absolutely everyone*," she said grudgingly, "there *was* another doctor who visited Miss Adams that first day."

"Dr. Westfield, perhaps?" Concordia asked, her voice deliberately neutral.

"Yes, that sounds right," the nurse nodded. "He said that he was a concerned friend of the family, and wanted to check on Miss Adams' condition. What is the matter? I kept her under close supervision, as I always do with my patients; I saw nothing untoward," she said defensively.

"Yes, of course," Miss Hamilton said soothingly. "Dr. Westfield is one of the college's trustees. He was more than welcome to visit Miss Adams."

"His concern does him credit, to be sure," Concordia responded acidly. Her mind was a whirl of conjecture; what had Dr. Westfield *really* been up to?

Chapter 35

Why do you dress me in borrowed robes?
I.iii

Week 13, Instructor Calendar
April 1896

"Signorina Wells! Do come in," Lucia Bellini said eagerly, when the maid had shown Concordia up to the second floor of DeLacey House.

"It is so kind of you, Miss Bellini, to help me in this way."

Concordia looked around the room, a standard size for the senior faculty but much larger than her own, as Miss Bellini opened an enormous armoire of ornately carved walnut. Such a piece of furniture would never fit in her tiny bedroom at Willow Cottage. The rest of the furnishings in Miss Bellini's rooms were typical of faculty quarters. Miss Bellini had personalized the space with photographs of stiffly-posed family groups, carefully placed in gilded frames, and a tapestry wall hanging that took Concordia's breath away. It was a beautiful work of art, a pastoral scene done in stunning detail. The colors were only slightly faded from the years, yet the richness of the fields and orchards, the farmhands and livestock, were still faithfully depicted.

Miss Bellini came over to Concordia, her arms full of gowns that swished and rustled. "It is wonderful, is it not? My mother gave it to me before I left Italy. This tapestry–and these pictures," she said, pointing to the table of framed prints, "are the only possessions left from my family's happier days in *Sicilia*."

"The tapestry is extraordinary," Concordia murmured, turning to face her. "But why 'happier days'? Did your family suffer some misfortune?" she asked.

Miss Bellini expression darkened, and her black eyes narrowed. "It was a misfortune that a number of families in *Sicilia*—the prosperous ones, with many acres of land—suffered. There were riots: peasants looting homes and setting fires, turning on the families who had given them—and their fathers and grandfathers before them— a good living. *Mio Dio! Selvaggios!* Savages! My mother grabbed her baby—me—the pictures, and this tapestry, and fled. My father, he—he was killed. I was too young to remember, of course, but she told me about it when I was older."

Concordia awkwardly touched Miss Bellini's sleeve. "I am sorry."

Miss Bellini gave a shrug. "People adapt, do they not? My mother, she lives with my aunt, in a tiny village outside of *Napoli*. They manage; they were even able to send me to school as a girl, and after that I earned a scholarship to Vassar College," she said proudly. "Then, I stayed in your country, to teach here. I am no longer—how do you say?—sick for home?"

"Homesick," Concordia said.

"Yes, yes, *homesick*. This is my home, now." She gave a disparaging laugh. "In the village where I grew up, the women marry farmers and raise chickens. But you and I—we have a better life, do we not?"

Miss Bellini laid out the gowns on the bed. "But we will speak of happier things. You must be pretty, eh? We will find for you the right dress."

Concordia looked at the profusion of richly-colored gowns spread out on the bed. Red, blue, rose, white, bronze. Satins, silks, velveteens. The blue dress was the color of sapphires, with a prim high neck and delicate ruching around the waist. The bronze gown sported enormous puffed sleeves, which ended in an elbow cuff trimmed in narrow satin ribbon. She looked in amazement at the collection. "What an array," she said at last.

Miss Bellini looked pleased. "Yes, they are wonderful. Several are out of fashion, of course, but men, they do not know fashion. And it is a man you want to impress, yes? Let us find a color good for you," she said, looking with a critical eye at Concordia's pale, freckled complexion, her red hair.

"The rose—no. And *not* the red." She set those down on the bed, holding up others.

"No... not the white. The blue, perhaps? No, no—it is too dark." She looked doubtfully at Concordia.

Concordia sighed. While she and Miss Bellini were of a size, she realized that their differences in coloring would pose a problem. Miss Bellini, with her dark eyes and hair, and her olive complexion, had selected gowns for herself in colors that complemented her own looks, but, unfortunately, were not at all flattering to Concordia.

"Ah! Wait—I forgot another!" Miss Bellini cried, flinging those dresses aside and pulling open a trunk beside her bed. Wrapped in tissue paper was a gown of pale green. "This one, what was I thinking when I bought it?" she said. "It makes my skin look yellow—see?" She held it up to her neck. "Ugh. It is quite new, too. I was planning to send it to my cousin. You try it," she said, stepping back to look at it against Concordia. "Yes, yes, that it definitely better, no?" She turned Concordia towards the mirror.

Half-heartedly holding the gown against her shoulders, Concordia was astonished to see that the dress did, indeed, look becoming. It had the effect of darkening her red hair to copper, of accentuating her green eyes and the creamy tint of her skin. The gown itself was beautifully made, and more in the current fashion, with barely a bustle at all. The form-fitting bodice, trimmed in pearl beading, glinted in the light. A short train draped gracefully along the floor. She would have to wear a tight corset in order to fit into it, she thought with a grimace. Miss Bellini had a smaller waist than she. But it would be worth it.

Miss Bellini was already on the floor, estimating length adjustments. "Yes, yes, there is not much to alter. Good!" She smiled up at Concordia.

When Concordia left Miss Bellini and that wonderful gown, her mind was full of the accoutrements she still needed. She had slippers already, an evening purse, and a cloak, serviceable but not glamorous. But that would be left in the cloakroom. Opera gloves? Jewelry? She would have to borrow those. She felt as if she were floating on a cloud.

Back at Willow Cottage, and preparing for bed, Concordia found herself reflecting on Lucia Bellini's family misfortune. The lady had successfully recovered from such an ill-fated start in life. And she had done so in her newly-adopted land. A resourceful woman.

Concordia also thought back to Mr. Bradley. They'd had a pleasant outing today, but her worry about Sophia had clouded it somewhat. She still found it puzzling that he had visited Sophia last week.

Why did that bother her so?

Then it came to her.

Mr. Bradley was supposed to have been in Boston.

Chapter 36

Say, from whence
You owe this strange intelligence?
                                        I.iii

Week 14, Instructor Calendar
May 1896

The week that followed brought with it the usual classes, student appointments, grading, and more play rehearsal. Miss Pomeroy was sharing Concordia's office now, as her own was in the fire-damaged wing. This simplified the necessary consultations between them regarding the costumes for the play, but unfortunately it made for crowded conditions, especially as Miss Pomeroy was rather slovenly. More and more of the room was being taken over by a jumble of fabric remnants, scissors, spools of thread. Concordia shoved aside the mess so that she could work at her desk while awaiting a student.

The boy who delivered mail and messages came in and dropped a packet of letters on her desk. "Thank you, Sam," Concordia murmured, sorting through the stack. Whistling cheerfully, he gave a nod as he moved on.

Casting aside the usual circulars and a Sage Allen department store bill, Concordia held up two letters, puzzled. She didn't recognize either one. The first envelope was made of high-quality paper, and had that satisfyingly substantial feel to it. Concordia didn't recognize the Boston address. Probably a life-insurance solicitation. She set it aside and fixed her attention upon the other letter. It was in a thin, cheap envelope, with what looked to be—tea stains?—in one corner. The writing on the outside was in a careful schoolroom hand which looked familiar. She slit that one open first.

It was from Annie. Concordia's heart beat faster as she started to read.

> *Dear Miss,*
> *I been looking for the missus jernal, and letters. They are not in her desk or room. I think they are gon but I will keep looking. Mister Henry looks bad. He has been acting real odd.*
> *Annie*

Concordia sighed in disappointment. Realistically, though, it was doubtful that any of Mary's correspondence would have been found after all this time had passed. She was puzzled by Annie's last comments: Henry "looks bad"— how? And he has been "acting odd"? She trusted the girl's instincts; if Henry's behavior was a normal response to Mary's death, Annie would not have bothered to mention it.

With an air of resignation, she picked up the other letter and slit it open. It was not life insurance, as she had supposed, but a letter from Dr. Samuels. Concordia sat up a little straighter. She had despaired of receiving an answer from him. How extraordinary that she should get both letters at once.

> *Dear Miss Wells,*
>
> *Please allow me to convey my deepest condolences for your sister's death. You have asked me its cause, expressing doubt about the death certificate. Let me assure you that your sister did suffer from endocarditis, an inflammation of the heart valve, and it can be fatal. There is not much beyond this that I am at liberty to share with you. I can tell you that there was no active malice or deliberate harm brought upon your sister. The condition which created the endocarditis is more widely spread than most people want to acknowledge. Your sister, however, was blameless.*

Unfortunately, Miss Wells, I cannot break patient confidentiality in this matter; I have already revealed more than I probably should. I do hope that you find the answers you seek.

Regretfully,
Bernard Samuels, M.D. "

An odd letter—clarifying and confounding at the same time, Concordia thought. Dr. Samuels seemed to have no doubt about the underlying cause of Mary's death. It was maddening that he would not reveal more. If she could trust what Dr. Samuels said, then at least Mary had not fallen victim to foul play, which gave her some peace of mind. But what "widely spread" condition was Samuels cryptically alluding to? And why would he refer to Mary as "blameless"? How did blame come into it?

Her thoughts were interrupted by the arrival of the student she had been expecting.

Concordia's schedule after dinner kept her occupied for the rest of the evening. After an hour of grading student themes in the library, she decided to visit Sophia before attending the costume fitting.

"How is your patient?" she asked the nurse on duty.

The nurse grunted. "Restless and irritable, as most convalescents are. But your visit will help, I'm sure."

Concordia found Sophia pacing, from window to bed. She was pleased to see that Sophia's current bandage was much smaller than the one before.

"Concordia!" Sophia said in delight. She sat on the bed, and gestured toward a chair. "Can you stay?"

"I'm sorry, Sophie, not for long." Concordia said with regret. Sophia's face lost its animation. She's not used to being idle, Concordia thought. The burden of secrecy was weighing heavily upon her.

"I'm… worried," Sophia said hesitantly.

"That's understandable, dear," Concordia said.

"No, that's not what I mean." Sophia sighed. "I still cannot remember anything from the week when I was attacked–not even the rally. This is agonizing. You have no idea."

Concordia tried to imagine what it must be like for days at a time to be a blank in one's memory, to try to will the thoughts to come to the surface, without success. "It must be frustrating," she said finally.

"Yes, but more than that–I feel that I had something very important to tell you… that morning." Sophia frowned in concentration. "But I can't remember any of it. Not at all."

Concordia nodded thoughtfully. "That's right, I recall it now; that's why you were coming to the cottage." So many things had happened since then; Concordia had forgotten about it, too. "You'll remember," she reassured Sophia. "I know you will."

She stood to plump up Sophia's pillow. "Why don't you rest for a while? It may do you some good."

"I suppose so," Sophia agreed, leaning wearily against the pillows. After making sure she was settled comfortably, Concordia left.

As she approached the auditorium, she found Julian Reynolds seated on an outside bench, chatting with a student. The last rays of evening light illuminated the meticulously-clipped blonde hair not covered by his derby.

"Concordia!" he called eagerly, getting up and walking over to her.

"Hello, Mr. Reynolds," she said, unsuccessfully keeping the chill from her voice. How could he greet her so familiarly now, after ignoring her for the past two weeks?

"The lovely Miss Osgood here," he gestured to the blushing senior still seated, "told me that you would be coming this way."

"Miss Osgood," Concordia chided, "you should already be inside the auditorium being fitted for your costume. Tell Miss Pomeroy that I will be there in a moment, if you please."

With a curious glance at the two of them, Miss Osgood went inside the building.

"I would appreciate it if you would not call me by my Christian name in front of the students," Concordia said stiffly. "It undermines my authority."

"Of course, my dear," he answered. "But there is something important I need to talk to you about."

"I know what you want to discuss. Now is not the time for such a conversation. And I really must go," she protested.

"No, it's not about that, although I do apologize for my behavior that night, and for neglecting you since then. Can you forgive me?" he asked.

When he looked at her so earnestly, with those sincere blue eyes, Concordia could not help but relent. "Of course. We can talk later," she said in a softer tone.

But Julian was not to be deferred. He led her over to the bench. "You should sit down. It's about that Bradley fellow. I had to warn you."

Concordia's eyes narrowed. "*Warn* me? Whatever do you mean?"

He gave a great sigh. "This is a difficult subject to bring up to a lady, and I do hate to do this, but it's for your own good, Concordia."

"Just speak your piece," she said impatiently. She had always been wary of what was said or done *for her own good*. It was rarely *good* at all.

"I was conducting business downtown yesterday," he began. "It was such pleasant weather that I decided to walk. My walk took me through a neighborhood where there are... questionable establishments. One house in particular," he said carefully.

Concordia gave him a blank look.

He took a deep breath and went on. "This house is known to be a... brothel. And, plain as day, I saw Mr. Bradley go in there. In fact, it was clear that the woman who opened the door knew him. She seemed to be expecting him."

Concordia shook her head vigorously. "No. That's impossible. You must be mistaken." She looked up at him, seeing his worried expression through blurred eyes.

Julian took her hand. "I'm sorry. But there is no mistake."

Miss Osgood came back outside. "Miss Pomeroy says she needs you *now*, Miss Wells," she called, her glance taking in the sight of them holding hands.

Concordia pulled away. "I have to go." She followed Miss Osgood inside.

The players were in various stages of dishabille, wearing partially pinned costumes, some of the pieces trailing upon the floor and getting stepped on. A flustered Miss Pomeroy, mumbling through a mouth full of straight pins, was fitting partially-sewn garments on the principal actors, while others in the cast picked through a pile of completed costumes.

"No, *I* get the scarlet cloak! Miss Pomeroy *promised* it to me!" one girl insisted.

This raised a hubbub of protest. Concordia quickly stepped into the fray.

"Miss Pomeroy and I have already decided upon the recipients," Concordia said firmly. She began handing out garments.

Miss Pomeroy glanced over in relief, and turned back to Lady Macbeth's hem. "Thand thill!" she muttered to the fidgety girl.

Finally, with the remaining costumes pinned and ready for their last round of sewing, Concordia and Miss Pomeroy sent the girls back to their cottages. It was nearly bedtime. Miss Crandall, as Head Senior, was not bound by the ten o'clock rule; she offered to remain behind to help clean up.

They would need all the help they could get during the three weeks remaining until the performance, Concordia thought. They needed more hands for sewing, especially for the time-consuming ornamentation of the "royal" garments. There was still the set to construct, although thankfully not an elaborate one.

"Props. Where do we keep the props?" Concordia wondered aloud. She turned to Miss Pomeroy. "I should at least look over the props tonight, just to see what we have to work with."

Miss Crandall noticed that the drooping Miss Pomeroy had removed her glasses and was rubbing her eyes. "I can show you where we keep some of them, Miss Wells," she offered. Concordia nodded, and Miss Pomeroy, looking grateful, said a weary good-night.

Miss Crandall and Concordia finished stowing away the costumes and turned out the lights. Concordia locked the door, pulling on the handle to assure herself that it was securely latched. A light rain was falling, and although not heavy enough to soak them through, Concordia hoped it would be a quick walk.

"Where to?" she asked Miss Crandall.

"The chapel," she answered.

"Are we praying for props?" Concordia quipped.

"Actually, the bell tower beside the chapel, Miss Wells. There is a little-used storage area," Miss Crandall explained as they crossed the quadrangle. "Not many people know about it."

The tower looked forbidding in the darkness. Since the bell tower and chapel had not yet been adapted for electric lights, Miss Crandall lit the lantern provided on a hook beside the door. They ascended the tower's spiral staircase, Miss Crandall leading, stepping gingerly. The stairwell was so cramped that Concordia could reach out with both hands and touch the damp stone walls on either side of her.

"Be careful." Miss Crandall called back over her shoulder. "This stair shifts. The mortar is crumbling away." Concordia cautiously stepped over it and followed Miss Crandall to the landing, where they stopped to catch their breaths.

"How could heavy, cumbersome props be kept up here?" Concordia asked.

Miss Crandall didn't answer, but pointed to a low wooden door, which she opened and ducked through. Concordia followed. They found themselves within a surprisingly spacious inner room, stacked with boxes holding all sorts of bric-a-brac, old draperies, rugs, and derelict equipment.

"We must be directly above the rafters of the chapel," Concordia mused, looking around.

"That's right," Miss Crandall said. "There is a wider staircase that connects to the room on the other side, but the door is warped and can't be opened. No one has bothered with it since, as far as I can tell. I would guess that the bigger items have been in here since then."

"How do *you* know about this place?"

"I discovered it when I was a sophomore."

Concordia looked puzzled as she surveyed the room. "This can't be all the props."

"No, the bulky wooden frames and sets that are reused every year are stored under the stage. I thought some of these other items might be interesting, though," Miss Crandall said.

Holding the lantern closer, Concordia began gingerly picking through boxes. It was an absurd collection of items. She tossed aside a water-damaged men's leather shoe, without a mate in sight. *Who would donate that.*

Ah, but here were some interesting pieces, she thought, setting aside costume jewelry, belts, wooden swords, and scabbards. She pulled out two daggers. The first was quite large, and dull-edged, with a plain black enamel hilt. The second had a shiny, narrower blade. Its red-lacquered hilt was more ornamental, and encrusted with a circle of rhinestones at its base. She held up the daggers for Miss Crandall to see.

Miss Crandall's eyes narrowed. "I've seen the red one before."

"Where do all of these things come from?" Concordia asked.

"Oh, students, parents, even professors have donated things over the years," Miss Crandall answered. She gestured toward the red-handled knife. "I'm not certain, but I believe that one belonged to Miss Pomeroy—she has given us several items over the years, I know. It's perfect for the dagger scene, don't you think?" She recited, in mock-dramatic fashion: *"Is this a dagger I see before me? Come let me clutch thee."* She waved her hand wildly in the air.

"Hmmm. Now I remember why you weren't cast in the lead role," Concordia said, making a face.

Miss Crandall smiled and passed Concordia a battered tiara.

Who on earth donated *this,* Concordia wondered, holding it up to the lantern. It looked like something belonging to a dowager duchess. Perhaps it would make a nice crown for Lady Macbeth. "We'll have to come back in daylight," she said, noting the windows.

She and Miss Crandall found an empty box and began putting in the items they would take away later.

"Aahh!" Miss Crandall flinched.

"What is it?" Concordia brought the lantern closer. Miss Crandall was sucking on her finger.

"That knithe ith very sharp," she said ruefully.

"Oh, dear. Will you be all right, Miss Crandall?" Concordia asked. The senior nodded.

"Well, we may want to use the dull-edged dagger instead, even if it doesn't look as good," Concordia said, taking a closer look at Miss Crandall's finger. "We cannot have the cast members slicing themselves. Ready to go?"

As Concordia turned towards the exit to the spiral staircase, she noticed what looked to be a service panel in the wall. "What's that?" she asked. She crouched down and gave it a tug.

"Hmm?" Miss Crandall held the lantern closer. She gave a chuckle. "Oh, you might as well have a look." She handed her the lantern. "But be careful—it's a long way down."

Intrigued, Concordia pulled the cover away and, mindful of spiders, leaned cautiously into the crawl space, holding the lantern aloft. Immediately below her was one of the sturdy rafters of the chapel's ceiling, and then—air. She caught her breath. She could see the whole interior of the chapel from this position. If she had wanted to (which she certainly did not), she could have traversed, beam by beam, the chapel's buttresses.

Of course.

Concordia pulled herself back into the room, dusting off her skirts. She stared in wonder at Miss Crandall. "*You?* You were part of the sophomore prank two years ago, when the gloves were suspended from the rafters?" Miss Crandall gave a sheepish nod.

"So *that* was how it was done. Amazing," Concordia murmured thoughtfully. "You were quite mischievous as a sophomore, Miss Crandall," she continued, as she restored the panel and they proceeded down the stairs, "it is extraordinary how responsible you have become in only two years."

"I have had to be," Miss Crandall said, jaw set in a stubborn line. She seemed preoccupied, so Concordia did not ask for an explanation. They returned the extinguished lantern to the hook before leaving the tower, and returned to Willow Cottage in silence.

Chapter 37

Twas a rough night.
II.iii

Week 14, Instructor Calendar
May 1896

Concordia thought she would have no trouble going to sleep after such an active day, so she was surprised to find herself still wakeful after several hours. The warm night air, fragrant with damp grass, did little to relieve the stuffiness of the room. Even in her lightest muslin nightdress, she felt uncomfortable. Her restless mind turned over the puzzle of what was revealed—and not revealed—in the letters she had received. She despaired of ever understanding how Mary died. During her occupied hours today, Concordia had managed to set aside her questions. But now, in the quiet of the night, there was no escaping them.

Then there was the problem of David Bradley, and what Julian had told her. Although she did not know Mr. Bradley very well, she had difficulty believing that he would be so base as to visit a brothel. But perhaps that sort of thing was not considered particularly wicked for a man to do. To her, it was loathsome. She knew she would have to talk with him about it, but how does a lady broach such a subject?

There was also the issue of Mr. Bradley's connection to Sophia Adams. Was he so concerned with Sophia's welfare that he would cancel his trip to Boston in order to visit her? He had allowed Concordia to believe that he had gone ahead with his plans, and that Sophia was practically a stranger to him. Perhaps *he* was the one making sure that Sophia Adams was unconscious after the attack? Was the "rescue" of Sophia in the rain that morning a blind?

Giving up on sleep, she groped for her spectacles and impatiently twitched aside the crumpled covers. She needed something to read. Perhaps Keats would serve to quiet her mind. Turning up the lamp in the sitting room, Concordia started to pull the draperies closed when something outside caught her eye. She leaned closer for a better look. Had there been a light? She looked up the hill toward the Hall. All was dark. No—wait, yes! A small point of light, moving steadily between the windows of the second floor, along the wing unaffected by the fire.

That had better not be one of my girls, was her first thought. Not after her stern talk with them about going out after curfew. Although more than a week had gone by since the fire, and all seemed quiet on campus, they still needed to be careful.

Who would be in Founder's Hall at– she checked the clock on the mantel– one o'clock in the morning? The light was now making its way up the stairwell to the third floor.

She had to know what was going on. Concordia rummaged in her wardrobe for an old lantern she kept for emergencies, and pulled on her coat. She slipped quietly through the door and out to the grounds.

The drizzle of the evening had stopped, but the wet grass soon soaked through her thin slippers as she approached the Hall. *Bother.* Why hadn't she stopped long enough to put on proper footwear, instead of rushing out in such a harum-scarum way?

Concordia tested the knob of the immense oak front door to the Hall: locked. She circled around to the side, where she found this door, too, to be locked. There was not a soul out on the grounds. Where were the extra watchmen hired by the college?

She would have to go in on her own. She unlocked the side door and stepped inside, easing it shut behind her. It settled in with a click that seemed as loud as a shot. She froze, listening. Nothing.

She now felt certain that the intruder was no student; with each of the outer doors locked, how would one of the girls get in? Yet someone *was* in here. Like her, it was someone with a key.

She crept through the library. She couldn't risk the side stairs immediately to her right; they were wooden, and creaked too loudly. It would have to be the front marble staircase. She still hadn't heard anyone moving about, but she and the intruder had an entire floor separating them.

Lantern held high, Concordia successfully navigated the Ancient Poets section, crammed with cumbersome, odd-sized volumes that jutted this way and that, unbridled in their eagerness to tumble from their shelves. She had nearly made it to the staircase when she walked into a low book cart. She grabbed at her wildly swinging lantern to stop it from creaking on its rusty hinges. It took a few moments for her breathing to settle down before she finally worked up the nerve to climb the stairs.

Once she gained the second floor landing, Concordia paused again. No glow of a lantern; perhaps the intruder had realized the risk and put it out? The clouds were clearing—enough moonlight was coming through the windows to enable someone to easily maneuver through the halls. Unfortunately, that would also mean she would be spied as soon as she got up there.

She heard a sound—the soft tap of heels on the parquet floor above. It came from the farthest corner, in the back hallway. She would have to take a chance, while the intruder was still far enough from the stairwell. Concordia extinguished her lantern and set it down. She wouldn't need it now. Pushing her spectacles more firmly upon her nose, Concordia crept up the stairs and along the hall, hugging the wall's shadows.

Although her slippers made no sound, the moonlight coming in through the long windows made her feel as exposed as a hunted doe. As she turned the corner, her heart lurched as she saw a tall, thin shadow—man, or woman?—moving in her direction. She quickly darted back around the corner. The hallway ahead of her was too long. She would not reach the stairs before she was seen—and pursued. The office doors along the hall were undoubtedly locked. She would waste precious time testing them.

She remembered the broom closet, which had no lock. As quickly and as silently as she could, Concordia skittered down the hall, praying, as she turned the closet's door handle, that the custodian kept the hinges well-oiled. He did. Looking over her shoulder, she could see the shadow at the other end start to stretch beyond the corner now, although she heard nothing but the wild pounding in her chest.

She slipped in and tried to ease the door closed. A mop handle got in the way. *Drat!* She didn't dare risk the noise of trying to shift it. She had to hope it would go unnoticed. The closet was cramped; a step-ladder, tarpaulins and buckets took up most of the space. She wrinkled her nose in distaste at the sharp odor of turpentine.

The footsteps were getting closer. Concordia burrowed as far back into a corner as she could, and wedged herself behind a drop-cloth thrown over the ladder.

She had scarcely bundled her skirts out of sight when she heard the door open. Her breath caught. There it was, the same tap as before. Undoubtedly a boot heel. A man's or a woman's?

She could *feel* the presence on the other side of the too-fragile drop-cloth barrier, hear the quiet breathing, not her own. He—she?—had only to reach a hand around to discover her. She waited, tensed, hardly daring to exhale.

After what seemed an age, the intruder left, soft taps barely audible along the hallway. She was alone. Her knees felt like gelatin, and she was shaking, but after a moment she willed herself to move. She had to get a glimpse, while she still had the chance. She swung the door outward.

Right into Miss Hamilton's face.

"Miss Wells!" the lady principal gasped, clutching her nose.

Before Concordia had time to apologize, or explain, they both heard a loud clatter and breaking glass, followed by a stifled oath, and the sound of running feet in the stairwell. The intruder had tripped over Concordia's lantern.

Without a word, Miss Hamilton ran faster than Concordia would have given her credit for, with Concordia right behind her.

They were too late; they heard the bang of the door as the prowler escaped.

"We can at least see who it was." Miss Hamilton rushed to one of the hallway windows. But luck was with the intruder; the sky had clouded up again, and they could see nothing in the blackness.

"Shouldn't we notify the watchmen?" Concordia urged.

Miss Hamilton sighed. "It's too late to give chase. I will report it, of course."

Miss Hamilton, rubbing her injured nose, looked over Concordia's attire with a sardonic eye. Concordia knew she must be a sight: shod in water-stained slippers, hair down over her shoulders, nightdress peeking below her coat and trailing at her ankles. Miss Hamilton, on the other hand, even at this late hour, was well-groomed and dressed in a plain, dark worsted dress, every button in place. Did she always keep such late hours?

"So, Miss Wells, would you mind explaining to me why you thought it wise to go prowling about so late at night?" The question could have been either a scolding or an amused observation; Concordia wasn't sure which.

Concordia bit off a retort about Miss Hamilton prowling in the dark, too.

"I saw the light, and thought that it might be one of the girls violating curfew. It seemed prudent to investigate."

Miss Hamilton considered this in silence. They walked together down the stairs, Concordia retrieving her broken lantern, stuffing the pieces inside its cavity.

They reached the front door. Miss Hamilton paused with her hand on the knob.

"I would ask that you not discuss tonight's events with the students or staff," she said to Concordia. "I don't want to alarm anyone unnecessarily."

"Yes, Miss Hamilton."

"And, further, Miss Wells, while your intentions were well-meaning, if acted upon rather hastily," this last said with an amused tug of her mouth as her eyes swept once more over Concordia's bedraggled appearance, "I expect my staff to refrain from wandering alone late at night in their sleeping attire. It is both dangerous and unseemly."

Concordia nodded. Tired as she was, she wondered which was more important to Miss Hamilton: safety, or decorum? She seemed to equate the two.

Back in her quarters, Concordia closed the sash, latched it, and climbed into bed. She had more questions now than before. The intruder, for instance. The muttered oath they heard sounded like a man, but she couldn't place the voice. What was he after? And what in the world was Miss Hamilton doing there at this hour? She had offered no explanation.

The more Concordia thought about it, the more convinced she was that Miss Hamilton had been looking for something. But what? And who leaves the electric lights switched off to search in the dark?

Only someone who doesn't want to be discovered, she thought reluctantly. Our Miss Hamilton has something to hide.

Concordia at last drifted off into an exhausted sleep, wondering how she was going to find out more about the woman.

Chapter 38

Look to the lady.

II.iii

Week 14, Instructor Calendar
May 1896

Concordia awakened to a spring morning that was sparkling clear. Perfect for a bicycle ride. She dressed quickly and, careful not to wake sleeping students, set out.

As she rode along the paths, quiet at this time of day, Concordia's thoughts returned to Miss Hamilton. Why had she been prowling the Hall after midnight, with the lights out? Was she looking for the intruder, as Concordia had been? But that made no sense, as Miss Hamilton's rooms did not overlook the Hall. Sycamore House blocked the view of the Hall from DeLacey House.

Unless Miss Hamilton had already known of the intruder's intentions?

The more Concordia dwelled upon Miss Hamilton's behavior, the more damning it seemed. Even the lady principal's dress—not the bright silk dress Concordia had seen her wear at dinner, but a dark wool dress. The better to prowl the halls in, so as not to be seen or heard? And who was the other person they both heard on the stairs?

Miss Hamilton was certainly someone's target, Concordia thought. The knife in the effigy; the ransacking of her private rooms; the attack upon Sophia, no doubt meant for Miss Hamilton; the fire set in her office. Why? Concordia remembered Miss Banning's outrageous suspicions regarding the seven unknown years in Miss Hamilton's history. *For all we know, she could have been in prison all that time.* While Concordia had difficulty imagining Miss Hamilton as a prison convict, something was not right about the lady.

Concordia knew she should probably seek advice about her concerns. But whom could she talk to? Dean Langdon? President Richter? She didn't know whom to trust. And what would she say? That she was suspicious of Miss Hamilton? For what—setting fire to her own office, stabbing her own doll? The idea seemed ridiculous. Concordia needed facts, not suppositions. And she was going to get them—today.

That afternoon, Concordia rang the bell of DeLacey House, book in hand, her stomach fluttering. *Let's hope this works.* A young housemaid opened the door.

"Miss Wells, hello!" she greeted her. "Are you here ta see Miss Hamilton?"

Concordia nodded mutely, her voice stuck in her throat.

"I'm sorry, miss, but she i'nt here. She's at the Senior Tea."

Concordia knew perfectly well where Miss Hamilton was. She cleared her throat.

"Oh! I forgot. How silly of me. She lent me this book, and I know she needs it today." Concordia held it out.

The maid reached for it. "I'll give it ta her."

"You are so kind," Concordia answered, passing it over. Then, as an afterthought, she added, "Oh, while I'm here, Miss Hamilton said I might borrow another book, from the house library. Would you mind if I come in?"

"O' course, miss," the maid responded, "but I have ta get back ta my work. Can you see yourself out when you're done?"

"Yes, thank you." Concordia tried to keep the relief out of her voice. She turned toward the library, waiting until the girl had disappeared into the rear kitchen. Concordia quickly headed for the stairs. She was in, but the next step was difficult. She had to get into Miss Hamilton's rooms.

Concordia had timed her search to coincide with the Senior Tea, which all of the DeLacey House senior faculty attended. The building was empty, except for the house staff. She had to hope that they would be otherwise occupied. This was her only chance to find out more about Miss Hamilton and what she was up to.

She tried the lady principal's door. It was locked, as might be expected. Time to find the housekeeping keys. Concordia had reasoned that the staff must need to change the linens and replenish the water ewers on a daily basis; she was counting upon the maids being lazy enough to keep the keys nearby, to avoid trudging up and down the stairs.

The linen closet was the most likely place. She began checking doors along the hallway until she came upon the deep closet at the end. At first glance, Concordia couldn't see any keys, but she searched anyway, feeling along the backs of the shelves and behind the door frame. She glanced over her shoulder, nervous that someone would come along and demand to know what she was doing there, probing among the sheets and towels.

It seemed like ages before her patience was rewarded. She sighed in relief when her fingers finally clasped cool metal. She lifted the key ring from a hook under the lowest shelf and quietly shut the door. Muffling the keys against her skirts, Concordia hurried down the hall, back to Miss Hamilton's door. The keys were not marked; it took several tries before she found the right one. With one last glance over her shoulder, Concordia put the ring in her skirt pocket and slipped inside, closing the door behind her.

Concordia cast her eye around the room, wondering where to start. Her heart was still beating wildly, and she was shaking. Was it anxiety about getting caught, or guilt about violating a woman's privacy? She wasn't sure.

Miss Hamilton's study seemed the logical place for correspondence and other documents.

Bright sunlight coming through the open drapes of the study cast shadows from the quivering leaves outside. Every moving silhouette made Concordia jump.

There was no doubt that Miss Hamilton was an avid reader, and a scholar. There were well-worn Greek and Latin primers, histories, a collection of Shakespeare plays. Another bookcase held volumes of Homer, Virgil, Milton, Balzac, Burke, Tennyson: both the classical and the modern engaged Miss Hamilton's interest, it seemed.

She turned her attention to the desk. It didn't look like the standard-issue furniture found in most of the faculty quarters. It was a solid oak, slant-top desk, at least fifty years old, she guessed. Perhaps it had been passed down in Miss Hamilton's family and she couldn't bear to leave it behind. Concordia had seen a desk just like this one, although she couldn't remember where. She began to carefully pick up papers, one stack at a time, so that she could replace them exactly where she had found them.

After half an hour of glancing over receipts, administrative paperwork, and letters from a sister in Chicago, Concordia was ready to give up. It would be imprudent to stay much longer; the tea would be over soon. She stepped back and looked at the desk again, frowning in concentration. What *was* it about this desk?

Of course.

Nathaniel Young once had a desk of this type. She remembered it from visits as a child. And…yes! Something that Nathaniel had shown her and Mary, ages ago, knowing it would delight little girls: the desk's secret panel.

With growing excitement, Concordia crouched down behind the desk, pressing along the ridge where the central cabinet's upper board dovetailed with the frame. After trying a few spots, she felt the board release, and she was able to slide it sideways. She leaned in for a better look into the cavity. It was only about two inches deep, but nearly as tall as the entire back.

Wedged into the space were neatly tied letters of correspondence, and a slim volume that looked to be a journal.

Now completely engrossed, Concordia promptly sat on the rug beside the desk and started to sift through her find. Miss Hamilton had made careful copies of her own letters, sent to a post office box in Chicago–not the same address as Miss Hamilton's sister, Concordia noted. The lady principal had also saved letters received from that same Chicago post office box. There were at least two dozen of them in all. She frowned over the cryptic letters, containing phrases and initials that made little sense to her.

She read the top letter of the pile, dated today. Miss Hamilton had apparently not yet completed it.

No sign of led. in FH.–interrupted. Presume destroyed by R.
W. bears closer watching

The letter stopped there. Concordia set the correspondence aside with a sigh and turned her attention to the book. It was not a journal after all, but some sort of log, divided into two sections. One section had times, dates, and more cryptic initials, and the other–

A card fluttered out of the volume. Concordia barely had time for a glimpse of the odd-looking symbol in the corner of the card–was that an *eye?*–when, to her horror, she heard the door opening in the outer room.

Concordia drew in a quick breath as the pieces fell into place...

An eye
watching...
We Never Sleep!

...as Miss Hamilton crossed the outer room in quick strides and flung open the study door. "You!" she cried.

Concordia looked up at the lady principal, her mouth open in shock. Both women were rooted in place, Concordia sprawled on the carpet, Miss Hamilton with her hand on the door.

"You are a *Pinkerton?*" Concordia exclaimed in disbelief.

Chapter 39

A pained look crossed Miss Hamilton's face, as she closed the study door behind her. "Not so loudly, if you please, Miss Wells." She let out a grim sigh. Stooping next to Concordia to gather the book and strewn letters, she wordlessly restored them to their hiding place.

Concordia watched her in silence as well, fitting it together. A lot of things made sense now: why Miss Hamilton would be targeted in the Glove Night prank, the attempt on her life that had failed with the assault upon Sophia, the fire in her office. Concordia also better understood Miss Hamilton's temperament—her cool-headedness, self-control, and quick mind were ideally suited to such work, and probably molded by it, too. It still seemed fantastic to Concordia that there was such a thing as a "lady Pinkerton." But why is a detective here?

"I can't give you a complete answer to that, Miss Wells," Miss Hamilton replied. Concordia didn't realize that she had spoken the question aloud.

Miss Hamilton sat down on a settee, carefully smoothing the folds of her cerise taffeta. She looked over at Concordia. "Why don't you sit in a proper chair, Miss Wells, instead of remaining ridiculously slumped on the floor?"

Concordia sheepishly scrambled to her feet, shaking out her skirts. "I'm sorry to have pried into your affairs. But I had to know. Your presence in the Hall last night was too suspicious. What is going on?"

With an air of resignation, Miss Hamilton waved her into a chair. "Please, sit down. This will take a while, I'm sure. I've become concerned lately about you discovering my secret, especially after last night."

W. bears closer watching

So that's why she wanted last night's incident kept quiet, Concordia thought.

"What were you looking for in the Hall?" Concordia asked. "Who was that man who ran away?"

"Dean Langdon is my guess," Miss Hamilton said.

"*Dean Langdon?* How is he involved? Why...?" Then Concordia began to see. "He was following *you*, wasn't he? Not the other way around?"

Miss Hamilton nodded.

Yes, that made sense, Concordia thought. Founder's Hall is visible from Sycamore House. Perhaps the dean had seen something, just as Concordia had, and investigated? But then, why would he run away?

Miss Hamilton broke into Concordia's thoughts. "I don't know how Edward Langdon is involved," she admitted. "He does suspect that I am not entirely who I seem to be, but I don't think that he realizes I am a detective. He may only be trying to protect the interests of the college. Or he may be concealing his own illicit acts."

Concordia remembered the argument she'd overheard in the arbor.

I know what you have been doing, and I will make sure you regret it. You are threatening the security of this college. The fury of Arthur Richter's tone had been clear. But what had he accused the dean of doing? She would have to give that further thought.

"Are you *really* a lady principal?" Concordia asked, recalling Miss Banning's suspicions.

Miss Hamilton made a face.

"I intended no insult," Concordia added hastily, "but I am astounded by the idea of a lady detective. I have never heard of such a thing before. How can you be both an administrator and a detective?"

"Well, it has been a challenge," Miss Hamilton said dryly. "Although it was some time ago, my credentials are genuine."

"Miss Banning said she could not find out anything about the past seven years of your life," Concordia said. "Is that because you were a detective back then, too?"

Miss Hamilton laughed. "Ah, Miss Banning. She would make a fine sleuth herself. She's a difficult lady to keep a secret from. But yes, you are correct, more or less. I've been involved with the detective agency in some capacity since I resigned as Forsythe's headmistress back in '88."

"So why become a detective?" Concordia asked, hoping the question didn't seem impertinent.

Miss Hamilton's eyes got a faraway look. "My husband—now deceased—was a detective. I started working for the agency, unofficially at first, while we were married, when he needed me for the occasional assignment. I found that the work suited me, and it was exhilarating."

"But it seems a sordid job for a lady," Concordia said, recalling unsavory stories of Pinkertons ruthlessly suppressing labor union strikes.

Miss Hamilton conceded the point with a nod. "Thankfully, my duties will never involve protecting the interests of industrial magnates, a most dangerous—and yes, *sordid*—endeavor. My husband Frank was one of those who died during the Homestead Strike in '92. The agency had been hired to provide security for Carnegie Steel Works—but you must remember the newspaper stories of that debacle." She sighed.

Concordia nodded. There had been conflicting accounts about who was to blame, or who fired the first shots—the agents or the strikers—but in the end, sixteen men from both sides were dead, the remaining Pinkertons surrendered in disgrace, and the state militia had to be mustered to control a rabble of five thousand who had entered the fray. It made the problems at Hartford Women's College seem minor by comparison.

Which brought Concordia back to the issue at hand. "You didn't answer my earlier question, Miss Hamilton. What were you looking for last night? It can't have anything to do with the recent incidents; they occurred after you arrived." A sudden thought struck her. "You are here because of the school's money troubles, aren't you? Was Miss Lyman involved? Does her death have anything to do with this?"

Miss Hamilton hesitated. "I will tell you that, yes, I have been charged with discovering who is behind the college's money losses. What I've been searching for, if I can find it, would prove the extent of the embezzlement going on, and the person—or persons—responsible. I believe Miss Lyman *was* involved—it's difficult to imagine her *not* involved, as bursar—but there is no concrete evidence to override the coroner's determination of suicide." She held up a hand to forestall Concordia's next questions. "I cannot tell you what I'm looking for, or who hired the agency's services."

Concordia considered this in silence. Miss Hamilton was looking at her expectantly.

"You wish me to keep all of this confidential, I suppose," Concordia said.

"It would put an end to my investigation, Miss Wells, if it were known," Miss Hamilton said bluntly. "The person responsible would no doubt stop, but would never be caught. The money would never be recovered, if that is even a possibility at this point. Further, I believe that most of the incidents over the last few months are connected to my investigation. We must catch the culprits, if the college is to have any peace again."

Concordia was torn. While she admired Miss Hamilton, she found the prying and subterfuge inherent to detective work distasteful. Yet, she recognized its necessity.

She stood to leave.

"Very well. I will keep your secret, Miss Hamilton."

Miss Hamilton suppressed a sigh of relief as she, too, stood. "Thank you. Oh, and one other thing," she said, holding out her hand, "may I have the housekeeping keys back?"

Chapter 40

False face must hide what the false heart doth know.
I.vii

Week 15, Instructor Calendar
May 1896

Concordia tried to draw a full breath, and found that she could not. She cast a wary eye at her reflection in the bedroom mirror. The corset had done its work, helping her fit into Miss Bellini's pale-green dress.

Oh, my.

Concordia made a face in the glass. She did not remember the neckline being this low-cut. Did she look like one of those women who took every opportunity to exhibit her feminine charms? She hoped not.

Well, it was too late now. She tried not to think about going through the entire evening– and early morning hours–depriving her lungs of the proper amount of air while her bosom experienced an excess of it.

How do women do this?

She turned from side to side, looking over the rest of the gown, momentarily forgetting her discomfort and delighting in the soft, filmy material that swirled and settled again gracefully in its folds.

Would Mr. Bradley like it?

Concordia glanced at the small hand-bouquet of white roses he had sent this afternoon. The note that had come with them had been penned in his usual light-hearted tone: *We will have a splendid time, even while keeping the youngsters from misbehaving.–D. B.*

Her smile faded when she remembered what Julian had said about him. Could it really be true? Julian could be mistaken about who he saw, or the house.

She wanted to give Mr. Bradley the benefit of the doubt, at least until she heard what he had to say about it. She resolved to talk to him tonight, even though a crowded ballroom did not lend itself to posing such a delicate query. But she needed to know, before she danced in the man's arms.

She wished she had someone to confide in. Mary would have understood her quandary. Concordia thought about her a great deal lately. She would have loved this event tonight, reveling in all the little preparation details. Concordia was only just beginning to appreciate the excitement and anticipation behind such an occasion, and to understand why Mary had enjoyed them so.

A knock on the door interrupted her thoughts.

"Yes?"

Ruby propped the door with a sturdy hip, juggling combs, brushes, and ribbons. Concordia went over to help. Through the doorway, she could hear the hubbub from the seniors upstairs, busy with their own preparations.

"*Where is my fan? Did that wretched Louisa take it?*"

"*No—you may **not** borrow my gloves! Those are the best ones I have!*"

Concordia chuckled and closed the door.

"How are you managing, Ruby?" she asked, turning to the harassed-looking matron.

"'Bout like you'd expect," Ruby answered, rolling her eyes. She stepped back to look at Concordia. "My, my, you look wonderful! That gown is right fetching on you. You'll be turning heads, for sure. Especially Mr. Bradley's," she said mischievously.

Concordia's cheeks grew warm as she murmured her thanks.

"Would you like some help with your hair, miss?" Ruby asked. "I'm done with the girls. They're fending for themselves now, and enjoying every minute of it."

"Oh, please," Concordia answered. "I don't know what to do with it."

Ruby sat her down and undid the multiple pins with nimble fingers. Concordia found her thick, wavy hair to be a nuisance; she usually pulled it straight back and up, twisting it into a tight knot on the top of her head and pinning it all madly in place. It seemed no matter how many pins she used, the arrangement managed to work itself loose again by midday. Today, at least, she had not stuck her customary pencil in there as well.

She tried not to fidget as Ruby experimented with combs and twists.

At last Ruby was finished, and held up the mirror for Concordia to see.

"How wonderful!" she marveled. Ruby had swept her hair back toward the nape in a softer arrangement, and entwined it with a pale green ribbon to match her dress.

"There's more of it," Ruby offered, holding up the rest of the ribbon. "Maybe you can wear a piece around your neck, with a brooch?"

"Hmm. I don't... actually, yes—I do!" Concordia answered. Rummaging in the dresser drawer, she pulled out Mary's pin, the one that neither she nor Henry, in going through Mary's jewel case the day after the funeral, had been able to identify. Until she discovered it in a skirt pocket a couple of weeks ago, she had forgotten about it.

Before passing it to Ruby, she looked at the filigree pattern, accented with a pearl in the center and in each corner, once more feeling the pang of loss. She would give anything to have Mary wearing this tonight, instead of her.

Once Ruby had the brooch threaded and tied in place, Concordia couldn't help but admire the effect. It nestled in the hollow of her throat, catching the light as she turned.

"There, now. Don't you look beautiful," Ruby said, smiling. "But there's one more thing," she added, reaching out with work-roughened fingers to gently remove Concordia's spectacles. "Yes. That's much better."

Concordia squinted in dismay. "But—I cannot *see* properly without my glasses!" she protested.

Ruby put her hands on her hips. "And what do you need to *see*, may I ask? You can see the faces of them that's dancing with you, can't you? You can see the floor under your feet. That's plenty. You'll get used to it."

Concordia gave up. "All right. But I'm bringing them with me." She didn't think she would last very long without her glasses. A squinty chaperone would be of little use.

Ruby was collecting the extra combs and pins when there was another knock at the door.

"I'll answer it," Concordia said. With great difficulty, she gathered her skirts and stood up. Apparently the knocker was too excited to wait; the door opened before she could reach it, and one of the freshmen poked her head in.

Ooh, Miss Wells, don't you look a treat!" she exclaimed.

"Thank you, Miss Bentham. Shouldn't you be getting to bed?" It was nearly ten o'clock. The flurry of senior preparations was making it difficult to maintain the routine.

"Yes, Miss Wells," Abby Bentham answered, "but this just came for you." She held out a small florist's box.

Concordia took it. "Thank you, Miss Bentham," she said firmly, not opening the box. "To bed now."

Ruby took over. "There now, you heard Miss Wells. Off you go!" She bustled the disappointed girl through the door, closing it behind them both.

The exotic fragrance and bright color of the single pink orchid inside the box assailed her senses as soon as Concordia lifted the lid. She squinted at the card inside, fumbling to put her glasses back on.

It was from Julian, as she had expected it would be.

"Will you forgive me? I throw myself on the mercy of your sweet nature. I hope that you will save a dance for me. Fondly, J."

Concordia sighed—to the extent that her dress would allow—and wondered what she was going to do about Julian Reynolds.

He had made his feelings for her quite plain, and she wondered why she resisted the attraction she felt for him. Perhaps she simply wasn't ready for that sort of commitment. She would have to trust her instincts, and see what happened.

Concordia knew that Julian was distressed over her friendship with Mr. Bradley. She and Julian had actually quarreled about it.

They had been enjoying an open-air carriage ride through Keney Park last Sunday afternoon when Julian asked to escort her to the dance. He was flabbergasted by her answer.

"You are going to the dance with *Bradley*? After what I told you I saw?"

"You don't *know* what you saw, Julian," Concordia said evenly.

"But I thought you would go to the dance with *me*!" The depth of his indignation surprised her.

"I don't recall you asking me before now!" she snapped.

"That was my intent, Concordia! I simply did not have the opportunity to do so before you *jumped* at the first offer you had!"

The words stung. How dared he? She was not some elderly spinster, desperate for an escort. And the cheek of the man, to assume that she would have no plans so close to the occasion!

The rest of the airing, considerably shortened, had been a silent one.

"Mr. Bradley has arrived," came Ruby's muffled voice through Concordia's door. Concordia hesitated. Carefully, she removed her spectacles again and put them in her reticule. She gathered up her other accoutrements—gloves, shawl, Mr. Bradley's flowers—and headed for the parlor.

The orchid was left behind to perfume an empty room.

Mr. Bradley's eyes widened when Concordia walked into the parlor. He tried not to stare as he admired the way her gown clung to the curves of her torso and hips. Her cheeks were becomingly flushed, and soft wisps of coppery hair framed her face.

He cleared his throat. "You look—most fetching, Miss Wells," he said at last. Recovering, he said with a twinkle, "I will have my hands full tonight, beating off your ardent admirers."

She gave a laugh. "Thank you, kind sir. You look quite presentable yourself, you know!"

He *did* look rather dashing, she thought. His black tail coat fit him well, without the creases and lumps of his customary hounds-tooth jacket. The crisply-starched white shirt, with its wing-tip collar and black bow tie, complemented his dark eyes and hair. The effect was quite elegant.

"Shall we go?" he asked.

The sounds of shuffling feet and excited whispers drew their attention to the second floor landing, where Ruby and several grinning girls were huddled. Even Ruby wasn't immune to curiosity, it seemed.

"By all means." Concordia smiled.

"Good night, ladies!" Mr. Bradley called out, steering Concordia toward the door.

Mercifully—as dancing pumps were quite impractical for walking about—it was a short walk to Sycamore House, where the Senior Ball was being held. They encountered a crowd of young men, on their way to Willow Cottage to pick up their companions. Several of them looked uncomfortable, although she couldn't tell whether it was from the tall, rigid shirt collars they were unaccustomed to wearing, or from nervousness.

Sycamore House had every light glowing, and looked wonderfully festive. The freshmen, sophomore, and junior classes had assembled teams of students to decorate the front entrance, ballroom, solarium, and dining room, in honor of the seniors. Torches lit the path up to the front doors, which had already been thrown open to guests. Beribboned garlands of ivy were draped over doorways and wrapped around pilasters. Pots of flowering shrubs brightened corners. Some of the plants shielded the seating clusters from general view, Concordia noted. Those areas would require particular attention.

"I'm glad we are arriving early," Concordia said. "Before we see Miss Hamilton about our chaperone duties, there is a confidential matter I must discuss with you."

Mr. Bradley gave her a worried look. "Is something wrong, Miss Wells? You're trembling."

But Concordia was already leading him out through the side door, to a decorative arbor where the gardeners stored their tools. Here they would be screened from curious passersby.

Concordia looked at him for a long moment before speaking. He shifted uneasily, waiting.

"Mr. Bradley—I don't know how to ask you this, but…" Concordia floundered.

Mr. Bradley took her hands in his. "You can ask me anything, and I will give you an honest answer. What is it?"

She blurted out, "someone saw you go into a house…of ill repute. Last week. I need to know if that's true."

Concordia could see surprise, anger, and unease flit across his features. He did not answer right away.

"Yes, it is true. I did visit such a house recently," he said at last.

She pulled her hands away and stepped back.

"I was not there for the reason that you suppose, however," he continued, his voice even.

"For what other reason would one visit such a place?" she asked coldly.

He took a deep breath. "I cannot tell you, at least not right now. I would be breaking the confidence of another. But you *must* trust me," he continued, in a pleading voice.

"I want to," she said, in barely a whisper.

"You can. I promise."

Concordia tried to read his face, and see where the truth lay. Could she really trust him? Should she also ask him about his aborted trip to Boston? It seemed less urgent. After all, the man had every right to change his plans, and to visit the woman he had helped rescue. The matter seemed silly, now, as she weighed what Mr. Bradley had just told her.

"Mr. Bradley, I…" she began.

"Signorina Wells! Signore Bradley!" Miss Bellini was approaching them, gesturing in excitement. Concordia quickly dabbed at her eyes with a handkerchief and put on a smile.

Miss Bellini looked at the gown with an approving eye.

"Does she not look *bellissima*, Signore Bradley?" she asked delightedly.

Bradley, smiling, obligingly cast his eye up and down Concordia's form. She felt a strange tingling sensation.

"*Molto bellissima*," he agreed.

"Y-yes, thank you. Miss Bellini—it—it is a wonderful gown," Concordia said.

Miss Bellini herself looked quite *bellissima*, Concordia noticed. She was dressed in a becoming satin gown the color of deep wine, cut flatteringly on a bias to emphasize her small waist. Her black hair was pulled smoothly back and gleamed in the light. She positively glowed with contentment.

In a change of topic, Concordia asked, "Have you seen Miss Hamilton?"

"Ah! How could I forget! She wants all of us to meet, *subito*—right away."

Linking her arm through Mr. Bradley's, Miss Bellini led them into the dining room, where the others were waiting.

Perhaps she should trust Mr. Bradley and set aside her worries about him, at least for tonight, Concordia thought, as they entered the dining room. She was at a festive event, after all. The outside world and its cares could wait.

Penelope Hamilton looked regal in a high-necked mauve silk gown, her graying-blonde hair plaited in a coronet around her head. She was talking with the other chaperones, among them the president, Dean, Gertrude Pomeroy, Nathaniel Young, and on his arm… Concordia's heart sank. *Her mother.*

Nathaniel, looking especially dignified this evening in his sleek black jacket and pin-striped trousers, smiled apologetically at Concordia, but then frowned thoughtfully as he looked over her dress.

Concordia paid him little heed. *"Mother?* How...? Why...?" she sputtered in confusion. Although still in the color of mourning, her mother had certainly dressed for the occasion, in what looked to be a new gown of shimmering onyx, with tulle elbow sleeves and the low square neck that was currently in fashion.

Letitia Wells' lip curled in amusement. "Nathaniel told me that more chaperones were needed, so I offered to accompany him." She leaned toward Arthur Richter and tapped him on the arm with her fan. "My daughter thinks I have no experience chaperoning young ladies. She rarely saw me in that capacity, of course, because she would not attend such events unless she was dragged to them. Always had her nose in a book. Just like her *father.*"

"And naturally, *Mary* gave you ample opportunities," Concordia snapped. How dare her mother intrude here, where she did not belong?

"Indeed. And may I say, Concordia, that you look much more attractive without those horrible eyeglasses perched on your nose?" her mother shot back.

President Richter, caught in the midst of this bewildering interchange, looked to the lady principal for rescue.

But it was the arrival of Miss Jenkins, accompanied by a gentleman whom Concordia didn't recognize, which provided the necessary diversion.

"Sorry we were delayed, Miss Hamilton," Miss Jenkins said.

"Good! Now we have everyone," Miss Hamilton looked up from her clipboard. Concordia could see a sketch of the ballroom on it, with what looked to be marked areas. The woman was unquestionably organized.

Miss Jenkins gestured to the bulldog-faced man standing beside her. "This is an acquaintance of mine, Merrill Clark," she announced. Mr. Clark gave a stiff little bow. "He's the director of physical education at Trinity College."

To Concordia, that last bit of background hardly seemed necessary. Mr. Clark looked as if he were more comfortable with a coach's whistle around his neck than the bowtie he was now sporting.

"A pleasure," he responded, his voice gravelly from what Concordia imagined to be years of shouting at thick-headed collegiate boys.

Miss Jenkins was wearing a dress that might be judged an unfortunate shade of Mandarin yellow, particularly when set against her blotched skin and deeply-lined face, but Concordia thought that the high color on the lady's cheeks and the sparkle in her eyes put Hannah Jenkins at her most becoming this evening.

After greetings were exchanged, Miss Hamilton, much like a general planning a campaign, outlined what they were to do.

Chapter 41

Have we eaten on the insane root
That takes the reason prisoner?
I.iii

Week 15, Instructor Calendar
May 1896

"Whew! It's getting warm in here," Concordia said, brushing aside a few damp strands of hair. Since she and Mr. Bradley were assigned to monitor students during the after-supper dance period, they decided to take advantage of before-supper dancing. Of course, it would not do to dance more than twice with her escort, but she found, to her surprise, that in between her dances with Mr. Bradley she had a steady stream of young men who sought to be introduced (the good-natured Miss Pomeroy was kept busy in that regard) and sign her dance card. She had also danced the quadrille with Dean Langdon, who was surprisingly light on his feet for such a large man, and more adept with the intricate movements than she.

"I'll bring you a cup of punch," Mr. Bradley answered, guiding her over to a bench by an open window. With a mock-chivalric bow, he headed for the punch bowl.

The light breeze felt refreshing as Concordia sank down on the bench in relief. She tucked a foot under her skirts and surreptitiously eased off her shoe. She would, no doubt, find at least one blister tomorrow. She fished out her spectacles and put them on; it was annoying to see people across the room as only blurry shapes.

The blurry shapes on the dance floor turned out to be students with their partners, assorted faculty, and Hartford's wealthy set: civic leaders, prominent businessmen, and their wives. It was a visual feast of bright lights and colors, of jewels glinting in the hair, around arms and throats.

Concordia noticed Miss Bellini, dancing with President Richter. Her cheeks were flushed and her hair was beginning to come out of its combs in the exertion of the round dance. The cuer called out the changes in steps and the couples on the dance floor performed them—or tried to perform them—simultaneously. At one point, President Richter missed his cue, but Miss Bellini didn't seem to mind; she threw her head back and laughed.

There were others, of course, who were not dancing. Concordia spied a knot of elderly men, cigars in hand, deep in conversation out on the balcony. One of them looked up and caught her eye. Dr. Westfield. He looked exceedingly cheerful, and flashed a wide grin in her direction. She nodded her head before turning away. Near the cloakroom, she saw her mother talking with Miss Jenkins.

Concordia still could not understand why her mother was here. This was the second time in the past few weeks that she had attended a campus event—first, the basketball game, and now, tonight's Senior Dance. Why? Her demeanor seemed too hostile for Concordia to suppose that a reconciliation was being attempted, but Mother had always been difficult to understand.

A pair of black-trousered legs was approaching.

"Oh, Mr. Brad—oh!" she broke off. It was not Mr. Bradley, but Julian Reynolds. He had come to the ball, after all. Concordia's heart beat a bit faster at the sight of his elegant form, and his dazzling grin.

"Good evening, Concordia."

He sat down beside her.

"You look wonderful tonight, my dear," he said.

"Thank you." Concordia stood uncertainly as Mr. Bradley came over to them, cups in hand.

"Here, Miss Wells," Mr. Bradley said, passing her a cup. "Good evening, Mr. Reynolds," he said, as Julian stood up.

"Bradley." Julian gave the barest of nods.

Concordia concentrated on drinking her punch.

The band struck up a waltz, and Julian offered his arm. "May I have this dance?"

She hesitated. Handing back the cup to Mr. Bradley, she let Julian whisk her away.

Julian proved to be an accomplished dancer, guiding her steps, one gloved hand firmly upon her waist. Much to her dismay, she found herself trembling in his arms. Really, the waltz is a rather decadent form, Concordia thought, a little unnerved. Few dances permit this sort of contact.

"Did the flower arrive?" he asked.

"Oh—yes, thank you, Julian."

"I really am sorry, Concordia, about the things I said, during our drive. It's just—I don't like this Bradley fellow. Even before I saw him go into that house. Well, we've been through all of that," he added, looking down at her compressed lips and clenched jaw, "I don't want to upset you further. But be warned. He could break your heart."

"We are merely friends." She looked over Julian's shoulder, and saw that Mr. Bradley was watching her. It was a long and lingering gaze, as if, at that moment, he considered her the most important person in the world. With a jolt, she realized that David Bradley had been looking at her in this way almost since they first met. Why had she not noticed it before?

"What about *us*, Concordia?" Julian Reynolds asked softly.

Embarrassed to realize that she had been thinking of one man while dancing in another man's arms, she flushed and looked up at Julian.

"Your friendship is important to me, it truly is. I don't know if there is more." She felt confused by a heady sensation whose origin she didn't understand. "I need time. Can we not leave it at that, for now?"

He expelled a breath. "I will give you all the time you need, Concordia." He smiled. "We have time."

Just before midnight supper, Concordia and the lady principal were chatting when they noticed a stir in the far corner of the ballroom.

"Miss Banning!" Concordia exclaimed, craning her neck. "Surely we were not expecting her? She must be feeling better."

"I understand that she is rather attached to these seniors," Miss Hamilton said. She did not seem surprised by Miss Banning's arrival. "Shall we greet her?"

Margaret Banning was already surrounded by people, her short stature nearly engulfed by the others. Several students were talking to her, gesturing excitedly. She was listening with an indulgent smile and thumping her cane enthusiastically. Concordia was struck by how pleasant the old lady looked when she smiled. Miss Banning made her way to a nearby bench, aided by Julian Reynolds and David Bradley, who seemed to be competing with one another to seat the old lady comfortably.

Miss Banning had exceeded herself in dressing for the occasion. She had replaced her customary lacy breakfast cap with a silk turban, its black ostrich feather cocked playfully to one side. Her gown was black moiré, with flounces jutting out nearly everywhere that a dressmaker could reasonably put one. The lady had topped the ensemble with a heavily-fringed oriental silk shawl, its scene depicting a leopard pouncing upon a peacock. The effect was startling.

"Good evening, Miss Banning," Concordia said. "How wonderful to see you!"

"So, how are you enjoying yourself, young lady?" Miss Banning asked, looking over at the hovering Bradley and Reynolds. "Are these gentlemen keeping you occupied?"

Before she could answer, a male voice interrupted them.

"What about you, Margaret; have *you* come to dance?" President Richter had joined their group. His teasing question was belied by a frown, and his complexion was pale: surprisingly so, Concordia thought, considering the warmth of the room and the vigorous dancing he had been doing.

Margaret Banning gave an unladylike snort. "Not likely, Arthur. I'm beyond the age where cavorting across the dance floor holds any appeal." Her eyes gleamed with—what? Banter, humor, malice? Concordia couldn't tell.

"I had to see my girls. I miss them. In fact, I've decided to return to my classes for the remainder of the year," she continued.

"But… but…" Richter sputtered, "surely you shouldn't take on too much, Margaret? Why not wait until next year?"

"Nonsense," she snapped, "Miss Hamilton and I have already worked out the details."

"I was not aware of this." *Now* Richter had some color to his face.

Miss Hamilton quietly observed the interchange. Concordia shifted from one foot to the other, wondering if she should attempt a graceful exit. She glanced over at Mr. Bradley. He seemed to be thinking the same thing. Richter was oblivious to all except Margaret Banning. He leaned in toward the old lady, his face now smoothed into a picture of concern. "Your office was quite close to the fire. I do not know what state it is in. Disagreeable odors may linger."

"We shall see," she retorted.

The supper bell interrupted them. As she entered the dining room on Mr. Bradley's arm, Concordia again noticed Nathaniel Young looking her way. Before she could catch his eye, he abruptly turned away, occupied with settling Mrs. Wells into her chair. Concordia noted with relief that she and her mother had different table assignments. At least she would be spared further conversation about her girlhood book-reading habits.

As this was an event attended by the city's notables, the supper offerings were more elaborate than Concordia had before seen: besides the usual wafer-thin sandwiches, cold meats, and chicken salad that one would expect, the savory aromas of duck *a l'orange*, veal mayonnaise, and oyster soup drifted by her chair as the waiters brought platters to the tables.

"I wonder how the college can afford such a dinner," someone at the table behind hers was murmuring.

Concordia heard a caustic laugh.

"Indeed, we may have to sacrifice a few faculty positions to pay for this. Perhaps we should take up a collection after the meal," replied another.

Concordia wished she could turn around to chide the pair of gossips, whoever they were. But her good manners—and her corset—made this impossible.

She looked around the supper room. Miss Bellini, seated at another table, looked sulky. Concordia had never observed the lady in a dark mood, and didn't know how to account for it. She had seemed so happy earlier.

Miss Bellini was seated between President Richter on one side and Miss Jenkins' escort, Mr. Clark, on the other. Merrill Clark had not taken his eyes off of Miss Jenkins, and seemed to hang upon her every word. Arthur Richter was engrossed in conversation with Dr. Westfield, Judge Armstrong, and a lady Concordia could not identify. Miss Bellini was left to pick at her food. Concordia didn't imagine that Lucia Bellini was accustomed to being ignored.

The dour Judge Armstrong was running true to type, considering the scowl that puckered his face. It was obvious, even from this distance, that he was peppering the president with questions. Considering the rigid set of Richter's shoulders and the napkin being twisted under restless fingers, the president did not care for the judge's line of inquiry. Concordia, for one, was grateful to be spared the judge's company, and pitied Arthur Richter.

Dr. Westfield, on the other hand, seemed oblivious to the tension around him. He was talking animatedly, his face flushed and nose reddened, making sweeping gestures that at one point knocked over his water glass. She couldn't help but notice that the water glass had been full, but the wine glass seemed perpetually empty.

"More salmon, Miss Wells?" Mr. Bradley offered, as the waiter hovered between them.

She shook her head. The courses had not yet come to an end, but her corset was tight enough already. Sadly, this meant she would have to forgo the elaborate desserts—the Charlotte-Russe, jellies, tarts, and ices. She noticed that Miss Hamilton and Miss Bellini had also set aside their nearly full plates. Most of the senior girls, on the other hand, were still tucking in. Where *do* they put it, she wondered.

"I wonder if they shall ever catch the arsonist."

Concordia looked around in surprise. She had not been paying much attention to the conversations taking place at her table, a decided lapse in manners. But here, perhaps, was a conversation worth listening to.

The comment had come from Dean Langdon, who was addressing Miss Hamilton, although in a voice that carried beyond their table. Concordia noticed other heads swivel in their direction.

Miss Hamilton clenched her jaw in annoyance. She took a sip from her water glass before answering.

"However should I know, Mr. Langdon? The police do not report to *me*, but to the president."

Langdon patted his lips with his napkin and replaced it in his lap, where it promptly disappeared under his pear-shaped belly. "I doubt if the police would share their progress. Particularly if they believe it is one of us. They would not want to alert the culprit and have him flee."

At this point, other conversations had died away, as guests at nearby tables shamelessly listened.

"No doubt," Miss Hamilton replied, "although I see no point in discussing the matter here."

"But do you not wonder *why*, Miss Hamilton?" Langdon persisted. "Why would someone set fire to your office? What hostility does the arsonist hold against *you*?"

"That's enough, Mr. Langdon," Julian Reynolds said sternly. "You are distressing the ladies. It is in bad taste, sir."

Concordia looked at Julian in surprise. Past gatherings had shown him to be a disinterested observer rather than a staunch defender. But then again, the fire was a sensitive subject for all of them.

Langdon flushed a deep red, but said nothing more. Gradually, conversations resumed around him.

Concordia's curiosity was aroused. Perhaps she would have the opportunity to speak with Dean Langdon on her own, and discover where his suspicions lay.

At last, the dessert course was finished, and the plates were cleared. The supper gathering dispersed, drifting back to the ballroom as they heard the band tuning their instruments once again.

Mr. Bradley offered his arm. "Our turn to make sure the children behave?"

"Indeed," she said with a smile.

The next few hours were occupied with Concordia and Mr. Bradley strolling between the alcoves, balcony, and side garden, alert for couples seeking secluded corners. Concordia noted, amused, that Mr. Bradley cleared his throat loudly as they approached likely nooks. This sometimes produced a muffled exclamation, and a young man beating a hasty retreat.

One couple out in the garden, however, was so engrossed in the delight of each other's company that they were not vigilant enough to flee before Concordia and Mr. Bradley came upon them.

"*Miss Crandall!*" Concordia exclaimed when they discovered the couple, seated, the young man nuzzling the young lady's neck, his hands in places where they ought not to be. They jumped apart.

"Mr. Blake, what in the *Sam Hill* do you think you are doing?" David Bradley demanded.

The young man murmured something unintelligible. Charlotte Crandall stood up, flushed but otherwise composed.

"We're sorry, Miss Wells." She turned to her companion. "I should go."

"I will get someone to accompany you," Concordia said to the girl. She certainly didn't want her to walk back to the cottage alone, or her gentleman friend to catch up with her along the way. "We will talk later," she added sternly.

Leaving Mr. Bradley to deal with the young man, Concordia escorted Miss Crandall back inside.

By the time Concordia had seen that the senior was taken care of, she could not find Mr. Bradley again. She returned to the garden, but didn't find him there, either.

"Concordia," a voice murmured close to her ear. She gave a yelp and turned. Nathaniel Young was standing in the shadow of the trellises.

"Nathaniel, goodness! You surprised me. Where's Mother?"

"In conversation with Miss Banning, I believe." He was certainly not as tidy as he had been earlier this evening, with his tie askew, trousers rumpled and graying hair standing on end, as if he had been running his hands through it.

"Were you looking for me?" she asked.

"Yes—uh, no!" he answered. "I was just getting some fresh air." He was looking at her gown again as he had before.

Concordia's patience had worn thin. "What is it? You've been acting strangely all evening, and my mother only has that effect upon *me*. Why do you keep staring at me?"

He hesitated. She followed his glance. It wasn't her gown; he was looking at her throat. She touched the brooch.

Why was he interested in Mary's brooch?

Mary's brooch.

Understanding flooded her. Her breath caught. *Of course.*

"Here, sit down. You look terrible," she said firmly, pulling him to a nearby bench. Wordlessly, he sat, looking down at his hands.

Concordia detached the brooch, holding it out. "This is your gift, isn't it? To my sister?"

He took it in trembling hands. "My wedding present to her."

"You were in love with Mary."

It all made sense to her now. The single life Nathaniel had maintained all these years. The close attention to Mary's illness. *This is the fifth such attack she has had, Concordia.* The blow that

Mary's death had been to him. The light in his eyes that had died.

"For how long, Nathaniel?" Concordia asked. Mary had been sixteen, just beginning to blossom into womanhood, when Concordia left home. Had he started *then* to see her with different eyes? When does affection turn into romantic love?

There was a long silence, punctuated only by a night creature rustling among the climbing roses.

Finally, he looked up at Concordia. "I don't know. It was not… dishonorable. I promise you. Although it was torturous to me," he said bitterly. "By the time I realized I loved her, it was too late. She was already engaged to be married." He sighed. "Perhaps seeing another man in love with her made me realize how I felt. I was a fool."

"You *are* a fool! And a cad, and a liar," came an angry voice.

Mrs. Wells stepped from behind the roses. "How *dare* you taint Mary's good name!" she cried.

Concordia looked on in astonishment as her mother, with the blazing fury of a lioness protecting what is hers, advanced upon Nathaniel, now standing, who waited for the blow.

"Mother, *stop!*" Concordia pleaded. "Mary didn't know. He never told her." It was a guess, but knowing Nathaniel's principled nature, she didn't doubt it.

Mrs. Wells hesitated, fists curled at her sides. "Is that true?" she demanded.

"It would have been abominable to tell her at that point," he said wearily.

But Concordia wondered if Mary had known, all the same. She remembered where she had found the brooch, tucked carefully out of sight, in the very back of the jewel case. According to Mary's husband, she had never worn it.

Mrs. Wells was still shaking in anger, which she now directed at Concordia. "Why did you keep this from me? You had no right!"

"Mother, I only just…"

"You always have to be *so* important, have to know things that others do not. You and your father both! Keeping secrets together, having your own special *jokes* that no one else understood. I have always *hated* that."

Concordia felt a lump form in her throat and could barely speak. "You are being grossly unfair," she croaked.

Nathaniel, recovering his composure, stepped into the fray, pulling Mrs. Wells' arm through his. "Come, Letitia," he coaxed. "I will take you home. You two can talk when you both are calmer," he added firmly, looking at Concordia. "We will get it all settled then."

The dance was coming to an end, with many of the seniors already returning to their cottages. After taking a few minutes to regain her poise, Concordia finally found Mr. Bradley. He was in close conversation with Miss Hamilton. Concordia had nearly overlooked the two of them, tucked in a corner by the balcony. The balustrade cast them in shadow, with only a bit of light illuminating Miss Hamilton's hair and reflecting off of Mr. Bradley's glasses. They were so earnestly engaged that neither was aware of her approach.

"That answer is not satisfactory, Mr. Bradley. Whyever were you—" Miss Hamilton was saying. Mr. Bradley, looking up and seeing Concordia, put a quick hand on the lady principal's arm. Frowning, Miss Hamilton turned around, and fell silent.

"Miss Wells, there you are!" Mr. Bradley said, giving her a bright smile. "I have been looking for you. I was just informing Miss Hamilton about the amorous couple she will need to deal with tomorrow." He looked at her more closely. "Weren't you wearing a brooch earlier?"

Concordia did not answer, her mind filled with questions about what she had just overheard. It did not sound as if they were discussing the "amorous couple" at all. Miss Hamilton looked decidedly unhappy with Mr. Bradley.

"If you will excuse me, I have to attend to other matters," Miss Hamilton said smoothly. As she walked away, Concordia noticed Judge Armstrong, alone on the balcony, smoking a cigar. He was staring after Miss Hamilton. His face was a collection of quick-changing expressions: surprise, and—was that fear? Perhaps relief as well?

Her imagination was running amok. Just because she had stumbled upon one secret tonight, surely that did not mean everyone else had something to hide. But she couldn't make any sense of it.

"I need to go home," she said. Her sticky-treacle thoughts were making her head ache.

He gave her a sharp, questioning glance. "Of course."

The pre-dawn glow made it easy for them to follow the path back to the cottage. Birds were already stirring, giving small trills from the shrubbery.

"Are you feeling all right, Concordia?"

"I'm fine—simply tired, that's all." Tired, but aware that he'd used her Christian name.

They came to her door.

"Thank you for—for a wonderful evening," she said. She looked up at him. *Could* she trust him? He may never tell her what she wanted to know. Was he an honorable man? Or would he break her heart, as Julian had said?

She took a deep breath. "Mr. Bradley, I—"

He pulled her toward him, gently. She could feel his warmth, his strong hands on her shoulders. He leaned in and kissed her cheek, his breath lingering in her ear. "The pleasure was mine. Sweet dreams, Concordia."

He smiled as he left, with Concordia staring after him.

Chapter 42

O, full of scorpions is my mind!
III.ii

Week 16, Instructor Calendar
May 1896

M ilton today.
Concordia prepared the classroom in advance of her students' arrival, spacing apart desks, laying out papers and pencils. The juniors were to be tested on *Paradise Lost*, part of their *Mastery in Classics* degree requirement. She had already been visited (*haunted* might be a better word) by a steady stream of students in her office this week, those seeking to compress half a term's worth of knowledge in the space of a one-hour tutoring session. A Herculean task at best.

What *was* it about Milton's *Paradise Lost*? Every year, the students fretted over it. Of course, they had eighteenth-century writer Samuel Johnson as a surprising ally in that regard:

We read Milton for instruction, retire harassed and overburdened, and look elsewhere for recreation; we desert our master, and seek for companions.

She chuckled, remembering a student unearthing the Johnson quotation and waving it gleefully before her.

"You see, Miss Wells? We are not the only ones!"

As the students worked, Concordia opened the windows. The scent of newly-mown grass wafted in, and sunshine sent prisms of color through the tilted lead-glass panes. Several girls stirred, restless.

Concordia's thoughts wandered to her conversation with Miss Hamilton nearly a week before, the afternoon following the dance.

"I must thank you for your assistance as chaperone last evening," Miss Hamilton had said, pouring them each steaming cups of tea. She passed the scones.

Concordia smothered a yawn. She had managed a small nap that morning, although it didn't seem like nearly enough sleep. But when the lady principal asks one to tea, "no" is not an alternative.

"What will happen to Miss Crandall?" Concordia genuinely liked the girl, but knew that Charlotte Crandall, Head Senior or no, could be expelled for her behavior in the garden.

"I have spoken with the young lady. She is secretly engaged to this Mr. Blake, against her parents' wishes," Miss Hamilton said. "They have another match in mind for her, apparently."

"But surely she is of an age to make her own decision?" Concordia protested. Miss Crandall seemed a sensible girl overall—except for last night's behavior, of course. But Concordia knew nothing about the young man. "Is there something objectionable about Mr. Blake?"

"That is not our place, Miss Wells," Miss Hamilton reproved. "We are not her parents."

"So what will you do?" Concordia persisted. "Miss Crandall is due to graduate in a few weeks. You would not dismiss her now? With her degree, she could be independent and choose for herself!"

"I am aware of that," Miss Hamilton said sharply. "But we must also safeguard the reputation of this college. No self-respecting parent will send a daughter here if we are perceived as tolerant of such behavior."

"Surely we can keep this quiet, and restrict her contact so that she is not compromised further? I would be willing to take responsibility for her," Concordia urged.

Miss Hamilton was quiet for a moment. "I will consider it."

Concordia knew not to push further. In a change of subject, she asked, "What were you and Mr. Bradley discussing last night?"

Miss Hamilton's features took on an expressionless quality. "We discussed many things, Miss Wells. I do not recall when you mean."

The conversation progressed little after that.

Now, in the quiet of the examination period, with only the scratching of lead pencil points and the rustling of papers, Concordia wished she had been more persistent. But Miss Hamilton had a skill for thwarting Concordia's best efforts at drawing out any information the lady was unwilling to relinquish.

Concordia had forgotten to ask her about Miss Banning's return. She strongly suspected that Miss Hamilton had something to do with that. The lady principal had not been surprised by Margaret Banning's arrival at the dance, nor by President Richter's flustered reaction to it. In fact, one might wonder if she was trying to produce that very response.

Did Miss Hamilton suspect President Richter of the incidents at the college? Yet his own office had been ransacked, and a threatening note left on his door. What would be the point of that? Perhaps she suspected him of something else, such as the embezzlement, the attack on Sophia, or Miss Lyman's death?

In Concordia's opinion, Dean Langdon could bear further scrutiny. She recalled the argument between Richter and Langdon the night after the fire. President Richter had accused the dean of–what? Did he believe the dean was responsible for the fire? Or the other incidents? And yet the dean himself had raised the issue of the fire during the midnight supper, so wouldn't that mean that he was innocent? Or was it a blind, to fool them all?

She must say something to Miss Hamilton. Perhaps they should be looking more closely at Dean Langdon.

Her thoughts were interrupted by the bell.

"Stop writing," she called out. "I will collect your papers here in the front of the room as you leave." Concordia heard mixed sighs of relief and resignation as the students escaped into the sunshine.

Chapter 43

"There now, miss," Ruby said, giving the gown a final shake and fluffing the folds, "the dress is all cleaned, and the creases came right out."

"What about the tear in the train?" Concordia asked, picking up the bottom of the skirt. She had been dismayed to discover a tear in the lace edging, but Ruby's repair was barely discernible.

"Whatever would I do without you, Ruby?"

The matron huffed in embarrassment and carefully folded the dress into its box. "I can have Sam deliver it this afternoon for you," she offered.

Concordia shuddered at the thought of the grubby 12-yr-old boy, amiable as he was, carrying around Miss Bellini's dress.

"No, no; I'll take it to her myself. I won't be long."

Concordia realized as soon as Miss Bellini opened her door that she had come at an inopportune time. The lady's eyes, usually bright and vivacious, were dull, watery, and red-rimmed; her face was pale. Her entire aspect conveyed agitation: hair carelessly pulled back rather than arranged in its usual soft waves, dress rumpled, shoulders drooping. Concordia had not seen Miss Bellini since the dance, and the difference was startling.

"I'm… I'm… so sorry to disturb you," she stammered.

"*Non importa.* Come in," Miss Bellini murmured, holding the door wider.

"I've brought back your dress. It was kind of you to lend it to me." Concordia laid the box on the bed. She looked again at Miss Bellini. Should she say something?

Concern prevailed over politeness. "Is there anything I can do for you, Miss Bellini? You look... unwell."

Miss Bellini sat down in a nearby chair, staring for a long time out the window. Concordia waited.

"Please, you must call me Lucia," she answered finally, looking up at Concordia. "We are friends now, are we not?"

"Of course—Lucia. What is wrong? Can I help?"

Miss Bellini shook her head. "No, no, *signorina*—may I call you Concordia? Yes?" She paused a moment.

"There is family trouble. You can do nothing. *I* can do nothing!" she said fiercely, getting up and beginning to pace in her agitation.

"There was one person who could have helped me—who *promised* to help me—but it was all empty words." Her voice choked. "He will not. Despite all we have been through together."

"Who, Lucia? Who would help? What do you need from him?" Concordia could not imagine anyone heartless enough to deny a woman in such obvious distress.

Lucia Bellini shook her head mutely. Her expression hardened into a glare, and her eyes flashed with their old animation.

"It is private. But I *will* act. He must know," she answered. She turned to the door and opened it. "*Grazie*, Concordia. You have helped me make up my mind."

Concordia left, confused. She had offered no advice; in fact, she had done nothing but ask questions. How had she helped? She felt like a spectator in a conversation that Miss Bellini had had with herself.

Concordia's thoughts were still full of the puzzle of Miss Bellini when she returned to Willow Cottage to find Annie, the Armstrong's maid, waiting in the parlor.

"Annie! Is everything all right? How is Davey?" Concordia asked. The maid's face was tense with excitement, and there was a fine bead of perspiration on her brow.

"Oh, he's fine, miss. Takin' to that woodworking they's teaching him like a fish to water, he is. But I'm so glad yer back. The waiting was enough to drive a body crazy. Look what I found!" With a flourish, Annie pulled out a crumpled sheet of paper from her pocketbook and handed it to Concordia.

Concordia smoothed it out and looked at it closely. It was heavy-weight paper, with a crisp gilt edge on three sides, the left edge was ragged and torn. Her heart fluttered with excitement. *Mary's journal!*

She looked over at Annie. "Did you find any more pages?"

Annie's face fell. "No, miss. Nancy and me, we looked nigh everywhere. Now don' worry," she added hastily, "I didn' tell Nancy why we was looking for the journal. I made out that it was sentimental, like, that yer wanted it. I'm the only one who seen this page."

Concordia glanced down at Mary's familiar, delicate writing, the feeling of loss tugging at her again.

> *January 15th*
> *I am feeling better today, but also quite worried. I have been ill for so long. Henry avoids me now. He doesn't touch me anymore. Is he disappointed in me? How can I be a proper wife for him when I am constantly unwell? What in heaven is wrong with me?*

There was a second entry, farther down the same page.

> *January 17th*
> *Sophia came to visit me today. Dear Sophia. She has been my comfort during this hard time. But, oh, how I wish she had not come today! What she had to tell me was most unwelcome. She cannot be right, but I fear she is. It is unbearable. Why must I suffer this way? What have I done to deserve this? What would Henry say, if I told him of my suspicions?*

And then, scribbled in agitation at the bottom, Mary wrote: *If she is right, then there is no hope for me.*

Concordia looked up at Annie, who had been quietly waiting, pity in her eyes.

"Where did you find it, after all this time?"

"It was under the rubbish bin, beneath the missus' writing desk. That no-account scullery maid, she's too bone-lazy to look around for rubbish that i'nt smack under her nose. She must 'a just dumped the bin and put it back without feelin' around for any scraps that fell out. And the desk prob'ly hasn't been used since then. Nancy and me, we was doing a lot of crawling around on our hands an' knees. That's how I finally found it."

Mary must have torn out the page from her journal and thrown it away, she thought. Her sister was probably afraid of how revealing it was, although, to Concordia, it wasn't revealing enough. And someone—Judge Armstrong, perhaps? Or Henry?— had later disposed of the rest of her journal.

She looked at Annie, impressed by the girl's resourcefulness. "Annie, you're wonderful! Your talents are wasted in service for the Armstrongs. Have you ever thought of getting a position elsewhere?"

Annie hesitated and looked around cautiously. She dropped her voice. "I been thinking on it, miss, believe me. I have a mind to take a typewriter training class. There's lots o' places here in the city that needs people who know how to use them contraptions, my sister says. And they pay the girls well, she hears."

The girl sniffed. "I'll be right sorry to leave Mister Henry. Not the judge, though! That man thinks he's the biggest toad in the puddle, he does."

Concordia stood and clasped Annie's hand. "I think it's an excellent idea. Do take care of yourself."

Annie looked at Concordia intently. "Are you all right, miss? Yer face is wet."

Concordia put her hands to her cheeks.

"Yes, of course I am. Good-bye," she managed to say, as Annie let herself out.

Chapter 44

Week 16, Instructor Calendar
May 1896

Concordia, I simply do not *know!*" Sophia angrily pushed back her chair and stood. She began to pace—door, window, desk, window—her tall, angular form crossing the small room in quick strides.

They were in Miss Jenkins' sitting room, adjacent to the infirmary. Now that Sophia had sufficiently recovered from her head injury, a more congenial location was deemed necessary. Here, in Miss Jenkins' quarters, Sophia could be more comfortable, yet protected. They had to assume that her attacker, still at large, might try again. The prolonged confinement was wearing on Sophia's nerves.

Mary's diary page fluttered to the floor. Concordia picked it up. One sentence stood out as she glanced at it again.

What she had to tell me was most unwelcome.

Concordia looked over at her friend, exasperated.

"Sophie, can you not remember *anything?* Or are you simply trying to shield me from the truth? What was wrong with Mary? You must tell me," she pleaded. She could not bear the thought of never knowing why Mary had been so pitilessly taken from them.

Sophia sank back into the chair, putting her head in her hands.

Concordia bit back her disappointment. She had so hoped that Sophia's memory would be roused by the sight of Mary's handwriting, her words.

Then something occurred to her.

"Perhaps we do not have to rely on your memory of specific people and events. Perhaps we can rely on your knowledge," Concordia said.

Sophia looked up. "What do you mean?"

"Based upon this entry," Concordia pointed to Mary's diary page, "we can safely assume that what you had to tell Mary was a surprise to her. My sister did not reveal a secret to *you*; instead, *you* came up with the answer. It must have come from your observations and knowledge, knowledge gained from your settlement house work, perhaps? Think! What do you know about the women you have worked with, their circumstances in life, the problems that they face? How might that apply to Mary? Where would this have led you?"

Sophia waved an impatient hand. "But Mary was not *poor*; she did not live in squalid conditions. What could *I* have figured out?" Sophia asked.

But Concordia was not ready to give up so easily. She was convinced that Sophia had the answer.

"Dr. Westfield and Judge Armstrong know something that they have worked very hard to conceal. Henry, too," Concordia answered. She recounted to Sophia the conversation she had listened to in the library the night following Mary's funeral.

By the time she had finished, Sophia was no longer paying attention; she was staring out the window, lost in her own thoughts. Tears started in her eyes.

Sophia looked at Concordia. "I know, now. My poor Mary."

"Tell me," Concordia urged.

When Sophia was done, neither of them spoke for a while, each struggling against a fresh wave of grief.

But Concordia knew they couldn't afford to wallow in their feelings. They had work to do.

A plan was beginning to form in her mind. Its success would depend on Sophia.

"How good of an actress are you?" Concordia asked Sophia.

Sophia dried her eyes and squared her shoulders. "As good as you need me to be."

"Good," Concordia had said. "You are about to become deathly ill."

Chapter 45

Week 16, Instructor Calendar
May 1896

...What in me is dark
Illumine; what is low, raise and support

Concordia encountered these lines as she struggled to grade the *Paradise Lost* examination papers in the quiet of her office. Her own wishes were echoed there; she needed as much illumination as she could summon.

There had been some light already, with the understanding of what had killed Mary. The cold fury brought on by that knowledge settled into her chest like a heavy stone. Nothing could be proved, but she knew those responsible must be confronted, not only for Mary's sake, but for Sophia's. Her safety depended upon it.

But would her plan work? Concordia conceded that it was an outlandish one. And they were up against a cunning and unscrupulous foe.

It was imperative that she talk to Miss Banning. She would need the old lady's help if this was to work. And she should inform Miss Hamilton, too.

Concordia looked out her office window. The day was incongruously bright and cheerful, with students sprawled on the lawn in their colorful spring dresses. Concordia recognized Miss Crandall, seated beside the fountain, scribbling upon a piece of paper, deep in conversation with Miss Pomeroy and Miss Bellini. Concordia was glad to see that Miss Bellini looked more like her animated self.

She heard snatches of laughter beneath her window as another group caught her eye. Mr. Reynolds, seated on the grass, was surrounded by the usual number of adoring girls. Once he lifted his head to gaze straight up at her office window. She pulled back hastily. Since the dance, she had been too busy to see him.

If she were honest with herself, she would admit she had been avoiding him. She didn't know if she could trust her feelings about him. Something was holding her back, and she needed time apart from him to think. But that was a luxury she didn't have at the moment, with all of the other turmoil going on in her life.

She glanced down at the ungraded pile of papers. Perhaps a short stroll to the pond and back would clear her mind.

Avoiding the crowd on the green, Concordia followed the stone path to the pond. Students were tossing crumbs to the ducks and exclaiming over the ducklings, mere puff-balls in the water behind their parents.

She smiled. How beautiful it was here. The water cast dancing flashes of light against the shore as the breeze ruffled its surface.

As she approached the overhanging low-limbed pine on the far side of the water, she noticed debris, no doubt tossed there by careless students. With a sigh, she began picking up the trash: a napkin, a wax paper wrapper, a *fork*, and, strangest of all, a shoe. Quite a grimy one, in fact. *Ugh.*

As she crouched under the pine bough to grab the shoe, one of the prickly cones scratched her forehead. *Drat!* She sucked in her breath sharply and winced, putting a hand to her head.

But she held onto the shoe as she moved away from the offending bough. Why on earth would a gentleman leave a shoe here, Concordia marveled, shaking out water and pine needles from it. It wasn't remarkable-looking, just a man's brown dress shoe, save for the irrecoverable damage done to the leather by being in the water for so long. But it looked familiar, somehow.

"Miss Wells, what do you have there?" a voice called.

Miss Hamilton approached, and stretched out a hand. Concordia willingly passed it over, and brushed off her palms.

"I found it just over there."

"By the tree?"

Concordia nodded. "It was caught in the leaf clutter. Rather odd to find a shoe here, don't you think?"

"Indeed. You seem to have gotten a nasty scratch, too." Miss Hamilton added, passing her a handkerchief. "Why don't you attend to it? I'll take care of this... item." She wrinkled her nose.

Exactly what Concordia thought, too. She checked her watch. Time to go back for more grading, anyway. She waved to Miss Hamilton, who was still looking thoughtfully at the shoe.

Chapter 46

Such welcome and unwelcome things at once
'Tis hard to reconcile.

IV.iii

Week 17, Instructor Calendar
May 1896

The tall windows of the auditorium illuminated the stage with an over-enthusiastic brightness. The glare hit King Duncan square in the face. The king squinted and held up a hand to shield her eyes.

"Miss Pomeroy, could you please draw the shades?" Concordia called over her shoulder. She had finally wedged the stiff, leather scabbard into position so she could secure the belt to it. She didn't want to let go now, dash it, or she would have to fuss with it all over again.

Miss Pomeroy, crouched at the hem of a student's costume, sighed, brushed straggling wisps of hair from her round face, and awkwardly got to her feet. Concordia offered an apologetic grimace from across the room. It seemed that there were never enough hands. Thank goodness the performance was tomorrow night.

Miss Pomeroy pulled on the stiff chain of the window blind, grunting with the effort. It wouldn't budge. Concordia abandoned the scabbard and went over to help, but even between the two of them, the rusty spring refused to yield.

"Ladies, allow me?" a voice offered.

Concordia turned, startled, to find Dean Langdon nearly at her elbow. The man was as quiet as a cat for someone so large. She nodded and stepped back.

He reached above the window frame—at least, as far as his hefty middle would allow—and yanked. It was an exertion even for Langdon, as he tugged on the chain and growled an ungentlemanly oath under his breath.

Concordia frowned.

She and Miss Hamilton had heard that same muttered invective in the stairwell of Founder's Hall.

So—Dean Langdon *was* their intruder, just as the lady principal had suspected! But *why* had he been there?

Langdon, still occupied with the shade, took no notice of Concordia. With a final screech of protesting old gears, the blind rolled down. He heaved a sigh of manly satisfaction, brushed off his hands, and made his way to the seats to observe the dress rehearsal.

Several teachers came in and seated themselves as well, along with Miss Hamilton.

Now was her chance. Concordia turned to Miss Pomeroy. "Would you mind terribly getting the remaining students into their costumes? I need to speak with Miss Hamilton. I'll only be a moment."

Nodding, the ever-patient Miss Pomeroy shepherded the stragglers backstage to dress. Concordia caught Miss Hamilton's eye—not difficult to do, as the sharp-eyed lady principal missed little—and gestured toward the wing.

The wing was empty and, with their voices lowered, relatively private.

"Miss Hamilton, I realize this is a bit unorthodox, but I have a favor to ask of you," Concordia began, when they had found a secluded corner. "I need to make a substitution."

Miss Hamilton listened intently as Concordia explained what she wanted to do, and why.

❦

"Hail, King of Scotland!"

The dress rehearsal was coming to a close as the new king was crowned. Only a few difficulties had arisen. Lady Macbeth still had a tendency to giggle during her sleep-walking scene, and Macduff's sword kept catching in its scabbard during the fight scenes. But tomorrow, they would be ready.

The seniors, flushed and pleased, accepted Miss Hamilton's and Dean Langdon's praises before heading to the storeroom with their costumes. Concordia asked why the president had not attended the dress rehearsal.

"It's a long-held tradition," Miss Pomeroy had explained. "Years ago, one of the senior classes had insisted that the president see only their finished product, and it has been that way ever since. The senior play is a source of great pride to them."

The spectators made their way out, a few giving Concordia superfluous, contradictory advice. Concordia thanked them—through clenched teeth—and privately wished them gone. Soon only the dean and lady principal remained behind, absorbed in murmured conversation, as Concordia closed windows.

A rhythmic *thump-bump, thump-bump,* punctuated by wheezing, and then a garbled yell, disturbed the quiet. Alarmed, they all turned to see Margaret Banning lumber into the room, brandishing a worn leather-bound book.

"I found it, heh, heh!" she cried, gesturing excitedly, cane poking madly through the air in their direction, "right under your young noses! Missed it, did you? A sad want of common sense, I'd say, missy," she finished, wagging the book lastly at Concordia, who stared, open-mouthed.

Without a word, Miss Hamilton, after a quick glance outside, firmly closed the auditorium doors.

"A bit more quietly if you would, Margaret. May I?" She reached for the volume in the old lady's hand.

Reluctantly, Miss Banning relinquished her treasure. Dean Langdon helped ease her into a chair, although she promptly waved him off after she was seated.

"I'm not incapacitated yet, Edward!" she snapped.

Dean Langdon gave Concordia a sidelong smile as he retreated to a safe distance.

Miss Hamilton had put on her spectacles and was thumbing through the pages. She looked over at Miss Banning.

"I congratulate you. It *is* indeed the ledger I have been looking for. Wherever did you find it?"

"Where I knew it would be, of course." Miss Banning's voice, although quavering with age, held a bit of a gloat. "In *my* office."

Concordia saw Miss Hamilton start in surprise, but she recovered quickly.

"Of course. What better place for concealment than an unoccupied office?" the lady principal thought aloud.

Dean Langdon interrupted.

"Would someone show me the almighty kindness of explaining why this—this—*ledger*—is so important, and *who* has hidden it in Miss Banning's office? I have a right to know what is going on here!" The dean's face was quite red.

"Of course, Edward," Miss Hamilton said soothingly, as though addressing a fractious child, "but do calm down."

Through her large bottle-glass spectacles, Miss Banning was watching the interchange with barely suppressed glee. Leaning heavily on her cane, she rose stiffly.

"*Humph.* I doubt, Edward, that you are as ignorant of the goings-on here as you say. Pretend if you like, but don't have a conniption fit about it." She turned to Miss Hamilton. "As for *you*, this is not some clever little puzzle to challenge your Pinkerton wits. *'There is a time when even justice brings harm.'* You should read your Sophocles."

And with that parting shot, she thumped and wheezed her way out of the room.

It was a long moment before anyone spoke. Dean Langdon looked in shock at Miss Hamilton. She returned his stare calmly, although her fingers were clenched around the volume, knuckles white.

Concordia looked from one to the other, waiting.

Langdon finally broke the silence. "I never imagined that you were a—did she say 'Pinkerton'? You are a *detective*? How can that be?"

Miss Hamilton gave a sigh. "It's true. I was sent here to find proof of who has stolen funds from the college. I was able to investigate without hindrance, for a while at least, until Miss Wells discovered my secret"—this said with a sharp glance in Concordia's direction—"and after that, I thought it worth the risk to take Miss Banning into my confidence. She knows every nook and cranny of this institution." She sighed. "I will have to impress upon her *again* the necessity of maintaining my confidence. I would also ask *you*, Edward, to keep this private. Only the three of you know who I am."

Dean Langdon nodded, still a little dazed. "Extraordinary. I never would have thought—"

Concordia broke in. "But Mr. Langdon, when you saw Miss Hamilton go into the Hall late that night, why did you follow her? You suspected she was in some way involved in the incidents, did you not?"

Langdon gave Concordia a puzzled look. "How did you—?" Abandoning the question, he continued, "I knew something was amiss, although I could not work out precisely what." He turned to Miss Hamilton. "I imagine you were looking for *that*?" He gestured toward the ledger.

Miss Hamilton nodded. "After the fire in my office, it was even more urgent that I find it, before it was destroyed."

"I had the impression a second person was in the Hall the night I followed you," Langdon said.

Miss Hamilton convulsed in laughter. Concordia flushed and looked at the floor.

"Our activity had drawn Miss Wells to the Hall," Miss Hamilton, said, in between gasps. "It was quite a lively evening."

Dean Langdon looked at Concordia, then back at Miss Hamilton. A small smile tugged at his mouth, and he chuckled.

"Land sakes, then, why didn't we sell tickets? We were practically a vaudeville act."

Concordia couldn't help but smile. The image of the three of them that night did seem absurd: separately prowling the halls, playing cat-and-mouse in the dark, each ignorant of the identity or intentions of the others.

But some questions about the dean's behavior still troubled her.

"Why did you search Miss Hamilton's private study?" Concordia asked abruptly, as the laughter died down. "Did you perhaps set fire to her office as well?"

Miss Hamilton frowned. Was she annoyed by the blunt accusation, or had that also occurred to her?

"No! I would never cause her harm!" Langdon protested. "But—yes, I did search her study," he grudgingly admitted. "I wanted to know what she was doing. I followed her to the Hall that night for the same reason."

Langdon continued, turning to the lady principal. "I was convinced that someone had involved you in something sordid. I was trying to discover who. I wanted to protect you."

"I can look after myself quite well, thank you," Miss Hamilton said frostily. She opened the book. "But I am curious about *who* you thought was corrupting me. These entries, here— and these *false* entries, here," she said, pointing to different pages, "are each in Bursar Lyman's hand." She continued scanning several pages in silence.

"She also uses initials, A.R.–Arthur Richter–for several payouts on one side of the ledger," Miss Hamilton mused aloud, "and numerous vendors listed here that I don't recognize. I'll have to check the official books against this one."

"How will you do so without President Richter finding out?" Concordia said.

Miss Hamilton gave a small smile. "I'll manage."

"How did Miss Lyman's secret ledger come to be hidden in Miss Banning's office?" Dean Langdon asked.

"I can imagine two possibilities: either the bursar herself hid it from her accomplice–let's be blunt here, I believe that person to be President Richter–or, Richter found the ledger after Miss

Lyman's death, and hid it in Margaret Banning's office. Either way, it was the perfect hiding place. It never occurred to me to look for it there, and I've been hunting for months. And if Richter indeed was the one who hid it there, I can only imagine that he anticipated his office would be searched. That suggests there is another confederate in this scheme that he was hiding it *from*."

Concordia listened with a strange feeling of detachment. Why was she not shocked by Arthur Richter being a crook? Too many things were happening at once. She needed time to think.

But first, she had another question for the dean. "I overheard part of your argument with President Richter the night of the fire," Concordia said. "Were you accusing him of misappropriating funds?"

Miss Hamilton looked surprised. Langdon flushed.

"We did, indeed, have words that night," he admitted. "I was trying to warn him to stop, without bluntly saying so. I long suspected that college accounts were being misused, but I couldn't be sure if Arthur was to blame. Several people, including the bursar and myself, have had a hand in directing the different accounts payable over the last few years. The accounts became horribly muddled when the college's investments lost money during the crash of '93, and we were forced to shift funds quickly from one place to another in order to cover our immediate expenses. No one kept a careful accounting during that period. The bursar claimed that she tried, but obviously she was lying to us."

"But during that conversation, President Richter accused you of something as well, Mr. Langdon," Concordia persisted.

The dean flushed. "Arthur saw me coming out of DeLacey House, after I had searched Miss Hamilton's study. When she reported the incident to him, he put it all together. He then suspected me of having searched his office, too, and leaving the threatening note. Which I did *not* do," Langdon said vehemently.

He hesitated, as if about to say something else.

"What is it, Edward?" Miss Hamilton prompted.

"It was the fire that worried me exceedingly," he continued. "That was the real reason I confronted him that night. Lord help me, I have wondered if he was somehow involved in *that*. That was also why I raised the topic of the fire so – prominently–during the dance supper. I was hoping to spur a reaction from him."

Miss Hamilton looked startled. "Arthur Richter! Involved in the fire? Whyever would you suspect him?"

Langdon rubbed the back of his neck in distraction. "He did not attend the basketball game until much later, and then he seemed quite agitated. It was only a short time after he arrived that we all heard the fire bell."

Chapter 47

Week 17, Instructor Calendar
May 1896

"Here, this may help," a soothing voice said.

Concordia, lost in thought, looked up to see Mr. Bradley holding the cup of tea that she had ordered. She gave him a wan smile as she took it.

"Do you work for Mrs. Gilly now?" she teased half-heartedly.

He smiled and sat down. "She has her hands full with patrons inside the shop. I thought I'd expedite things."

At Mr. Bradley's insistence, they had gone to the Canton Tea Shop, several blocks from Hartford Women's College. "You need to get away from the school for a little while," he had told her.

With so much still to do, Concordia had resisted at first, but now she was glad she had given in. She hadn't been here in years. The shop offered a vast array of teas from around the world, and Mrs. Gilly, the proprietress, baked the most divine lemon tarts she had ever tasted. The tea shop was especially pleasant this time of year, when one could sit outside beneath the brightly-striped awning, as they were doing now, and watch passersby.

They drank their tea in appreciative silence, Mr. Bradley casting frequent glances her way.

Concordia felt some of the tension draining away. He looked on, nodding in approval.

"Much better. You were looking rather pale," he said. "Do you want to talk about it?"

Concordia hesitated. She had to be careful not to give away Miss Hamilton's identity.

"Mr. Bradley, I don't know where to begin. There is so much happening."

He leaned forward. "You can begin by calling me David. That's so much better, don't you think? Easier to confide in someone named 'David.' I've had considerable experience with the name—I know what I'm talking about."

A laugh bubbled out of Concordia. He certainly knew how to raise her spirits.

He gave her time, gazing idly around him.

Finally, Concordia dropped her voice and leaned closer. "A ledger has been found, hidden in Miss Banning's office."

He raised an eyebrow in surprise. "Not hidden by Miss Banning, I gather?"

Concordia rolled her eyes. "Do be serious, David!"

He smiled to himself.

"How is this ledger significant?" he asked.

"Miss Hamilton says that it reveals the individuals behind the misappropriation of college funds."

"Did she tell you who they were?" David asked.

Concordia hesitated. "I cannot say."

To her surprise, he did not push the question. Perhaps he had already guessed. "What happens now?"

"Miss Hamilton is checking further, gathering more proof. Apparently she doesn't believe that the ledger alone is sufficient evidence. It won't be long, though, before she will present the information to the board of trustees."

"Should not President Richter fill that role? After all, he has been at the college much longer. He would have more credibility with the board. He's also a man," he added, as an afterthought.

Concordia frowned. Why did gentlemen so readily believe that they were the only persons capable of understanding financial matters? How did a pair of trousers imbue one with worldly experience? She would dearly love to argue the point, but she could not tell him that President Richter was one of the guilty party, and that Miss Hamilton, as an investigating detective, carried far more credibility than any of the male administrators.

There was a long silence. Concordia heard rustling sounds behind her; birds often foraged for pastry crumbs along the open windowsill.

"That is something that's already been arranged," she finally answered.

"But it is not the ledger that troubles you," David challenged.

She was silent for a few moments, twisting her napkin in her lap.

"You're right. It is something else altogether," she said finally. "Dean Langdon believes that President Richter may have had something to do with the fire."

David shook his head in disbelief. "Surely not!"

"Well, according to Mr. Langdon, the president didn't arrive at the senior-junior basketball game that day until quite late. The fire bell sounded shortly thereafter, he said."

"He could be mistaken," David said dismissively.

"Perhaps," Concordia acknowledged. Tears started down her face. "But don't you see? Even if President Richter did *not* set the fire, he had to have been *outside* the gymnasium building when we were all shouting for help; he may have been outside even while I was scrambling down the vines. How could he not see, or hear, any of that? Founder's Hall sits atop a hill, clearly visible from the gymnasium. Why did he not help? He and my father were close friends. I used to adore him as a child."

David patted her arm, but Concordia was not to be comforted.

"Concordia. You don't know this," he said earnestly. "Think about it. When all of you were leaning out the window, trying to summon help, did you see *anyone*? You've told me that there was not a soul out on the grounds that day. They were all at the game by then. Surely, if Richter had been outside, able to see you, would *you* not have been able to see *him* as well?"

He pulled out his pocket kerchief and gently dried her eyes. She smiled through the last of her tears.

They heard the abrupt scrape of a wood chair from the other side of the window. Startled, they looked toward the source, and glimpsed a tall, lean gentleman as he left his table inside the shop and rushed out the side door to the street.

"That fellow seemed in a hurry," David commented.

Concordia, from her position under the window awning, craned her neck for a better look. It was too late. The man was gone.

Chapter 48

Now does he feel his title
Hang loose about him, like a giant's robe
Upon a dwarfish thief.

V.ii

Week 17, Instructor Calendar
May 1896

There was an air of gaiety in the auditorium the next evening, as students, faculty, and townspeople wandered up and down rows, some searching for seats, others circulating among family and acquaintances. Within a short time, there was barely room to move. The custodian set up more chairs along the back and sides to accommodate the crowd.

The playgoers were attired in their best finery, bright silks and jewels shimmering in the glow of the footlights on stage and the lamps bracketing the walls. Behind the curtain, Concordia cautiously peeked out at the crowd, at least what she could see of it from her position.

So many people! The front rows, reserved for the administrators, senior faculty, and trustees, were nearly filled. Judge Armstrong and Dr. Westfield were already seated, along with Nathaniel Young, and others whom she knew only by sight. President Richter, Dean Langdon, and Miss Hamilton were conspicuously absent. David and Julian had each promised to attend, but there was no sign of either gentleman.

"Psst! Miss Wells!" a voice whispered from the wing.

Concordia turned around and saw Miss Hamilton, wearing an elegant dress of deep lavender for the occasion. It made Concordia's own serviceable china-blue cotton, one of her favorite light-weight skirts, look rather ordinary.

"Miss Hamilton? What are you doing back *here*? Why are you so late?"

She beckoned Concordia farther away from the curtain before she spoke.

"We cannot find President Richter anywhere. Dean Langdon and I have been searching for the past hour." Miss Hamilton wore a worried frown.

Concordia was confused. "Is he ill? Perhaps he had some emergency that called him away?"

Miss Hamilton was skeptical. "Without notice of any kind, to any of his staff?" She sighed. "I wish I could slip into his rooms and see if he has packed, but he recently put a new lock on his door that I cannot open."

"You suspect that he has fled?" Concordia asked incredulously.

"He may be aware of the ledger's discovery. Miss Banning was none too discreet about waving it around, as you may recall." Miss Hamilton glanced over her shoulder to where Margaret Banning, perched on a stool along the opposite wing, was giving enthusiastic instructions to the girls.

"Perhaps, too, he fears that we suspect him of killing Miss Lyman," Miss Hamilton added.

Concordia looked startled. "We suspect *what?!*" she exclaimed. Several heads backstage turned her way. She lowered her voice to a whisper. "Do you really think he killed the bursar? How do you know?"

"I know it's an unpleasant thing to contemplate, Miss Wells, but we must face facts. The ledger ties him to her too closely. They had been working together on this scheme. The circumstances of her suicide could have been easily contrived. The shoe you found by the pond, a gentleman's dress shoe, had no business being there. It was so sodden and deeply stained, it could have easily been there since the winter, trapped under the ice, and eventually caught in the underbrush after the spring thaw."

"That does not mean it's Arthur Richter's shoe," Concordia persisted. She couldn't believe what she was hearing. It couldn't be true.

But then she remembered she *had* seen that shoe before—or, more properly, the mate to it. In the tower storage room, among the donated props.

"I make it my business to notice such unique features as clothing, hair, faces, voices," Miss Hamilton answered. "Arthur Richter has a tweed suit that he seemed to favor pairing with brown dress shoes. Over the past few months, however, I have seen him wearing the suit with *black* shoes."

"There could be another explanation for that, surely? That doesn't mean that's his shoe," Concordia said.

"I grant you, it is a relatively nondescript style. But there is more. Do you remember the day after Miss Lyman was found? Richter's severe laryngitis, as one gets when out in the cold and damp for too long? And consider the scratch we all saw on his forehead that day." Miss Hamilton gently touched the wound that Concordia had incurred two days ago, at the pond. "It was just like yours. I believe it was caused by the same low-hanging branch, near where Miss Lyman was found. Richter, in carrying Miss Lyman's body, couldn't duck low enough to avoid the branch hitting his face."

Concordia reluctantly conceded that Miss Hamilton's evidence, while individually minor, collectively provided something damning. Things were looking very bleak for President Richter, and the college. "What will you do?"

"I strongly suspect that at least one other person is involved in the embezzlement scheme, if not in Miss Lyman's murder, so I am not yet prepared to act. There is more that we must learn. I've also been making inquiries into Miss Lyman's past, but we are running out of time." The lady principal sighed. "I may have to go to Lieutenant Capshaw with an incomplete set of facts."

Concordia could tell that Miss Hamilton's professional pride was warring with the need to foil President Richter's escape.

"We are ready, Miss Wells!" Miss Pomeroy called out. She and Miss Banning were looking at her expectantly, as the players took their places.

"The prudent course, for now, is to continue with the play," Miss Hamilton said. She squeezed Concordia's arm and smiled. "I regret that I cannot stay to watch the performance. I have much to do. But I believe they say in the theater, 'break a leg.'"

"Good luck to you as well, Miss Hamilton," Concordia murmured, watching her leave the auditorium. She gave a signal to the stagehands and retreated backstage. For the time being, her responsibility was here. The lights were dimmed, the curtains parted, and the play began.

"O, treachery! Fly, good Fleance, fly, fly, fly! Thou mayst revenge."
The dying Banquo's words to his son in Act III were Concordia's cue. With a final tap on Miss Banning's shoulder to signal her intent, Concordia slipped quietly out of the dressing area backstage, exiting through a side door of the building.

The usher, absorbed in the play, paid Concordia little attention when she re-entered the auditorium through the vestibule doors. She stood against the back wall, watching both play and audience. How would events unfold in the next few minutes? It was out of her hands now.

"Which of you have done this?" Macbeth looked suitably startled as the ghost of Banquo, who had just appeared on stage, stared back at him silently. The other players pretended oblivion to the specter.

The audience was reacting as expected, leaning forward intently as Macbeth struggled to keep his composure.

"Thou canst not say I did it. Never shake thy gory locks at me!" Macbeth chided the ghost, while trembling in anger and fear.

As well Macbeth should; the stage makeup looked fittingly ghoulish on the young lady playing Banquo's ghost, her face unnaturally white, dark makeup around her eyes, red streaks dripping along her neck. She wore a wig of straggling locks and her clothes were bloody, torn rags. Concordia had arranged for a specially-fitted electric light to illuminate the ghost from the balcony above. Charlotte Crandall, one of the stagehands, kept it trained on the specter as it moved.

Concordia continued to wait, her heart pounding and her mouth dry. She watched the audience, now, more than the action on the stage.

There! A stirring at the end of the second row.

"Avaunt, and quit my sight! Let the earth hide thee! Thy bones are marrowless, thy blood is cold." Macbeth was shouting now.

Two forms separated themselves from the gloom, making their way toward Concordia and the back of the auditorium. She could not see who they were yet. But they were coming closer, one with a familiar waddling gait, the other walking unsteadily, even with a walking stick and the other man's arm to lean upon.

"Dr. Westfield," Concordia whispered, as they approached. "Let me help you. This way." She hurried ahead to open the vestibule door, casting a final glance at the stage, where the ghostly Sophia Adams was making her exit.

Well done, my friend, Concordia thought, looking over at the ashen-faced Judge Armstrong, still leaning heavily on the doctor's arm. *Thou mayst revenge.*

The lights in the vestibule were blinding to their dark-adjusted eyes as Concordia helped Dr. Westfield guide the judge into the reception room. They eased him into a chair. Judge Armstrong struggled for breath through bluish lips.

"That woman…how is she…" the judge gasped.

"Shh, Matthew. You mustn't agitate yourself so," the doctor admonished nervously. Gone were his wide smile and cheery, booming voice.

Concordia looked on as he broke some sort of ampule under the judge's nostrils.

"What's that?"

"Amyl nitrite," the doctor, answered, without looking up, "we have started to use it recently for angina patients." Dr. Westfield felt Judge Armstrong's wrist.

Guilt twisted in her stomach. She had not known about a heart condition. Although on the day of the rally the judge had looked a bit ill, he seemed fine on other occasions.

It was true that she had hoped for—even counted upon—a violent reaction from Judge Armstrong when he saw the woman he had nearly killed and believed to be at death's door, alive and conscious, on the stage. Concordia remembered the judge's face, a few weeks before, when he had glimpsed Miss Hamilton in the half-shadows of the dance floor: the look of shock, then fear, and lastly, relief. The judge had briefly mistaken Miss Hamilton for Miss Adams.

Soon the judge's color returned, and he was breathing more easily.

Closing the door for privacy, Concordia braced herself to follow through with the plan. She, too, had a part to play.

"What woman were you speaking of, Judge Armstrong?" she inquired solicitously.

With his strength sapped, the judge's glare lacked its usual ferocity.

"It is nothing," Dr. Westfield said quickly. "In cases like these, the patient's mind can wander during an attack."

"I thought perhaps the judge was referring to the presence of Sophia Adams on the stage. She has made a miraculous recovery, has she not?" Concordia asked, turning back to Judge Armstrong.

"To whom, pray, are you referring?" the judge demanded, his breathing easier, and some of his former bravado returning.

Concordia would not be intimidated. "Do you mean, sir, that you did not recognize Sophia Adams, the activist who spoke at the Women's Suffrage Rally last month? The young woman who visited your daughter-in-law during the worst of her illness, nearly every day? My goodness," Concordia said,

"Miss Pomeroy must have outdone herself with the stage make-up this year. Congratulations are in order."

"Of course, of course," Judge Armstrong harrumphed, sitting up straighter, "I remember now."

Concordia pressed the point. "Most certainly you should, seeing that you sent the good doctor here to check on Miss Adams' condition shortly after she was taken to the infirmary."

Westfield cleared his throat. "We were already on the grounds that day for the trustees' breakfast. It seemed only natural that I should look in and see if I could be of assistance. The assault upon the young lady was most tragic."

"But you tried to visit again just a few days ago, did you not, doctor? You were no doubt told that Miss Adams' condition was so grave that only her attending physician could see her."

Dr. Westfield looked confused. "How–?"

Concordia gripped her hands tightly together in an effort to keep her voice calm. "I must confess that you were deliberately misled. Miss Adams has been conscious, and *talking*," she emphasized, noting the look of alarm on Judge Armstrong's face, "for the last couple of weeks. Miss Hamilton, Miss Jenkins, and I realized that whoever was responsible for the attack upon her might try again if it were known that she had awakened. Miss Adams was safe as long as the perpetrator believed her to be unconscious. And you wanted to make very sure that she was in fact unconscious, is that not so?"

The doctor sputtered in indignation. "I have never laid a hand on the young lady!"

"True," Concordia conceded, "but you *have* protected the guilty party."

She snatched up the judge's walking stick before he could react. It was the one she remembered him carrying at the rally, with the lion's head gold knob.

"Give that back," the judge snapped, but he lacked the strength to stand up and pluck it from her hand.

"In a moment," Concordia answered, holding it up to the light. It was clean and newly polished. Her stomach lurched when she saw the misshapen side of the knob, flattened where it should have been curved.

She pointed the stick at Dr. Westfield. "You are just as guilty as if you had wielded this yourself, doctor. You *protected* this man—after he committed violence upon a defenseless woman. And you protected him before, when he stood by and did *nothing*"—Concordia's voice broke—"to help *another* woman, one even more vulnerable. My sister." She gave Judge Armstrong a withering look, still addressing the doctor. "Is it not time to stop protecting him?"

The judge, ignoring Concordia, looked warningly at Westfield. "Say... nothing... or...I will... destroy you," he gasped, chest heaving in his agitation.

Dr. Westfield gave a bitter laugh. "When this is known, anything you have to say against me will hold little weight. I am tired of this charade."

They were interrupted by a tentative knock on the door. Concordia opened it to find Nathaniel Young outside. She waved him in, closing the door behind him. She could hear the sound of wild applause. She hadn't much time.

"Is everything all right?" Young asked the doctor, with a glance at Judge Armstrong. "When you two didn't return, I grew worried."

Concordia pulled him over to a chair beside her. "Do sit down. You need to hear this, Nathaniel. You were close to Mary, and deserve to know the truth."

She gave the judge an icy stare. "I'm giving you one more chance to tell us what happened."

Armstrong's dark brows drew together in anger. "This is absolutely absurd. I want my carriage brought around immediately. I have nothing more to say to any of you." He pressed his lips together in a mutinous line.

"I will not keep you much longer tonight," Concordia said, and turned away from him.

"Doctor? *You* must tell us what caused Mary's illness and death."

Dr. Westfield sighed and looked at Concordia with weary eyes. "I am so sorry, Miss Wells. I tried to help her, and still protect the Armstrong family." He passed a trembling hand over his forehead before continuing.

"Your sister was suffering from a gonococcal infection. That is a venereal disease," he explained, looking over at Young.

"Dear God," Nathaniel said, "my poor Mary."

"*Who* gave it to her, doctor?" Concordia asked fiercely, although she knew the answer.

Dr. Westfield hesitated. "You must understand, Miss Wells, that men and women have different needs, different expectations, when it comes to marital relations…"

"*Who, doctor?*"

The judge spoke at last. "It was *Henry,* damn him!" He sat back, drained and white. "His friends decided, before his wedding, that my son needed to go to his marriage bed with *experience.* They took him, reluctant though he was, to a brothel. Young fools!"

The doctor nodded somberly. "I have been treating Henry for the same malady, with an equal lack of success, I'm afraid. He has little time left. In each case, I have tried all of the antiseptic irrigation treatments I know, but we in the medical community simply have no cure for this."

These evils eventually come home to roost, Sophia had said to Concordia, during their trolley ride to Mary's house. It certainly had come home to her sister, Concordia thought. She felt dizzy, and took several deep breaths.

"If Henry had it first, why did Mary get sick so quickly?" Nathaniel asked, voice shaky.

Dr. Westfield grimaced. "That is what makes the spread of the disease so difficult to contain. It can take longer for the symptoms to be apparent in a man who has been infected. He unwittingly passes it on to his wife. Henry did not know until it was too late."

Nathaniel put his head in his hands.

There was something Concordia didn't understand. "If there is no cure, why did you consult the specialist?"

The doctor looked uncomfortable. He cast an angry glance at Judge Armstrong before he spoke.

"Dr. Samuels is the best in his field. He said that there was one last chance. He could perform surgery to remove Mary's reproductive organs, and possibly prevent the infection from spreading to the blood. God help me, I let Matthew dismiss the man and send him back to Boston. The Armstrong family reputation was paramount," he said bitterly. "The judge feared discovery."

"What about Henry?" Concordia asked. "Did he know there was a chance to save his wife?"

The doctor looked down at his shoes in silence.

Concordia remembered what Annie had told her about that final meeting, when Dr. Samuels had stormed out in anger. *All* of them had been there. Henry too.

She blinked back the hot tears that stung her eyes. "You have much to answer for. *All* of you," she said, through clenched teeth.

She was interrupted by another knock on the door.

"Miss Wells, are you in there?" a high-pitched voice asked.

Concordia opened the door to a flushed and exuberant Miss Pomeroy. "Ooh, Miss Wells, we have been looking for you! You must come! The play is a rousing success!"

Concordia attempted a smile, then gestured behind her. "Judge Armstrong has taken ill. Can you call for his carriage, Miss Pomeroy? I will be right with you."

After Miss Pomeroy left, Concordia touched Nathaniel Young's shoulder. "Are you well enough to make sure that they return to the Armstrong house—and stay there for the time being?"

The man's composure was returning. He nodded. "Yes. I can manage."

Concordia turned to look once more at Judge Armstrong.

"I must consider what I will do—what Mary would want of me."

With that, Concordia turned on her heel and walked out.

Chapter 49

The night is long that never finds the day.
IV.iii

Week 17, Instructor Calendar
May 1896

"Sophie, you were wonderful!"

Sophia grinned. "I was a bit nervous, I must say. Fortunately, I didn't have any lines." She resumed rubbing the last of the stage paint from her neck with a piece of old flannel. "And Miss Pomeroy outdid herself in making me look ghastly."

The two had slipped away from the cast party and were settled in front of a cozy parlor fire in DeLacey House, where Sophia had a guest room for the night. She would return to the settlement house, and her charity work, tomorrow.

"You should have nothing more to fear from Judge Armstrong, now that the truth has been exposed," Concordia said. She had already recounted to Sophia what had happened after her stage exit.

"But Concordia, there is something that I don't understand," Sophia said.

Concordia suddenly stood up and went over to the parlor door, looking at Sophia and putting her finger to her lips. Eyes wide, Sophia remained quiet, waiting.

Carefully, Concordia opened the parlor door and peered into the hallway. Empty. The air felt damp out here, but that was all. Shaking her head, she closed the door and returned to the fire.

"What was it?" Sophia asked.

"Nothing. My nerves must be on edge. I thought I had heard someone in the hallway." Concordia took off her glasses and wearily rubbed the bridge of her nose. "I'm sorry, Sophie— what were you saying?"

"I was about to say that I cannot understand why Judge Armstrong would want to harm me. How could he know that I understood the true nature of Mary's illness? Although my memory is still hazy, I'm certain that I would not be foolish enough to tell him what I knew without proof."

Concordia had wondered about this, too, but then had remembered something about the day of the rally.

"I think I can guess. During the post-rally reception, you spoke with Miss Hamilton about forming a junior suffrage league, and you said"–Concordia closed her eyes, and quoted, "'Women are being exploited every day; their health and even their reason are suffering as a result.' The judge heard you. He looked quite startled, in fact."

Sophia sighed. "I wish I could remember. But even so, that doesn't seem sufficient reason to assume I knew about Mary."

"I think we should keep in mind that this is a man for whom power and status are all," Concordia said. "Such a secret, once revealed, would create a dreadful scandal. It would ruin all that he holds dear. His beloved son is dying from the same disease that killed Mary. The stress of it seems to have unbalanced him, so that even such an innocuous comment could have prompted him to violence. He obviously feared what you knew. "

Sophia shook her head. "So what do we do now?"

Concordia stared at the fire. *There is a time when even justice brings harm.* Miss Banning's warning rung in her ears.

"I don't know. I honestly don't know," she murmured.

Concordia was still thinking over the question as she hurried back to Willow Cottage. A storm had been threatening all evening, and now the wind and rain had begun in earnest. The campus grounds were empty of students and visitors so long after midnight. Concordia wished that she had not stayed out late talking.

With her rain hood over her head, and bent over against the gusting rain, she nearly missed it: off to her left, a flickering glow. She stopped. It was coming from the bell tower, its door ajar.

Concordia frowned. No one should be in there at this hour. She and the cast had agreed that it was too late tonight, and they all were too tired, to put away the props that would be stored there. That task was left for later. She hesitated, preferring the comfort of her bed, but redirected her steps to investigate.

The lantern, still lit but sputtering, was lying on its side as she pulled the door wider. Concordia picked it up and the flame sprang back to life. She pushed straggling wet strands of hair from her face to look at it closely. Its glass was cracked—had someone dropped it where it lay, or had it somehow been knocked over?

She held the lantern over her head, trying to see up the narrow, winding stairs of the tower. The light could not penetrate very far into the blackness. Reluctantly, she picked up her already-sodden skirts and proceeded to climb.

The space within the staircase had the distinct chill of damp stone. Concordia once again experienced the uncomfortable sensation of walls closing around her, as if she were being enclosed in a tomb. She shivered. She could hear the rain, falling more heavily now, beating against the outer walls of the tower. Still she climbed, carefully stepping over the crumbling stair that she and Miss Crandall had found when they had last visited the tower; past the storeroom, which she briefly checked—no one in there; past the lookout window halfway up the stairs—no one out-of-doors; then, up to the belfry, whose bell had been taken down long ago, where she stopped to catch her breath. She was nearly to the top of the tower. She had seen no one. She felt on a fool's errand; who would come up here without the lantern? Yet something felt wrong. She would check the open parapet at the top, just to be thorough. But she needed to rest a moment; her legs felt like lead.

Concordia set the lantern on the floor and wearily propped herself on a low beam, sitting as far from the belfry's open sides as she could; the rain was blowing in with steady force now. Her gaze idly followed the beam of light cast by the lantern on the floor.

She saw a foot.

Her heart in her mouth, she grabbed the lantern and rushed over to find a figure in a heap behind the gear apparatus. The lamp sputtered—*drat!*—its kerosene running low. She held it over the form.

President Richter stared back at Concordia, hands clenched around a red lacquer knife hilt protruding from his chest.

The lantern flared briefly, and went out.

The scream ringing in Concordia's ears seemed to come from a voice other than her own. She flung herself headlong down the twisting stairs, stumbling on her skirts, scraping her hands as she caught herself on the walls to keep from falling, finally making it to the front door, and out.

And into the arms of a startled Nathaniel Young, who caught her as she staggered.

"Concordia! Was that you screaming?"

"Oh, Nathaniel, you *must* help me!" Concordia gasped. "I just...it's President Richter... he's...." She gulped down a sob.

"Steady there," he said, rubbing her shoulders as she gave an involuntary shudder. The rain was drenching them both.

"We need help—and lamps," Concordia said, pulling herself away from his grip. "I fear he's... he's dead, but my lantern went out before I could be sure." She looked at him with a puzzled frown. "Why—are *you* here?"

Nathaniel Young looked grim. "I just came from the Armstrongs. It's Henry... he's dead, Concordia."

The second shock was too much for her, and he just had time to catch her as she fainted.

Chapter 50

I 'gin to be aweary of the sun,
And wish th' estate o' the world were now undone.

V.v

Week 18, Instructor Calendar
June 1896

The blackness thinned. She heard voices, one raised sharply, others a murmur.

Where was she?

She felt a drowsy warmth, and would have drifted asleep if not for the uncomfortably hard plank she seemed to be lying upon. She turned and banged her head. It was a pew.

"Ow," she muttered, sitting up and rubbing her forehead. An overcoat slid to the floor.

Everything looked blurry.

Oh. She groped for her spectacles, finally finding them tucked in her skirt pocket, and put them on. Much better.

The rain had cleared, and the weak light of early dawn was just starting to touch the windows. But what was she doing in the chapel?

Then it came back to her. The tower. President Richter.

Concordia!" Julian Reynolds exclaimed. He hurried over. Nathaniel Young and a policeman, standing in the nave, turned. Concordia recognized the gaunt form and bright red hair of her old friend Lieutenant Capshaw.

"Thank goodness," Julian breathed, taking her hand and sitting beside her. "I was so worried about you. How do you feel?"

"I'm still a bit light in the head," Concordia answered, giving him a wan smile, "but I'll be all right. What are *you* doing here?"

Before Julian could answer, Lieutenant Capshaw approached them.

"I'm glad to see you're awake, miss."

She looked up at the policeman. "President Richter is—dead?"

The lieutenant nodded. "I'm afraid so."

Concordia shuddered. So the president had not fled.

Julian put a protective arm around her shoulders.

Capshaw reached for the water pitcher and glass that had been provided. "Here, miss, drink this—you'll feel better."

"Now," Capshaw said, when she handed back the empty glass, "I have some questions for you, Miss Wells, as you might imagine." Did he sound faintly disapproving, or was it merely her imagination?

Concordia looked over to where Nathaniel Young was standing and watching. "May I speak with Mr. Young first? It will take me only a moment."

"*After* my questions, please," Capshaw said firmly.

Concordia did not have the strength to argue. "Very well, lieutenant." She sat up straighter and smoothed her skirt.

"What brought you to the tower? What time was it?"

She hesitated. "It was absurdly late, I remember. I'm not certain of the exact time. Two this morning? Three? Miss Adams and I were talking into the late hours, and then I left her at DeLacey House—"

"*Miss Adams?*" he interrupted, startled. "She is awake? Why was I not informed of this?"

"Oh!" Concordia had forgotten about their little deception. "It was...recent. There has been so much going on. I'm sorry, lieutenant," she said feebly.

Capshaw gave her a stern look. "We will discuss the matter at length later. In the meantime, continue with your story, please."

"Let me see... oh yes. As I was walking home, I noticed a light coming from the tower. The door was open. I thought it was odd, so I crossed the quadrangle to see what was going on."

"You went to see *what was going on*," Lieutenant Capshaw echoed. He gave a heavy sigh and shook his head. "Miss Wells. I have dealt with a fair number of young ladies in my years with the city, but never have I encountered one with such insatiable curiosity, or an aptitude for discovering trouble. You placed yourself in a dangerous position, miss, if you don't mind my saying so."

Julian, sitting next to Concordia on the pew, patted her hand. "You see, my dear? You take too much upon yourself. It would have been more prudent to get help."

Concordia gave an unbecoming snort. "You would have me awaken Mr. Langdon, perhaps, in the wee morning hours because of an overturned lantern? Sometimes expediency must supersede prudence. Had I not investigated, who knows how much longer President Richter would have lay there, his whereabouts unknown."

She turned to the policeman. "Except for the parapet above the belfry, I climbed the entire staircase, lieutenant. I can tell you for certain that no one else was there."

"Anything else?" Capshaw asked.

Concordia thought. "Well–the knife. I only caught a glimpse of it before my lantern went out, but I believe I've seen it before."

"Where, Miss Wells?"

"In the store room of the tower. Amid the props. We were going to use it for our play, but I deemed it too sharp to be handled safely, so we used another dagger instead."

Capshaw made a *tsk, tsk* noise of disapproval under his breath. "How many daggers does one find lying about a ladies' college?" he asked of no one in particular. "Never mind. So, Miss Wells, you believe that the murderer retrieved the weapon from the store room first, in preparation for murdering President Richter?"

"How would I know that?" Concordia snapped, her mind reeling. That could not be the correct conclusion to draw, for Miss Crandall was the only other person besides Concordia who had known of the red-handled dagger. The idea that Charlotte Crandall could be mixed up in the murder was ludicrous.

"I could be wrong, Lieutenant. The knife I'm thinking of has a circle of rhinestones around the base of the handle."

Lieutenant Capshaw scribbled a note on his paper. "Very well, miss. Not to be indelicate, but there was a great deal of blood around the hilt, so I did not see any stones. I will take a close look at the knife at my next opportunity."

He beckoned to Nathaniel, who drew closer to the group. "Mr. Young, you say that you heard Miss Wells scream?"

"I did not know who it was at the time, but, yes, I was on the grounds, heading to Willow Cottage, when I heard a lady scream," Nathaniel said. "I ran to the tower, and had just reached it when Miss Wells burst through the door."

Capshaw was murmuring to himself as he wrote. "I'll never understand college people. Walking about in the rain; clambering out of windows; out in the wee hours, when decent people are in bed...."

He finished his notes, and looked intently at Young. "Why were you visiting Willow Cottage so late, Mr. Young? It seems a curious hour to pay a call upon a young lady."

Nathaniel flushed an angry red.

"I had an urgent family matter to discuss with Miss Wells," he answered curtly.

"And the nature of that 'urgent family matter', if I may ask, Mr. Young?"

"No, you may *not* ask, sir."

They were interrupted by sounds of a horse's hooves outside and the jingling of a harness.

"What on earth...?" Concordia said. Horses didn't typically come trotting up to the chapel.

Capshaw walked over to a window and looked out. "I will have more questions for you later. If you'll excuse me," he said, and abruptly left.

Puzzled, Concordia went to one of the side windows. Outside, a horse and dray had pulled up to the tower. The dean and lady principal were outside, talking with Lieutenant Capshaw. They looked expectantly at the tower door, as two uniformed men emerged, carrying a heavily-shrouded form. Concordia turned away.

"They've come for President Richter," was all she could manage to say.

Nathaniel and Julian stayed with Concordia throughout the morning, until Capshaw had no more need of her. Once at the door of Willow Cottage, however, Nathaniel sent the hovering Julian on his way.

"Thanks, Reynolds, dear fellow, but Concordia and I have family matters to discuss. I'm sure you have affairs of your own to attend to. Good-bye."

Concordia suppressed a laugh at the look on Julian's face as Nathaniel closed the door on him. "I wish I could manage that," she said. But she felt sorry for him, too. After all, Julian had only wanted to help.

"I don't doubt it," he answered. "He's an agreeable fellow, and certainly useful in an emergency, but he can be most persistent."

"What was Julian doing at the chapel to begin with? Was this last night?" she asked.

Nathaniel pursed his lips thoughtfully. "I did think it odd. After you fainted, I carried you to the closest shelter from the rain–the chapel–and when I went back out to get help, I found him standing there, just outside the door. He said that he was bunking in Sycamore House after the play, and noticed a light through his window. Apparently he was concerned that something was amiss."

"Hmm." Concordia didn't know what to think of that.

"Actually, it was providential that he was on hand," Nathaniel said. "I didn't want to leave you alone to get help, so he offered to stay with you, and also to keep an eye on the tower entrance, in case…" his voice trailed off. Would the murderer really have returned to the scene of the crime, as they did in the mystery stories?

Concordia suppressed a yawn.

Nathaniel steered her into the parlor and sat her down on the chaise. "I'm going to get your housekeeper to fix us some good strong tea before you fall asleep on your feet. We have to talk."

But the ever sharp-eyed Ruby had already put the kettle on the stove, and proceeded to fuss over them both until they were settled comfortably in the parlor with their tea. She left them to talk in private, closing the door quietly behind her.

Young drew a deep breath.

"It was unforgivable of me to have shocked you so, Concordia. I should never have blurted out the news of Henry's death."

"What happened at the Armstrong house, Nathaniel?" she asked, gripping her cup more tightly. Nothing he could tell her would shock her now.

"After we left you at the theater last night, I rode in the judge's carriage, as you know, with the doctor accompanying us, back to the Armstrong house," he began. "The house was in an uproar when we arrived. Henry had been found dead in the library. The staff was at sixes and sevens, unsure of what to do. It took quite a while to sort everything out."

"What caused his death?" she could barely whisper the question, but she had to know.

Nathaniel seemed lost in his own thoughts, and was staring into the fire. Finally, he spoke. "Henry Armstrong was suffering from a terrible guilt, leading an intolerable existence," he mused aloud. "I see that, now."

"You didn't answer my question," Concordia said firmly.

He looked at her. "I'm sorry." He paused. "Henry killed himself, Concordia. He used one of the judge's pistols and shot himself in the head."

The truth was brutal, but not a surprise. She blinked.

"Thank you, Nathaniel," she said simply. She stood. "I need to be alone now."

Concordia fell into bed soon after, fully clothed, and slept.

Chapter 51

Week 18, Instructor Calendar
June 1896

"You took a considerable chance, Miss Wells," Miss Hamilton said, as she and Concordia sat in the drawing room of DeLacey House later that day. News of President Richter's death had made its way through the college. With final examinations nearly finished, some students had already left campus for the summer, so the ripples of shock over the news would take some time to fully spread.

Why did everyone keep telling her that she was taking too many risks, Concordia thought wearily. And Miss Hamilton, of all people. "I didn't consider it dangerous at the time. Last night, it seemed as if we had solved many of the mysteries: the murder of Miss Lyman, the attack on Sophia, the intruder in Founder's Hall, the search of your rooms, and the prank in the chapel. And you achieved your objective of discovering those responsible for the missing funds."

"It is never wise to be overconfident, Miss Wells," Miss Hamilton said reprovingly. "I am still not convinced that the scheme was confined to President Richter and the bursar. In fact, there are still a great many things we do *not* know: who set the fire in Founder's Hall, or who searched the president's office and left a threatening note on his door. And now, of course, we have a murder to solve."

To Concordia, it seemed like pulling on an inconsequential thread, only to find other threads coming unraveled, until the fabric falls apart. For every answer they found, more questions sprang up to take their place. And now, Richter's murder superseded them all.

"*We* have a murder to solve? Should not the police perform that task?" Concordia asked skeptically.

"I don't think they would object to a little help," Miss Hamilton answered.

Concordia wasn't so sure. Lieutenant Capshaw seemed the prickly sort.

"I grant you that I will need to step carefully," Miss Hamilton admitted. "Lieutenant Capshaw would not allow me to look through Richter's belongings, but he did confirm my suspicion that Richter was preparing to flee. All he would tell me was that Richter's suitcases were packed, and he was carrying a significant amount of cash on his person. I feel as if we are very close to an answer."

"Did you tell him about Miss Lyman?" Concordia asked. "That he had most likely murdered her, and made it look like a suicide?"

The lady principal nodded. "Lieutenant Capshaw merely said he would share my theory with the detective originally in charge of investigating Miss Lyman's death. But he didn't seem terribly shocked by the news. Most likely, Richter's murder automatically calls into question *any* death on campus.

Or perhaps, given Capshaw's comments about "college people," the policeman assumes the college is a den of iniquity, Concordia thought. It had certainly seemed so lately.

Miss Hamilton continued. "I must admit that, professionally, it is quite embarrassing to have a murder happen right under one's nose. Especially when the victim was about to be charged with embezzlement and the possible murder of another! It reflects badly upon me, and other women detectives."

"But why *women* detectives particularly?" Concordia asked.

Miss Hamilton sighed. "We are under a special sort of scrutiny, by agencies and potential clients. Assignments such as this are rare. It was a bold move on my employer's part, and it took quite a bit of doing. Most of the time, women in my position are used as mere spies, because we can go places where men cannot. Once we have gathered the needed information, the men take over the case. They do not believe us capable."

"But it was not your fault that President Richter was murdered!" Concordia exclaimed. "You accomplished what you were sent here to do. You were not hired to guard Arthur Richter."

"Fair or not," Miss Hamilton said, her hazel eyes narrowing stubbornly, "the only way that I can redeem my professional reputation is to find his murderer."

"You shouldn't do it alone," Concordia said. "I want to help." She could not bear the thought of Miss Hamilton facing her employer in disgrace.

Miss Hamilton shook her head. "I think this is best left to me."

"Do you have any ideas about who is responsible?" Concordia asked, deciding not to argue the point for now.

"It seems reasonable to assume that whoever murdered President Richter was his partner in the embezzlement scheme, and killed him to prevent discovery. The murder could have been provoked by Richter's plans to leave," Miss Hamilton said.

"Yes, that makes sense," Concordia said. "And some of the earlier incidents, such as the fire and the president's office being searched, could be explained by the presence of another confederate, besides Miss Lyman. If that person suspected a ledger had been kept, he would have been desperate to obtain it, and searched Richter's office."

"But it does not explain the threatening note on Richter's office door," Miss Hamilton pointed out. "Why would such a man—or a woman, I suppose, is a possibility—searching in secrecy, put the world on notice that something was amiss? And why did he not take the money Richter was carrying before he fled the murder scene?"

"You have a point," Concordia said. "But there's something else I don't understand. Why would Miss Lyman have kept a ledger of this sort to begin with, something that would incriminate her and her cohorts if it were found? And how did you know about it?"

"I wasn't *sure* of its existence at first," Miss Hamilton admitted, "but in my experience, there are several reasons why embezzlers do this. Some assuage their consciences by convincing themselves that they will pay back the money, and so they need to keep a record of it. Others are collaborating with another party, and wish to protect themselves with a little blackmail. Still others concoct such an elaborate system of moving funds between accounts in order to avoid detection that they require a written record of it."

"Oh," was all Concordia could manage to say. What a sordid world Miss Hamilton navigated.

They were both quiet for a while.

"I believe I know a way to bring the murderer out of hiding," Miss Hamilton said. She looked at Concordia thoughtfully. "Perhaps, Miss Wells, you are right: I could use your help. I have to warn you, however; there is some risk."

Concordia, the image of President Richter's open, unseeing eyes ever-present in her mind, didn't hesitate. "What do you need me to do?"

Chapter 52

By the pricking of my thumbs,
Something wicked this way comes.
IV.i

Week 18, Instructor Calendar
June 1896

The dining hall of Sycamore House was full once again with administrators, staff, and trustees, but Concordia managed to secure a chair next to Margaret Banning before the meeting began. Despite the warmth of the evening, Miss Banning was dressed in her usual layers of petticoats, dress, shawls and cap, perched askew. Tufts of orange cat hair clung to the folds of her skirt.

"Good evening, Miss Banning."

The lady looked at Concordia over the rim of her glasses, keen eyes bright with interest. "Humph. I can't see what's good about it, young miss," was the tart response. "I hear you're the one who found the president. Is it true?"

Miss Banning certainly got right to the point. Her voice, as usual, was rather louder than it should be. Several heads turned their way.

"Yes, unfortunately, it was I who found him," Concordia answered. She looked around the room. David Bradley was here—she caught his eye and smiled to him—and Julian, who frowned when he noticed the interchange. Nathaniel, looking tired and subdued, was talking with several other trustees. Miss Bellini, pale-faced and quivering, had buried her hands in her crumpled shawl, and stared down at her lap.

Miss Banning gave her a poke and leaned closer conspiratorially, although her voice wasn't any lower. "So, do you think he was killed because of the ledger we found?"

Concordia made a frantic hushing gesture as even more heads turned their way. "Please, Miss Banning! The ledger is safely locked away in Miss Hamilton's desk. No one else is supposed to know about it!"

In her excitement, Concordia realized that her own voice had also gotten louder than it should. She flushed in embarrassment, and noticed that most of the eavesdroppers politely turned their heads away, trying not to appear to overlisten. Good.

"No need to get into a snit," Miss Banning shot back. "I can keep a confidence as well as anybody."

Soon Miss Hamilton and Dean Langdon arrived, each wearing somber black, although the dean's suit looked a trifle dusty.

Miss Hamilton cleared her throat as the room settled down. "We have contacted President Richter's family—he has a brother in New Hampshire—and they will make the funeral arrangements. There is a family plot in Nashua, apparently."

"Surely, we should do something here at the college to honor his memory?" Miss Pomeroy protested.

Miss Hamilton made a face that would pass for distress, though Concordia knew that the lady principal held President Richter in little esteem at this point.

"Naturally," Miss Hamilton answered. "A memorial service will be held in the college's chapel on Saturday. Dean Langdon is making those arrangements." She looked at Langdon, who nodded.

"I will share the details with everyone as soon as possible," he promised.

"On a related topic," Miss Hamilton said, "you are all no doubt aware that I am serving as the acting president of the college until a replacement is appointed. In that capacity, I must go into town tomorrow to fulfill certain obligations. I will return in the evening. Dean Langdon will be in charge during my absence."

It was ironic, Concordia thought, that President Richter, who staunchly believed women should have a limited role in public life, and who also believed that the purpose of a women's college was to prepare girls to better fulfill their domestic responsibilities, would by his death place a woman in charge of Hartford Women's College, if only temporarily.

The next day, as Concordia waited in Miss Hamilton's study, she thought back on the meeting. Miss Hamilton had handled herself well. She was, after all, navigating dangerous territory, with an ongoing police inquiry and the college's reputation at stake. The lady principal had been careful not to mention Miss Lyman's death, the ledger, or her suspicions of President Richter, and blithely ignored questions which strayed into that territory.

Concordia's thoughts were interrupted by a creaking floorboard outside Miss Hamilton's door. She quickly ducked behind the sofa. She heard the jingle of housekeeping keys and the swish of the maid's skirts, diminishing as the girl continued down the hall. Concordia breathed a sigh of relief.

"Miss Hamilton," Concordia whispered to the figure coming out from behind the window curtains, "I feel ridiculous."

Miss Hamilton crossed the room in quick, long strides, cracked open the door, peeked down the hallway, and closed it again. "It is quite necessary, Miss Wells, I assure you. You have played your part beautifully. You are quite sure that you and Miss Banning were overheard before the meeting started?"

Concordia nodded.

"Well, then, the guilty party will know I have the ledger here," she pointed to the desk drawer where she had secreted the book, "and now he believes that I am gone for the day. We haven't much longer to wait."

Miss Hamilton looked soberly at Concordia, putting a hand on her shoulder. "This may be difficult for you. Are you certain that you do not want to leave it to me?"

Concordia was puzzled. "I don't understand."

Miss Hamilton shook her head. "Never mind. Remember, wait for me to come out from hiding first. I want to give the culprit a chance to incriminate himself, so that there is no doubt. And under no circumstances," she added sternly, "are you to make a sound until I do, *no matter what you see or hear.*"

"Yes, Miss Hamilton," Concordia promised.

They didn't have long to wait.

When the floorboards in the hallway creaked again, Miss Hamilton and Concordia resumed their hiding places. Concordia's heart was hammering in her chest but she stayed absolutely still, taking only quiet, short, shallow breaths. After some scraping and fumbling noises, she heard the knob turn and the door swing open.

The silence seemed to scream in her ears, as she strained to hear the next sound, wondering what was happening. She could see nothing yet from her position. Was she really in the room with a murderer? What if he changed his mind, and left, and they could prove nothing?

She heard the faint creak of shoe leather, but the footsteps themselves were muffled by the Persian rug. From under the settee, she could see shoes now, and the bottom of trouser cuffs. A man, then. The shoes were carefully polished, and the cuffs had a beautiful crease to them. The sight gave Concordia a vague feeling of uneasiness.

She could hear the man opening and closing desk drawers now. After a pause, there was a wrenching sound, and the splintering of wood. He had broken open the locked drawer. Concordia realized that Miss Hamilton had deliberately made it more difficult to get to the ledger, in order to avoid arousing suspicion of the very trap that was set. Unfortunately, she had to sacrifice her antique desk to do so.

Concordia heard a sigh of satisfaction. He must have it by now. Her guess was confirmed when she heard the quick turning of pages.

When was Miss Hamilton going to come out and confront him? Hadn't it been long enough? The suspense was killing her.

And yet, that uneasy feeling persisted.

Finally, there was the *swish* of fabric, and then the steely voice of Miss Hamilton.

"Set that down, sir, if you please."

When Concordia jumped out of her hiding place, the first startling sight to meet her eyes was that of Miss Hamilton by the window—holding a *derringer*, of all things. She had never seen a woman wield a pistol before.

Then she saw the man.

For the second time in as many days, she felt she was going to faint. She gripped the back of the sofa for support.

"Julian!" she cried.

Chapter 53

What, can the devil speak true?
I.iii

Week 18, Instructor Calendar
June 1896

Julian Reynolds stared back at Concordia in dismay. No one spoke for a moment. Then he broke the silence.

"Concordia, please, let me explain," he pleaded.

Miss Hamilton, still holding the derringer, gestured to a nearby chair. "Be seated, Mr. Reynolds. We have much to discuss before the police arrive."

At the mention of "police," Julian paled. He sank into the chair, and put his head in his hands.

Miss Hamilton looked at Concordia, who was struggling for composure. "I told you this would be difficult," she said softly. "Step into the hall if you please, Miss Wells. The housekeeper should be awaiting our instructions."

As Concordia opened the door to the hallway, she heard Julian say, "This was all a trap?"

Just as Miss Hamilton had said, the housekeeper was standing at the end of the hallway, waiting. She looked expectantly as Concordia approached.

"Shall I git the policeman now, miss, like Miss Ham'lton said ta do?" she asked.

"Yes," Concordia said, "and hurry, please." She didn't want to spend any more time with the man than was necessary, but she had some questions. She went back into Miss Hamilton's room.

"Ah, Miss Wells," Miss Hamilton said as Concordia returned. She was now seated comfortably in an armchair across from Julian Reynolds, ledger and pistol resting in her lap. "Do sit down."

Except for the weapon, the scene looked oddly like a cozy fireside chat, Concordia thought, choosing a seat close to Miss Hamilton. That lady was leaning back in her chair, her expression strangely serene. Julian's composure had returned, Concordia could see, although his handsome face was a guarded mask and he sat warily. His gaze rested on the gun in Miss Hamilton's lap.

"Is that really necessary, Miss Hamilton?" he protested. "You treat me as a common criminal. You have nothing to fear from me."

"Oh?" Miss Hamilton said contemptuously. "I have nothing to fear from President Richter's murderer? What kind of fool do you take me for, Mr. Reynolds?"

Reynolds faltered, and looked confused. "You think that I–*I* had something to do with Arthur's death? That's absurd! Why on earth would I do such a thing?"

"Why indeed?" Miss Hamilton said. She opened the ledger. "The entries here, and your actions today," she gestured to the broken desk drawer, "reveal your complicity with President Richter and Miss Lyman in misappropriating college funds. You knew of the existence of this ledger, and were desperate to find it, and destroy it. You knew suspicion was centering upon the president, and that he planned to flee and leave you to shoulder the blame. You had sufficient motive to kill him: self-preservation, revenge, perhaps both."

Concordia listened in silence. Julian shook his head vehemently.

"No, I did *not*! I admit that I wanted to examine the ledger, and discover what was in there that might implicate me. But that is all."

"Oh, there is a great deal in here that implicates you. You are the owner of the Signal Printing Company, are you not?" Miss Hamilton asked, looking up from the ledger.

Concordia started. *The Signal Printing Company.* That name had been stamped on the back of Reynolds' photograph albums.

Julian shifted uneasily.

"Of course, you are not *named* as the owner," Miss Hamilton continued, "there were several trails of orphaned companies I had to follow before I found your name. Over the past two years, Bursar Lyman and President Richter authorized rather sizeable payments from college accounts to Signal Printing."

Julian turned to Concordia and gave her a pleading look. "It was only temporary, I assure you, Concordia. I was going to pay it back, as soon as the business revived."

Concordia remembered the neglected back rooms of Julian's house, filled with worn furnishings and cold hearths; the immigrant maid, speaking little English, inexperienced in basic parlor maid duties; the costly photography hobby; Julian Reynolds' impeccable wardrobe. It was an expensive pretense to maintain. She understood it now, but wondered at how she could have mistaken the façade for the man.

Miss Hamilton broke the silence. "But you would *not* have been able to pay it all back, would you, Mr. Reynolds. Not with Arthur Richter and Ruth Lyman also taking a share of the money."

Julian shrugged. "Perhaps. But the funds were only divided between Arthur and myself."

Miss Hamilton raised an eyebrow. "Miss Lyman helped you steal, but kept none of it herself? But why? You are sure of this?"

"Arthur told me himself. He had deliberately hired her for the bursar position because he knew he could compel her to adjust the books for him. She had done it once before, at another school, without getting caught. Arthur found out, somehow. He threatened to ruin her if she didn't comply. She didn't want to. Arthur laughed at her assertion that she was reformed. Once a criminal, always a criminal, at heart. Perhaps she was assuaging her conscience by refusing to touch the money? She tried to thwart us at every turn, I do know that."

How horrid, Concordia thought. Poor Miss Lyman.

"Do you know why Arthur did it?" Miss Hamilton asked.

"He lost a great deal of money in the market failure of '93—more than is widely known. He was planning to retire soon. I had the impression that he was giving part of his share to someone else, too, but he would never confirm that."

"But was this person aware of the scheme?" Miss Hamilton asked.

Julian grimaced. "I had hoped he wouldn't be so foolish, but it concerned me greatly."

"Do you know why Richter killed Miss Lyman?" Miss Hamilton asked, changing the subject.

Julian started. "She did not kill herself?"

"No. I am convinced Richter killed her elsewhere—perhaps by means of that head wound the coroner noticed—and dumped her body, weighted down, in the pond. But the weight broke away, and that's why she was found sooner than he had planned. You knew nothing of this?"

Julian shook his head vehemently. "Arthur told me that she had grown despondent, and had taken her own life because she couldn't deal with the guilt."

"Even if that were the case, Mr. Reynolds, you would still bear responsibility for her death," Miss Hamilton said sternly.

"But it makes no sense," he protested. "Why would Arthur have murdered her? The scheme was working so well. He would not have wanted to jeopardize it by killing her."

That made no sense of Concordia, either. But other mysteries were becoming clearer to her now, as she looked at Julian. "You targeted Miss Hamilton—with the knife in the doll, and the fire in her office. Why?"

Miss Hamilton raised an eyebrow in silent appreciation.

Julian flushed. "I believe I have said enough," he said curtly.

Concordia, in a cold fury, stood up, leaning over him. "Nine of us were trapped in that burning building. It is only by the grace of Providence that we escaped. You, sir, are despicable." She started toward the door.

"Concordia, no, please!" Julian cried, face growing pale. "I will—I will tell you—everything."

Concordia looked at him for a long moment, then resumed her seat.

Reynolds continued. "After the trustee meeting in January, I happened to overhear a conversation, hinting that a private inquiry agent was placed at the school, to discover who was behind the money losses. It did not take me long to realize who that would be—Miss Hamilton, of course." Despite his current circumstances, Julian Reynolds looked pleased with himself.

Miss Hamilton gave him a steely look. "So the knife, placed in my likeness after the students had orchestrated their prank, was intended to frighten me away from my investigation? How did you know what the girls were planning?"

Reynolds snorted. "Really, Miss Hamilton, those young ladies fall all over themselves to get my attention. It was a trifling matter to discover what they were up to."

You ladies are not very good at keeping secrets, Julian had once told her.

Concordia felt her stomach clench at the arrogance of the man, even as he was caught *in flagrante delicto.* She gritted her teeth.

"But you did not frighten easily," Reynolds continued, "so I had no time to waste. I knew Miss Lyman kept a ledger—the transactions were too complex to keep track of otherwise. But I was concerned about how incriminating it could be. After her death—remember, I thought she committed suicide—I worried that she intended to expose us through a suicide note and the ledger, to be found afterward. So after Miss Lyman's death I went to Arthur, who assured me that the book was safely hidden. But I was suspicious. Each time I asked he refused to produce it."

"I decided to take matters into my own hands," Reynolds continued. "I planned to begin my search for the ledger in Arthur's office, naturally. But I found that the room had already been rather sloppily rummaged through"–this said with a condescending look in Miss Hamilton's direction–"so I assumed that *you* had it, Miss Hamilton. I would think, as a professional, you would be more discreet in your methods. But perhaps you lack the skill and experience a *man* would have."

Concordia gave Miss Hamilton a puzzled look, but neither of them volunteered the fact that Miss Hamilton had already searched both the bursar's office and President Richter's office months before. Who then, had searched Richter's office in February, when Reynolds had found it in disarray?

"Did you put the threatening note on the door?" Concordia asked.

Julian shook his head, and plucked an invisible speck of lint from his trousers. "There was no note on the door until later–when we all discovered it there. I confess to being quite confused about that."

"Perhaps the president did it himself, to deflect suspicion?" Concordia suggested, looking over at the lady principal.

Miss Hamilton shrugged. "Perhaps." She turned to Julian.

"You searched my office next," Miss Hamilton prompted, "on the day of the basketball game."

Concordia listened in silence. It made sense now: the sound she and Miss Landry had heard within the lady principal's office. It must have been Julian knocking the book to the floor. And her sense that there was something out of place that she could not identify. It was a *smell* that did not belong there. Of course–his cologne. Why hadn't she realized it before?

Julian nodded. "It seemed an ideal time to search, when everyone else was occupied. Or so I assumed."

"You must have stood just behind the door when I looked through the transom," Concordia interjected. "I couldn't see you at all."

"You nearly had me there," Julian admitted.

"Why did you set fire to my office?" Miss Hamilton demanded.

Reynolds lips trembled, and he looked at Concordia, now staring down at her clenched hands. "I had no idea you would be trapped. You must believe me. I would never do anything to harm you. Concordia, I swear!"

Still, Concordia would not look at him.

"You did not answer my question, Mr. Reynolds," Miss Hamilton said.

Julian hesitated. "I had no more time to search. My prolonged absence at the basketball game would have been noticed. I set the fire so that, if the ledger was indeed in the office and I missed it, it would be destroyed. I also wanted to throw suspicion upon the college's mysterious mischief-maker."

Down below, they heard the bang of the front door.

Miss Hamilton stood. "The police have arrived for you, Mr. Reynolds."

Chapter 54

The green fields whizzed by in a blur, air rushing over her face and through her hair. Concordia pedaled her bicycle, past the grassy hills, over the old sheep tracks, beyond the college grounds, beyond people, as hard and as fast as she could endure. The sun was out with the full force of late afternoon, and her blouse was soon damp and clinging to her back.

Finally, exhausted, she stopped, lay down in the grass, and wept.

She was much calmer when David found her, at the top of Rook's Hill, watching the sun stretch lingering rays of gold and crimson across the campus grounds below.

He sat down beside her, careless of the damp grass staining his trousers. "The news has spread throughout the campus—and beyond it now, I'm sure—about Reynolds. I came to find you when I heard. I thought you might be here. Are you all right, Concordia?"

She glanced up at him with a wan smile. "I will be." She shook her head. "I was so wrong about him. How can I trust my own judgment anymore?"

David put an arm around her shoulders. "He fooled us all. It was impossible for you to have known."

"It's still confusing. I accept that he was responsible for a great deal of wrongdoing—the doll, the fire, the stolen money—looking back now, it all makes sense, the little things that I didn't understand at the time. But the murder? I'm not sure what to think."

Concordia looked at him steadily. "And I am tired of secrets, David."

He knew what she meant. "You want me to explain why I was in that—questionable establishment."

"Yes. And why you visited Sophia Adams, instead of going to Boston, and kept it from me."

"You know about that, too?" David shook his head. "They are each connected to the other, actually."

Concordia looked skeptical.

"No, truly," he protested. He was silent for a moment.

"Did you know I have a younger brother, Lawrence? I have never talked with you about him, for good reason."

Concordia started. *Lawrence Bradley*. Sophia had mentioned that name.

"Lawrence has been spoiled his entire life," David went on. "He never had to work for anything. He fell into dissipated habits, along with other such men he called his friends. Any entertainment and stimulation would do: gambling, drinking, music halls—and—and brothels."

Concordia began to see. "So when Julian saw you at that house—"

"—it must have been the day I finally found Lawrence and went to get him," David finished. "He had been missing for a week. I was planning to seek him out among some of his favorite haunts in Boston, when I discovered that he was still here in Hartford. *He* was the man who created the disruption at the rally, Concordia. I learned about it the day after the attack on Sophia."

Concordia looked at David in surprise. "The man at the rally is your *brother*?"

David nodded. "He has little memory of the time. That's not surprising, as he was still drunk when I found him. If Reynolds had watched the house for just a while longer, he would have seen me dragging him out."

"But why would your brother go to the rally in the first place? And how is Sophia connected—no wait, I remember—she *recognized* him. They know each other, don't they?"

David grimaced. "Miss Adams and my brother go back a long way. They were childhood friends. He is a few years older than she, and she idolized him like a big brother. He let her follow him around. I ran with a different crowd, so I didn't really know her. They drifted apart, of course, as they grew older, but she must have learned of Lawrence's dissolute behavior. A few weeks before the rally, she took it upon herself to visit him in his rooms. Unaccompanied. To give him a good talking-to, no doubt. She's a very headstrong young lady."

Concordia nodded. "That is Sophia's way."

David sighed. "Lawrence was inebriated, and angry, when she called on him. He was abominable to her. Shouted terrible things, called her a meddling spinster, even threatened violence, before she finally left. In a fit of remorse, he told me about it, at least what he could remember of it."

"So why…?"

"Don't you see, Concordia? When you and I found Miss Adams that morning, Lawrence had already been missing for days. He had threatened her with violence once already, and then I learned that he had disrupted the rally as she was standing upon the stage. I have known him to hold grudges and become uncontrollably angry while intoxicated. I thought the worst. I felt guilty for…not keeping a better watch over him." He faltered, and fell silent.

"You decided to visit her in the infirmary," Concordia prompted.

"Yes. I'm not even sure why, myself. Perhaps to apologize for Lawrence, even if she could not hear me? It seems absurd, I know."

He continued. "You were not the only person to notice my visit. The night of the ball, Miss Hamilton practically interrogated me. It was difficult to evade her questions."

So that was the conversation Concordia had interrupted.

David gave a shaky laugh. "I was actually *glad* to learn that Lawrence was at that–establishment–the entire time in question. It was a relief, at least, to know that he could not have attacked Sophia."

Concordia was quiet for a while. Finally she spoke. "What will happen to him?"

"Our parents have decided that it is best to get him away from the bad influence of his friends. They are sending him on a South American tour. He sails with my uncle next week."

Concordia looked down at the peaceful-looking campus below, and shook her head. "That's a heavy burden to carry. At least you won't be responsible for him now."

David took her hand in his. "Then you *do* believe me, Concordia? I know that others have shaken your trust, but I promise you that I will not."

"Yes. I believe you," she answered absently. His words had brought her thoughts back to Julian.

He looked worried. "Are you sure? You don't sound convinced."

She focused steadily on the horizon. The sun was sinking lower, and a cool breeze was beginning to dry her damp blouse. It would be dark soon.

"I'm thinking again about President Richter's murder. The more I consider it, the harder it is to believe Julian killed him."

"I know you have feelings for Reynolds, Concordia, but–"

"No, it's not sentimentality," she interrupted. "There are some pieces to this which do not make sense. Why lure President Richter to the tower, for instance, and kill him there? And, if Julian was the murderer, why would he return that night? Wouldn't he want to be as far from the place as possible? And why use a knife? It's a very messy way to commit the deed, and Julian is meticulous in the extreme. Would he not have chosen a cleaner way to do it?"

David was silent for a while. "I'm beginning to see your point. But that would mean that we still have a murderer among us."

Concordia shivered. "That's exactly what it means."

She lay awake long into the night, listening to a chorus of tree frogs in the distance, one question uppermost in her mind.

Who murdered Arthur Richter?

She turned over restlessly, tugging at her nightgown, which was hopelessly bunched and twisted. There had been so much death this year. First Ruth Lyman, then Mary, and Henry, and now President Richter. They had nearly lost Sophia as well. All the ugly attributes of human nature—lust, greed, fear, bitterness, self-preservation at the expense of others—each of these had been laid bare.

And yet... the brighter side of humanity had revealed itself to her this year, too. She had seen courage: in her students, as they faced being trapped in the fire; in Sophia, playing her part on the stage in front of her would-be murderer; in Miss Hamilton, doing what Concordia had seen no other woman do, staring down a criminal over the barrel of a pistol. Concordia had also seen loyalty and compassion: in David, in Ruby, in Miss Bellini, in Nathaniel. And yes, even her mother has shown her softer side, she thought, recalling the day of the fire.

Amidst it all, people laughed, they loved, they danced....

What a set of contradictions we are, she thought. Miss Banning's words about Macbeth drifted back to her: *He is human, like the rest of us. No matter how kind, well-intentioned, or amiable we may be, we are each equally capable of malice, under the right circumstances.*

What were the "right circumstances" to provoke a murder? The threat to one's safety, perhaps? Had Arthur Richter threatened anyone with physical violence? Perhaps he had posed a different sort of threat. Who else besides Julian, Richter's co-conspirator, would have felt threatened by him?

Or was he murdered for the sake of vengeance? But that didn't narrow the field. Had he not wronged them all?

She fell asleep, her dreams alternating between couples, waltzing along ballroom floors, and murderers, knives held aloft, waiting in the shadows.

Chapter 55

Thou sure and firm-set earth
Hear not my steps, which way they walk, for fear
Thy very stones prate of my whereabouts.

II.i

Week 18, Instructor Calendar
June 1896

Concordia went through the next day in a state of distraction. She was aware of saying goodbye to students, some of them facing a several-days-long train ride home, and of helping Ruby air out mattresses and beat rugs, but she felt as if she were sleep-walking through most of it.

The last task of the afternoon jolted her out of her reverie. She had to brace herself to approach the tower again, Miss Crandall and Miss Pomeroy in tow, as they packed away the last boxes of stage props in the storage room.

"I'm fine, really," Concordia insisted, after catching the two exchanging anxious glances. "Let's get this finished before we lose the light."

They sorted the items into orderly piles, to make the task easier next year. Concordia stiffened when she pulled out the black-handled dagger.

"I'll put that away, Miss Wells," Charlotte Crandall quickly offered. Concordia passed it over.

"Where is that other dagger you were describing, Miss Crandall?" Miss Pomeroy asked. "I'd like to take a look at it."

Concordia stared at Miss Pomeroy in disbelief. How could she *not* know that was the weapon Richter had been killed with?

News of it had circulated widely enough. Gertrude Pomeroy needed to get her nose out of her books.

But the tactless question made one thing clear to Concordia. *We should have been paying more attention to the dagger.*

With a sinking feeling at the pit of her stomach, she realized she knew who the murderer was. And that she had to do something about it.

After supper, Concordia sought out the messenger boy, who was settled under a tree, cheerfully tucking into the last of his meal. As she approached, he wiped his mouth with the back of his hand and awkwardly brushed crumbs from a particularly grubby pair of knee pants.

"Ev'nin, miss."

"Good evening, Sam," Concordia said. "I have an errand for you." She held out two envelopes. "Can you deliver these for me? After you've finished, of course," she added politely.

The boy glanced down at the envelopes. "But, miss, the lady princ'pl i'nt back yet from town."

"Oh!" Concordia said, startled. "Do you know when she is expected?"

"Not sure, but I 'spect it'll be soon. I heard one of the teachers say she's s'posed to be back already." Sam gulped the rest of his sandwich.

"I suppose you will have to leave it for her at DeLacey House then, but be sure to deliver the other letter personally. It's quite important. And you needn't say who it's from; it's a... surprise." She gave the boy a coin.

He grinned. "Right away, miss."

As the evening hours went by, Concordia waited in her quarters, pacing restlessly between the mantel clock at one end and the French doors at the other. She had tried to read, but couldn't focus upon the words. Instead, she reviewed the pieces of the puzzle, looking for contradictions or flaws in her thinking. Most of it fit together. But there were some things that she didn't understand, and these gaps troubled her. What if she were wrong?

Concordia started when the clock sounded its tinny chime in the quiet of the cottage. Where was Miss Hamilton? She should have read the note and been here by now. Concordia felt the first stirrings of doubt. Did she really consider herself capable of setting a trap for a murderer? Was this the consequence of spending too much time in the company of a detective, like the contagion one risks in a measles ward?

But Concordia knew that Miss Hamilton was wrong about Julian murdering Arthur Richter. The real culprit was still free. This was the only way she could think to catch the killer. She was hoping she didn't have to do so alone.

She looked at her watch. Ten-thirty. She couldn't wait any longer. With a last wistful look at the safety of her room, Concordia grabbed her lantern and slipped out of the cottage into the foggy darkness.

The night air felt clammy as she hurried to the bell tower. Once she was at the massive iron-hinged oak door, Concordia struck a match, carefully shielding the flame, and lit her lantern. She slipped inside.

The humidity of the outside air was magnified ten-fold within the dank stairwell. Concordia was loath to touch the dripping stones. She wished again that Miss Hamilton were here, even to dissuade her from carrying out her plan.

Concordia went all the way to the top this time. She crouched behind the parapet and looked out. The fog was lifting, and the moon cast a clear light across the grounds.

No one coming yet. But she stayed where she was, watching.

After what seemed an agony of waiting, she saw a figure hurrying across the quadrangle. Her breath caught. Perhaps it was Miss Hamilton, after all?

But no—the form did not have Miss Hamilton's long strides. Concordia's heart sank. She descended the flight of stairs to the belfry, tucked herself behind a buttress, shuttered her lantern, and waited.

She heard the creak of the door below, and then footsteps, cautiously, softly, up and up. The figure stopped at the belfry and approached–closer, closer.

In a swift movement, Concordia stepped out, directing the full light of her lantern upon the figure. It was, indeed, the person she had been waiting for.

"Hello, Lucia," Concordia said.

Chapter 56

We fail?
But screw your courage to the sticking place
And we'll not fail.

I.vii

Week 18, Instructor Calendar
June 1896

Lucia Bellini shaded her eyes and swung her own lamp in Concordia's direction. She was wearing a dark dress, bare of ornamentation. Her olive complexion was sallow in the lamplight, and her black hair was pulled back tightly at the nape of her neck. Concordia was surprised to see that her right hand was clumsily bandaged. Miss Bellini's lantern quavered, throwing bobbing shadows about the room.

"Concordia?" she answered tentatively. "It is *you*?" Her other hand curled around the slip of paper that Concordia had sent earlier.

The words on the paper, so carefully composed, were etched in Concordia's mind: *I know you were responsible. Come to the belfry at eleven tonight. We must talk.*

"Yes, Lucia, I figured it out," Concordia said, trying to keep her own voice steady. "*You* killed Arthur Richter."

Miss Bellini sagged against the wall and Concordia stepped forward to help her.

"*No!*" She said, dark eyes blazing, and groped for the cross beam to sit upon.

Concordia retreated, but said, gently, "You have been under a great deal of strain, more than any woman should have to bear. Won't you tell me about it?"

Miss Bellini gave a hollow laugh. "Signorina Wells, I am merely responding to a—what do you say?—ah, yes, *cryptic*—note, anonymously written. Curiosity would be natural, would it not? Especially when I am being accused of something, no?"

The woman had nerves of steel. This wasn't going well, Concordia thought. What could she say to get Miss Bellini to tell the truth? She had hoped that confronting her in the tower, beside the very spot Richter died, would be enough. Obviously Concordia's knowledge of criminal behavior was woefully lacking.

Lucia Bellini flushed with triumph. "See? This is absurd. How could *I*—and *why* would I—murder that poor man? Surely a *pazzo*—madman—has done this."

Concordia nodded thoughtfully. "I do think that President Richter's killer was quite desperate—perhaps unstable. Shall I tell you what I think happened?"

Miss Bellini gave a theatrical sigh. "If you insist, *signorina*."

"Very well. Call it intuition, if you will, but there have been little hints—glances, gestures, the way you and Arthur Richter danced together—that I did not realize the meaning of at the time. But later, after some reflection, it all made sense. The two of you were much closer than merely two professionals working together, weren't you? You were… lovers. And then something must have happened. During the ball? Or after? Your entire demeanor changed. When I came to return your dress, you were angry, vengeful, and determined to act. How had you been betrayed, Lucia? What had he done?"

But Miss Bellini shook her head, her eyes gleaming with unshed tears.

"I think I know, at least some of it," Concordia went on. "Julian Reynolds—who is now in police custody for conspiring with Richter and the bursar to steal college funds—said there was someone else the president was giving money to, although he did not know who. It was *you*, Lucia, wasn't it? Your family trouble back in Italy—money trouble? But then he got frightened, and refused to give you more."

There was one person who could have helped me—who promised to help me—but it was all empty words. He will not. Miss Bellini's tormented words came back to Concordia.

Miss Bellini's eyes flashed with the old anger.

Concordia waited for her to speak, but when she stayed silent, continued. "He was worried about being caught. Miss Lyman's death, with a successor as bursar, would make it impossible to steal more."

Impossible to steal more. The methodical, rational college president would never have killed Miss Lyman. Her death essentially cut off his funds. Unless... Concordia sucked in her breath.

"Miss Lyman threatened to turn herself in, didn't she?" Concordia asked. "Along with Richter and Reynolds. She was tired of being blackmailed, and forced to steal from the college she loved."

Miss Bellini tossed her head, dark eyes glittering in the light. "You are guessing, are you not? You have no proof we learned what she was planning."

"Ah, I see. You *discovered* her plan. How? Did you catch her in the act of writing her confession? Or did she confide in you, not knowing that you and Richter were lovers? Did you bash her over the head when her back was turned, this woman who sought you out for help? Did you then run to Richter to clean up your mess?"

Lucia Bellini's face contorted in hatred, although she said nothing. But Concordia was sure she was right. She could picture Miss Bellini, in a panic, hitting the woman, leaving her where she lay, and seeking out Richter for rescue. Then Richter would have had to improvise, carrying the body to the pond in the middle of the night, in the process striking his forehead and losing his shoe in the dark, and getting laryngitis from exposure to the icy pond. Discarding the single shoe, which later made its way into the school's collection of props.

"I don't think proof will be a problem. A ledger has been discovered," Concordia said. "Miss Lyman—already under duress to misappropriate college funds—made careful entries in it, implicating Richter and Reynolds. I'm sure the police will be able to prove your complicity, given time." That was a guess, but Concordia had faith in Capshaw's abilities.

"But it's no wonder Richter had to stop taking money," Concordia continued. "There were too many incidents, too much police presence at the college. Questions were being asked. Someone had been searching his office. You. You also left the threatening note on his door, to shift the blame toward the student pranksters. Were you looking for the ledger when you searched the president's office?"

Lucia Bellini hissed through gritted teeth. "Yes! I searched his office. Arthur had told me he had Miss Lyman's ledger, safe. But he no longer trusted me; he would not tell me where it was hidden. I wanted to go through the book, work out how it was done. All was not lost! Could we not have continued with the plan?"

She stood up, agitated, and began to pace in front of Concordia. "But—ah!—I found *nothing*. I was... *arrabiata*—angry! I tore the room apart. And then, someone was coming, so I left quickly. I did not see who it was. Afterward I thought, what might Arthur do if someone threatened him? Perhaps I could gain control that way. I went back and put the note on the door."

"Did that work?" Concordia asked. Richter had probably suspected, at first, that the note was Julian's, which would have put them at each others' throats for a time.

Miss Bellini grimaced. "For a little while, yes. He looked to me for support, said he admired my strength. He said he would help me, no matter what. *Bah! Men!* Never can they keep their promises."

"What happened to change his mind?"

"At the dance—oh, I was so happy then!—later that night, afterward, he was worried, distracted. Something about

Margaret Banning's return. He kept talking about her. But he was making no sense. He said he did not dare take more from the college. It was over."

Concordia remembered the dance, and Miss Banning's announcement of her return. No doubt the news had unnerved Richter. His hiding place for the ledger—Miss Banning's office—was no longer secure. He knew that, if he couldn't get to the ledger first, Miss Banning was bound to find it. Which she had.

"Why did you kill him, Lucia? Was it merely for spite, because you could no longer get what you wanted? Or did you worry that he would reveal that *you* killed Miss Lyman, and lay the blame upon you for everything?" Concordia was reluctant to be deliberately cruel, but she needed to keep Miss Bellini talking.

Where was Miss Hamilton?

The barb had its intended effect. Miss Bellini stepped closer, face contorted, releasing a stream of foreign invectives that Concordia was glad she didn't understand. She resisted the urge to shrink back.

"*You,*" Miss Bellini pointed a finger accusingly at Concordia, "stand there and judge *me*? You understand *nothing*. It was an accident. I did not mean…to kill her. Arthur did not blame me for that."

"So why kill him?" Concordia asked. There was something here she was missing, something crucial. But what? She had to be careful not to provoke Miss Bellini beyond endurance. Help was too far away.

But Lucia Bellini shook her head stubbornly, glaring at her.

Concordia frantically thought back to what she knew of the woman's personal life. It was precious little. The day she had returned Miss Bellini's gown stood out in her mind, certainly. Lucia had been distraught, talking almost to herself.

I will act. He must know.

Know what?

The missing piece came to her at last. Concordia looked intently at Miss Bellini.

"Lucia, you are…with child, are you not? Arthur's child."

Miss Bellini heaved a deep sigh, as if a burden had been eased from her shoulders. Concordia waited. Night creatures rustled between the beams.

"Yes, it is time, perhaps," Miss Bellini said. She looked at Concordia. "And we are friends, yes? I can tell *you*."

"Tell me," Concordia said.

"You were right about us. I loved him," she said. "Even when he failed me, I loved him still. By the time of the dance, I knew that I was carrying his child, but to tell him—I was afraid. If I did nothing, I would be ruined, my career gone."

"So you had to act," Concordia prompted.

Miss Bellini nodded. "If he would marry me, would that not solve the problem? We could move away from here, start at another college, where the gossip could not reach. I would be a good wife to him. And I could bring my mother and aunt here to live with us, and *they* would have a better life."

"So you arranged to meet him here. Why here, in the tower?" Concordia had been puzzled by this.

Miss Bellini smiled. "It was here that Arthur first kissed me. It seemed—romantic. Perhaps it would soften his feelings, and remind him of the old days, before the worry about money."

"But it didn't happen that way," Concordia guessed.

Miss Bellini's smile was gone. Her face hardened. "No. I didn't recognize him. He was cruel. Hateful things he said to me, when I told him about *his* child! Laughed in my face, said it was my own fault. I was nothing but trouble, damaged goods, and the product of all that he hated about educated women. Can you imagine that? He, president of a women's college, hating educated women?"

She drew a ragged breath. "A respectable wife would never carry on the way I do, he tells me. Headstrong. Willful. Like a man. A *man*, he says!" She began to weep.

"What happened then, Lucia?" Concordia asked, a spasm of pity tugging at her.

"I stabbed him," Miss Bellini answered fiercely.

"With the knife from the store room downstairs," Concordia said, feeling a little sick at the memory of Richter's lifeless body. She struggled to maintain her composure. She needed to stall for time, not faint dead away.

"You found out about the dagger from Miss Crandall," Concordia said, remembering Miss Pomeroy's question: *Where is that other dagger you were describing, Miss Crandall?* Miss Bellini had been part of the conversation with Charlotte Crandall and Miss Pomeroy. Concordia had seen the three of them together by the fountain, looking over a piece of paper.

"Yes." Miss Bellini gave a puzzled shrug. "She thought it belonged to Miss Pomeroy or me–she even drew a sketch of it. Why would she care? I do not know."

Concordia didn't understand that, either, but she ignored it for the time being. She gestured to Miss Bellini's bandage. "How did you injure yourself?"

Lucia Bellini looked at her hand. "The knife, it was very sharp. Arthur tried to get it away from me, and it slipped in my hand. I managed to pick it up again before he lunged at me. We both fell, and the knife–" she faltered, "was thrust into his chest."

"You had your shawl in your hands during the recent meeting. You needed to hide your injury," Concordia said, almost to herself. Miss Bellini nodded.

"But I don't understand why you took the knife with you in the first place," Concordia continued. Hardly an act to inspire romantic feeling.

Lucia Bellini gave Concordia an anguished look. "I knew, before he came. For Arthur and me, it would either be a new beginning for us, or an end. An end of *my* choosing."

She shrugged in resignation. "It hardly matters, now. That night, I lost the child. Now I have nothing of Arthur left."

And then she ran for the stairs.

Concordia, taken by surprise, was slower to respond. "Lucia!" she called after her. She could hear her on the steps–going up. Why *up*, if she was trying to escape?

Oh no.

Concordia sprinted up the stairs, breath heaving in gasps, desperate to catch up.

"Lucia! No!"

She heard a fading cry as she reached the uppermost stair. Concordia threw herself against the wall of the parapet, and looked down.

From the top of the tower, she stared down in horror at the broken shape illumined by a cold, indifferent moon. Arms, legs, head–all sprawled at impossible angles, like a ragdoll flung to the ground when a child tires of it. Concordia's stomach lurched as the ground tilted and her head reeled.

The heavy stone balustrade felt rough under her hands, and she gripped it like a lifeline. *She should go for help.* But she couldn't force her legs to move.

Taking deep breaths, Concordia steeled herself to look down again, desperate for an impossible sign of life.

There was nothing. Lucia Bellini was dead.

Epilogue

Tomorrow, and tomorrow, and tomorrow...
V.v

Summer Recess
June 1896

A warm breeze fluttered the curtains of the French doors in the lady principal's study, thrown open to reduce the stuffiness. Miss Hamilton quickly anchored the skittering papers, and turned back to her packing.

"Where will you go next, Miss Hamilton?" Concordia asked, as she crouched beside a low shelf, putting books in a box.

"I'll stay with my sister in Chicago, until the agency has another assignment for me."

Which no doubt would be soon, as Miss Hamilton was back in her employer's good graces. She had, in fact, been awarded a bonus for successfully solving the murders of both Arthur Richter and Ruth Lyman. Despite the lady principal's objections, Concordia had insisted that Miss Hamilton take sole credit.

"Wouldn't the board of trustees offer to have you remain as our lady principal if you ask them?" Concordia could not imagine them refusing her anything, now.

Miss Hamilton smiled. "They already asked me to stay."

"Oh." Concordia, confused, turned back to the box.

"I considered it," Miss Hamilton said. "Heaven knows the college has lost an extraordinary number of staff already. It will be a challenge to replace three trustees, a dean, bursar, lady principal, mathematics teacher, and history teacher–Miss

Banning tells me that she has *absolutely* decided to retire–all at once."

Concordia sighed. It would, indeed. The campus felt different already, now that summer was upon them and Dean Langdon had taken over as the college's president.

"However," Miss Hamilton went on, "the college will be the better for the changes, and it is time for me to move on." She looked closely at Concordia. "I assume *your* decision is final as well?"

Concordia had been astonished when the Pinkerton Agency offered her employment. "We are impressed by your contributions to the investigation, as detailed in Miss Hamilton's reports. Another lady operative of your talents would be of value to us," the letter had said. Apparently, Miss Hamilton had *not* been reticent about Concordia's role.

Thank heaven her mother would never learn of it.

"Oh, yes," Concordia answered firmly. "I am a teacher, *not* a private detective. I have not the heart for that sort of work." To elucidate a mystery was one thing, but to deal with the consequences once the tangle had unraveled itself was quite another.

Lieutenant Capshaw had questioned Concordia exhaustively after Miss Bellini's death: when did she realize that Miss Bellini had murdered President Richter? What about the murder of the bursar–when did she know that Miss Bellini was responsible for that? How had she come to that conclusion? Why did she not contact the police with her suspicions, or at least wait for Miss Hamilton's return, instead of confronting her herself? Capshaw had looked particularly disapproving when he asked that last question.

Concordia had tried to explain her thinking, but her reasons were based more upon impressions: the light in Miss Bellini's eyes when she danced with Richter, the array of expensive ball gowns and jewelry she owned on a teacher's salary, the depth of her anger the day after the ball, with her grim words–*I will act.* And after the play, when Concordia and Sophia were in the parlor of DeLacey House talking, Concordia was certain she heard the front door opening, and felt a draft of damp night air in the hallway. It must have been Miss Bellini, returning from the tower. Then there was the fact that only four people knew the existence of the dagger and where to find it: Miss Crandall, Miss Pomeroy, Miss Bellini, and herself.

"None of that was any sort of *proof*," she had told Capshaw. "She was by nature an impetuous woman, ruled by strong emotions. I thought it necessary to surprise her, and provoke her to admit what she had done. But if I had told you my suspicions and I was wrong, I could have done irreparable harm."

It takes many good deeds to build a good reputation, and only one bad one to lose it.

Splendid. Now she was thinking like Miss Banning.

"And I didn't even know that Miss Bellini was involved in Miss Lyman's death until I confronted her in the tower," Concordia continued. "Even Miss Hamilton had assumed that Richter was responsible for the murder. He was the one who put Miss Lyman's body in the pond to make the death seem a suicide. But Richter killing her didn't make any sense, as Reynolds had pointed out: why kill the bursar, when she is the one getting the money? Her death would only complicate the embezzlement scheme. A heat-of-the-moment act was the better explanation. Miss Bellini had made several panicked decisions lately, including stabbing Richter."

And, finally, jumping from the tower, she added to herself.

Even now, Concordia kept thinking of Miss Bellini, wondering whether more harm had been done by confronting her. If she had not been cornered, perhaps she would not have been so desperate as to take her own life.

But the woman had killed two people. She could not just walk away.

Further, Miss Lyman's death would have remained a suicide, and Julian would have been tried for Arthur Richter's murder.

Despite all he had done, Concordia could not turn her back and allow him to be punished for such a heinous crime.

Not that Mr. Reynolds had many scruples. As soon as he'd had the chance, he jumped bail, sailing off to parts unknown with a wealthy widow of recent acquaintance. Concordia doubted if the authorities would apprehend them. But perhaps that was better than a lengthy, sensational courtroom trial. All of the other principals in the matter were dead. There was no avoiding the publicity, of course, but one could hope that the ill effects of the scandal would dissipate over time.

Strange as it might seem, Concordia missed Lucia Bellini. She had been a bright, vivacious, passionate person, bringing life and color to everything around her. In her day-to-day life, she had been kind. That was the woman Concordia was determined to remember.

Coming out of her reverie, Concordia looked over at Miss Hamilton, who was sliding the last of the boxes to the corner by the door. The sunlight caught the glints of silver in her blond hair, pulled back in its usual no-nonsense chignon, but she moved with the grace and ease of a younger woman. She wore a bolero cape-style traveling suit of brown and gold, its collar and lapels appliquéd in rows of soutach braid. It must have been a *generous* bonus, Concordia thought. Incongruously, she wondered where Miss Hamilton had packed her derringer.

Miss Hamilton's derringer reminded Concordia of something else.

"Miss Hamilton," Concordia asked, "why was Miss Crandall so interested in the dagger? Last week, she mentioned speaking to you about it, but then she had to run to catch her train."

Concordia had been relieved when Charlotte Crandall managed to graduate without further mishap. The young lady decided to postpone her engagement to Mr. Blake, and planned to teach at a nearby girls' boarding school in the fall.

Miss Hamilton gave the box a final shove with her foot before answering. "Miss Crandall suspects that the knife is a seventeenth-century European bodice dagger. It may be valuable. Which would certainly be a boon for the college," she said.

"*What* is a bodice dagger?" Concordia asked in amazement.

Miss Hamilton chuckled. "They were actually common in Renaissance Europe, and were designed to be carried in either the bodice—which was quite a structured garment in those days—or the top of one's boot. This one seems rather more ornamental than most. Perhaps it was carried by a lady of the upper class?" She shrugged. "Dean—pardon me, *President*—Langdon is having a curator friend examine it."

"How on earth does Miss Crandall know of such things?" Concordia did not recall a course being offered in seventeenth century weaponry.

"Our dear Miss Banning often digresses in her curriculum plans, particularly when she is enthusiastic about her subject."

"Amazing," Concordia murmured.

"Well, that's the last of it." Miss Hamilton stood and brushed off her skirt. "And just in time," she added, as they heard voices at the end of the hall.

To her surprise, Miss Hamilton reached over and hugged her. "I do hope that you will write. You must tell me of all the doings here." She sighed and looked around the room. "I *will* miss this place. And all of you."

Miss Hamilton opened the door at David Bradley's knock. He was followed by a less-rumpled-than-usual Edward Langdon, his hair freshly parted and slicked back. He clutched an enormous flower bouquet, which he thrust toward Miss Hamilton.

"Th… these… are for you," he stammered.

Concordia recognized the roses and brown-eyed susans from the garden at Sycamore House. She glanced at David, who winked back at her. He was looking cool and comfortable in an ecru suit of crash linen. She couldn't help but notice that his clothes seemed to fit him better these days.

"We'll be outside when you are ready," Concordia said, steering David out.

"Your idea?" Concordia asked, with a glance at the fresh scratches and green stains on his hands.

David grinned. "One can never go wrong with flowers for a lady."

They were waiting with the driver beside the carriage when Miss Hamilton came out to join them. Langdon, carrying her valise, set it down. Tight-lipped, he walked away without a word.

Miss Hamilton smiled ruefully as her gaze followed Langdon. "He tried to convince me to stay. He is disappointed that I'm not changing my mind."

David consulted his watch. "Speaking of that, if you wish to catch your train, we should leave now."

Fortunately, Union Depot was a block from the Capitol Building, barely two miles away, and they reached the station in good time.

Concordia typically found train stations to be unnerving and exhilarating at the same time, and today was no exception: hectic with the press of people, baggage, crying children, and porters; the good-bye waves and hearty handshakes; the thunderous vibrations beneath one's feet, and the acrid smoke in the back of one's throat. Many were traveling to new places; some of them, separated by distance, responsibilities, or finances, might never again see the loved ones waving good-bye to them as the train pulled away from the platform.

"All aboard the 2:10 for New York City!" the conductor announced, pacing up and down the platform. Miss Hamilton gave Concordia a slip of paper.

"Read it when you are home. Good-bye, dear."

She gave them both a quick wave as the porter took her case and helped her up the step.

Concordia looked on with blurry eyes. "Good-bye, Miss Hamilton," she whispered.

On the ride back to campus, David finally broke the silence. "I saw Sophia Adams the other day."

Concordia looked up. "Oh? How is she? I haven't seen her in a few weeks. I understand she is quite busy these days."

And no wonder. Sophia Adams had added another cause in her mission to improve women's lives: educating them about venereal disease. She and several prominent doctors in the city were discussing the formation of a social hygiene association, modeled after those in Chicago and Philadelphia, to change behaviors and dispel misinformation. Concordia knew that, if anyone could do so, it would be Sophia Adams.

"She's fine," David answered. "Seems to be fully recovered." He hesitated. "She told me that you had worked out who had attacked her, but she would not tell me anything else. She suggested that I ask you." David's brown eyes were full of curiosity.

Concordia sank back against the carriage cushions. Sophia had brought news of Judge Armstrong the last time she visited. His health and reason had rapidly deteriorated since Henry's death. He was now in the constant care of nurses, and there was talk of moving him to a sanitorium.

Sophia had other news as well.

"Would you believe it?" Sophia had said, eyes dancing in amusement. "Doctor Westfield is moving to the Oklahoma Territory."

Concordia gave a bark of laughter. "He'd make an unlikely cowboy."

Sophia grinned. "Apparently a family member has a land claim. The boom towns always need doctors."

"Let's hope he provides better care to his patients out West," Concordia retorted.

She was still angry at them—Judge Armstrong, Henry, Dr. Westfield—for neglecting a vulnerable woman in their care because of fear and pride. And then, there was Judge Armstrong's despicable attack on Sophia.

Even so, Concordia's desire for revenge had burned itself out. Revenge, or justice? The line between the two seemed to blur. *There is a time when even justice brings harm.*

She would never know Mary's wishes. She had discovered the truth, and confronted the judge with it. Would Mary have been satisfied with that? Providence seemed to take the rest out of Concordia's hands; she and Sophia agreed to leave it that way. Judge Armstrong was suffering the loss of his only son, and he might not survive the blow. Certainly, he was no longer a danger to anyone.

Concordia did share what she had learned about Mary's death with her mother. She couldn't bring herself to do so in person, though. She wrote her a letter, which Nathaniel offered to deliver. Mother had the right to know the truth behind Mary's death, even though it was a painful truth. And her words in the garden during the dance still weighed heavily on Concordia: *You always have to be so important, have to know things that others do not. I have always hated that.*

Perhaps she was right. If so, Concordia had her own share in what was wrong between them.

So far, her mother had not responded to the letter. Was she so hurt and angry that she could not acknowledge what Concordia had gone through to finally get to the truth? The silence stung.

Concordia realized she had allowed her thoughts to wander, and that David was anxiously watching her. She looked over at him and smiled in apology.

"It's a long story, David. Perhaps I will tell you someday."

Back at Willow Cottage, Concordia had her own packing to finish. She planned to stay with Sophia at the settlement house during the rest of the summer recess.

There was a knock at her door, and Ruby poked her head in. "A visitor, miss."

Puzzled, Concordia went to the parlor.

"*Mother?*"

Mrs. Wells was perched tentatively on the settee. She had changed out of her customary mourning clothes, and wore a plain white shirtwaist and simple skirt of dove gray.

To her surprise, her mother came eagerly forward, clasped Concordia by the arm—Mother's hands were surprisingly strong, for all of their delicacy—and drew her over to the settee.

"Nathaniel gave me your letter. Your news was such a shock, it took me a while to accept what really happened." Struggling to maintain her composure, she looked down and plucked at her skirt. "But at least I *know*. I wanted to thank you, Concordia, for all that you have done for Mary. For me."

"Of course," Concordia said, stiffly.

Calmer now, Mrs. Wells met her eyes. "There is something I wanted to ask of you."

Concordia braced herself. What now?

"Will you stay with me during the summer recess? We have much to talk about."

"We do?"

Mrs. Wells smoothed her skirt and sighed. "I don't necessarily *approve* of your choice in life, Concordia. I have been trying to understand it better, but sometimes it just makes me shudder. Girls playing basketball in bloomers, studying ancient Greek, living communally in such *casual* quarters..."

She held up a hand to forestall Concordia's protest. "*But*—I cannot deny that this seems to suit you. You are happy here. And for all their hoydenish ways, your girls are charming. They look up to you. So, perhaps I can become accustomed to the idea. I will try. Will *you* try, as well?"

She looked at Concordia expectantly.

Concordia hesitated, her throat tightening and nose prickling.

Finally, she nodded mutely, feeling as if she had recklessly plunged off a cliff.

After her mother left, Concordia composed herself with a cup of strong tea. The cottage was quiet and empty, with Ruby the only other occupant. She couldn't believe she was missing the students already.

As she stood to resume her packing, the crackle in her pocket reminded her of Miss Hamilton's note. Curious, she pulled it out.

My dear Concordia,

Since Frank died, I have always worked alone. This experience has taught me that I can rely upon a trustworthy few without sacrificing my self-sufficiency. I am grateful to you, for everything.

Perhaps, one day, we will work together again.

Sincerely,
Penelope Hamilton

Concordia smiled and took out her battered copy of *The Tragedy of Macbeth*. Out of it fluttered the card that had accompanied David's flowers, and the torn sheet from Mary's diary. She slipped the note inside with the rest, put the volume in a box, and resumed her packing.

THE END

Don't miss the next Concordia Wells adventure! Coming soon:

Unseemly Pursuits

A deadly secret that won't stay buried...

It is the fall of 1896, and Hartford Women's College has survived the "unfortunate" events of last semester. In fact, things are looking up for the college, which has started a new antiquities exhibit, attracting donors and talented faculty to oversee it.

Professor Concordia Wells welcomes this new normal, even with the usual student high-jinks on campus and the endless round of responsibilities: for her classes, the clubs she oversees, and the lively college girls she lives with.

However, two new arrivals soon trouble the day-to-day routine: first, there is the popular and exotic Madame Durand, a spirit medium who leads the school's "Spirit Club," and gives private séances for the bereaved clients of Hartford's affluent social circles—including Miss Wells' mother. Then there is the new lady principal, Olivia Grant, whom the students have nicknamed "the Ogre." The woman seems bent on making Concordia's life miserable, and keeps a watchful eye on the young lady professor's every move.

In the midst of this tension, events take a truly disturbing turn when an Egyptian amulet donated to the college mysteriously disappears, and the man who had contributed the item, the father of Concordia's best friend Sophia, is found murdered. Soon Sophia is arrested for killing her own father. But why won't she cooperate with the police, and try to save herself?

Concordia races against time to find answers. Could the missing amulet be the key to the murder? Her inquiries begin to unravel a 20-year-old secret, once closely guarded by men now dead. But such secrets can be dangerous for the daughters left behind, including Concordia herself. Can she make sense of the mystery that has bound together their fates, before someone else dies?

Bruce County Public Library
1243 Mackenzie Rd.
Port Elgin ON N0H 2C6

CPSIA information can be obtained at www.ICGtesting.com
Printed in the USA
LVOW10s1809110216

474714LV00022B/602/P